G000166039

The K   Stone

To John and Liz

THE
KNOWLEDGE
STONE

A Trilogy of Mystery

Jack McGinnigle

with all Blessings

Jack

Jan 2014

First published in Great Britain by Piquant Fiction in 2012.
PiquantFiction is an imprint of Piquant.
PO Box 83, Carlisle, CA3 9GR, UK
www.piquanteditions.com

ISBN 978-1-903689-82-0

British Library Cataloguing in Publication Data
 McGinnigle, Jack.
  The knowledge stone : a trilogy of mystery.
  1. Paranormal fiction.
  I. Title
  823.9'2-dc23

  ISBN-13: 9781903689820

Cover design and typesetting by ProjectLuz.com

Contents

PROLOGUE

Deep in the Earth, the Stone *was*. Not buried, for it was part of the fabric and makeup of the Earth, part of the unity that is the World we know. Yet it was also a separate entity among the many separate entities that make up Earth. Part of the whole that itself comprises many parts of a whole that is part of a universe of wholes … and outwards to inexplicable infinity.

The Stone was not alive, for we all know that stones have no life. Yet it would be wrong to define the Stone as "dead", for that word implies a previous existence of life. Instead, it may be designated as inert, unchanging in its basic being.

However, physical changes must be chronicled, as the Stone was subjected to movement, to radical and gigantic heaves, thrusts and judders; to sliding, grinding, rearing and plunging, at times augmented by heating to incandescence or cooling to absolute frigidity. All this happening within the mass of changing plasma that is the World and its environs, cycling within uneven patterns of space and time, its composition lurching from dense solid to viscous liquid, to vapour and beyond.

So in this mystery of time and space, the Stone was unmade, fractured and rent apart with variable violence, moulded and shaped, ground down and reformed in a myriad of ways. But during all these eons, there was yet a constancy in the kernel of its entity.

In the being of the Stone, there was no concept of time. No beginning, past, present, future or end. Such things do exist, at least as a gossamer timeline in the fertile minds of higher life forms, albeit imperfectly expressed and understood. Yet the Stone was associated with what we understand as a history, a past mysteriously blended with significance. For the Stone had not always been an assemblage of gritty, pseudo-inert particles; it had been something quite different, an integral part of a large formation in which there had been a sensation of life, movement and meaning.

There was no life in the Stone, certainly not in any individual sense. It had never had the tinge of sentience, either. But in the nucleus of its being, it was mystically *aware*.

PART ONE

Joachim

'I'm really glad I live in modern times.' The boy always woke well before first light. It was his special time, his only opportunity for luxurious musing. There was no question of thinking at the end of the day when he clambered into his narrow bunk in the hayloft of the barn. By then he was so tired he could barely keep awake; a whole day of almost continuous manual labour had totally exhausted his thin, wiry young body. But this time in the morning before first light was different, especially precious and magical to him.

As he drifted upwards through layers of sleep, on the journey towards full wakefulness, his initial thoughts continued, 'I'm really glad the bullock cart has round wheels and not square ones like the carts of olden times.'

This thought had come from Old Malik the day before and it had obviously been sufficiently striking to be the first subject of his early morning muse.

Approaching full wakefulness, the boy now recalled exactly what Old Malik (his master, the farmer) had said. The words were embedded within an unpleasant and frightening incident but Joachim was well used to such events on the farm. He had been told to move the bullock cart across the farmyard to the field and the solid wooden wheels of the heavy cart had sunk into a depression of viscous mud left by an overnight rainstorm. The cart was stuck fast and the boy was trying his best to extricate it, wrestling with the powerful bullock harnessed to the cart, shouting loudly, pulling at its head ropes and beating the back of the unfortunate animal with a stick.

Old Malik had heard the commotion and appeared out of the barn. As his gaze rested upon the scene in the farmyard, his face twisted into a familiar pattern of anger.

'Be quiet and stop thrashing that bullock,' he roared.

Old Malik did not actually care about the beating the bullock was receiving, since he himself often beat his animals savagely. The reason for his reaction was even more cruel; every day, he revelled in making the boy's life a misery: 'Listen very closely to me, you stupid little fool,' he snarled menacingly, 'you're really lucky this is the Year of our Lord six hundred and fifty-seven (Old Malik knew such things); in olden times, bullock carts didn't have round wheels like this one, they had square wheels that just dragged along the ground, like a sled.'

Joachim, still straining at the head of the reluctant bullock, was silent for a moment. As Old Malik turned away in contempt, the boy ventured: 'But surely …'

The man froze. Then he wheeled around, paced forward and thrust a furious face close to Joachim, eyes narrowed and blazing, purple veins etched on his forehead. 'What? Are you arguing with me again? I'm *telling* you the way it was in olden times. I'm giving you the benefit of my knowledge about the past. I'm telling you the wheels of the bullock carts were square; they just dragged along the ground. Life then was much more difficult than it is now. The trouble with you is that you are a stupid, ungrateful, utterly useless wretch. No wonder I need to beat you so much.' He looked around for a beating stick.

The boy recognised a familiar danger and bowed his head immediately, stumbling backwards and mumbling apologies in an attempt to appease the farmer. Fortunately, the bullock had been frightened by the violence in Old Malik's voice and had pulled the cart free from the mud with a series of convulsive terror-fuelled heaves. Thus, a grateful Joachim was able to beat a hasty retreat from the scene – as hasty as a slowly lumbering bullock cart could achieve! This particular moment of danger had passed but the boy lived his life with the constant fear of such happenings.

Still stretched out in his narrow bunk and becoming aware of the first tinge of deepest blue through gaps in the barn wall, he now reflected about the comment he had inadvertently started to make to Old Malik. Of course, he blamed himself for what had happened. He knew it had all been his fault. In a moment of forgetfulness, he had just thought aloud and he should not have done that.

But surely his thought was true? Even if the wheels had started off square, the constant dragging would rub away the square corners and eventually the wheels would begin to turn, very clumsily and unevenly at first; then, the more they turned the rounder they would become, eventually becoming round wheels like those of modern times!

Elated, the boy clapped his hands with joy: 'I'm sure that's right – but I'll need to keep quiet about this.' He knew better than to try to mention it to Old Malik, or indeed to anyone else on the farm; they would tell the farmer what he had said and Old Malik would come looking for him with a stick in his hand.

'I've just got to keep it a secret,' he decided.

The boy's thoughts now drifted to his past life. His memories of living with his own family in the next village had diminished although he remembered he had been the eldest child in what seemed to be an ever-growing family; there were already five younger siblings and another was expected soon. They were always extremely poor; their living conditions were extremely cramped and they never had enough to eat.

In this land, it was commonplace for poverty-stricken parents to seek to solve the dilemma of a growing family by arranging for their elder children to be apprenticed to a local farmer or businessman. In fact, this was not an apprenticeship at all but a financial transaction where the employer bought the child for an agreed sum paid to the father. Thus the father gained a welcome sum of money for the family and the cost of maintaining the apprentice was transferred to his or her employer, who then became responsible for feeding, clothing and housing the child. In truth, this was child slavery and, at the employer's behest, that slavery could be extended throughout the whole of adulthood.

When Joachim was around eight years old, his father had sold him to Old Malik as an apprentice farm worker and, since then, the boy had never been able to visit his home and make contact with his family. Remembering this sadly, he thought wistfully of his mother, a quiet kindly woman, always tired and prematurely aged by hard work and child-bearing: 'Mother was nice; how I wish I could see her now. I could always speak to her about anything. She would have liked to hear about the bullock carts of olden times.'

His eyes filled with tears. He knew a visit to his village was impossible, because Old Malik never allowed him to have a free day or even a few hours to himself. The only time he ever left the farm was in the company of Old Malik when heavy or bulky items had to be fetched from or taken to the village. Then, he was the labourer who loaded or unloaded the cart while Old Malik drank beer at the alehouse with his friends. Woe betide Joachim if the work was not done when Old Malik returned, often drunk and even more ready to be violent towards him.

The thoughts about his family took the boy's mind back to the day he was brought to the farm. This was something he used to think about often – in fact he used to have nightmares about it. Nowadays, he thought about it only occasionally, although when he did, the memory was still pin sharp.

He remembered travelling to the farm in a very bumpy cart. Following the financial transaction with his father, Old Malik had lifted him into the back of the cart and growled, 'Sit there, don't move and be quiet.'

So the little slim boy arrived at the farm, cowed and frightened, clutching a very small, pathetic bundle of possessions. From the start, Old Malik treated him roughly. When the frightened boy started to weep, the old man was callous: 'Stop that,' he snapped, 'I don't allow snivelling. You're mine now and you better do exactly what you're told.'

The boy was taken to the farmhouse and Old Malik called for his wife to come out. 'This is a farm boy I've bought,' he grated, making no mention of his name, 'he'll live in the barn.'

The fat, slovenly woman (Joachim later discovered her name was Maretta) looked at him with dull, disinterested eyes. 'More work for me,' she muttered, 'who needs another mouth to feed?' Then she turned away and re-entered the farmhouse, slamming the door behind her.

Old Malik seized the boy by the shoulder, causing him to cry out with fear and pain: 'Listen to me,' he said, 'you are not allowed in the farmhouse. You live in the barn over there, in the hayloft, and you better look after all the farm tools in the barn and see that nothing gets stolen. Now come with me.'

The boy was dragged around to the fetid privy at the back of the farmhouse and thrust inside. The privy was just a stinking pit in the ground covered by a slimy plank of wood pierced with a hole. Users of the privy were screened from sight by screens of flimsy coarse rush matting that also provided a sparse roof.

'When you need to, you do it in here – nowhere else, you hear?' the man growled.

'Yes, Master,' the boy whispered tearfully.

'And another thing, you'll be cleaning it out every few weeks and you had better do it properly.'

Old Malik then propelled the boy back to the farmhouse. 'Right,' he said harshly 'I want to see you here at first light tomorrow. And you better be clean, tidy and ready to work. If you aren't, you'll be sorry.' The man turned on his heel and stamped into the farmhouse, slamming the door loudly behind him.

Joachim remembered how he trudged pathetically across the yard to the barn. It was getting dark and, when he got there, it was difficult to see inside the barn. When his eyes had adjusted to the dim light, he could just make out a rough ladder leading to the hayloft above. He climbed up gingerly, taking his little bundle with him. Most of the hayloft was stacked with bales of hay but he could just make out a narrow bunk made of rough planks of wood set along one wall. There was a single worn blanket in it.

He remembered how exhausted he felt as he stripped off his shirt and breeches and put on his spare shirt – the only other garment he had in his bundle. Putting a generous layer of hay into the bunk, he climbed in and covered himself with the thin blanket. Then, he cried himself to sleep, fearful of what the next day would bring.

The boy's mind now snapped back to the present. Work always started very early on the farm and he knew that Old Malik would be shouting angrily for him very soon if he did not appear, scrubbed clean and ready for a full day's work when the light became strong enough for the farm activities to start. The boy reflected with regret how easy it was to make Old Malik angry – in fact he seemed to be angry all the time. When the anger was directed at the boy, which it frequently was, the situation often developed into physical beatings; Old Malik would seize the nearest stick (he had a number of beating sticks placed at strategic points around the farm) and lay it across the shoulders, back and legs of the unfortunate boy.

Such an event had happened the day before.

'Well, it was my own fault,' the boy thought ruefully 'I did drop that bag of grain and it split open.' In fact the bag had been far too large and heavy for Joachim's slight frame but, despite this (or perhaps deliberately), Old Malik had ordered him to pick it up and stack it in the barn.

The subsequent beating had been very painful and the boy hoped that the wheals on his back had not been bleeding in the night. If they had, he knew from experience that his shirt would be sticking to his wounds and that the bleeding was likely to restart when he pulled the shirt off. His back would then be very painful all during the day and make it difficult for him to do his work as quickly as normal. He shivered at the prospect. Old Malik might notice and become angry again, putting him in danger of more beating.

'Oh well, I'll soon find out if I've been bleeding,' he thought ruefully, still snuggling deeply into the straw.

Remarkably, despite the harshness and periodic brutality that marked his daily life, the boy was not downcast or frightened. Lying in his bunk, for now warm and comfortable, he looked around the cramped, dimly-lit hayloft that had become his home since he came to the farm. 'Life really isn't too bad,' he thought, 'I'm not beaten every day and the food that Maretta gives me is usually quite good, although it's never enough.' Then he paused and added to his thought, 'but I've learned how to survive.'

He smiled secretly as he thought of the extra food he sometimes managed to take when no-one was looking. Neither Maretta or Old Malik ever suspected he would do such a thing! So small pieces of bread or cheese, sometimes even an apple or pear, were quickly taken and hidden in his clothes, later to be eaten on an "official" visit to the privy.

The boy knew that the dark, dirty and fly-infested environment of the privy was highly unsuitable for eating food but it was the only place where he could be alone and was unlikely to be disturbed suddenly. He smiled again, this time quite cheerfully. 'Yes, life is really quite good. Maybe Old Malik will not be angry with me today. I'll try my best to do exactly what he tells me. I'll try to be really good.'

Joachim now judged it was time for him to get up. He sat up gingerly and stepped out of the bunk, easing his shirt from his back and pulling it off over his head. In the dim light, he examined the garment.

'Only one little streak of blood,' he thought, 'I'm really lucky.' Naked, the boy climbed lithely down the rickety ladder to the earthen floor of the barn. Stepping outside, he paused and looked around with great care before slipping around the side of the barn, out of sight of the farmhouse. Here he urinated quickly on the ground – something Old Malik had expressly forbidden him to do. As he did so, he recalled how unpleasant it was to go to the privy.

There were several reasons for this. On the daily occasions he found it necessary to use the privy, he often found it occupied by Old Malik, Maretta or even Giana. Giana was a scrawny, graceless girl several years younger than Joachim, who had been acquired by Old Malik some months before. She now worked for Maretta in the kitchen or farmyard. Joachim was forbidden by Old Malik to have any contact with Giana or even approach her anywhere on the farm.

Of course Old Malik and Maretta took precedence at the privy and must never be disturbed when they were occupying it. However the boy could not understand why Giana also took precedence over him. After all, he was older than her and had been at the farm much longer. 'It's not fair,' he thought. At the same time he felt sorry for Giana because it was obvious that she was treated unkindly by Maretta. 'Even so, it's not fair that she is allowed to use the privy before me,' he thought again, still standing naked by the side of the barn.

Then an impish grin lit up his face. He looked down at the wet patch on the ground before him and whispered: 'But I've certainly solved that problem for this morning!'

At the doorway of the barn, a large barrel of scummy rainwater provided the boy with the only means he had of washing himself. Shivering a little, he scooped away the algae and threw cupped hands of icy water over his head until the whole length of his body was glistening; he winced as the water stung the red and purple wheals on his back. Scrubbing himself clean with a rough cloth, he then rolled in the straw to dry his wet and reddened body. Finally, he plunged the blood-stained shirt into the water, scrubbed the blood stain and rinsed the garment out before hanging it up on a high beam: 'I hope that will be dry by this evening,' he thought, 'otherwise I'll have to sleep in my skin.' He hoped this would not happen because the straw in his bunk would be prickly and hurt the healing scars on his back. Climbing the ladder to the hayloft, he dressed quickly in shirt and breeches and then combed his hair flat with a roughly-hewn wooden comb that he had carved from a flat branch. The light strengthened. He was ready.

He knew he had to hurry now. Old Malik only allowed him a few minutes to eat the food and drink that Maretta angrily threw down for him every morning. Running, he arrived just as Maretta tossed the familiar small wicker basket down on a flat stone just outside the door of the farmhouse. He tried to thank her but she ignored him, muttered something under her breath and slammed the door shut.

The boy had tried very hard to please Maretta when he first arrived but she either rebuffed him icily or shouted angrily for him to go away, sometimes slapping his face if he didn't move fast enough. At first, this harsh and unkind treatment made him cry but he had long become hardened to it. Nevertheless, he had made it a rule to be scrupulously polite to

Maretta; maybe someday she would be in a better mood and smile at him – or better still, let him have more food.

As he perched on the fallen tree trunk where he ate his morning and evening meals, he heard loud shouting from the farmhouse. Obviously, poor Giana had done something wrong and the shouting was punctuated by the sharp crack of a hard hand hitting soft flesh. Joachim dropped his head in compassionate fellowship but at the same time was pleased that the sound was not the so-familiar muffled thud of a heavy stick bruising and cutting into taut flesh and muscle: 'I'm glad they don't beat her with a stick,' he thought, 'slaps are really sore but they don't injure you so much.'

In the past, the boy had tried many times to show friendship to Giana. He was forbidden to talk to her but inevitably they met at times because the area of the farm was not very large. Meeting face to face, he had smiled at her a number of times but his smile was never returned. She looked either blank or cross.

'In fact,' Joachim remembered, 'there was that day when we met on the narrow path to the field and she pushed me right into the mud, whispering: "Get out of my way, you horrible boy!"'. Momentarily, he felt rather sad that everybody hated him.

Meanwhile the boy ate quickly from the scarred wooden bowl perched on his knees. This morning there were two slices of coarse brown bread and a small piece of hard cheese, all made by Maretta from their own farm produce.

'This tastes pretty good,' the boy thought as he ate, 'I just wish there was more.' He was always hungry and sometimes experienced quite sharp pains in his stomach. She had also given him a large earthenware cup of goat's milk and he drank that down quickly.

It was always a problem for him to find enough to drink. Sometimes, he was driven to drink water from the small muddy stream that crossed the farm at the bottom of the field. Before drinking the water from the stream, he always examined it carefully, meticulously removing any dirt, insects or rotting vegetation; even then he knew from past experience that the water might still make him sick.

'The trouble is, you can't see the evil spirits,' he always reminded himself, 'I wish I was like Old Malik and never had to drink this water.' While working, Old Malik drank from bottles of beer that Maretta had brewed for him. He never offered any to the boy and Joachim knew better than to ask for some.

The door of the farmhouse opened with a crash and Old Malik appeared. Without looking at the boy, he spoke harshly: 'Get moving. You're ploughing today. Get started at the top of the field and make sure your furrows are deep and straight. I'll be examining them and they had better be right.' As he spoke he tossed a cloth bundle towards the boy – this was Joachim's daytime meal, to be eaten during a very short break in work when Old Malik gave permission.

The boy deftly caught the bundle before it spilled its contents on the muddy ground; this was an important skill he had learned after many occasions of scavenging his precious food from the stinking dirt. He tied the ends of the cloth around his belt, already moving towards the pen where the bullocks were kept. Old Malik kept two bullocks for heavy work on the farm; the boy was directed to use the smaller animal with a lighter plough to deal with the rather poor, stony soil at the top of the field while Old Malik used the larger beast with a heavier plough which was more suitable for the lower field where the ground was softer, more fertile and much easier to plough.

Fortunately, both bullocks were quite docile creatures and the boy usually had little trouble with them. In addition to the animal he was to use, it was also his job to fasten the harness around Old Malik's bullock, so that it was ready to be hitched to the plough.

'Better do his bullock first,' he thought, 'otherwise I might get into trouble.' He made soft clucking noises to reassure the bullocks as he approached with the sets of harness ropes and had no problems putting them on, achieving this just before the arrival of Old Malik.

The farmer glared at him and growled, 'You still here? Get moving and make it quick.'

The boy immediately left the pen with his bullock as quickly as he could, avoiding the kick that Old Malik aimed at him as he passed. As he led the bullock along the packed earth of the path that led up to the top of the field, he delighted in the crisp, sunny morning and hummed a little song he had learned from his mother when he was a little boy. 'At least the bullock likes my singing,' he thought with a little smile, 'even if no-one else does.'

The wooden plough lay at the edge of the field where it had been left at the end of the last ploughing season. Its metal parts were rusty but the boy knew that the rust would be cleared away as soon as he started ploughing. Heaving and straining, he pulled the plough upright and propped it up with a stick. Then he manoeuvred the bullock round to the front of the plough and fastened the harness ropes to the cleats. Holding the plough upright on its single wooden wheel and keeping the ploughing blade clear of the earth, he tapped the bullock on its back with a stick, calling for it to walk forward. The animal complied and, in due course, they reached the top of the field where they turned around and were ready to begin ploughing.

There were times when the boy really enjoyed his work on the farm and this was one of them. Despite his inexperience, lack of strength and diminutive stature, he knew he did a good job of ploughing.

'Not that Old Malik ever says so,' he thought ruefully, 'but the fact he doesn't complain means that he must be satisfied. I do wish he would be nice to me, just occasionally.' He sighed wistfully.

As expected, the ground was dry and difficult. The plough stalled and jammed many times and the bullock had to heave with all its power to pull it free. There were some occasions when even the strength of the bullock was insufficient and then the boy had to dig around the large jagged stones and heave them out of the furrow. Some stones were so big and heavy that the boy could not lift them and they had to be rolled laboriously, end over end, to the edge of the field. Soon, his hands became reddened, bruised and sore.

When the boy eventually reached the end of the first furrow, he looked back to admire his work: 'Not bad,' he thought, 'quite straight and it looks to be deep enough.' He hoped fervently that Old Malik would be satisfied with his work.

The plough was turned around and the second furrow made in the same agonisingly slow way. These first two furrows were followed by the third, the fourth and the fifth, all neatly parallel to each other. The sun was now high in the sky. The boy stopped and mopped his beaded forehead with a rag, squinting upwards at the blazing sun.

'Whew! It's really hot now,' he said aloud. Then he jumped as the harsh, strident tones of Old Malik's voice pierced his delightful reverie.

'Talking to yourself, are you? Just about what I expect. You'll grow up to be a madman – that is, if you live long enough to grow up!' Old Malik thought this a very good joke and laughed loudly and unkindly. By this time he had walked to the top of the field where he scrutinised Joachim's furrows narrowly.

The boy waited in silence, trembling a little.

Old Malik stood completely still and said nothing for several minutes. Then, he turned on his heel and walked off down the hill. 'You can eat after you give that beast a drink.'

Standing some distance away, Joachim barely heard the rapidly fading words, carried away on the wind. Obediently, the boy visited the stream and fetched water for his bullock; he also watered Old Malik's animal at the bottom of the field. Although Old Malik had not ordered him to do this, he knew from bitter experience that he would be in trouble if he did not attend to the other beast. At times, Old Malik used such tricks as an excuse for beating the boy.

'I hope this will please him,' Joachim thought. He also fed both animals by laying down a pile of sweet-smelling hay for each. Then, sitting under the thin branches of the spindly tree in the top corner of the field, he spread out his daytime meal on the cloth. The boy observed with gratitude that the slices of bread were thicker than those he had been given in the morning. There was a thick piece of cheese and a small pat of butter, too. To drink, Maretta had included a pot of mead, made from the honey produced on the farm.

'What a feast,' the boy thought, 'I'm really lucky to be given such good food.' Within a short time, the midday meal had been consumed and the boy prepared to have a short rest before starting again on the exhausting task of ploughing. 'Anyway,' he thought, 'my beast needs to rest.'

The boy knew that Old Malik always returned to the farmhouse for his midday meal and that he would be absent for quite a long time – much longer than the brief respite that Joachim was allowed. Because of this, the boy knew that he could rest safely for a time, which he could measure by the creeping shadow of the tree across the ground. He knew he must be hard at work when Old Malik returned to the lower part of the field. He marked the position of the shadow, lay back and stretched luxuriously. 'Yes, life is good,' he thought.,

'I'm not hungry or thirsty, my back is only slightly sore and I can be alone and relax for a little while.'

Time passed and Joachim's thoughts wandered gently. Then a feeling of unreality crept over him slowly, a feeling he had never experienced before. It was strange but not unpleasant so he was not frightened or worried by it. He felt almost connected to the earth rather than lying upon it. He heard, or rather, sensed the start of a gentle sound. At first he could not identify what it was but then he realised it was like the rustling of many leaves when the wind blew through a large broad-leafed tree. The sound strengthened progressively until it pervaded his mind. A deep peace descended upon him.

Time passed.

'Crack!' A dry twig below his shoulders snapped, a tiny sound that exploded in his mind like a clap of thunder. The boy sat bolt upright, his eyes wide and fearful, focussing with difficulty to scan the field before swivelling round to check the position of the tree shadow.

'Not much movement,' he breathed gratefully. However his sudden awakening had shaken him considerably and he also felt peculiar, as if something special had happened. Scanning all around, he could not see anything untoward; still the fine sunny day, the quiet field and, thankfully, no sign of Old Malik. 'A funny dream,' he concluded, 'I wonder what it means.' The boy knew that dreams could be messages from the spirits.

As he continued to sit quietly on the ground, he felt there was still something he must do, but he couldn't think what it might be. Again, he looked around carefully – nothing different or strange. It was when he turned to admire the straight furrows of his ploughing that he saw something odd. There, some distance away in the bottom of his last furrow, was an intense, sparkling light. Of course the boy had seen things reflecting the sunlight before; some stones sparkled, or sometimes water droplets on the grass reflected the sunlight in beautiful pinpoints of light – but this was different – bigger, brighter.

'What can that be?' he asked himself and went to investigate.

The object proved to be unremarkable. A small pale yellow stone projecting vertically from the ground, roughly cylindrical in shape but with two smooth depressions on each side of the cylinder towards the top. He stretched out a hand and picked it up, his forefinger and thumb slipping naturally into the smooth cavities. As he did so, he imagined he felt a peculiar little jolt deep in his body.

'Must be the effect of the mead,' he thought. He examined the stone from all angles and noted that it was quite light in weight. At first he thought it was completely plain and smooth but closer examination revealed shallow striations from end to end and it was from these shallow marks that the sun reflected brightly. 'Maybe it's magic,' he thought, but he smiled as he said this because, unlike the people in olden times, he did not believe in magic stones. 'But it's really quite nice; I'll keep it in my pouch. It can be my secret,' he thought, and felt quite pleased that he had something in his possession that no-one knew about.

Now he walked back to the tree and checked the shadow.

'Better get started again,' he thought, 'Old Malik will be coming back soon.' He felt particularly calm and rested. The bullock was roused, re-harnessed to the plough and work restarted.

Not long after, when Joachim was about halfway along his new furrow, the burly, grizzled figure of Old Malik appeared at the lower corner of the field.

Old Malik

Replete from his ample daytime meal, washed down by copious quantities of farm-brewed beer, Old Malik strode towards the field, his large booted feet tramping angrily on the path.

'That boy had better be working hard when I get there,' he thought, 'otherwise he's in trouble.' He smiled unpleasantly at the thought. He kept a beating stick at the top of the field and would not hesitate to use it on the boy.

Other men might feel satisfied and good-humoured after a good meal with plenty of beer to drink but Old Malik's life had settled into bitterness and anger many years before. He and his wife had long ceased to have any close relationship and now they barely tolerated each other. Nevertheless, he recognised that he was dependent on Maretta. Although he would never have admitted it, he knew that it would be impossible to run the farm without her.

For many years in the past, his only "pleasure" had been in bullying and beating the unfortunate men and women who worked on his farm. When the farm was more productive, several men and women worked for him and he had always been quick to abuse them. In recent years, these adult workers had gone and he could only vent his spleen on the unfortunate Joachim and, to a lesser extent, on the girl Giana. Old Malik had long translated his constant unhappiness into violent behaviour towards those who worked for him.

'They need beatings,' he muttered with perverse satisfaction, 'they need to know who is in charge.'

In his life, Old Malik had actually had four names. He had been born on the farm and, as the firstborn son, had followed the local tradition of taking his father's name. Thus, the sturdy baby who grew into a small boy was called Little Malik, his first designation. Later, as he grew up to become a strong and muscular boy, his name was changed to Young Malik. Two decades later, on the death of his father, Young Malik became the owner of the farm and became plain Malik for many years. In time, his lined, weather-beaten face and grizzled hair transformed him into Old Malik, arguably his final incarnation. However, no-one ever called him Old Malik to his face (no-one would have dared!); in the local villages where he appeared occasionally to buy, sell or barter, his few acquaintances would shake his hand and call him Malik.

On the farm, Maretta spoke very little to him and, these days, never spoke his name; for many years, she had addressed him only as "Husband". Likewise, he addressed her as "Wife". Of course Joachim or Giana were not entitled to speak the names of Old Malik or Maretta but acknowledged them as Master and Mistress on the very few occasions they were required to speak. Normally, Old Malik did most of the talking and no response was required or expected!

Old Malik was a man who lived in the present; he gave little thought to the future and seemed to have no interest in the past. In fact his childhood had actually been happy and secure. Although his father set the Young Malik to work on the farm at quite an early age and required a good standard of work from him, he was always pleasant and fair to him. He loved his son and wished him well. Young Malik was strong and physically well-coordinated so he did not find his work on the farm onerous.

However, the academic side of Young Malik's training never went so well. His father was an educated man who could read and write well; in addition he had enough skill and understanding of figures to keep the farm accounts meticulously. Naturally, he wished to pass on all these talents to his son and spent many long hours teaching him reading, writing and basic numerical skills, as well as passing on the considerable general knowledge he had acquired during his life. With dogged persistence, Young Malik eventually was able to read and write and became sufficiently numerate to deal with simple accounting procedures.

His mother was a cheerful, energetic woman who doted upon her first-born son. She spoiled him when she could and clearly favoured him over her other children. She arranged that he sat next to her at family meals and surreptitiously fed him the best bits of food from the communal dishes before the others could take them. During the day, she attended to him assiduously any time he was present, making sure his clothes were always in good repair and putting delicious tit-bits in his food bag when he left for work.

The two younger children, twin girls, would sometimes protest to their father about this favouritism but he would smile at them warmly, saying: 'No, you're wrong. Your mother loves you all equally and so do I.' Then, to prove it, he would give each of his children an equal share of food and a small cup of beer. Of course the younger children were unconvinced but as members of a happy family, they accepted the situation with equanimity on most occasions.

The years passed and Young Malik grew into one of the most physically attractive young men in the area, receiving many admiring glances from the young local girls when he accompanied his father to the surrounding villages. Also, the people of the area treated him with increasing respect, since they recognised him as the heir to the farm, which, in these days, was one of the finest in the region. In this country, it was the norm for the eldest son to inherit family-owned land from their father;

if the land had a farm operating upon it, then the inheritance became the farm in its entirety.

Old Malik's father was a very successful and progressive farmer, knowledgeable in all matters of cultivation. In addition, he was notably shrewd in business and particularly good at dealing with people. Unlike the many tenant farmers in the region, he actually owned his farm. Many years before, he had been able to buy the farmland from the local landowner; rumour had it at the time that some sort of favour had been involved with the deal but the exact details of the transaction were unknown.

Naturally, the handsome eldest son of a local farm owner was especially attractive to those families who had daughters in the appropriate age range! In the local community, there were quite a number of families who were anxious for their daughters to become known to the attractive Malik; this even included the family of the rich landowner who had sold the farmland to Malik's father. This important family lived in a large stone house in the middle of a large tract of forested land. Young Malik's mother was ambitious for him and, as mothers do, she did all she could to direct him in the direction of the landowner's daughter.

On the other hand, Young Malik's father was indifferent to this possible union of families. He was interested in the continuation of the farm under the ownership of his son and he had for years done his best to train him in all the various skills and techniques he would need. Although he recognised that his son certainly had the physical stature to handle all aspects of the farm work, he was disappointed that Young Malik was slow to learn the more complex skills of farming and business. In truth, Young Malik could not comprehend the more complex ideas his father wanted him to understand. The teaching was repeated many times but progress was slow and unreliable. Young Malik continued to be confounded and confused while his father despaired.

Time passed and, after very delicate negotiations between the two families, Young Malik had been introduced to the daughter of the local landowner. Unfortunately, she proved to be a thin, dull and insipid girl with an extremely haughty manner. Young Malik's mother was highly delighted; she had worked long and hard to achieve this situation and now all her plans were coming to fruition! She calculated that the status of her family would be greatly enhanced by this union. Who knows, maybe her husband could use his knowledge, skill and charm to become an important landowner himself, instead of just a farmer. She could see herself living in a big house with many servants: 'Oh, life could be so wonderful!' she cried in delight – and danced around the room!

Her husband, poring over some accounts at a table in the corner of the room, looked up and gave her a wan smile. He guessed the train of her thoughts. He wished that Young Malik could acquire his farming skill or business sense or, at least, some of his mother's sparkle. In his father's company, the young man seemed particularly slow and dull: 'Maybe he's a really good match for that pathetic girl,' he thought sadly. But in his heart he knew better, because he knew that the wife of a farmer needs to be strong, dedicated and hard-working. From what he had seen of the landowner's daughter, she would certainly not fit the bill as a wife for his son. Putting down his pen, he sighed.

More months passed and it was now arranged that Young Malik should make visits to the landowner's house to become acquainted with his daughter. He would arrive each time with a small gift for the girl, giving it to her nervously as she sat waiting. On each occasion, she would set the gift aside without comment. She made no attempt to make conversation, merely indicating that he should sit down. Of course the two young people were never allowed to be alone together.

The visits normally involved Young Malik seated rather uncomfortably on a carved wooden chair in the large and dark main room of the house with the girl sitting on another chair some distance away; a third chair was always occupied by a chaperon – the girl's mother or another female relative. Their stilted, very sparse conversations were monitored carefully. Very occasionally, if the weather was particularly fine, they would be allowed to walk outside for a short time but were never allowed to be close to each other; the chaperon was always nearby, watching and listening carefully.

As the weeks and months went by, Young Malik became increasingly disquieted by these visits. He felt uncomfortable and unwelcome in this large pretentious house and he had no liking for the people who occupied it. When he met the landowner and his wife, they treated him with disdain and almost ignored him. Even worse, he found nothing attractive about the appearance or attitude of their daughter, who seemed to be totally uninterested in anything he tried to say or do.

After a number of these visits, he complained to his mother, suggesting that it was all a mistake.

'These are very early days,' his mother replied brightly, 'there is no way you can get to know much about their daughter in such a short time. Just give it time. You'll see. I'm sure she's an absolutely lovely girl and you will be very lucky if she agrees to marry you.'

Young Malik thought about these words and was increasingly depressed. He was trying his hardest. He had been on his best behaviour with her. He had tried what he considered to be his best wiles. He had smiled at the girl many times, using his most winning smile, but she looked either bored or slightly alarmed. He had tried to be witty and charming but she had remained impassive or grimaced ever so slightly – probably in disgust, he thought. If she responded to anything he said her answer consisted merely of monosyllables.

So it was unsurprising that Young Malik became increasingly disconsolate as he trudged along the rough roads to the landowner's house. His route took him past a barren tract of land where the poorest people of the area lived in tumbledown shacks, attempting ineffectually to scratch a precarious living from tiny infertile smallholdings. He did not lift his head as he passed these pathetic places; he did not know any of these people – and did not want to, either!

'If they get to know who I am, they might accost me and try to beg money from me,' he thought.

However, one very hot day as he was trudging back from another extremely depressing visit to the big house, he was startled to hear beautiful singing. Surprised, he lifted his head and found himself abreast of one of the poorest and most ramshackle smallholdings. As he looked, he saw a tall young girl with flowing dark hair feeding a few scrawny hens in a tiny pen. As she threw meagre handfuls of grain to the hens, she continued to sing in a haunting, tuneful voice. Young Malik noted that she was dressed incongruously in a worn and rather ragged black dress that was clearly too big for her.

'An old dress of her mother's,' he thought, wryly. Suddenly aware, the girl turned and looked straight at him with large questioning eyes. 'She's beautiful,' he thought, 'actually, I think she is the most beautiful girl I have ever seen.'

This totally unexpected thought struck Young Malik dumb for a moment; then, collecting his scattered wits, he faltered: 'I'm very thirsty, do you have any beer?'

The girl hesitated and frowned.

'I'll pay,' he added hastily. Her face lit up with a fleeting smile and Young Malik's heart leapt!

'Wait,' the girl said quietly and disappeared into the shack, reappearing a moment or two later with a pot of foaming beer, handing it to him over the rough fence. He took a coin from his pocket and she accepted it gravely, examining it carefully. 'It's too much,' she said, 'but I have no other money to give you.'

'No, I want you to have it,' Young Malik replied, his eyes never leaving hers.

Close up, he thought she even more beautiful still: 'What a pity she is a low serf, suitable only to be a slave worker,' he could not help thinking with regret. The beer was good and he drank it quickly. 'I thank you,' he said gravely. She took the pot from him and was silent as he walked away, his mind in a turmoil. Suddenly he stopped and turned; she had not moved and was watching him intently.

'What is your name?'

'Maretta,' she replied quietly.

Young Malik's mother noted that her eldest son had suddenly become happier and more eager to visit the big house: 'Something must have happened,' she concluded wisely, 'I knew it would – these things take time.'

Little did she know how accurate her conclusion was; certainly something had happened – but it was something she could never have imagined! Every depressing visit to the big house was now a preface to a subsequent meeting with the beautiful girl from the poor smallholding. Young Malik became increasingly enchanted by her beauty and he found her personality absolutely delightful. He looked forward eagerly to their every meeting.

At first, the excuse was Young Malik's thirst as he walked back from the big house. She would wait for him to come and when she saw him would run to fetch his pot of beer. As he drank it very slowly, they would talk of many things. Her life of grinding poverty had taught her little of the world but he was astonished at her quickness of mind as he imparted his knowledge to her. He loved to watch her face. There was in her a vital freedom which fascinated him: 'She is like a wild bird,' he thought, 'perhaps an eagle or a falcon.' This thought filled him with wonder and delight.

Young Malik's sterile visits to the big house continued without any material change. Meanwhile his friendship with Maretta blossomed. At first, Maretta's mother was puzzled by the change in her daughter but judicious questioning soon revealed that a young man had come into her daughter's life. Her mother was not surprised because she knew that her daughter was very beautiful. But who was this young man?

In the end, Maretta told her mother the whole story and this became quite a dilemma for the older woman. She knew that Maretta's relationship with such a high-status young man was fraught with danger and could easily result in retribution against her family. She recalled that such things had happened to others in the past and shuddered as she remembered how a poor family had been attacked at night by men armed with swords and clubs. Men, women and children had been killed, injured or abducted as slaves. Their pathetic smallholding had been razed to the ground.

Maretta's mother was in no doubt that the attractive young man's family would be very shocked by his relationship with her daughter and she was wise enough to know that any prospect of wedlock was out of the question.

'His class never marry beneath them,' she thought. However she hoped it might be possible for her daughter to become a servant at his farm – in this way, Maretta could have a better life than she had. So, although fearful, the mother turned a blind eye to her daughter's friendship with the handsome stranger.

Thus, no restrictions were placed on Maretta and soon she and Young Malik took to walking in the forest nearby, sometimes talking seriously, sometimes laughing together or chasing each other through the forest like children at play. He became more and more enchanted with her and he knew that she loved to be with him.

So it was that the two young people set out to walk and talk in the forest on a fine, warm summer's day. He was dressed neatly in his best clothes – only the best was good enough for his visits to the big house! His boots and breeches were of fine leather and his shirt a soft linen, the rolled up sleeves revealing the powerful muscled arms that Maretta loved. By contrast, she was dressed in the only clothes she possessed, the baggy, worn black dress made of heavy, coarse material; a dress that had indeed belonged to her mother in her younger days. On Maretta, the dress was voluminous, covering her shoulders and hanging loosely around her, almost covering her slim bare feet.

They had talked seriously, gazing ever more deeply into each other's eyes. They had held hands. They had laughed together at little private jokes. Suddenly she sprang up to enact a game they had played many times before in the forest.

'You can't catch me,' she cried and ran off as fast as she could.

Joyously, Young Malik sprang to his feet and raced after her, calling: 'Bet I can!'

So the game proceeded as always, down the paths, round the trees, through the bushes; she dodging and ducking, he pretending that he could not catch her.

When she began to tire, the game always finished in the same thrilling way. Maretta judged the moment when her pursuer had drawn close, then threw herself face down on a soft bed of leaves. She would utter a little scream as he flopped down beside her, his arm falling across her back.

'Caught you!' A cry of triumph. Then they would lie together for a few moments, breathing hard, blissfully enjoying this moment of contact.

This time, however, something very different happened. When Maretta launched herself onto the bed of leaves, the heavy black skirt was caught by a sudden gust of wind and billowed up around her upper body, entangling her arms. The heavy material dragged with it the only other piece of clothing she was wearing – the long linen under-garment worn by all the girls and women of the region.

Unaware that anything had happened, Young Malik flopped down beside her as usual, crying the familiar "Caught you" and throwing his bare muscular arm across her waist. Almost immediately, he realised that his arm was not touching the familiar coarse material of her dress but the living warm softness of her flesh. Astonished, he turned his head and saw the length of her slim naked body fully revealed.

Young Malik had once seen a tree struck by lightning. A terrifying blue arc like a rope of fire had momentarily connected the black cloud to the fragile tree. Instantly, the tree had burst into a ball of fire, transforming it in seconds to a fragile skeleton of black ash. Then there was an eerie silence, a silence of suspended reality, before the air exploded with a noise greater than anything he had ever heard; surely a noise make by God himself?

This was exactly how Young Malik felt now. The flash and explosion occurred like a hammer blow within his head as his eyes focussed upon her body. Time was arrested; he and the girl were a frozen tableau in a timeless world. Then, the world sprang back to life; some sense of normality was reasserted as the normal forest noises encroached into his consciousness.

Wild-eyed, he snatched his arm away and sprang to his feet. She did not move or make any attempt to cover herself. At first he was dumbfounded by this but then a flash of understanding energised him into explanation and action: 'Of course! She is entangled in the heavy folds of the dress and cannot make any movement.' As he thought this, he seized the hem of her skirt now lying in folds across her shoulders and quickly drew it down to her ankles, covering up her nakedness. As he did so, he was careful to ensure that that no part of his hand came in contact with her soft flesh.

The next weeks and months were cataclysmic. The visits to the big house ceased. Young Malik was adamant that he would go no more to meet the daughter of the landowner. There were a number of meetings between Young Malik's father and the landowner, formal, difficult, delicate meetings; angry meetings at which furniture was thrown. Later, there were conciliatory meetings when the farmer applied his personal negotiating skills to the situation; this also included a brief mention of past favours done for the landowner, an element that seemed to inject a welcome calmness into the discussion.

Eventually, working relationships between the farmer and the landowner were re-established, although they remained uneasy and fragile for many years. Young Malik's mother was at first devastated by the failure of all her careful work. However, in the end she was persuaded by her husband that the landowner's daughter would not have been a good match for her beloved son. Deep in her heart, she had known this all along.

Meanwhile, Young Malik's relationship with Maretta became common knowledge in the region. Of course his mother was opposed to his relationship with this poor serf girl.

'You must not marry beneath your class,' she told him severely on a number of occasions.

He received similar advice from many of his village friends. 'Be sensible, take her on as a servant,' they suggested, 'then you can have her anytime you want.' And they laughed uproariously, augmenting this mirth with the usual coarse indicative gestures that young men are prone to make.

Young Malik ignored them all. He was resolute. He had gone to see Maretta the day after the incident in the forest.

Looking deeply into her eyes, he was blunt, firm and direct: 'I want you for my wife.'

At first, she demurred.

'You should not,' she told him, 'you know I am a poor serf and my family has nothing. I cannot possibly be a fit wife for you. Go away and forget me.'

'No,' he replied. 'We are betrothed and I will marry you.'

There and then, he gave her a ring to wear to mark their betrothal. They continued to meet frequently but Young Malik never touched any part of her body; they touched only when they held hands or when they kissed briefly.

In due course, the bride price was paid by Young Malik to the father of the poor serf family.

This action caused quite a scandal in the region; many thought that the normal marriage arrangements should not apply to such an odd union.

Following their betrothal, Young Malik provided new clothes for Maretta, the first new clothes she had ever possessed. He also gave her money so that she could buy all the things that a wife would need. He told her that he was building a new wooden shack for them at the farm and that this would be ready when they were married.

Maretta was delighted and deeply in love with Young Malik. Now she could walk into the village with her head held high and buy from the merchants there. When she did so, no-one spoke to her or acknowledged her new status but Maretta did not care.

Some weeks later, the reluctant village priest was persuaded (by the offer of a greatly increased marriage fee) to conduct their marriage ceremony in front of a handful of people. Unlike the usual village weddings, which were events that lasted for days and involved much singing, dancing, eating and drinking, the wedding of Young Malik and Maretta was a very muted affair, attended only by a few family members. There was no celebration, no music or dancing. Deeply in love, Young Malik and Maretta hardly noticed. They had eyes only for each other.

After the wedding, the bridegroom took his new bride to the farm and installed her in the new shack he had built for them, a small one-roomed structure that smelled deliciously of sweet new wood. He was particularly delighted when Maretta told him that she had never before seen such a beautiful house, so clean, neat and new.

Young Malik was also very pleased when his father came to welcome his wife as a new member of his family. He knew his mother was still tight-lipped about his marriage to Maretta but was convinced that in due course she would be charmed by his new wife's beauty and wonderful personality.

Thus began the married life of Young Malik and Maretta. They were ecstatically happy together. She looked after all his needs assiduously and he treated her with love and great kindness. They both looked forward to the long evenings after work, when they could snuggle up together! Like all young married couples, their love-making was joyful, energetic and frequent.

At breakfast the arrival of their children would be discussed on many occasions. As Young Malik spoke humorously of a farmer's need for many workers, Maretta's answering smile was the timeless face of the "Creator Mother", intensely beautiful and filled with the purest form of love.

The months, then the years passed and Young Malik became deeply worried that new life did not form in Maretta's body, despite their constant attempts to make this happen. He called upon many physicians and apothecaries for advice and, at considerable expense, these experts came to the farm and examined Maretta many times. Each consultation produced a remedy of some type and Young Malik took on the responsibility of administering these to his wife. Sometimes the remedies were unpleasant and Maretta was opposed to taking them.

'No use complaining,' her husband would say without pity, 'you must follow orders. I have paid a great deal for these remedies.' And so the pills would be swallowed and the ointments applied despite her protests.

As more time passed, Young Malik began to blame his wife for her lack of fertility, at first secretly, then openly and with increasing acrimony. He became increasingly withdrawn and spent less and less time with her. Then one day, Young Malik decided that his wife should be examined by the village midwife. 'She deals with these matters all the time, so she should be able to find out what the problem is,' he thought.

Of course he did not discuss this with his wife but went to see the midwife the very next day. Having explained the situation to her, he requested that she come to the farm and examine his wife. 'I want many children and she is barren,' he stated with his customary bluntness. Having agreed to pay the midwife's fee for this service, he arranged to transport her to the farm on the following day.

'The midwife is here to examine you,' Young Malik said to his wife the following morning when he appeared at the farm with the old woman. 'Make sure you do everything she wants and tell her the truth, you hear?' Displeased and stony-faced, Maretta held the door of the shack open and the midwife entered.

Young Malik waited outside and time crawled past.

'This is taking a long time,' he complained, 'let's hope it does some good.' Like all men of these times, he was of course totally convinced that the infertility was Maretta's fault.

After a whole hour, the midwife appeared and they sat down and talked together.

'I've asked her many questions and I've examined her very thoroughly,' the midwife said, 'and I cannot find anything wrong. Of course, that doesn't mean that all is well, because there are many reasons for a woman to be barren.' Then she added: 'If you want to have many children, you gentlemen should be very careful who you marry. The women you marry need to be good breeding stock, you understand?' The midwife looked at him significantly but Young Malik did not understand her words.

'What do you mean?' he asked in some bewilderment.

'I mean that your wife is *not good breeding stock*,' the midwife replied waspishly. 'If you want many children, you need a woman from good breeding stock.' Young Malik was dumbfounded and completely taken in by the midwife's artful explanation. His face flushed deeply with embarrassment. He had never given any thought to this aspect of marriage.

Now in his confusion he felt his fury rise – Young Malik reacted to most situations with anger: 'How could she have duped me like this?' This thought struck him like a physical blow, sending his mind reeling. In this moment, his love for Maretta was choked off by his fury. Sitting beside him, the midwife observed his reaction and her face became set in an ugly smirk of satisfaction.

Several years passed. The farm continued to be successful and fertile under the leadership of Young Malik's father. The older man had now given up trying to teach his son the essentials of good farming and Young Malik's farm work was that of a labourer rather than the trainee farmer he should have been. Every evening, Young Malik took himself off to the village tavern, where he drank noisily with his companions.

One evening, not long after a violent storm had affected the area, a man entered the tavern and told him there was a woman outside who wanted to speak to him urgently.

'Who is it?' Young Malik asked.

'I don't know,' the man answered, 'but she says she has come to solve your problems.'

With the bad grace of a drunken man, Young Malik went outside, shouting:

'Who wants Malik?'

'I do. I'm here to solve your problems.' Young Malik recognised the village midwife.

'What do you want?' He spoke testily.

'I have worked very hard for you and your wife. I have found for you exactly what you want,' she replied. 'Look, a baby!' She held out the small bundle she was carrying in her arms.

'A baby?' he queried, completely taken aback, a shadow of remembrance flitting across his face.

'Yes,' the midwife continued, 'a very good baby, not long born, fit and healthy – and high-born, too (The midwife was a skilled and inventive liar). You won't find a better baby than this one! Her parents are dead – uh, they died in the storm last week.' She thought quickly. 'A tree fell on them, that's what happened.' She paused: 'A special baby for you and your wife and a special price for you, only ninety-five Ourtz.' This said quickly.

Young Malik was silent, introspective. Suddenly he shook his head as if to clear it:

'No,' he said.

The midwife was nonplussed: 'But I have taken it into my care especially for you. And I've come here on this cold night just to see you about it,' she protested.

'No,' he said again.

'Look,' the midwife spluttered in confusion 'Because I know this baby is the right one for you, I will give you a very special price, only seventy-five Ourtz.'

'No.' The man turned his back on her and re-entered the tavern.

That evening, Young Malik was unusually quiet when he returned to the shack. Maretta, dozing in a chair beside the fire, did not notice his return. For some minutes, he stood looking at her, seemingly poised to speak, then suddenly he turned on his heel and went out again.

It was shortly after this that a tragedy befell the farm. Young Malik's mother fell ill with a serious fever and within a very short time she had succumbed to this illness and died. Her eldest son, sunk in his own selfish misery, regarded the death of his mother as an unreasonable inconvenience and dealt with the burial arrangements in a callous and perfunctory manner.

He was equally callous towards his father who was understandably devastated by the death of his wife of so many happy years. In the months that followed, the father became increasingly withdrawn and began to lose interest in the farm, which had always been the passion of his life. Within the year, despite knowing that his son lacked the skills to be a good farmer, both in agricultural knowledge and as an employer of people, he had passed over the running of the farm to his son and withdrew to pottering around the farm, doing odd jobs here or there, often ineffectually.

It would not be long before tragedy returned to the farm once more. One cold and blustery day in the following year, one of the young farm labourers ran with considerable trepidation to inform Young Malik that his father had been found lying injured on the floor of the barn. On hearing this, Young Malik, who was working to mend a section of fencing, struck the young man with a violent punch and knocked him to the ground, not because of the news he had brought but because he had interrupted the work Young Malik was doing.

Leaving the man bleeding on the ground, Young Malik stalked off to the barn, bellowing his anger. The other workers cringed in fear at his approach and fell completely silent as he stamped into the barn. His incandescent gaze, at once furious and contemptuous, rested briefly on each of the workers now pressed against the walls of the barn.

'What's happened? Where is he?' The oldest labourer, a quiet and gentle grey-haired man, gestured timidly towards the centre of the barn.

Young Malik's father was lying in a twisted heap on the hard earth of the barn floor, with the hayloft ladder on top of his body. He had obviously been climbing the ladder for some reason when it had broken free from its fastenings. It was immediately obvious that he was dead. Having fallen from a considerable height, he had struck his head violently on the metal blade of a plough which had been brought into the barn for repair. This blow had shattered his skull.

In complete silence, Young Malik took in all the details of the scene before erupting into absolute fury. He seized a stout stick and began to lash out at the totally blameless men and women who were present. Screaming, they ran from the barn in terror but not before some had been injured by the farmer's murderous and totally unjustified attack.

Somedays later, Young Malik attended his father's funeral with the same truculent disinterest that he had exhibited when his mother died. He made no effort to respect the memory of his father and shocked many by wearing his normal dirty work clothes. Maretta did not attend the funeral; her husband had not mentioned it to her and, even if he had, it is unlikely she would have been there – it was too much trouble.

His father had been a very well-respected and popular man in the region and many people attended the funeral, all wearing their best clothes. The village elders and many of the other leading local citizens came to offer their condolences to Young Malik but all were treated with casual rudeness. Even when the rich landowner, still smarting at the farmer's rejection of his daughter, came forward to offer his condolences,

Young Malik's only response was: 'Never mind that, just make sure I get the farm title passed to me as soon as possible.' (As the King's Justice, the rich landowner had some administrative responsibilities for the area.) These brutal words shocked many people who were present and most vowed to have nothing to do with the farmer from that moment on.

Nevertheless, the farm now belonged officially to Malik, notably no longer "Young". On returning from the funeral, he told Maretta that they were moving into the now empty farmhouse. He would turn their shack into a store. Maretta objected. She told him that she did not wish to move; that she was perfectly settled where she was. Characteristically, Malik ignored her wishes. When all their belongings were moved to the farmhouse, he placed her bed into the smaller room and set up a truckle bed for himself in the main room, underlining their complete separation.

Under Malik's management, the farm continued to go downhill. Over the years, incorrect management of the soil reduced its fertility markedly and crop output decreased considerably; sometimes, the crops failed completely. Simultaneously, poor husbandry of the farm animals meant that many of them became sick and died.

Inevitably, Malik blamed his workers for all these problems and became even more unpleasant and abusive towards them. When he resorted to striking them on a regular basis, one by one they started to leave; they were free men and women and could do so. The oldest workers stayed on for a time, loyal to the memory of Malik's father, but eventually even they could not tolerate Malik's increasing violence.

Left without help on the farm, it was then that the aging Malik bought Joachim to work as a farm boy: 'I'll soon whip him into shape,' he thought, smirking unpleasantly at the prospect.

"Old Malik" had arrived.

The farmer narrowed his eyes and squinted towards the top of the field where he could see the boy ploughing.

'Good thing for him,' he grunted, rather disappointed. He was also disappointed to find that his bullock had been watered and fed. Soon the animal was hitched up to the plough again and the work restarted. Hours passed; the shadows moved and lengthened and all was quiet apart from the muted noises generated by the ploughs, the panting of the straining bullocks and the occasional shouted commands of their drivers.

Suddenly, there was a great commotion from the top of the field. A large bird had flown up from a ground nest in front of Joachim's bullock and the startled animal had reared and plunged in sudden panic. The heavy plough was knocked over, pinning the boy's leg to the ground. He struggled to free himself but could not.

A few minutes later, Old Malik approached the scene, shouting angrily and brandishing his heavy bullock whip. This sight filled the boy with absolute terror. Old Malik had only once before struck him with a whip; not only was it the most agonising punishment he had ever experienced but the wounds were so severe that his flesh took many weeks to heal. He struggled to free himself with redoubled efforts so that he could flee.

'If he whips me while I'm trapped here he might kill me!' The boy burst into terrified tears.

Old Malik seized the bullock and calmed it. Then, cracking the heavy rawhide whip, he turned his attention to the trapped boy:

'You stupid useless little fool,' he snarled, 'this is all your fault and now you're going to pay.' The boy whimpered as the man stepped towards him, raising the heavy whip.

Suddenly, still several metres from the prostrate boy, the man stopped. He stood stock still. His fury disappeared, as quickly as a candle flame is extinguished by a sudden gust of wind, to be replaced by a powerful feeling of peace and calmness which pervaded his whole being. He had not experienced such a feeling for decades. Unnoticed, the bullock whip slipped from his thick, powerful fingers to fall on the ground. He looked away from the boy pinned below the plough and let his gaze run along the neat furrows that the boy and his plough had produced, finding his thoughts turning unexpectedly to the beauty and precision of that work.

After some moments, Old Malik's gaze returned to the trapped boy. Stepping forward, he lifted the heavy plough and set it aside, revealing that the boy's leg was deeply embedded into the soft ploughed earth below. Released from the dead weight of the plough, the boy scrambled free, carefully lifting his leg from the earth while keeping a very wary eye on his master. The leg came free with ease and the boy rose slowly to his feet, testing his weight upon the limb, rather gingerly at first, then with increasing confidence, finding he could move it without pain or tenderness: 'I'm really lucky,' he thought gratefully, 'that heavy plough could easily have broken my leg.'

Now, he was in a quandary. Should he run away to avoid Old Malik's fury or should he just stand still and pray to the spirits that he would not to be killed? Should he try to explain what happened – how it was not his fault but the fault of the bird suddenly frightening the bullock? Or should he restart his ploughing work again to try to please his master with his dedication?

Meanwhile, the man was still and silent, looking at the standing boy with a strange neutral expression that Joachim had never seen before.

In fact, Old Malik was looking at the boy with almost sightless eyes, his mind in bewildering turmoil. Strangely, part of his mind was calm and serene, a long-forgotten condition for him, and part was a racing tumult of almost totally-forgotten memories. Finally, Old Malik looked around him, a look of appraisal, a careful scan of the farm as if seeing it for the first time. Then he smiled, a rather bewildered but genuine smile quite unlike his usual cruel leer. Bending down abstractedly, he scooped up the bullock whip and tucked it neatly under his arm. Then, without a word, he turned around and walked back down the hill, striding purposefully towards the distant farmhouse.

Maretta

'He knows so much,' she thought ecstatically, literally hugging herself in her delight, 'and I have so much to learn.' The girl just loved to sit close to the handsome (to her, beautiful) Malik as he spoke in what to her was a clear, educated voice. She had no idea that the world was filled with so many things; how could this wonderful young man know so much? He had told her so many amazing facts that it almost made her head spin.

Dreamily, she called to mind some of the wonders he had told her about: strange and dangerous places far away that could only be reached by crossing huge oceans of water in gigantic boats filled with hundreds of men! … fierce wars between huge armies which lasted for many years. In these conflicts, there were numerous heroic deeds done by brave knights dressed in armour of bright metal and sitting astride mighty battle horses! … victorious kings and lords who lived in impregnable castles. Some also had gorgeous palaces filled with priceless treasure – more gold, silver and precious stones than she could ever imagine! … incredible lands where the mountains were so high that they were permanently covered with deep white snow that had fallen from the sky (he had to explain to her what snow was).

Why, he even knew about the sun, the moon and the stars!

She quivered in delight as she thought of the way he clasped her hands so tenderly as he told her these things; his broad and strong hands were always so warm and alive. Sometimes, she managed to be so close to him as they sat on a grassy knoll that she could feel the warmth of his firm thigh against hers. As he spoke, she could not take her eyes away from his; not that she wanted to – not for a minute, a second. His beautiful brown eyes were filled with such intelligence and strength. She was in love with this most remarkable of men and being in love was the most wonderful thing that had ever happened to her in her life!

He was so delightfully playful, too, she reflected. They both enjoyed laughing together, telling each other about the extremely funny events they had seen: the ropes of that heavily-loaded hay cart breaking and the road completely blocked with many bundles of hay; it had taken such a long time to reload the cart and no-one could pass by for hours! … the old fisherman overbalancing on the bridge and falling into the water among the fish he was trying to catch. How wet and furious he had been! … the village merchant's carefully built display of apples, so lovingly and painstakingly constructed into a high tower outside his shop, suddenly collapsing catastrophically. How hilarious it had been to see the fruit rolling away in all directions! How funny to see the merchant dashing this way and that to retrieve his precious produce! Did you see? Some of the apples had even rolled away down the hill!

Oh, how they laughed until the tears ran down their cheeks.

Her mind now turned to the part of their tryst that she loved most: their special chasing game. How thrilling and exciting it always was to dash breathlessly around the trees, avoiding his outstretched arms, until that moment when he caught her. That glorious moment when his arm fell across her body! She recalled how they had played this wonderful game many times and the pressure of his arm on her back was the culmination of their amazing time together. It filled her with such yearning and suffused her with a feeling of absolute peace.

Then her smile faded to solemn introspection as she recalled the day before. They had had gone to the forest as they usually did. Their chasing game had been played with all its energetic joy and the time had come for that moment of unified peace. Her old dress was so loose on her body that she was completely unaware of its billowing travel from feet to shoulders at that moment when she threw herself down on the leaves. She only realised that something unusual had happened when she found large copious folds of thick black material underneath her hands, arms and upper body. Certainly she would never have expected the closer-fitting undergarment to be lifted up too, to reveal her body almost completely.

So instead of the usual light pressure of his muscular forearm across the loose waistband of her dress, it was a surprise, though certainly in no way unpleasant, to feel the touch of his warm flesh upon her own. It was then, registering his unexpected touch along with the distinctive caress of cool air upon the complete length of her lower limbs that she realised fully what had happened. At such moments, the human brain works remarkably quickly. On this occasion, the age-old wisdom of womanhood took over. She did nothing. She made no movement. She lay completely still.

Wisdom can be instinctive and some wisdom is exactly that. But most wisdom is garnered and honed by the experience and learning that the progression of life brings. Maretta was the second child in a very poor serf family; her elder brother was a few years older and a younger brother had followed her. Family life had always been very hard. They lived precariously on a very small patch of infertile, rocky land which was, in fact, common land.

The family were aware they had no rights to live on this common land and so were in constant fear of eviction. They knew that such evictions happened periodically and, if it ever happened to them, they knew they would be driven out of the area with anger and violence. Members of serf families had been injured or even killed in the course of such evictions.

The five members of the family lived in a rude shack built on this land and they attempted to grow root vegetables and keep a few animals on the extremely poor soil surrounding the shack. This was mainly unsuccessful; the crops were stunted at best and the only animals that survived were a few thin and scrawny hens, providing them with infrequent eggs.

Maretta's father and mother were absent throughout the length of the day, having to take any labouring work they could find at neighbouring farms or businesses, their pay usually being in the form of some food to feed the family in the evening; mostly, the food they were "paid" was inadequate and, in consequence, the family was almost always hungry. With the absence of her parents, Maretta was looked after by her elder brother throughout the day.

By the time Maretta was around eight or nine years old, her mother had felt it appropriate to inform her daughter that girls and boys were *very different from each other:*

'You need to be careful,' the mother warned her daughter, looking at her significantly. However, she did not elaborate further. This lack of explanation did not surprise Maretta, because serious conversations with her parents were very infrequent and invariably brief. By the time the adults returned from their day's labours, they had little energy for conversation and the whole family retired to their sleeping areas as soon as the meagre evening meal had been consumed.

Later that evening, lying in her narrow bunk, Maretta recalled her mother's teaching. What had she meant, "very different"? The girl turned her thoughts to her little brother who was around five years old at this time. Like Maretta herself, the little boy was in the care of her elder sibling during the day; this care included giving him his daily wash in a large wooden tub, set down in front of the shack and filled to a shallow depth from their supply of collected rainwater.

This was a routine that had previously been applied to Maretta when she was younger; of course she was now much too old to need someone to wash her and these days her ablutions were carried out carefully and in private. In her mind, she now scrutinised her little brother's naked body as he stood in the tub, examining it slowly and with great care to establish all the significant differences between his body and her own.

No "big sister" of a baby boy is unaware of the physical difference between baby boys and themselves. On first sight of the child being bathed or changed, their curious eyes are drawn to that peculiar (ugly?) little tube of flesh set in the groin and, in response to their questions, spoken or unspoken, their mother explains that "all boys are made like this". It is common for the girl to accept this explanation with pensive neutrality.

Remembering this scene some years before and now visualising the familiar sight of her little brother standing naked in the tub, Maretta could not identify any other physical differences; in fact, as far as she was concerned, all other parts of the little boy's body were identical to her own. Head, neck, shoulders, arms, body and legs were just like her own.

She puzzled about this for a while, then she thought: 'Maybe it's *other* boys who are "very different". How can I find that out?'

Despite her young age and disadvantaged life, Maretta was an intelligent and resourceful little girl, well used to solving her own problems. Now she lay quietly and wondered how she could solve this particular problem. Suddenly, she brightened: 'I know exactly how I'm going to do it!' she whispered triumphantly and turned over to go to sleep with a little smile of satisfaction on her face.

The opportunity to put her plan into action came several days later when her elder brother took his sister and brother into the village to buy a small quantity of salt for the family. The previous day, his father had been paid a few coins for his day's work and the family needed to replenish their small stock of this essential item, used for cooking and flavouring.

The day was perfect for Maretta's purposes, being very hot and still. On such a day, she knew it was highly likely that some of the village boys would be swimming and splashing in the river near the bridge; they usually did this if the weather was very hot. Because she knew that the boys always played naked in the water, this would offer Maretta the perfect opportunity to make a detailed inspection of their bodies.

On reaching the village, Maretta told her brother she would sit down near the road to the bridge and enjoy the sunshine while he went to the village store.

'I'll stay near here,' she assured him artfully, already hearing the shouts and laughter of the boys playing in the river nearby.

'All right,' her brother replied. 'Stay there and I won't be long.'

As soon as her brother was out of sight, Maretta crept down to the river and concealed herself in a large bush growing beside the riverbank. Sure enough, several naked boys were playing in the river and she had a completely clear view. As the boys dived from the bank, swam in the water or stood up and wrestled with each other, shouting, screaming and fighting each other with various degrees of violence, the hidden girl examined each one with great care.

After ten minutes or so of detailed study, Maretta judged that her mission had been accomplished and withdrew from the cover of the bush, skipping quickly back to the crossroads where she had arranged to wait for her brother. Once seated there, frowning with concentration, she recalled all she had seen and formulated her conclusions: 'Now I know for certain,' she thought with satisfaction, 'all boys look like that. They're all just the same as my little brother. There's just that one little difference between each one of them and me – and I know exactly what it is.' She felt quite sure of the result of her investigation.

Then her smirk of satisfaction faded: 'But why did Mother tell me they were very different? And why must I be careful?' Now she felt confused again.

For some time, the girl sat quite still with her eyes tight shut, frowning and concentrating as hard as she could on this difficult problem. Then, in a sudden flash of understanding, she remembered the behaviour of the boys in the river – weren't they so rough with each other? Weren't they always jumping upon each other, pushing each other beneath the water, fighting, shouting and screaming?

'That's it,' she thought, her frown cleared from her face by a wide smile, 'they *are* very different, because they're always fighting and they're so very rough. And that's why I need to be careful.' At last she understood!

After this, in the weeks and months that followed her great investigative adventure on the riverbank, Maretta often looked down at her own smooth, streamlined body as she stood naked in the tub and, with a gentle smile of satisfaction, remembered the rough behaviour of the boys in the river and whispered that traditional mantra of femininity: 'I'm glad I'm not a boy.'

There comes a time when children (quite suddenly, it seems) become taller, quite elegant creatures and seem to leave much of their childishness behind. Time had passed and it was now obvious that Maretta had crossed that mysterious threshold. It was then that a new routine was introduced into her life by her elder brother.

One day, just after she had made a visit to the privy, he led her behind the shack and told her he needed to check that she was cleaning her body properly after such a visit. Maretta was completely unperturbed by his request. She loved and admired her elder brother; he was like a second father to her – in fact he was more like a father to her than her real father, who was absent all day, every day. So she happily lifted up her clothes and exposed her body to him. At first, his examination was restricted to a perfunctory visual check but soon he began to touch her soft intimate flesh.

In the weeks and months that followed, these examinations were called for periodically and Maretta chattered quite happily to her brother as his hands probed her with increasing thoroughness. Gradually, however, she found herself becoming more reluctant to submit to these examinations. She began to feel that her body should be private and she was sure she was perfectly capable of keeping her whole body clean, including these parts that he insisted in examining. On the other hand, she did not want to offend her brother; after all, he was only doing this for her own good, wasn't he?

Then came the day when the usual inspection was called for and Maretta was conducted to the familiar spot behind the shack. On this day she was unhappy, now very reluctant to bare her body and she communicated this to her brother in no uncertain terms. Her brother insisted. It was his responsibility to look after her, he said. She should not be so ungrateful. He was very disappointed in her.

Thus rebuked and hanging her head in shame, Maretta complied with his wishes but winced as his hands touched her. This time, the examination was particularly thorough: 'This is taking a long time,' she thought, wriggling uncomfortably, 'I wish he would hurry up.' Hard on the heels of this thought, there came a sudden blinding flash of revelation that made her lift her head suddenly and look deep into her brother's eyes. It was in the depth of those eyes that she *saw the truth*.

In an instant, her brother's face flushed deeply; then he broke away from her accusing gaze and mumbled something incomprehensible before stumbling away. This was the last inspection of her body that Maretta had to endure. More importantly, at that moment Maretta the girl-woman had gained a timeless wisdom about men and women and life.

It was that same wisdom that kept her body motionless on that day in the forest, lying prone upon the soft bed of leaves, pretending to be tangled in the folds of her dress and fully aware of the astounded gaze of her beloved and beautiful Malik.

Maretta was more than happy to leave the next move to Malik. Whatever it was, it would be the right action for the moment, she told herself. Nevertheless she was a little disappointed when the heavy material of her skirt wafted away the intoxicating caress of the cool air on her sensitive skin before moulding itself to the contours of her body.

Within seconds, his strong arm had lifted her to her feet. For a moment they stood close together, looking at each other with new and knowing eyes.

Finally he spoke quietly but with great firmness: 'Not until we are man and wife. I love you too much for that.'

She understood and loved him all the more, hardly realising that he had just made a proposal of marriage. That night, she had agonised over what had happened in the forest and eventually decided she must set him free. She was not a suitable wife for such an important man. She was a poor serf who would never be anything else. And she wept the night away.

When they met on the following day, she blurted out her decision to part from him but he held her arms gently, looked straight into her eyes and rejected the suggestion with such force that her resolve shattered into delightful submission. From that time her life turned into a whirlwind of preparation, anticipation and joy, all spiced with a tinge of fear.

At the farm, Maretta was delighted with her new home and settled in to become the new and loving wife who worked tirelessly to make everything perfect for her handsome and attentive husband.

'What very happy days these are,' she thought as she cleaned the shack and its surrounds until everything was neat and bright.

She was deeply grateful to Young Malik's father who had welcomed her into the family with open arms. She had become very fond of the old man.

With a woman's instinct, she knew why her mother-in-law acted at first with stiff formality towards her and she right away began to work hard to forge a friendly, slightly subservient relationship with the older woman. In the event, this proved to be quite easy. Maretta was quick to help with the many chores of a farmer's wife and this, along with her ready humour and attractive beauty, soon won over the older woman. In fact the quick transition from tension to friendship was due not only to Maretta's efforts. Young Malik's mother knew that her beloved son was deeply in love with his new wife, and she was pleased to see him so happy.

Maretta looked forward eagerly to being pregnant. She did not care whether her first baby was a boy or a girl – after all, there would be so many more! However as the months and then the years passed, it became increasingly obvious that the blessing of pregnancy was not being visited upon her. She tolerated all the visits from the physicians and apothecaries; she knew her husband was trying his best to solve their problem and bring the blessing of babies to their family. The remedies they gave her often tasted horrible and some of them made her sick. Some of the ointments and tinctures were also foul-smelling and some were injurious, irritating or even burning her skin. Nevertheless she was always obedient, firstly because it was what Young Malik wanted her to do but also because she was desperate to present him with the son he yearned for.

Then came the day when her husband arrived with the village midwife. Maretta was washing some clothes when she heard a harsh, unfamiliar voice outside the farmhouse door. She had opened the door to find the midwife with her husband. She was a stooped old woman who wore a permanently sour expression and spoke angrily all the time.

Maretta knew the midwife by reputation; she was well-known among the poor serfs of the area, not only for refusing help to them with any birthing problems, even when payment was offered, but for speaking out against them in an attempt to stir the villagers into violent action against their poor neighbours. 'We don't need their kind here,' the midwife would say inflammatorily, 'they are nothing but a band of thieves, cheats and liars. We should drive them out. Who cares if they live or die?'

At her husband's bidding, Maretta reluctantly invited the midwife to enter. The interrogation proved to be unkind and unsympathetic. There were many questions, some worryingly embarrassing, but out of loyalty to her husband, Maretta did her best to answer them all to the best of her ability. The physical examination was even worse, ranging over every part of her body and conducted in a far from gentle manner. Finally, it was over.

'Do I have a problem with my body? Why cannot I make a baby?' Maretta addressed the midwife's back as she was packing away her cloths and tools.

'My answers are for your husband,' the midwife spoke contemptuously without turning around, 'not for you.'

Young Malik and the midwife spoke for a long time in the farmyard. Maretta strained to hear what was being said but could only make out an occasional word. After some time, the midwife climbed upon the cart and they left for the village.

Maretta waited with great impatience for the return of her husband. She was desperate to hear what the midwife had told him. Maybe if they followed her advice, everything would be all right. Maybe a baby would grow in her body – twins, even! Maretta felt a great rush of delight within her: 'Yes,' she thought, 'maybe it could even be twins. This could be a new start for us.' She felt a great surge of love for her husband, remembering those far-off days when they were so ecstatically happy, so much in love. 'Oh, how I wish he would return!' She strained her eyes into the distance.

Late in the evening, Young Malik finally returned, drunk and aggressive. He barged noisily into the farmhouse, calling loudly for more beer. Maretta opened a flagon and poured some for him. He took it without a word and quaffed it noisily, ignoring her completely. She sat quietly, waiting.

After some time, she spoke: 'What did she say?' Her voice flat and expressionless.

For some moments, he did not move. Finally he looked at her and she was shocked and repelled by the look of rejection in his eyes. Still he said nothing.

'What did she say?' she repeated. 'Why can't I make a baby?'

'She said she could not find anything wrong,' Young Malik replied slowly, almost inaudibly.

Maretta was overjoyed. Her optimism had been justified!

'But that's wonderful,' she cried ecstatically. 'We can try…'

'No.' His voice crashed through her words and shattered them. A shocked silence followed.

'Why not?' she whispered finally. 'If there's nothing wrong…?'

Another silence for several moments. Then: 'She says you are not good breeding stock.'

The world collapsed in upon Maretta. She felt totally numb, hardly able to draw her next breath. She had no idea how long she existed in that room with these eight words spinning around in her head, incising virtual grooves inside her skull. Eventually, very slowly, she came back to life. She was alone. He had gone from the room, she knew not where. She was left alone with these razor-sharp, devastating words: "She says you are not good breeding stock."

Maretta sat for some time in the apparent stillness of assessment and interpretation. Then came a burst of incredulous understanding, like the explosion of a rocket in the sky. She recognised with complete certainty that the midwife's words were part of a vendetta against her and against her unfortunate people. Now she spoke aloud, quietly and without expression:

'She examined me and could find nothing wrong. So she decided to poison my marriage because I am a poor serf.' Tears filled her eyes, part rage, part grief.

In the following days and weeks, Maretta tried to speak to her husband about the real meaning of the midwife's assessments and comments but he refused point-blank to engage in any conversation. Despite her best efforts, she could not penetrate the wall of dislike that was now his attitude towards her. As time passed, his demeanour deteriorated further to become constantly withdrawn and even more bad-tempered. It became the norm for him to be very drunk every evening.

From the farmhouse next door, Young Malik's father continued to be kind to her in a gentle, absent-minded sort of way but his mother withdrew her goodwill, firmly taking sides with her son.

'I knew it would never come out for the best; I told you you should never marry below your class.' However these words were not spoken in triumph because Young Malik's mother knew that her son was now very unhappy.

As the situation deteriorated further, Maretta became deeply depressed. Left all alone every day, she started to seek solace in the beer which in the past she had brewed for Young Malik with so much love. Soon she spent much of her days in varying degrees of alcoholic haze and in consequence become slovenly and uncaring in her habits. Her face became set in a vacuous, ugly scowl. Young Malik hardly noticed. As they sat at the table together, he bolted down the food she prepared for him and never raised his eyes to look at her.

Imprisoned in her world of unhappiness and alcohol, Maretta was vaguely aware of changes at the farm. The one she resented most was being compelled to move from her home into the farmhouse next door. Why did she need to move? She was perfectly happy where she was. She knew that both of Malik's parents had gone, died, she thought: 'I wonder what happened to them?' She sometimes puzzled about that but could not remember.

She also knew that all the farm workers had gone – again, she didn't know why and she didn't care; after all, it was her husband's business. On one occasion she had asked Malik about it but, as usual, he had just ignored her. Also, she remembered that Malik had bought a little boy to work on the farm – that was years ago. He was sent to live in the barn and she knew he was still there because she had to prepare food and drink for him. She had absolutely no interest in this boy and usually could not remember his name. All these thoughts constantly swirled around in Maretta's addled brain.

Then one evening, one of her unfocussed reveries was rudely interrupted as the farmhouse door crashed open, heralding her husband's usual drunken arrival. Normally he was taciturn and did not speak.

However this evening was a rare event. As he entered, he asked her a question: 'Do you want this?' He grated these words as he pushed a small ragged child across the room.

'What is it?' Maretta, half asleep and absorbed in drinking beer in her favourite chair by the fire, could not be bothered to raise her eyes.

'It's a child that came with a market deal I did this afternoon,' the man replied, 'you've been nagging me for a servant.'

Maretta could not remember any conversation on this matter. Nevertheless, her interest was slightly aroused and she stirred herself, squinting across the room blearily: 'Is it a boy or a girl?' she enquired.

'It's a skinny little girl,' he answered disinterestedly. 'Do you want it or not?

Maretta heaved herself out of the chair and seized the child rather roughly by the arm, pulling her closer to the light of the fire where she peered closely at her face, then lifted her clothes to inspect the small pathetic body below: 'Goodness, it's really skinny – and it's absolutely filthy, too! Couldn't you get a cleaner one than this?'

These comments infuriated Old Malik.

'Look,' he snarled in reply, 'I told you it was skinny. Have it or not as you want. What's all this about dirty? If it's dirty – wash it. What's wrong with you?' So saying, he left the farmhouse in his usual bad humour, slamming the door loudly.

There was complete silence for some minutes. The child did not move and waited with frightened eyes fixed on Maretta. Sighing wearily, the woman rose unsteadily to her feet and fetched a small wooden tub from a cupboard in the corner of the room. After some water had been poured into the tub, the cowed, feather-light girl was lifted into the water; in the same movement, the dirty, ragged dress that was her only garment was stripped from her and thrown aside.

Maretta set to work. Firstly, dirt and grease was washed out of the girl's matted hair, her face was washed several times, then all other parts of her emaciated body were scrubbed until they were clean. All this time, the girl made no sound. Maretta stood back to admire her handiwork.

'She does look a bit better when she's clean,' she thought.

'Sit over there,' her very first words to the child were sharp and unfriendly, 'while this disgusting thing – she held up the small ragged dress – is washed.' The garment was plunged into the tub where it was scrubbed energetically and hung up to dry near the fire.

'Haven't you got any other clothes?' was Maretta's next question to the small huddled figure of the girl. The child shook her head. 'Well you'll just have to stay like that until the dress is dry.' Maretta sat down heavily on her chair and picked up the pot of beer, drinking deeply from it and totally ignoring the child.

Once again, there was complete silence in the room. After ten minutes or so, the woman looked up and spoke: 'Have you got a name?' When the little girl did not respond immediately, the question was repeated, more sharply: 'Wake up! What are you called?'

'Giana,' the girl whispered.

'Giana, is it?' Maretta repeated, almost to herself. 'Funny name, no-one is called anything like that around here.' The child was silent. 'What work can you do?' the woman asked, sharply again.

'Anything you want me to do, Mistress.' The girl's voice was barely a whisper.

'Anything?' Maretta's voice was derisive and raucous in comparison. 'Let's hope so!' she quipped grimly, momentarily enjoying her unkind joke.

This was the manner of Giana's eventual arrival at Old Malik's farm.

Giana

It had been a long night of vicious weather. Now the dim light of dawn revealed churned, saturated ground peppered everywhere with deep pools of constantly rippled water. The wind, a ferocious, howling gale during the night with stinging, near-horizontal rain that chilled and soaked in an instant, had now given way truculently to a lower order of storm. Even so, the day had still dawned raw and angry, a bilious scudding grey augmented by cruel gusts of icy rain, driven pitilessly against those unfortunate enough to be out.

The woman (though in truth hardly more than a girl) had by chance stumbled close enough to the mouth of a low, dark cave in the hillside and taken blessed refuge there at the height of the storm the night before. Although cold, the cave was dry inside and sheltered from the worst of the wind.

As soon as she had penetrated far enough into the cave to escape the weather, the woman sank to the floor in a paralysing haze of increasing, pulsating pain. She was filled with terror as she realised her time had come and now she scrabbled around ineffectually with her hands, trying to prepare for the arrival into the world of the life that had been beating inside her for so many months.

The night developed steadily into an unbearable, all-pervading crescendo of pulsating pain, worse than anything the woman could ever have imagined. Her shrill screams echoed in the cave but were quickly snatched away by the banshee howls of the wind outside.

By morning, it had been fulfilled. The woman lay exhausted, desperately calling into the void for help, while trying to stem the crimson stream that flowed from her body. Her baby lay where it had been delivered from her womb; in her pain and exhaustion, the only thing the mother had been able to achieve was some padding layers of blanket below the tiny body, with the ends drawn up to enclose the baby in a loose cocoon.

The child was alive, crying thinly but at the same time demonstrating that unique determination of the new-born. Despite her most powerful desires, the mother had no capacity to respond. Time passed. The crimson flow did not slacken. The mother's cries for help weakened. The baby clung to life, protesting its innocence with increasing hopelessness. The cries emanating from the cave mouth diminished.

'What a day!' The travelling merchant muttered these words to himself as he and his family trudged along the narrow muddy track that would eventually take them to the village. When the weather was like this there was no question of anyone riding in the large covered wagon – not even the children.

Years before, when this heavy wagon was being built for him, the merchant had wisely specified stout wide wheels; they were usually effective on muddy roads. However, this track was proving to be a serious trial. It was in poor condition and heavily pocked with deep potholes, now filled with slimy mud. The merchant sighed as one of the large rear wheels sank deeply into a pool of mud, bringing the heavy vehicle to a shuddering halt, despite the best efforts of the two strong mules harnessed to the front shaft.

Like his father before him, the man was a travelling merchant in cloth; he and his family spent most of the year on the road, travelling widely around the country villages, selling from the extensive stock of cloth carried in the wagon. Each of the large bundles of cloth was very heavy and it was of course necessary to carry a comprehensive selection of material for sale.

As he travelled across the country, the merchant also bought cloth from village weavers and sold this on at a suitable profit to individuals and other merchants further along his route. This had been a steady and successful business in the family for many years.

'People always need good cloth for hangings, covers and clothing,' the merchant often said, 'and everyone knows I sell nothing but the best of cloth.'

With one wheel stuck firmly in the deep mud, the merchant wearily fetched his shovel and began to dig out a ramp in front of the trapped wheel; if the excavated ground was firm enough, this would allow the wheel to roll up to ground level when the mules exerted all their strength to pull the wagon forward. His wife helped to throw the excavated mud over to the roadside with a smaller shovel.

Meanwhile, their two children, a boy and a girl, did as children always do – they ran whooping up the hill, laughing, shouting and jostling each other with that mysterious joy of living that children have. On the track below, the cloth merchant now judged that the wagon was ready to be pulled from the mud so he returned to the heads of his beasts to tug at their head ropes, clucking his tongue to encourage them to pull forward. The powerful beasts strained forward and the wheel came free with a reluctant squelch and rolled up the excavated ramp to return to ground level.

Ready to resume their journey, the merchant replaced the shovels in the wagon and called for his children. After some moments, the boy and girl came running back. His wife took one look at their little faces and, as mothers always do, knew something was very wrong. She caught the boy by the arm and enquired urgently: 'What's wrong? What has happened? Have either of you hurt themselves?'

Eyes wide, gasping and white of face, the boy mumbled a reply: 'It's up there, in the cave. We thought it was a bird but I think it's a baby. It's all bloody.'

The boy burst into tears and his little sister immediately howled in sympathy. The adults looked at each other blankly, shock mirrored in their eyes. Extended seconds ticked by.

'It's not our business, nothing to do with us,' the man said uncertainly, 'we've got enough problems of our own.' He looked as if he wished he was somewhere else – somewhere very far away!

However the woman was more practical and decisive: 'No, we can't say that. We can't just walk away. The boy has told us what he saw. We need to investigate, to see what has happened.' Still the man did not move. 'Go and see what has happened. Go quickly.' The woman was adamant.

Reluctantly, sighing and muttering to himself, the merchant climbed up the hill to the cave. After a few long minutes he reappeared and returned to the wagon. The adults held a whispered conversation, observed fearfully by their quietly sobbing children. Then both adults climbed up to the cave, the man carrying his shovel.

The baby was still alive, though now so weak that it was reduced to almost inaudible whimpering, its breathing rapid and uneven. The woman lifted the pathetic scrap of life from the ground, still wrapped in the blood-soaked blanket and carried it down to the wagon. There, she tended to it, washing away the blood and dirt and wrapping the tiny body in clean, warm cloth. Meanwhile, the man carried out his grim task on the hillside near the cave, digging a shallow grave and burying the small pathetic body of the mother therein.

When the man returned, his wife asked about the identity of the mother – who she was, where she came from, where she might have been going.

'I looked everywhere,' he replied, 'but there was absolutely nothing to identify her. We don't know anything about her.' Then he looked worriedly into the bunk bed where the baby lay. 'What about the baby? Do you think it will live?'

'Well, I'm going to try my best,' his wife answered briskly, now busying herself with the preparation of some warm milk. 'We'll see if she can be persuaded to have a little of this milk. If I can get her to take some of this, she will have a chance of survival. We don't want to have to deal with two deaths in the same day.' The reality of this thought passed a shadow across each of their faces.

The following hours brought blessed progress. The baby responded well to the care of the merchant's wife and started to feed with strengthening enthusiasm, moving its tiny limbs with increasing energy. By the end of the day, the family were congratulating each other on their success at saving the baby's life – an undeniable truth.

From the start, the children had been fascinated by the baby; they had never seen a child so small and they were amazed by the power and enthusiasm that was displayed when the bottle of warm milk was offered. They pleaded with their mother to be allowed to feed the tiny infant and were delighted when the milk disappeared quickly from the bottle. Now that the child was thriving, the children were informed by their mother that the baby was a girl: 'Just like you!' She pointed at her daughter.

'What's her name?' The children had cried excitedly.

'She hasn't got a name but I'm going to give her one,' their mother replied. 'I'm going to call her Giana, after my own great-grandmother who lived a long time ago in the Old Country.'

The slow journey of the heavy wagon continued and it was several days later before the merchant and his family reached the village that was their next destination.

'The first thing we need to do is find the midwife,' the merchant said to his wife. 'Obviously the baby will need to be left here, because we cannot travel around the country with such a young child. The midwife will be able to find someone to look after her. Maybe someone who wants a baby but can't have one … perhaps a family whose baby has died recently.' His wife was sad about this, for in these few short days she had established a loving bond with the child. Little Giana was now thriving well, despite her traumatic and near-fatal entry into the world.

Enquiries were made of passers-by and the shack of the midwife pointed out. The merchant pulled up the wagon nearby, climbed down and knocked at the door.

'Who is it?' An unpleasantly raucous voice was heard from within.

'I'm a stranger, a passing merchant who has important business with the midwife of this village.' The door was flung open with a crash. The midwife was a stooped old woman who wore a permanently sour expression.

'What is your business with me?' The midwife spoke angrily.

'I have a baby to discuss with you.' The merchant smiled his most winning smile, the one he always found effective in difficult commercial transactions. 'Can my wife and I speak to you?'

With bad grace, the midwife permitted the man, woman and baby to enter her shack.

'What's all this about?' She addressed them sharply, look-ing aggressively at them both. So the sad story of Giana was told and the midwife's scowl deepened. 'What am I supposed to do? How can I find someone?' The old woman continued to complain bitterly, while stripping and examining the baby with practiced but far from gentle hands. Giana squawked in protest but the examination was soon over. The midwife then thrust the naked baby and its clothes back into the arms of the merchant's wife.

'There's nothing wrong with this baby though she could do with more flesh on her,' she stated disagreeably. 'If you want me to find her a home, you'll need to pay me. I don't do all this for nothing, you know. People don't want to look after stray babies and it can take me months to find someone. Anyway, what's her name?'

'Giana,' the merchant's wife ventured.

'Giana?' The midwife repeated the name raucously. 'What sort of a name is that? No-one is called anything like that around here. Why don't you call her something normal?'

'Giana was my great-grandmother's name; she lived in another country far away,' the woman replied uncertainly.

'Well, it's a stupid name to give a child,' the midwife grunted, 'but why should I care?'

There was silence for a few moments. Then the midwife turned to the merchant: 'I want fifty Ourtz.'

The man shook his head: 'It's too much,' he replied, automatically falling into his merchant negotiating mode.

'Really,' the old woman sneered, 'then take the baby and go.' She turned away and made to leave the room. The man was nonplussed. He was not used to such unpleasantness in commercial transactions. To him, this was of course a commercial transaction.

'What about forty?' This said with decreasing hope.

The midwife swung round and thrust her face close to his: 'I said fifty and I meant fifty. Take it or leave it.' Then she turned away abruptly, muttering curses.

Shamefacedly, the man counted out the coins and, without another word or a backward glance, left the room.

His wife was distressed. She did not wish to leave baby Giana with this unpleasant old woman – but she knew she had no choice: 'Please be kind to her,' she said quietly, as she turned to leave with tears in her eyes.

'What?' The midwife spoke so loudly and sharply that the child started violently and began to wail with fright. 'Now look what you've done, you stupid woman,' the midwife yelled, 'get out, the baby's mine now and I'll do what I like with her.'

The merchant's wife left the midwife's shack with great sadness and rejoined her husband to begin the business of trading cloth in the village. As the wagon trundled slowly along the road, both adults were strangely quiet, part of their introspective selves back with Giana, the little girl that had touched their lives so dramatically.

'Girl!' The midwife shouted into the back room of her shack.

'Yes, Mistress,' a small voice instantly replied.

'Get in here. You've got another baby to look after until I find it a home. And you had better keep it quiet while I'm sleeping.'

The girl, a thin, rather clumsy teenager with downcast eyes, sidled into the room: 'Shall I take it to the nursery room now?'

'Of course,' snapped the midwife, 'what do you think I'm calling you for?'

The girl, a simple kindly soul, immediately felt sorry for the baby, obviously abandoned by its parents – of course she did not dare to ask the midwife what had happened, since this would only elicit anger and even a beating with the stick. The girl had been sold to the midwife as a servant several years before and she knew she had to keep quiet and do exactly as she was told. She did not even dare to ask whether the baby was a boy or a girl but she hoped the midwife would tell her the baby's name.

'Take it and go,' the midwife rasped, 'it's a girl and the stupid people that brought her in called her Giana. What a stupid name! And I told them that, too. Anyway, it'll very likely grow up to be a stupid girl, just like you, so she may as well have a stupid name too.' The midwife cackled unpleasantly at this, greatly enjoying her joke.

'Get on with your work,' she said, pushing the girl violently towards the baby. The girl picked up the baby gently and left the room.

'It's not a stupid name,' she thought. 'Giana is a nice name but I've never heard of anyone else called Giana.' She held the baby close and spoke gently: 'Giana is a very nice name. I love it – and I love you, too.'

In the other room, the midwife sat down to recall her triumph over the cloth merchant.

'Oh, I really handled that well,' she chortled, 'making him pay for giving me the baby – and fifty Ourtz is nearly a week's work for me. I certainly duped these two!' She was absolutely delighted with her performance. 'And it's not over yet. I told them it would take me a long time to find someone to take the baby but I know exactly where it can be placed. And they will need to pay, as well!' She almost hugged herself with delight.

Several days later, the midwife's mood had changed. She had planned to sell the baby to that rich farmer Malik, the one with the barren wife. She looked forward to making a lot of money out of this transaction. She knew he drank at the tavern on most evenings. Her plan was to go there and complete the transaction. Then he could take the baby home to his wife and everybody would be happy. Especially herself! She planned to sell the baby to Farmer Malik for 100 Ourtz – a very nice amount of money. She felt sure she could talk him into it; she would tell him what a wonderful baby this was and he would be happy to pay that amount – two whole weeks work for her!

In the event, her carefully worked out plan had been a total failure, a real disaster. She had done her best and applied her finest persuasion but Malik had just said "No." She could not believe it. No one had ever said "No" to her before in such circumstances – it must have been the fact that he was half-drunk.

Should she try again, she wondered? She considered this for a while but, remembering Malik's angry and aggressive attitude, decided that she would not succeed. Anyway, it would look bad for her. She was an important person in this community and could not be seen to be crawling back for a second attempt.

'No,' she decided, 'I'll just have to find someone else to buy the baby.'

The following weeks showed that this would be no easy task. The midwife had given the matter a great deal of thought and put subtle feelers out among the village community.

'I need to be careful with my reputation,' she thought. 'That's more important than getting rid of any stray baby.'

On a number of occasions, the midwife skirted around the subject with people who might possibly be amenable to acquiring another member for their family but nothing positive emerged from these approaches. Finally, the midwife was becoming desperate: 'I really can't keep this baby for much longer,' she thought, 'it isn't suitable for me to do so and it's too much trouble.'

So on the following morning the midwife called to see the village handyman and his wife, taking the baby with her. She would certainly not have chosen this family for the baby since they were known to be stupid and feckless, living from hand to mouth and already with no less than four badly-behaved children, all loutish boys. On the other hand, the midwife thought she would be able to persuade them to solve her problem. At this stage the midwife had long given up any thought of financial reward for herself.

On arrival at the squalid smallholding occupied by the handyman's family, the parents received her as an honoured guest – in the past, she had helped with birthing, for suitable recompense, of course. With feigned sadness, she showed them the baby and explained the fabricated circumstances of her orphan status, emphasising her high birth. Of course the baby (her name was Giana – a beautiful name, don't you think?) now needed a new family. She had considered the matter very carefully and chosen them for this very important task.

The handyman and his wife were greatly flattered and indicated that they would accept. Just one thing, they asked, was there a financial settlement with the baby, by any chance?

'Unfortunately not,' the midwife regretted, 'she has already cost me many Ourtz for clothing, food and other essentials and I have paid for all this from my own income. So you understand…'

The handyman and his wife "understood" and now accepted the baby with a certain reluctance.

'Fine,' the midwife concluded briskly, 'you are good people and I know you will look after her well.' With that, she left, leaving Giana in the care of this dysfunctional, unpleasant household.

Giana was brought up with her four elder "siblings"; she was never treated as an equal but rather as a servant. By the time she was old enough to be able to carry out household tasks (she was probably around five years old when this began) these were piled upon her by the adults and their children. So poor Giana found herself allocated to all the most difficult and unpleasant tasks, cleaning the privy, keeping the filthy smallholding clean and tidy, looking after the scrawny animals, fetching the water for the household from the well far away.

In addition, she was treated cruelly. If any member of the family was displeased with any aspect of her performance, they would slap her hard or even beat her with a stick. As a consequence, Giana's small body was always covered with blotchy bruises and scratches.

Their cruelty extended to her sustenance, too. At mealtimes, Giana could only eat and drink when all other members of the family had finished and had their fill; frequently this meant she had only scraps or crumbs to eat and sometimes there was nothing left at all. Her clothing was always poor and inadequate. All she ever had were the worn-out rags passed down from older members of the family. So for many months and years of her young life, Giana had a truly miserable time, always hungry and thirsty, always dirty and treated like a slave.

As a leading member of the village community, the midwife knew very well what was happening to Giana as she grew up but she had absolutely no interest in the girl. Despite her early involvement with her, she felt absolutely no sense of responsibility for what had happened. In fact any time she met the unfortunate Giana in the village, struggling with heavy water containers or sweeping and cleaning at the smallholding, she either ignored her or exhorted her to work harder. 'Do your very best,' she would say to the thin and exhausted child, 'you owe it to your adopted father and mother who look after you so well.' This said complacently to the poor dirty, ragged child, grey of face and suffering from malnutrition and dehydration.

One day, the feckless handyman sought out his wife and said: 'I think it's high time we got rid of that girl. The more she grows the more expensive she is to keep.'

In reply, his wife laughed unpleasantly: 'Who would have her? Just look at her. She's disgusting!' She pointed to Giana, dirty and ragged, brushing the dirt energetically in an attempt to clean the yard.

'Yes, I agree,' said her husband, 'but I have an idea. I'll include her in a deal. Farmers are always looking for manual workers. As she grows up, she'll become stronger and will be able to do more work. I'll tell them what a good worker she is. I'll tell them a convincing lie.' He smiled artfully. The handyman was very pleased with this strategy; he had worked it all out by himself!

'All right,' agreed his wife. 'It'll be a good thing to be rid of her. She always has been a nuisance.' Thus, Giana's fate was sealed.

Several days later, the girl was told to get into the cart and go with the handyman. When she enquired where they were going, the handyman slapped her face hard.

'Don't speak until you're spoken to,' he said angrily. Giana was silent, rubbing her bruised face. The cart stopped in the centre of the village where a number of farmers and various tradesmen were gathered. This was a market for farm work contracts and it was here that the handyman sometimes managed to obtain work.

'Stay there and don't move,' he said to Giana, 'or I'll slap you again.'

The handyman joined a group around several farmers. He recognised a large burly man as Farmer Malik and approached him.

'Good morning, Master,' he said respectfully, 'do you have any work for a good handyman?'

'I might need a good fence, 100 pics,' the farmer growled, regarding him critically.

'Master, my fences are the finest,' the handyman replied eagerly.

'Really,' the farmer sneered, 'I'm not so sure about that; your reputation is not very good.'

'Master, I use good wood and I have a special contract to offer. Thirty-five Ourtz…'

'Too much,' the farmer bellowed 'I would not pay over twenty…'

'Master, please let me finish … Thirty-five Ourtz for the fence and a free child worker for your farm. A very good worker, very well trained by me and brought up in my own home.'

'Where is this child?'

'Sitting in my cart,' the handyman answered, 'come and see …'

Giana cut a pathetic figure in the cart, dirty and dishevelled. She looked fearfully at the handyman and this large burly man with him.

'Stand up, child,' Malik snapped and the little girl obeyed immediately. He looked into her eyes and ears and told her to open her mouth, inserting a thick finger to check her tongue and teeth. Then he lifted her clothes with one large hand and explored her limbs and body with the other, examining her critically just as he would any young farm animal he was considering buying.

'Thin as a rake,' he observed, having noted the prominent ribcage and the spindly limbs, 'don't you feed your servants?' He looked angrily at the handyman, who blenched and was silent, hoping that the farmer's anger would not prejudice the sale.

'Right,' said the farmer, 'I will pay twenty-three Ourtz for the work and the child. Take it or leave it. Take it and you start tomorrow.' He turned away abruptly and made as if to leave.

'Wait,' the handyman wailed, 'I'll take it.' The agreement was recorded and the handshake sealed it.

'Be at my farm at first light tomorrow,' Malik ordered, 'and don't be late.' Then he turned: 'Child! Waken up and come with me.' He walked away.

The girl climbed from the handyman's cart and ran to follow the farmer through the crowds.

He pointed to a bench beneath a tree. 'Sit there, and stay there till I come back.'

Malik disappeared into the tavern and it was several hours before he returned, by now in a rather drunken state. By this time he had forgotten all about the little girl he had acquired but fortunately had his memory jogged when he saw her sitting quietly on the bench where he had left her. 'You,' he shouted. 'Come here.' She ran to his side and looked at him fearfully for further instructions. 'Can you speak?'

'Yes, Master,' she whispered.

'Come with me.' He led the way to his bullock cart nearby. 'Get in,' he instructed, leaving her to scramble up with difficulty on to the high cart.

During the journey, Malik did not speak a word to the child. Eventually they arrived at the farm and Giana was greatly startled when Malik bellowed "Boy" at the top of his voice. A farm boy ran from a barn nearby and, without instruction, came to attend to the bullock cart, holding the beast's head as the farmer climbed down.

Malik ignored the boy and turned to her: 'Get down and come with me,' he growled.

In the fading light, he pushed her towards the farmhouse door, and, opening it violently, thrust her ahead of him into the smoky and dimly-lit interior.

Giana had been frightened by the introduction to her new mistress, who did not seem at all friendly towards her. She did not like being stripped naked and scrubbed; it had made some places on her body quite sore. On the other hand, it was lovely to be clean. It seemed to her that it was a long time since she had been clean. At the handyman's house, she had never been allowed to wash herself or her clothes. She could only clean herself, occasionally and rather perfunctorily, on brief visits to the river.

As she sat naked beside the fire, waiting for her dress to dry, she thought: 'It would be nice if I am allowed to keep myself clean.' At the same time, she was worried about many other things. Where would she sleep? Would the farmer and his wife feed her? If they didn't, she would die – and she didn't want to die! She couldn't help her eyes filling with tears.

Then, a new and awful thought! Where was the privy? She had forgotten all about that! Her knees squeezed together involuntarily. She hoped she did not need to ask her new mistress where it was; disturbing her might make her angry and who knows what might happen then?

'Wake up!' Her employer had spoken and, deep in her introspection and worry, she had not heard her. She felt a pang of panic.

'What are you called?' This loudly and sharply.

'Giana.'

Her mistress thought it was an unusual name. Her next question: 'What work can you do?'

'Anything.' Giana desperately hoped her reply would please her mistress.

Her mistress laughed but Giana did not know whether she was pleased or not. Maretta heaved herself to her feet and checked the dryness of Giana's ragged dress.

'You can put this on now,' she said, passing it to the girl, 'you might not look so scrawny with some clothes on.' Then the woman went over to the food store and returned with a bowl and a pot of milk. Without a word, she handed these to the girl and returned to her seat.

'Thank you, Mistress.' Giana knew the value of politeness.

Maretta did not look up.

'This is good food,' Giana thought as she ate the bread, butter and cheese in the bowl and drank the milk from the pot. Clothed and with food now in her stomach, Giana began to feel less worried and frightened. 'Maybe they will be nice to me here,' she thought. 'I must try my best to do good work for my mistress.'

Maretta's voice penetrated her thoughts: 'Girl,' she said, without looking up, 'you will sleep with me in the next room. And you had better be a quiet sleeper!'

'Yes, Mistress, thank you, I'm a very quiet sleeper.' Giana did not know whether she was a quiet sleeper on not. At the handyman's she had been forced to sleep on the hard earth floor under a table.

There was silence for some time, then Maretta spoke again: 'Girl!'

'Yes, Mistress.'

'The privy is round the back of the farmhouse. Make sure you use it!'

'Thank you, Mistress.' Giana felt wonderful. Now she knew everything. At that moment, her life was complete!

That night however, it was inevitable that Giana would sleep rather fitfully, afraid to disturb her irascible mistress who had made it clear that any disturbance would result in punishment.

'Just lie quiet and don't disturb me. If you do, I promise you'll regret it.' Maretta had growled this to the girl as they prepared for sleep in the side room of the farmhouse.

At the same time, the prospect of sleeping on a soft mattress was a luxury for Giana. This would be the very first time she would enjoy the warmth and cosiness of a real bed. In her whole life she had known nothing other than the hard, cold floor at the handyman's tumbledown shack, where she had always been in danger of a stray kick from any member of that extremely unpleasant family.

Preparing to go to bed in that strange room, Giana was in something of a quandary about what she should wear in bed – the quandary being that she did not have a special item of clothing for that purpose. Before combing her hair, her mistress had changed into a long linen shift. Giana had no other garment to wear other than her old worn-out dress, washed by Maretta earlier that evening. She could choose to sleep in this as she always had done in the past but now she was afraid this would make it very crumpled and this might easily make her mistress displeased and angry. In the end, she waited until the flame was extinguished and then slipped naked into the bed, a brief shadow of a pale nymph.

Very early in the morning, while Maretta still slept heavily, sprawled across most of the bed, Giana rose to make herself ready for the day. The side room had its own door to the farmyard so there was no risk of disturbing Old Malik who could be heard snoring noisily in the main room next door. Giana was very grateful that she did not have to exit through that room since disturbing Old Malik was not only unthinkable but a very frightening prospect. Giana shivered at the thought. She was frightened of Old Malik and hoped she would be able to keep out of his way as much as possible.

In the half-light of dawn, the morning was cool and dry. After a cautious but necessary visit to the privy, she found a tub of water behind the farmhouse where she was able to wash herself quickly. She was considerably alarmed when Old Malik suddenly appeared around the side of the farmhouse but he ignored her totally and stalked by. Running back to the front of the farmhouse, Giana now found that her mistress had risen.

'Where are you, girl?' A call of irritation.

'Here I am.' Giana was quick to reply and stood with downcast eyes in front of her mistress.

Maretta looked at the little thin girl with ill-tempered disapproval. 'Where have you been?'

'Washing myself, Mistress,' the girl replied humbly, 'I thought you would want me to be clean.'

The woman said nothing but turned and walked into the farmhouse. When Giana did not move, she called over her shoulder: 'Why are you still standing there? Are you stupid? Come with me at once!'

They entered the farmhouse and Maretta propelled the girl to a corner of the room where food and utensils were kept in a cupboard. Fixing her with an unfriendly eye, she said to the girl: 'Listen very carefully. You had better remember what I am about to say. This is where I keep the food and drink; also the bowls, platters and knives are here. First thing in the morning after the Master rises, you will prepare our first meal. The Master and I will sit at the table over there. I will tell you what food and drink you will serve. You will wait upon us and make sure we have everything we want. When we are finished you may have your food – I will tell you what you may eat and you will sit on that stool over there.' She pointed to a rough, rickety stool against the wall. 'You will eat and drink quickly so that you may begin your work as soon as possible. I hope you understand all I have told you because I don't like stupid people.'

'Yes, Mistress,' the girl whispered meekly.

'So do it.' The command was sharp. 'We will eat bread, butter and cheese; and we will drink some mead.' She indicated a thick stone flagon on the floor.

Giana ran to do her bidding, placing a large platter of bread, butter and cheese in the middle of the table and two smaller platters in front of the chairs, each with a knife. The smaller platters were flanked by two pots and the large flagon of mead placed on the table. Giana stood back to admire her handiwork and waited for her Mistress's approval.

'Crack!' Disorientation followed by sharp pain. Maretta had come up behind her and slapped her hard on a bare leg. Giana screamed, partly with pain but mostly with shock.

'Stupid girl,' Maretta said, 'take that large flagon off the table. Such a vessel is always put on the floor – here.' She pointed.

'I'm very sorry, Mistress.' A distressed Giana gasped, wanting to rub her bruised leg to alleviate the pain, 'I'll never do it again.' She removed the flagon from the table and set it down at the place indicated by Maretta.

As part of the routine, Giana was also instructed to prepare a small morning meal for the farm boy, all items to be placed in a wooden bowl. When it was ready, Maretta took the bowl, checked it and placed it outside the door. Giana wondered why her mistress seemed to be so angry about this – after all, the farm boy was not doing her any harm, was he?

At the same time, another meal was made up and placed in a cloth bundle; Giana understood this was the midday meal for the farm boy which he would eat later during a short break from his work. The bundle was left just inside the farmhouse door.

The girl was relieved that no other incident occurred during the morning meal. Old Malik stumped into the farmhouse shortly after and he and Maretta sat at the table to eat their morning meal. Giana stood respectfully nearby and carried out any supplementary orders issued by her Mistress. The farmer ignored both the girl and his wife. When the food had been eaten, he rose and left the farmhouse without a word, lifting up the prepared food bundle by the door.

Through the open door, Giana heard him shouting angry instructions to the farm boy who was sitting quietly outside. She was shocked to see him throw the food bundle carelessly in the boy's direction and was relieved when, by dint of quick movement, the boy was able to catch it before the food spilled out on to the ground.

Maretta now indicated that Giana should clear the utensils away and take them outside to be cleaned. After this had been done, she indicated the food that Giana should eat as her morning meal and included a pot of fresh milk. Obediently, Giana sat on the stool by the wall and consumed her first morning meal quickly. After her rather shocking and painful experience this morning, Giana concluded ruefully that she would need to be very careful at Old Malik's farm.

After the morning meal was finished, further detailed instructions were given to Giana. These referred to her many other duties – helping her mistress with cooking, baking, dairy and butchery work; looking after the farmyard animals, collecting the eggs, milking; attending to the kitchen garden and storing the vegetable crops; and finally, general cleaning within and without the farmhouse.

Giana could see that she would be kept very busy. On the other hand, she recognised that her food and sleeping conditions were better that she had experienced in her earlier life. And if she was very careful and hard-working, maybe she would not be punished very much. She was well used to painful punishment but Maretta's hard slap earlier this morning had been an unexpected shock.

'I'll just have to try my best to be good,' she thought.

There was one other instruction, greatly emphasised by her mistress. This referred to the farm boy. Giana had caught several glimpses of him since she had come to the farm the day before and she had thought that he looked like a nice boy, completely unlike the loutish children of the handyman who had always been so unkind and cruel to her. She thought the farm boy was probably a few years older than herself and had looked forward to speaking to him, servant to servant, (equal to equal?). However, it seemed that this was not to be. Maretta was forceful and unequivocal on this subject.

Giana was to have nothing to do with this farm boy, whose name was Joachim – Maretta spat the name out with contempt and Giana wondered why. The farm boy worked only with the Master and he was a lazy good-for-nothing; he often had to be beaten by the Master, he was so idle and stupid. She, Giana, was not to speak to the farm boy, ever, even if they met face to face. If she disobeyed, she would tell the

Master to beat her, just like he beat the farm boy. With a big thick stick, all over her body. Did she understand? There was only one answer to that question!

'Yes, Mistress, I will never speak to him or have anything to do with him.' Giana spoke fearfully and with extreme subservience.

In fact, Maretta's hatred of the unfortunate Joachim was first of all an attempt to alleviate her own deep misery by transferring it to another. This is a common and invariably unsuccessful strategy that has been attempted by human beings down the ages.

However the second reason was more experiential, rooted in that particular series of long-past events that involved herself and her elder brother, where her innocent naked body had been used for his sexual gratification. Within her confused mind, the boy Joachim had been placed into the role of her elder brother and now the girl Giana became the innocent victim that had been herself. The outcome of all this was the almost hysterical forbiddance placed upon Giana.

Giana was a simple girl who was happy enough to obey commands. Clearly, she had no experience of normal life, where relationships are often loving and respectful; her experiences were confined to obedience and punishment if her "superiors" were not satisfied with her work or any aspect of her attitude. Therefore she just concentrated on whatever task or activity she had been directed to do at that moment, without giving thought to anything else. Her only concern was to give satisfaction so that punishment would not come her way.

So the months and years passed and Giana worked hard every day, often finding it difficult to complete all the work in the allocated time. Satisfactory work was received by Maretta with no comment while mistakes or uncompleted work were met at least with anger and often by hard slaps to her face or various parts of her body; occasionally, if the offence was judged to be grave, more serious beatings were administered by a hard hand or a thin switch. Nevertheless, many days passed relatively peacefully for Giana and proper feeding soon built up her health and strength, making her physically strong and healthy as she grew.

Giana was now dressed in simple clothes of robust quality. Within several weeks of her arrival at the farm wearing her only ragged and worn-out dress, her mistress had returned from a trip to the village and called the girl to her: 'These are for you.' Two plain dresses of stout grey material were placed on the table along with two lighter undergarments. There was also an extra chemise for bedtime, and the "wardrobe" was completed with a pair of sturdy leather sandals. Giana was dumbfounded. She had never had any new clothes in her life!

'Mistress, thank you. You are so good to me.' She burst into tears of joy.

Maretta frowned: 'Put them on, girl,' she said testily and Giana complied.

The fit of all the garments was reasonably good and Giana was absolutely delighted. She felt so elegant. Didn't the new cloth feel so good and smell so nice? What a lucky girl she was! In her simple joy, she pirouetted around the room.

Maretta smiled thinly and briefly.

'Listen, girl,' she said, 'when your dress gets dirty, change it for the other one while you wash the dirty one, you understand? I can't have my servant running around in dirty ragged clothes. And always wear your sleeping garment in bed.'

'Yes, Mistress,' Giana delighted, 'I will never forget. Thank you so very much.' That day, Giana's work was done even more thoroughly than usual and completed in good time.

Despite the strict instructions (dire warnings!) she had received about contact with the farm boy Joachim, it was inevitable that they would have sight of each other quite often, for the farm was quite small. For instance, the boy sat not far from the front of the farmhouse to eat most of his food; on these daily occasions he was no more than two cart-lengths from her, separated only by the barrier of the farmhouse wall.

There were also occasions when their work inadvertently brought them together, on the paths around the fields or meadows of the farm or around the farmyard itself. From the start, he had always looked at her with a friendly expression and greeted her pleasantly in a quiet voice. These occasions had terrified Giana, especially at first, and she ignored him completely and scuttled off as fast as she could. The prospect of being beaten by Old Malik with a long stick completely terrified her. On one dreadful occasion, she had come upon the farm boy being beaten by Old Malik and been totally horrified by the blood-streaked wheals being laid upon his body.

However, as the seasons and years went by and Giana became older, she became a little more relaxed about inadvertently meeting Joachim, although, for her own sake, she still maintained a strict policy of "no contact". He still spoke to her quietly when they met and smiled at her, but she was too frightened to reciprocate and always walked on as if he was not there.

In fact, there was one occasion when they met on a narrow path and she deliberately pushed him into a deep puddle of mud to give her enough room to pass – that was how she tried to rationalise it to herself afterwards. Also, she had been very rude and called him a 'horrible boy' – in a whisper, of course. The recollection of this event worried Giana considerably and she hoped fervently that the Master or the Mistress would never find out about it. The prospect of the Master's big beating stick always made her shudder!

Joachim

The boy subsided slowly until he was seated upon the earth, his eyes fixed on the retreating figure of Old Malik.

'Is this a dream? Will I awaken in a moment to find myself in my bunk at the barn?'

These thoughts, and many others, raced through his mind at lightning speed. He was totally bewildered, yet there was a sense of elation, too. One moment, he had been pinned to the ground by the heavy plough, literally a terrified sacrifice awaiting death – or unbearable pain, at least – and the next moment, here he was, sitting on the ground, alive and well, in no pain of any kind: 'Well, perhaps my leg is just a little sore.' This incongruous thought leaping from his racing consciousness brought a shadow of a smile to his lips.

One thing was clear to him. Something had happened to Old Malik at the instant he was approaching with that terrifying whip held high; something that had transformed him completely.

'That something saved my life.' The boy was serious as he thought that. 'I've never seen him change like that. I've never seen him act like that. I've never seen him look like that, either. What could have happened? Did the spirits take him over to save me?'

Joachim thought that unlikely. As far as he could remember, the spirits had never done anything for him in the past; in fact he was always a little nervous when he brought them to mind.

'You need to be careful what you say or even think about the spirits,' he thought, 'you never know what they are thinking about you, so it's better to be safe than sorry.' Instinctively, he looked around – just in case the spirits were gathering around him!

Uncounted time passed as the boy sat thinking. Gradually his whirling mind slowed its pace and re-assembled itself back into a more normal, practical mode. He looked around him; the light was beginning to fade and it was clear that the ploughing work of this day had come to an end.

'Old Malik has gone to the farmhouse, so I'll need to attend to his plough and take his beast back.' This was no problem – something he had done many times before. He rose to his feet to make a start on this essential work. He talked quietly to his bullock as he unhitched it from the plough and then led the animal down the hill to where Old Malik's plough stood in the furrow he had been working on when Joachim's unfortunate accident happened. A shiver ran through the boy's body as he relived the memory of his terror.

It took just a few moments to unhitch the second beast and the two large animals were soon on their way to be fed, watered and bedded down for the night in their pen. On arrival, the hitch ropes were taken off and, after checking that plenty of sweet hay and fresh water was available for them, Joachim patted each animal and spoke to it gently: 'You've done well, today. Have a good rest.' He believed that farm animals should be treated kindly. 'After all, we need them just as much as they need us.' He often thought that.

Now, in the rapidly fading light, he couldn't help feeling uneasy. It was time for the evening meal. Normally, this was placed outside the farm door for him, just like the morning meal. Joachim was increasingly worried as he drew nearer and nearer to the farmhouse. What if Old Malik was still angry with him for the mistake he had made at the field? As usual,

Joachim had begun to blame himself for the event. What if he was waiting in the farmhouse to rush out and administer the beating he had promised the boy when he was pinned under the plough?

Joachim found that he was trembling with fear as he approached the farmhouse; his pace become slower and slower and he wondered whether he should hide in the barn and forgo his evening meal. As he tried to decide what to do, his faltering steps brought him ever closer to the farmyard.

Suddenly the farmhouse door was thrust open and the light from the lamp inside streamed out to illuminate the figure of the boy. Joachim gasped, looking fearfully for the powerful figure of Old Malik striding out to seize him in a painful grasp, as he had done so many times in the past. However relief flooded over him as he recognised the familiar figure of Maretta framed in the doorway. As usual, she stepped forward and put down his platter and bowl on the stone beside the door, as she did every evening. Then, unusually silent (she often muttered curses as she put out his meal) and without looking up, she turned to re-enter the farmhouse.

The boy was about to move forward to collect his meal when he realised that Maretta had stopped. She was standing quite still in the doorway with her back to him. He also stood quite still, waiting to see what would happen next. Then, very slowly, she turned around and gazed at the stars. Long seconds ticked by.

Next, something incredible happened; Maretta dropped her gaze slowly until she was looking straight at him. The boy was transfixed and his mind raced once again. What was happening? Was he in trouble? She never looked at him. She had not done so for years. At the same time, another channel of his mind registered a very surprising fact – her eyes were dark pools of beauty!

Now confused, his brain raced through the facts of his relationship with Maretta, in the hope that this would start a process of understanding. These days, she ignored him, although sometimes there were muttered curses or even a slap on his face if he came too close. In the past, when he was much younger, she had hit him often and told him many times that she hated and despised him. He had never known why but her looks either of blazing anger or withering contempt had made him very unhappy. But now, at this moment, her eyes did not transmit the hard look of hatred or anger – her gaze was soft and gentle, wistful and unfathomable.

So the world stood still … until …

'Good evening, Mistress.' To his astonishment he heard his voice say these words, softly, timidly; the words followed by a gut-wrenching pang of panic, physically real, as he realised he may have made a terrible mistake by speaking. Another silence. Then her response; not words of reply but an inclination of her head and a brief smile – the first smile he had ever seen on Maretta's face. Then she re-entered the farmhouse and closed the door gently.

The boy stood absolutely motionless as his mind tried to process what had just happened. Then, remembering his evening meal, he tip-toed forward cautiously and lifted the dishes from the flat stone and withdrew quickly to the imagined safety of the fallen tree trunk where he sat to eat most of his meals. Here, he uncovered the food in the bowl and felt a wave of pleasure: 'I'm lucky tonight,' he whispered. In addition to thick slices of good wholesome bread, butter and cheese, there was some meat stew – a rare treat. Incredibly, there was also a flagon of beer to drink. Joachim settled down to enjoy this excellent meal, possibly the best he had ever had!

'This is wonderful,' he said to himself, 'I know Old Malik will have returned to his usual angry self by tomorrow but, whatever happens, at least I will have really good food in my belly.' The boy felt deep contentment and resolved to work extra hard for his Master on the following day. 'If I work well, maybe he will forgive me for the accident with the plough. Maybe he will not be so angry with me.' Joachim, filled with good food and beer, now felt quite optimistic!

In fact, although Joachim could not have known it, there had already been very dramatic happenings at the farm. Earlier that evening, Old Malik had strode back from the field to the farmhouse. Opening the door, he called for his wife but the room was empty. Maretta and Giana were working in one of the outhouses – a spacious barn that housed the dairy and the bakery.

They had been very busy for some hours and a large batch of loaves cooled beside the wood-fired oven in one corner of the barn, filling the surrounding area with the delicious aroma of freshly-baked bread. Guided by this most pleasant of aromas, Old Malik had made his way to the bakery out-building. As he approached, he could hear sounds of activity from within.

Maretta was startled and taken aback by the sight of her husband in the doorway – she could not remember the last time he had come to any of the farm outbuildings where she carried out her tasks.

'Women's work!' he had always growled, 'I have no interest in women's work or where it's done.' Normally, when he returned from work, he went straight to the farmhouse, washed at the tub around the back and then settled down with a flagon of beer. Woe betide anyone who disturbed him before the evening meal! The woman paused and looked at him with questioning eyes while the girl ran to cower in a far corner of the room.

'Wife,' he said, looking straight into her eyes, 'we need to talk. At the farmhouse. Now.' This last word spoken not with his normal aggression but expressed in an urgent tone which contained a hint of pleading. She looked at him in great astonishment. Firstly, he was actually looking at her! Looking at her face, into her eyes. She thought that many years had passed since he had done that. Secondly, he had made a request to her, admittedly spoken bluntly but nevertheless containing none of the anger or harsh derision that usually pervaded his words to her. He was treating her with respect!

Was he ill or injured? She looked at him carefully. Certainly there was something different about him but he looked fit and healthy enough, she thought. Had there been a disaster on the farm? Again, she looked at him and did not think so. A disaster would have resulted in fury and she would have heard him coming from afar. A mysterious happening? A sign from Our Lord? He would just have ignored anything like that, she thought, wryly! What could it be?

Her emotions were mixed. She was curious, though filled with trepidation, too. At the same time she became acutely aware of her unkempt and slovenly appearance; he never looked at her these days so she had lost interest in her appearance. Now, under his gaze she felt grubby and ashamed.

Another scene paused in time. He, unmoving, waiting, his eyes fixed on hers. She, looking at him, physically still also but mind racing, sifting possibilities. The girl, crouching in the corner, terrified at his sudden appearance but aware of a strange tension in the room; hoping fervently that this would not culminate in anger towards her.

'I will come.' Maretta spoke quietly and his face relaxed.

The woman then turned to Giana and spoke sharply.

'You are to clean up here, girl, and make everything tidy. Then you can churn some milk for butter. Make sure you do it properly.'

So saying, the man and woman left to walk the short distance to the farmhouse.

Increasingly aware of her unkempt appearance, Maretta said: 'I must clean myself before we talk.'

'No,' he said quietly, 'first, we talk. It will not take long.'

Intrigued, the woman followed him into the farmhouse.

He indicated they should sit at the table. When she sat down, he reached across and grasped her hands, firmly but with gentleness, too. Even so, surprise and some alarm could not stop her uttering a little cry. Still looking intently into her eyes, the man was now having difficulty speaking, difficulty in choosing the right words which would express what he felt he must now say.

'Wife.' He paused.

'Maretta ...'

She started. He had not spoken her name for a very long time!

'I have wronged you.'

She looked at him carefully. Yes, his features were lined and coarsened but in them she could recognise the Malik she had married, the Malik she had loved so much. She saw he had tears in his eyes! In response, she felt a rebirth of that love she had for him.

However, Maretta did not disagree with what he had just said. He had wronged her but if, for some inexplicable reason, he now understood even a tiny part of what she had been through, then this could be the start of a new life for them. She did not have to consider her response for long: 'We can start again, if it is your wish?'

This was spoken as a query. She knew instinctively this was the right response although with the wisdom of woman she acknowledged to herself that the way was unlikely to be easy and the result unpredictable. Nevertheless, if there was effort, good will and, yes, love, a course around most of the dangerous rocks of destruction and disillusionment could possibly be negotiated.

'There is more,' the man said, without averting his gaze. 'I have also been a bad farmer and a bad master, too; these things must change and I will need your help to change them. We must talk about these things and consider them very carefully.'

'You will have my help, if these are things you wish to do,' the woman answered immediately. Despite her doubts, a cautious wave of optimism coursed through her. 'In any event,' she now thought, 'surely some good will come out of this.'

Still with his eyes fixed on hers, the man felt a great love for this beautiful woman. Having virtually ignored her for many years, he was seeing her anew – and his gaze did not reveal the ravages of age and neglect but travelled with ease through to the beauty beyond, the beauty he remembered so well.

'We will clean ourselves from the dirt of our work and change our clothes. Then we will eat,' he said quietly. 'Afterwards, we will talk more.'

Maretta was relieved that this intense conversation was over, although she was also cautiously elated at what had happened.

'I pray that his new mind will continue,' she thought.

For the first time in many years, she felt happy as she rose from the table, looking forward eagerly to being clean and dressed neatly in fresh clothes.

In the dairy room at the outbuilding, Giana had worked hard with the butter churn. She had produced a good quantity of butter in the way her mistress had taught her. She now scooped the butter out of the churn, heaped it upon a large dish and covered the whole with a cloth. After draining overnight, the fresh butter would be ready to be divided into blocks and stored. She had also poured the residue of buttermilk from the churn into a large bowl and placed a heavy cloth over the top.

When the churn had been thoroughly cleaned, Giana stepped back and admired her work with a good deal of satisfaction: 'I have worked long and hard. I do hope the Mistress will be pleased with me.' However, the girl thought it very unlikely that she would receive any praise for her work. 'The best I can hope for is a "no comment",' she thought ruefully.

Soon afterwards, the girl walked slowly from the dairy to the farmhouse in the rapidly diminishing daylight. She was musing on the dramatic conversation she had witnessed between Old Malik and Maretta. Giana did not understand what had happened but she thought the Master had been "different".

'Very different,' the girl whispered. Then her thoughts continued. Ever since she had come to the farm, her Master and Mistress had seemed to dislike each other intensely. They were together only at mealtimes when they largely ignored each other; any words spoken seemed to be uttered in anger or contempt. 'I think they must always have hated each other,' Giana thought. 'It's very puzzling. The village handyman seemed to like his wife, even if he was unpleasant to his children and especially to me. I wonder why the Mistress married the Master if they hated each other so much.' The girl could not fathom it and shook her head sadly.

As she approached the farmhouse, daylight had been all but extinguished, so she was unaware of Joachim sitting silently in the deep shadows where he had eaten his splendid meal. If she had known he was there, she would have hurried past with a pointedly averted gaze, because she was strictly forbidden to have anything to do with him; she knew she had to be careful when she was so close to the farmhouse because it was possible that her mistress would be watching. Also, as a simple and impressionable girl, Giana had long accepted her mistress's opinion of the boy and, in consequence, was convinced that poor Joachim was very stupid and completely lazy; a bad boy who deserved to be beaten by the Master.

Hidden by the darkness, the boy saw and heard her progress but kept silent, knowing that she would not want to see him. It was then that something very strange happened. Suddenly the girl felt she had to stop and look around her. She felt she must scan the darkness which now surrounded her and, as she did so, that scan came to a stop at one particular spot in the deepest of the darkness; in fact, she was looking directly into the face of Joachim, sitting motionless and watching her with bated breath. As Giana continued to look intently at this one spot in the darkness, an incomprehensible feeling of happiness came over her.

Overwhelming happiness was a feeling that Giana had never really experienced before. From the time she had become sentient, her life as a child had been one of suffering, either by the internal pains of hunger, thirst or general neglect, the sharp agony of ill treatment or the debilitating hopelessness of being unloved. Although her suffering had diminished to some degree when she came to Old Malik's farm (at least she was fed adequately and slept in a bed), she still had to face the periodic pain of punishment and the despair of indifference towards her.

As Joachim watched, transfixed, he saw her smile, a smile of pure joy, a smile directed straight into his eyes. However he knew that she could not possibly see him: 'If she could see me, she would not be smiling, she would be scowling,' he thought sadly.

After some moments, the girl turned away and resumed her journey, still bubbling with joy. Arriving at the farmhouse, she slipped through the door unobtrusively, hoping that no-one would see her and angrily demand a full account of her work.

To her surprise, she found the Master and Mistress sitting at the table, deep in quiet conversation; she noticed immediately that they were both dressed in neat, clean clothes and was surprised to see that the Mistress looked quite different; yes, attractive, even. From the shadows, Giana looked at Maretta carefully; it was not only the dress she was wearing, it was the expression on her face. She was listening intently to the Master and her expression was soft, gentle and radiant.

Then the girl noticed something else. The evening meal had been prepared – and the food for the farm boy was not in its usual place, ready to be taken out by the Mistress. Giana was astonished. The preparation of the food was a routine task that she had to carry out after she had finished her work in the farmyard. But this evening, the Mistress had already prepared the meal; the platters and bowls of food were all ready to be taken to the table and she must have already put out the food for the farm boy. It did not occur to the girl that Joachim would have been eating in the shadows when she came back from the dairy.

'Girl!' Giana started in fear but the Mistress's voice was soft and calm, 'will you bring the meal to the table?'

'Yes, Mistress.' The girl had learned to be quick and efficient, carefully placing the various items precisely in their correct places and standing back to await further orders.

'Thank you, Giana,' Maretta spoke softly again. The girl was astounded; her jaw literally dropped open. The Mistress had thanked her! And she had called her by her name!

'Mistress,' the girl mumbled, her face flushed with deep confusion.

Maretta smiled at her.

'You may go to have your food,' she said. Giana stumbled from the table. What had happened? Why was the Mistress speaking kindly to her. This had never happened before. It was wonderful, yes, but why? *Why?*

Now the girl had taken her meal and sat upon her stool. The food was delicious and plentiful. The milk was fresh and cool. And Giana was elated, filled with happiness at what had just happened and filled with the joy she had received mysteriously in the darkness outside: 'I've heard people talk about the spirits,' the girl thought, 'but I never thought the spirits would ever bother with someone like me, just a poor farm girl.'

She felt awed at the thought and wondered if it could possibly be true. Then, practicality returned: 'The Master and Mistress seem to like each other at the moment – but it won't last. Everything will be back to normal by tomorrow and I'll soon be in trouble for something!'

Although these were her conclusions, nevertheless the girl felt that something very special had happened to her and she still felt happier than she had ever been in her whole life.

Outside in the rapidly cooling evening, the boy replaced his utensils by the farmhouse door as he did every evening and withdrew to his quarters in the barn. On arrival, he lit a small oil lamp and climbed up into the hayloft. As usual, a complete day of very physical work had made him very tired and he was more than ready for sleep. As he started to undress he remembered his strange find earlier in the day.

'I do hope I still have it,' he thought as he felt in his cloth waist bag. At first, the strange stone eluded his search but he eventually found it lodged into a corner of the bag. Bringing it out, he examined it once again by the light of the lamp, noting again how the strange striations along its length sparkled with multicoloured light. 'It's really quite beautiful,' he thought, and found that his finger and thumb had once again slid naturally into the depressions at one end of the stone. As this occurred, he felt again that little jolt, the same odd sensation he had experienced when he picked up the stone in the field, a strange feeling of power and awesome significance quite unlike anything he had felt before.

'This must be a very special stone,' the boy thought, 'maybe it's a gift from the spirits. I must keep it safe.' He found a small piece of clean, soft cloth and wrapped the stone in it. Then he put it back carefully into his bag and secured the top tightly with the drawstring. 'Whatever it is, I'm going to think of it as my good luck charm. Let's hope that's what it is!' He grinned happily as he thought that.

Moments later, he was stretched out in his bunk, tired and warm. Physically still and completely relaxed, his mind returned naturally to the day now ended, recalling all the amazing things that had happened and trying to work out the meaning of each. Inevitably, it was not long before sleep overtook him, certainly long before he was able to come to a conclusion about even one of the day's very unusual events.

The next morning, the boy awoke at his normal early hour and mused further on the strange happenings of the day before, without making any further progress on their meaning or implications.

'A new day,' he thought, 'and everything will be back to normal. It won't be long before I'm in trouble again.' He sighed. 'I really do try my best but sometimes my best just isn't good enough.'

The boy had come to exactly the same conclusion as Giana had the evening before. Yesterday had been strange and some wonderful things had happened but now all that was over. Now it was back to hard work and no appreciation from the Master or Mistress. He stretched his body and sighed again. In fact, the boy and the girl could not have been more wrong.

Joachim followed his normal routine and appeared outside the farmhouse at the usual time, neat, clean and ready for a day's hard work. When Maretta appeared with his morning meal, she placed it gently on the stone and gave a brief smile before going back inside. The boy was very surprised.

'She's in a very good mood this morning. I wonder why?'

Also, his morning meal was better than normal and much more plentiful. The boy ate and drank gratefully. Shortly after, he sprang to his feet as Old Malik appeared.

Looking directly at the boy – normally he looked contemptuously the other way – the farmer said: 'We'll continue ploughing today and should finish the field in three days.' As he spoke, he handed the boy's midday meal to him, neatly tied in a clean cloth. The boy was surprised to be told details of plans and even more surprised that he did not have to scramble to catch his midday food before it spilled over the ground.

'Yes, Master, thank you, Master,' he replied respectfully and left to prepare the bullocks. Both beasts were ready by the time Old Malik appeared at the pen. He said nothing as he led his beast away with Joachim following close behind.

Because of the stoniness of the field, the boy's ploughing towards the top of the field continued to be difficult and slow. Mercifully, however, the morning's work was uneventful. At the bottom of the field, Old Malik was making good progress as his plough sliced through the softer, more fertile soil. The boy kept a wary eye on him but the man rarely looked his way.

'We don't want a repeat of yesterday.' The boy was absolutely sure of that!

'Boy!' Completely engrossed in his work, Joachim had not noticed the approach of his master. Now his voice close by made the boy jump with fear.

'Yes, Master,' he stammered, bringing the plough to a stop.

'You may stop and eat.' His master spoke quietly and calmly, in a voice quite unlike his normal bullying tones. 'Will you look after my beast?'

The boy was astonished. Old Malik was actually *asking* him if he would do something!

'Of course, Master,' he replied in mystified tones.

'Good,' the man responded and strode away down the hill towards the distant farmhouse.

The beasts were quickly dealt with; unhitched, fed and watered. Then the boy settled down beneath his usual tree and unpacked his midday meal.

'What a feast,' he breathed. A generous hunk of good bread, plenty of butter, a large slice of excellent cheese and even a small piece of dried beef. Best of all – a flagon of farm-brewed beer, just like the ones Old Malik drank every day. Joachim shook his head in wonderment: 'I am truly blessed; I must be sure to thank the Mistress for this.' Joachim felt like a king. 'I'm sure kings don't eat any better than this!' The boy's knowledge of kings was rather scanty, gleaned from comments made by Old Malik, who had been educated in such things by his father when he was young.

The rest of the day passed without incident and good progress was made. As the light began to fade, Old Malik arrived at the top of the field to inspect Joachim's furrows. Joachim stood by respectfully, scanning his master's face and hoping that his work would be judged satisfactory. The farmer examined the neat furrows narrowly. Apart from his episodes of fury, the farmer was a man of few words, so the boy was pleased but not surprised when the man said nothing – although Joachim thought he saw a brief nod of approval.

Then the man spoke quietly: 'Good progress today, we should finish the field tomorrow.' Joachim was grateful that the words were spoken in a quiet, almost neutral tone. There was no hint of anger or contempt in the farmer's voice and, to Joachim's great relief, there was no threat of violence either.

'Yes, Master, I will work hard tomorrow.'

The man looked at the boy for a few seconds and then smiled briefly.

In the following days, the farm work continued without incident or problem. The boy noted that the Master and Mistress spent every evening talking quietly together; they seemed to have a considerable amount to say to each other. The boy observed that their faces were relaxed and happy; in particular the face of the Mistress exuded an aura of great serenity.

Joachim had tried again and again to work out what had happened on that day of the "accident" but each time he had to abandon the attempt with a rueful shake of the head. Meanwhile, the boy was deeply grateful that his meals continued to be generous and of good quality. Sitting alone outside the farmhouse, he recalled with astonishment that Old Malik had not spoken harshly to him for four whole days!

The next day, the farmer had sent him to harrow the field, to break down the soil lumps and prepare it for planting the crop. This was a much less onerous task than ploughing and the boy made good progress back and forward across the field, guiding the harrow behind the powerful bullock.

From his vantage point high in the field, he was able to see that Old Malik had a visitor, a man who he recognised as a neighbouring farmer. On his visits to the village, Joachim had seen this man several times and knew that he was treated with a great deal of respect by all the other farmers. He had heard it said that this man was the best farmer in the region.

Joachim saw that the two men had toured every part of Old Malik's farm and, when they came to the field, Old Malik waved to the boy to stop his harrow and indicated he should come down to them.

'I hope I'm not in trouble,' the boy thought. However, because of the presence of the other farmer, he did not think so. Nevertheless, he approached Old Malik with some care.

'This is my farm boy, Joachim, the boy I have been telling you about,' Old Malik said. Turning to Joachim, he said: 'This is Farmer Sistas, who is the best farmer in the region.' Joachim removed his cap.

'Good day, Master,' he said.

'Holat, Joachim,' the man said, taking the boy's hand and shaking it. The boy was taken aback. The farmer was shaking his hand as if he was a man!

'Is the work going well?' Old Malik looked into the boy's eyes with a friendly gaze.

'Yes, Master, it will be finished today.'

'Good. You can carry on with your work now.' Old Malik and Farmer Sistas turned away.

Once again behind the harrow, Joachim was confused once again. What was happening? What did that strange meeting mean? Why was this farmer at the Master's farm and why was he, just a farm boy, being introduced to such an important man? Once again, Joachim was at a loss to work it out. Suddenly, he grinned in his cheerful way.

'Whatever it all means, it's all much better than it was a week ago. I hope it continues this way. It would be wonderful if it did.'

Meanwhile, Giana was equally confused but extremely grateful. From that day when the Master came to the bakery, her mistress had changed completely. She was now always neat and clean and drank very little beer. More importantly from Giana's point of view, her treatment of the girl had altered radically. She was kind and fair to her and usually addressed her by her name, instead of calling her "Girl" and ordering her around angrily.

Moreover, when the girl worked hard and well, Maretta would now thank her and compliment her on good work done. When the girl made a mistake, the Mistress would point out her error and calmly show her how to do the task correctly. There had also been a significant change in domestic arrangements. The day before, Maretta had said to the girl: 'The Master will sleep with me in the side room, Giana, and you will sleep here in the main room.'

This change pleased Giana very much. At last, she had a bed of her own where she could spread out and bounce around all during the night!

'Yes, Mistress, I will move my clothes from the side room immediately.'

There was one other major change. One day while they were working in the dairy together, Maretta had spoken about Joachim: 'Giana, listen to me, please. The Master now tells me that the farm boy Joachim is a very good worker and knows his farm work well. In fact he is so satisfied with him that he no longer needs to beat him. I think all this has happened because the Master is so good at training farm boys. So I am now treating Joachim as a good and faithful worker and I want you to do the same. The Master has told the boy he may speak to you and you may now speak to him if you want. But don't do anything stupid. Boys are very different from girls, you know.'

As she said this, Maretta felt she had heard these words somewhere before. 'Where could it have been?' She puzzled about this for some time. 'Oh, I can't remember, maybe it will come back to me some time.' So saying, the query passed from her mind.

Two weeks had now passed since everything had changed at the farm and Joachim was still puzzled by many things that had happened. However the time had now arrived when at least some of his questions would be answered. Although the boy now had a very good working relationship with his master (for instance, he had noted with great relief that all the beating sticks around the farm had disappeared), he was worried and a little frightened when Old Malik mentioned at the beginning of their working day that they would have a "serious conversation" that evening at the farmhouse.

This worried Joachim more and more throughout the day. What if Old Malik had decided his work wasn't good enough? Maybe that he should be replaced by a man who would be stronger and able to do more work? If he left the farm, where would he live? What would he do? How would he survive?

He did not think he would be welcome at home – after all, his father had given him away to Old Malik many years ago. As the day progressed, Joachim became more and more convinced that Old Malik was going to cast him out of the farm. Then, an even worse thought came to him. What if he was to be sold as a slave? Sold to someone who would treat him badly and starve him and whip him? So, by the time evening came, Joachim was ashen-faced and trembling in fear.

'Come in and eat in the farmhouse,' Old Malik said, 'come and sit with us at the table.' Joachim was terrified. He had never been in the farmhouse in all the years he had been at the farm and now, even worse, he had to eat his food with the Master and Mistress at the table! With great reluctance, the boy entered and did as he was bid.

The food was excellent but, this evening, it tasted of ashes in his mouth; he could hardly stop his jaw trembling as he waited for the axe to fall. A flagon of good beer helped him to relax a little but he still felt like these bad criminal men must do as they waited to have their heads cut off by one sweep of a very heavy sword. Joachim had heard that this was the method of execution in this land.

Finally, the meal was over and the bowls and platters cleared away. Joachim now closed his eyes and waited for the dreaded blow to fall.

'Joachim, as you know, things at the farm have changed. But now they need to change a lot more.' Old Malik's voice was solemn. Maretta sat impassively across the table, looking at Joachim. 'The changes I am now going to make affect you considerably,' the man continued, ominously.

Joachim nearly burst into tears. He considered throwing himself upon the floor at his master's feet and begging for mercy.

'I knew it. I'm done for. He's selling me as a slave.' These thoughts played at deafening volume in his mind, blotting out everything else. His sightless eyes eventually refocused.

Old Malik was looking at him quizzically: 'Do you?'

Joachim looked at his master with wild, uncomprehending eyes.

'Sorry, I ...' he whispered.

Old Malik recognised confusion but could not guess at the cause. He repeated the question: 'Joachim, do you remember meeting Farmer Sistas?'

'Of course, Master.' The boy's voice was barely a whisper.

'You are to go to his farm for at least one day in every week. He has agreed to train you to be a farmer as good as he is. You will learn all the modern methods of farming from him. He will teach you how to choose the best workers and how to treat them so that they are happy and work very hard. And he will teach you about the money of farming, too. And when you have learned everything, we will do all of it here and make this farm great again. What do you think of that?'

Joachim was completely overwhelmed for a number of reasons. He was not being sold as a slave. He was not being sent away. He was to be trained to be a good farmer. Could this be true? He was to be trained to be a good master of people – and became a money handler. But he knew nothing of people and words and numbers and money!

His eyes staring, he blurted: 'But, Master, I am not worthy. I have no knowledge of people or words or numbers or money.' He could not stop his thoughts pouring out like a torrent through a broken dam.

The man placed his large hard hand on the boy's clenched fists, feeling the tremor within them. 'Yes, Joachim, you are worthy. You know how to work hard and you will do so. I know you have no knowledge of these things but Farmer Sistas will teach you all about farming and people and I, Malik, will teach you how to read and write, how to count numbers and handle money. I will teach you many other things, too.'

The boy looked at the man wide-eyed. He knew that Old Malik knew about these things for he had seen him reading and writing. He had seen him counting numbers in a big book and he knew that this man knew many things about the world. An image of the peculiar bullock carts of olden times flickered briefly in his conscious mind. A sudden rush of joy coursed through him: 'Yes,' he thought, 'maybe I could do this if I tried my hardest. If I worked hard at my studies maybe I could do it. Maybe I really could learn about farming and people and words and numbers and writing.'

The boy's words of reply tumbled out: 'Yes, Master, of course I will do this – and I will make you proud of me, I will work so hard at all these things.'

The man smiled: 'I know you will, Joachim.'

At the other side of the table, Maretta smiled too, warmly and gently.

'There is one other matter,' the man continued, 'you are to leave the barn. You are to make your home in the shack next door that we use as a store; it is the house that the Mistress and I lived in when we were first married, when my parents were still alive and lived here in the farmhouse.'

Joachim was astounded. A house of his own? How could he be so lucky?

'Master,' he stammered, 'you are too good to me …'

'No,' Maretta replied, speaking for the first time, 'it is the right place for you and we want you to live there. You should realise that you are almost a man, now.' It was true. Many years had passed since the little boy Joachim came to the farm and now he was a tall, increasingly sturdy young man only several years from adulthood.

'The decision is made.' Old Malik spoke. 'Tomorrow, we will clear the stores from the house and you will live there. I will make sure you have what you need. You will be able to study there and I will come to you to teach the things I have spoken about.'

Once again, Joachim's mind was is a spin! Moments ago he had thought he was being sold as a slave and here he was now, being given all these wonderful gifts. In his mind, he listed them: special teaching from Farmer Sistas to become a very good farmer; teaching to read and write – anything he wanted to! teaching to be able to count numbers and know money; information about the world, the skies … all the things the Master knows about. And a house of his own, to live and study in.

The boy sat quite stunned but deeply elated. His mind raced back to the day of the "accident" several weeks before. Then, he lived a closed, precarious life of worry and deprivation, a life which stretched into the infinity of time, unchanging, going nowhere; just the constant prospect of fear and pain every day. Now, his life path was gleaming in front of him like the rays of the sun, filled with hope, joy and purpose, dazzling him with its very brilliance.

He turned to the adults with shining eyes: 'Master and Mistress, I will not let you down. You may ask anything of me and I will do it. I am such a lucky boy to have such a good master.'

As he spoke the word "lucky" his brain instantaneously connected him with his earlier spoken words "lucky charm" and he remembered the beautiful stone nestling deep in his pouch. 'No,' he concluded immediately, 'nothing as good as this could be created by a lucky charm!'

His master was speaking again. 'Listen, Joachim, from now on you will eat here with us in the farmhouse, here at the table. This is what the Mistress and I want.'

'Yes, Master.' Surely the ultimate honour. The boy was awed – but also just a little worried. He had always eaten his food alone and was concerned that his manner of eating might not be satisfactory in front of his Master and Mistress.

Maretta, watching him closely, said with a smile, 'Don't worry, Joachim, we will not be watching you eat!'

He looked at her gratefully. 'Thank you, Mistress.' He felt much better. However he resolved to be very cautious and watch how they ate their food; then he would copy them exactly.

The following day, Old Malik was as good as his word.

'Before we start the day's work, we will clear your house.' Working quickly, the small house was soon cleared and Joachim seized a brush to give the small room a very vigorous sweep out. When he had finished, he looked around in pleasure and wonderment.

'What a beautiful house,' he said out loud, 'I will be so happy here.'

Old Malik heard him speak and smiled. The man felt very happy about this, too. He was confident that the decisions he had made about the boy were absolutely correct. Now he found himself thinking: 'Why didn't I think of all this before? It is so obvious that I must plan for the future.'

In fact, Old Malik had never planned for the future. Down the years, he had never even thought about the future once.

Later that day, after the farm work was done, Old Malik said to Joachim: 'Now we must prepare the house for you to live in.' They went to the barn and set to work building some of the basic items of furniture that the boy would need. Using some smooth wooden planks and stout netting, Old Malik constructed a generous bed and then made a large soft mattress, stuffing it with large quantities of fine wool. Meanwhile, Joachim constructed several simple seats. These items were taken to the house along with several large boxes to be used for storage.

Finally, Old Malik, who was quite a skilled craftsman in wood, made a large table, sturdy yet elegant, carefully planed to be absolutely smooth on top and then polished with oil. 'This will be a good study table for you,' he told the boy, who was very impressed by the quality of Old Malik's work.

'I never knew he could make such very good furniture,' the boy thought before answering his master. 'Master, this table is very beautiful and I am sure I will work upon it with great happiness.' He was surprised when the man's face flushed with pleasure.

Maretta and Giana appeared with various other items for the house; blankets for the bed, lamps to light the room, water jugs, basins, etc. and all these items were placed on the table. The woman looked around with pleasure at what had been her home for a number of years.

'It's good to see my old home being used again for its real purpose. Did you know that this house was built by the Master? He did it all himself and in only a few weeks, too.' Joachim had not known this although, after seeing Old Malik's skill in constructing the bed and the table, he was not at all surprised.

While everything was being made ready, the boy noted that Giana was solemn and withdrawn, avoiding his eyes and looking rather upset. Joachim wondered why. When he had smiled at her and thanked her for bringing essential items for his house, her response was minimal and she left at the earliest opportunity without saying goodbye. This disappointed Joachim, because he wished to share his happiness and good fortune with Giana. She was, after all, the only person at the farm who was near to his own age and whose status as a servant was similar to his.

However the boy now remembered that he and Giana did not know each other very well. Since they had received permission to speak to each other, the two young people had spoken on only a few brief occasions and those conversations had tended to be rather stilted and hesitant. A relaxed and genuine friendship would take more time to develop.

'Maybe that's the problem,' he thought, 'maybe she still feels awkward talking to me.' Yet he felt there was something more, almost as if the girl was unhappy and resentful at the turn of events on the farm. 'I don't know why she should feel unhappy,' the boy mused, 'after all, her life has changed very much for the better, just like mine. The Mistress is not unkind to her and doesn't punish her any more when something goes wrong. So why isn't she happy, like I am?'

Joachim was very puzzled and resolved to raise the matter with Giana at an appropriate moment.

'The trouble is, she's always working with the Mistress and I rarely see her alone. We need to have a private conversation about this and it cannot be in the farmhouse with the Master and Mistress listening in. The first time I see a suitable opportunity, I will talk to her.'

So the new routine of Joachim's life soon settled down into a comfortable rhythm. He and Old Malik continued to work together on the farm but the farmer was now quite friendly towards him, praising good work and calmly correcting him when this was occasionally necessary. The boy worked hard and applied himself intelligently to the tasks he was given, rarely making mistakes.

During breaks from work, they now sat together. Old Malik was not a man who said a great deal but sometimes he would recount a story from his youth or tell the boy some facts about the world. Joachim would listen to the old man with rapt attention and marvel at his knowledge and experience.

After that "serious conversation" in the farmhouse, the weekly visits to Farmer Sistas had commenced. On these days, Joachim would get up especially early to give himself time to walk to the neighbouring farm just as the morning light was beginning to fill the sky.

'I wonder why the sky is so beautiful and filled with colour?' the boy thought. 'I must ask the Master about this. He is sure to know.'

On arrival at their neighbour's farm, he was always received in a most friendly and informal way by Farmer Sistas. 'Holat, young Joachim,' the man would say, shaking Joachim's hand vigorously and smiling broadly, 'come in, let's get started with the good work.'

The teaching had started with a comprehensive tour of the farm. Joachim was very impressed. Everything was neat, clean and in good repair. The crops in the fields were strong and healthy and Joachim noted that the condition of the soil was excellent. Likewise, the farm animals were all in peak condition, whether these were work animals or those that were kept for their milk, eggs, wool, skin or meat.

Over the weeks and months of Joachim's visits, the farmer taught the boy everything about the proper care of all the animals, in terms of feeding, shelter and the maintenance of their health. After detailed instruction, the boy was given the task of caring for each type of animal and his work was supervised carefully by the farmer.

At the end of this process, the farmer was pleased with Joachim's progress. 'Right now, he would make an excellent livestock farmer,' the man thought.

As the seasons progressed, the farmer taught Joachim the essential principles of modern arable farming, showing the boy how to choose the best fields for growing particular crops and how to look after the crops as they grew. He also taught him how it was necessary to rotate various categories of crops around the different fields while leaving one field unplanted for a season. The unplanted field was referred to as "fallow". 'It allows the soil to rest,' the farmer explained.

When the farmer was satisfied that the boy had grasped all the principles of agriculture and could manage fieldwork to a high standard, he turned his attention to farm maintenance, general management and employment practices.

Meanwhile, Old Malik had started to teach Joachim to read and write, coming to his house on several evenings each week. Joachim proved to be an apt and enthusiastic pupil and Old Malik, who had struggled with these things as a boy, was astonished and impressed by his rapid progress.

When he complimented him on his good work, the boy would answer: 'It's because you are such a good teacher, Master,' and Old Malik would need to turn his face away to hide the tears of joy filling his eyes.

In a remarkably short period of time, Joachim could read and write to a good standard, partly because he was a bright and intelligent pupil who was desperate to learn and partly because he practiced these skills so assiduously in the evenings when he was alone. Old Malik now turned his attention to figure work and, over the following months, taught the boy about the meaning of numbers and how to manipulate them by means of addition, subtraction, multiplication and division. These were difficult concepts for Joachim to grasp at first but he persisted with great determination and finally understood exactly what the various mathematical manipulations achieved.

Knowing how difficult all this was, Old Malik was once again delighted with the boy's progress. Joachim's understanding of numbers and their manipulation made his introduction to money very simple. Old Malik showed him all the coins that were used in their country and very soon the boy had completed with competence the various exercises and tests that Old Malik set.

'I think you're now a better money handler than I am.' Old Malik laughed and regarded his pupil with pride.

'No Master, I could never be better than you,' was the boy's reply. The two looked at each other with twinkling eyes of affection – two people linked by the common bonds of knowledge and respect.

At the neighbouring farm, Farmer Sistas had examined Joachim's knowledge of farm maintenance and found that the boy had been well taught by Old Malik. The boy was familiar with the maintenance and repair of the various pieces of farm equipment that were used to prepare the ground; also with the animal harnesses which attached the work animals to the equipment. The farmer set him tests and the boy passed these with flying colours. The farmer found also that he knew how to build a good, stout fence, driving the posts precisely into the ground and nailing the horizontal rails neatly. He could also build a secure gate and carry out repairs to the foundations, walls or roofs of any type of farm building. He could even build a fireplace and chimney.

'You have taught the boy to do these things well,' the farmer told Old Malik during one of his regular visits to report upon Joachim's progress.

Old Malik was extremely pleased to receive such a compliment, especially since it came from a man so well-respected in the community. Reflecting with pleasure on Farmer Sistas's words later that day, Old Malik's face darkened as he recalled how much of his earlier teaching of farm work tasks had been accompanied by anger, contempt and physical violence. He shook his head sadly as he recalled beating the boy and recoiled at the recollection of tender skin striped with purple wheals and crimson blood.

'I was mad then,' he whispered, 'but I have changed, thank the Lord.' He lifted his eyes heavenward.

Sitting outside his house on a warm evening, Joachim was supremely happy with his life.

'I have it all.' His thoughts were filled with joy. 'I live here in this most wonderful of houses. I enjoy my work with my Master. I'm good at my work but every day, I'm getting better and better. I can read, write and count numbers and I also know money very well.' He thought affectionately about Old Malik. 'He has taught me so well and now he is teaching me all the other things he knows about the world. And now Farmer Sistas will start to teach me about people and how to make them work with contentment.' He felt he would burst with happiness and was desperate to share it with someone, because unshared happiness is an ache, an agony, almost physical in its intensity.

A slight sound made him look around and there was the slim figure of Giana walking towards the farmhouse.

'Giana,' he called, 'come and speak to me.' He remembered his resolve to have a private conversation with her. Now he had found his chance.

The girl hesitated, then replied: 'No.'

'Why not?' he persisted. 'It's not yet time for the evening meal.'

'No,' she said again, 'I don't want to.'

He was surprised. 'Giana, please come and speak to me. I want to tell you about all the things that have been happening to me.'

'I don't want to hear about it.'

He was taken aback by this forthright reply. 'What's wrong? Come and sit here. I want to speak to you about your sadness.'

After a moment or two of indecision, the girl walked over slowly and sat down gingerly on the edge of the chair beside him.

'What's wrong?' he repeated his question.

Now she looked at him, a flash of anger in her dark eyes: 'It's all right for you, with your lovely house to live in and being taught to be a good farmer.'

He was mystified.

'But your life must be very good, too, Giana. The Mistress is kind to you, you have a bed of your own and everyone is nice …' His voice trailed off.

'Listen,' she said, her tone now hard-edged, 'your life has changed in so many different ways but mine hasn't. My life is just the same. I'm still a servant to the Mistress. All day, every day, I have to do everything she tells me to do. She may not be unkind to me like she used to but I still have to be obedient, all the time. Unlike you, I'm still treated as a little servant girl. No-one gives me a house and beautiful furniture. And I don't eat at the table or talk as an equal to them.' Having said this Giana burst into loud and bitter tears.

'I don't talk as an equal …' the boy faltered. He was dumbfounded at what Giana had said – but he was beginning to see the logic of it. 'I've never really looked at it from her point of view. Maybe I can begin to see what she means, now.' His thoughts were a revelation.

'Giana, I never thought …' Again his voice faded away and he leaned forward to comfort her.

'Don't touch me,' she snapped, 'I don't want your sympathy.' On saying this she jumped up from the chair and ran off towards the farmhouse. He looked after her sadly.

'I should have known this. I should have been able to work it out.' Joachim was blaming himself. 'I must think what to do.'

The following day, while doing his farm work, he thought about Giana's unhappiness many times and racked his brains to see how he could best help her.

'Maybe I should discuss this with the Master.' He looked across at the old man and thought how he would approach the subject with him. At the same time, intelligently, he tried to work out what his Master's reaction would be. 'I don't want him to be angry with me. He might say it's none of my business and then I won't have helped Giana at all.'

Reflecting further upon speaking to Old Malik, the boy thought it most likely that the man would grunt something like: 'Giana? Giana is the Mistress's servant. I have nothing to do with her.' That would be the end of the conversation and, again, Joachim would have solved nothing. 'Better that I should speak to the Mistress myself,' he concluded, feeling rather nervous at the prospect.

Although Joachim and Maretta had a friendly enough relationship these days, they did not usually speak on "serious matters". She might not be pleased with his interference in her affairs:

'I'll need to think of a gentle way to introduce the subject,' he thought.

By the end of the day, Joachim had decided how to approach Maretta but he knew he had to find the right time to speak.

'It will need to be a time when Giana is not present,' he told himself.

That very evening, the perfect opportunity presented itself. He had cleaned himself and had arrived at the farmhouse for the evening meal. Maretta was making preparations for the meal but both Old Malik and Giana were absent from the room. The boy knew that his Master was outside washing himself at the tub and so would not return for some minutes: 'Mistress, where is Giana?'

'She has gone to the dairy for some milk, Joachim.' The boy noted that this was said in a friendly voice and decided to put his strategy into action.

'May the Lord be with me,' he whispered. Old Malik had recently converted him away from the spirits and he now worshipped "The Lord" like the Master and Mistress. 'Mistress, I must speak about Giana. Will you permit it?'

Maretta was surprised. What could the boy possibly have to say to her about Giana?

'Yes, Joachim, you may speak.'

'It is possible that Giana may eat with us at the table? I feel unhappy that she is not sharing all the wonderful privileges you and the Master have given me. But I recognise I am like Giana. I am just a servant on the farm, like her.'

Maretta was very surprised. This had never occurred to her because, unlike Joachim who clearly was approaching manhood, she thought of Giana as just a little girl. It was true that Giana was several years younger than Joachim and was not yet showing the signs of becoming a woman. She looked searchingly at him and he blenched nervously under her gaze. She found she was touched by the concern of this young man for someone who was weaker than he was.

'Joachim, I will think about this and discuss it with the Master.'

'Mistress, I hope I have not displeased you.' He was worried that he may have made things worse.

'No,' she reassured him, 'it is right that you should have spoken – and, Joachim …'

'Yes, Mistress?'

'There are things you do not know about – but, in time, you will.'

'Yes, Mistress.' Joachim did not understand this enigmatic comment but was grateful that all seemed to be well. 'I have done all I can,' he thought.

The very next day, when the time of the evening meal came, Maretta laid a fourth place at the table. When Giana brought the platters and bowls, she was puzzled by the extra place at the table and enquired: 'Mistress, do we have a guest for the evening meal? You have not mentioned it and I have not prepared extra food.'

'No, Giana, we have no guest,' the woman replied with a smile, 'the Master and I wish you to sit at the table with us. We want you to have all your meals here from now on.'

Giana was astounded. 'But, why?' the words stumbled out.

'Because you are now a grown up girl and soon you will be a woman. And because you are a good servant.'

The girl could not believe her good fortune and tears of joy filled her eyes. 'Oh thank you, Mistress, thank you Master.'

Maretta glanced significantly at Joachim, sitting quietly (and innocently) in his place, and nodded imperceptibly. The boy flushed with pleasure. He hoped fervently that this would make Giana happy. He looked at her now, settling down in her place at the table, and was glad to see her face wreathed in smiles.

Farmer Sistas and Joachim were now concentrating on the most complex parts of farm management – strategic organisation and people. Now that the boy could read, write and count, he kept the farm accounts and dealt with many aspects of money, making only very rare mistakes. He was also taught how to work out the best strategy for the farm and set everything out in the Farm Book, so that this could be constantly reviewed and, if necessary, amended during the seasons.

Where many farmers in the region planned their activities virtually on a day-to-day basis, Farmer Sistas was a meticulous strategist; this was why his farm was so efficient and known to be easily the most productive in the region. This was the position formerly taken by Old Malik's farm when it was managed by his father. So Farmer Sistas trained Joachim rigorously, testing him to the limit on strategic matters. The boy was quick to learn and the farmer was delighted with his rapid progress.

'I have trained others for this work,' the farmer told him, 'but you are easily the best of all my pupils.' Of course both Joachim and Old Malik were delighted to hear this.

Finally, Farmer Sistas came to the employment and management of workers on the farm.

'Joachim, this is a very serious part of farm work,' he told the boy, 'and it is of great importance that the right workers are employed on fair terms. You must now learn how to handle people and how to motivate them to give you the best work they can give.'

Joachim was awed at this prospect – in fact, it terrified him!

'But Master, I am only a young farm boy. How can I make grown men work well?' His heart thumped within him. He had not been awed by any of the things he had learned from Farmer Sistas and Old Malik. It had been very hard work but it was wonderful to be able to do all these things well. But how could he, Little Joachim, hope to command workers, grown men, much bigger and stronger than he?

Farmer Sistas smiled, looking across at this sincere and increasingly impressive young man, not only acquiring new knowledge each day but rapidly growing towards powerful adulthood.

'Joachim, I will teach you and then I will prove to you that you can do it – and do it well.'

The following weeks were filled with teaching about employing and handling workers.

Firstly, Joachim was taught and tested on recruitment and command: 'So how many men will you employ?'

'I will consult the strategy and see how many I need,' the boy answered immediately.

'How much will you pay?'

'I will find out the level of pay in the region and then I will pay according to their ability and experience.'

'How will you treat your workers?'

'I will expect them to work well. I will be firm and fair and treat them with justice and respect.'

'How will they treat you?'

'They will treat me with respect and do what I ask them to do.'

'And if they don't?'

'I will warn them and give them a chance to reform. If this fails I may have to terminate their employment.'

'Will you need to supervise every worker personally?'

'No. If I have a large number of workers I will form them into teams with a leader. The leader will be responsible to me and I will pay him more money.'

'Will you train any of your workers in new skills?'

'Yes, I will always want to develop my workers. The better they are the better the work they will do for me.'

Farmer Sistas was delighted with the results of his teaching. Joachim passed all his tests with flying colours.

On Joachim's next visit to the neighbouring farm, the farmer said: 'Joachim, your teaching is now complete and I am confident you can apply all the skills of a very good farmer.' Joachim flushed with pleasure. Old Malik would be very pleased when he heard. 'The only thing you lack now is actual experience of commanding workers. Come with me, please.'

Rather mystified, Joachim followed the farmer across the spotless farmyard and round the edge of a field. In the distance, Joachim could see three men, offloading posts and thick planks of wood from a cart. These were big, burly men, bronzed and stripped to the waist, their well-developed muscles rippling as they handled the heavy wood with ease. As the farmer approached, the men stopped work and greeted him.

'Good morning, Master.'

'Good morning, men,' the farmer responded. Turning to Joachim, he continued: 'We are building a new fence along the bottom of this field; the old one was rotten and was removed yesterday. If you look here, you will see the line of the fence; it is about 300 pics long.'

Joachim thought this was very interesting but wondered why the farmer was telling him all this. The farmer's next words revealed why.

'Joachim, you are to take charge of this work and these men. I expect the work to be finished by the end of the day. I don't expect you will have any problems but, if there are, I will be at the farmhouse.'

Joachim felt as if the world had collapsed on him! How could he command these men? They were all much bigger and stronger and older than him. Then, memory of his training diminished his fears to some degree.

The farmer turned to the workers: 'This is Joachim, your overseer for today. He is responsible to me for the work. You will call him "Master".'

With a pleasant smile to Joachim, the farmer walked away quickly, leaving a very apprehensive Joachim facing three pairs of hard eyes boring into his.

The boy's brain started working again as he rapidly surveyed the work to be done. The task was simple enough but it was a long fence so work had better start immediately.

'Let's get started,' he called to the men and walked to the place where the first post had to be driven. To his surprise, he found he was alone. The three men had sat down on the ground and were looking at him with rather derisive expressions. Joachim walked up to them slowly.

'Let's get started, men,' he repeated.

The oldest of the three spoke laconically: 'We thought we'd have a rest first!' The man flashed a smirk to his fellow workers as he said this.

Joachim locked eyes with this man. A few moments of silence passed. Bodily, the boy's stomach was churning with fear but his mind was calm, analysing the situation, sifting actions. After a few moments, the man flushed and broke away from the boy's gaze.

'What is your name?' Joachim asked the man quietly.

'Karval.' The man spoke loudly, too loudly.

'Karval … do you wish to work today?' The boy's voice was softer still.

'Yes.' This in a more uncertain voice.

'Then, get up, and come with me.' The words were still quiet but now hard-edged.

The man jumped as if struck physically, then scrambled to his feet.

'Yes, Master,' he mumbled.

'Karval, will you drive the first post,' Joachim instructed. The work was started and the first post was driven into the ground, Karval holding the heavy wood upright and the other two men wielding long heavy hammers. Flexing their large muscles ostentatiously and sneaking derisive glances at Joachim's relatively slight frame, the workers stepped back and prepared to start the second post.

'Stop!' Joachim's voice. 'This is bad work. The post is not vertical. Do you not know how to drive a post properly? Remove it from the ground.' In silence, the men removed the heavy post with difficulty and looked towards him.

'I think I need to show you how to drive a post,' the boy said, stepping forward. They gave way to him and stood aside, confused.

'How can he drive a post?' Their thoughts unspoken.

Joachim lifted the post, propped it exactly vertical using other posts to hold it steady; then, with smooth and accurate hammer blows, drove it into the ground to the correct depth. Little did they know that Joachim had driven many posts in the past and had acquired the technique to do it easily and accurately.

'Now get to work and do it properly. I will inspect each post and rail.'

Joachim had no more trouble with the workers and the work was completed in good time.

With all completed, Joachim addressed the workers: 'Thank you for your day's work. When you have cleared the residue and taken the cart back, you may finish your day's work and be paid.'

'Thank you, Master,' they said respectfully.

The boy returned to the farmhouse where Farmer Sistas was working.

'The fence is completed and all is well,' he reported.

'Good,' the farmer replied, 'will you now pay the men? Here is the money chest and the book. You will find the contracts in there.'

Joachim took the items and found the three men waiting outside. He placed the book and the chest on a table and found the page for today's work. Each man was to be paid three Ourtz for the day's work. Joachim paid the money to two of the men but when Karval came forward, the man said: 'Master, I am to be paid four Ourtz.'

Joachim checked the book again. 'It says three Ourtz in the book,' he said, 'why do you think you should be paid more than the others?'

'Because I am the overseer.'

Joachim looked into his eyes. 'Today, you were not the overseer.'

'Master, I am always the overseer – if you ask the Farmer, you will see.'

'The Farmer is busy and will not be disturbed. Anyway, you were not the overseer. I was the overseer.'

The man was silent, looking resentful.

'Listen,' Joachim said firmly, 'answer this question. Were you the overseer today?'

The man looked shifty. 'I am always …'

Joachim interrupted. 'Answer the question. Were you the overseer today?'

Silence. Then: 'No, Master.' The words mumbled.

'Who was?'

'You were, Master.'

'Thank you. Here are your wages. Three Ourtz.' Joachim entered the wage amounts in the book and rose to his feet. 'You may go now. Thank you.'

The men left and Joachim went back into the farmhouse.

'Well, Joachim, did you have any problems with the work or the workers?' the farmer greeted him.

Joachim smiled. 'No Master, nothing I could not put right.'

The farmer laughed knowledgeably and patted the boy on the shoulder. 'Now I have taught you all I know and you have learned it well. You are a very good farmer now. You know how to run a farm properly, you know what to do about the crops and the livestock and, most importantly, you know how to deal with workers, how to be fair and how to be firm. You are a great success and you are finished here. I will tell your Master that he can trust your knowledge and you actions fully.'

Joachim was very pleased but was sorry to hear that he would not be coming to Farmer Sistas' farm any more. 'I will miss coming here and speaking with you, Master. I have enjoyed it very much.'

'Don't worry, Joachim,' the farmer replied, 'we will meet often in the village and we will drink a flagon of beer together as good friends.'

Joachim flushed with pleasure. Farmer Sistas was treating him as a friend – and a man!

Back at Old Malik's farm, the old farmer was delighted to hear that Joachim had completed his training with Farmer Sistas and passed all his testing with flying colours. Likewise, the boy had become very competent at reading and writing; for some time now, Old Malik had put him in change of the farm's accounts and did not hesitate to seek his advice on farming matters. 'You are now a better farmer than I am,' he told the boy.

Although this was undoubtedly true, the boy always said: 'No Master, I am not. But together we will make the best farm in the region.'

Under Joachim's influence, the farm improved dramatically and both crops and livestock were more productive.

Soon, the farmer said: 'Joachim, we have need of more workers here. Let us review the work to come and then you will tell me how many workers we need. When we have done this, I will leave it to you to find the workers and agree with them their wages.'

Joachim was delighted to do this and a week later, after a number of discussions with Old Malik, he proposed that they should employ four men for the farm work. Then he asked a question: 'Master, have you asked the Mistress whether she is in need of more help with the work that she and Giana do? With more workers on the farm, there will be more work for them.'

Old Malik was pleased that Joachim should have extended his thoughts to the women. 'This is a good thought. I will ask the Mistress.'

His enquiry was received with pleasure at the farmhouse. Maretta replied: 'Yes, I would like to have one extra worker for the farmyard.'

Joachim added this requirement to his list.

The following week, Old Malik said: 'Joachim, it is time to employ the new workers we have decided upon and I leave you to do this. You will be much better than I would be at this task. You will go to the village on the next Market Day when workers present themselves for work contracts.' The old man continued: 'Now there is something else I want you to do for me. From this day you will not call me Master, because now you are a farmer here, my assistant. You will call me Malik and the mistress wishes that you will call her Maretta. This is important now that we are to have new workers on the farm.'

Joachim was deeply honoured and said so. However he recognised that this was a necessity if he was to be a leader of the new workers on the farm.

On the next Market Day, Joachim went alone to the village to look for workers. As in any small community, the elevation of Joachim to the status of Farmer was common knowledge and the fact that he had come to employ workers was well known. At the place in the centre of the village where workers were hired, Joachim was approached by many men. He spoke to each one in a friendly tone and established their skills and experience, noting all this in a book which he had brought with him. He was calm and unhurried in all he did and made no quick or hasty decisions.

During the afternoon, he called four men to him and one by one negotiated their wages for work on the farm. He gave each one a note of their agreement; most of the workers could not read but they took the paper and stored it safely in their clothing. The men he employed were all strong, fit and of good character and each one had different farming skills. In addition, he spoke to a number of women and eventually chose a teenage girl as a worker for Maretta. This girl had experience of farmyard work and was strong and willing.

The following day, the five new workers came to the farm and Joachim received them. Leading them to the farmyard, he introduced them to the other residents of the farm: 'This is Farmer Malik, the Master of this farm. This is his wife, the Mistress. And this is Giana, who, like me, has worked at this farm for many years. As you know, I am Joachim, Farmer Malik's assistant. We all hope you will work hard and honestly for us. We also hope that you will be happy; if there are any questions or problems (he looked at the men), you may come to me. You (he addressed the girl) will of course be working for the Mistress. Now, let us all start the day's work. There is much to do.'

That evening while they were eating their evening meal, Old Malik said to Joachim: 'For the next few days, I will be away from the farm. I have important business with the land-owner and others. You will need to take full charge of all the work here.'

Joachim knew this would be no problem for him. 'I will look after all the farm work until you return, Malik. I will merely follow the schedule of work that you and I have drawn up.'

In fact, the schedule of work had been drawn up by Joachim alone but he always insisted that Old Malik should approve it. At the same time he couldn't help being curious about what Old Malik had said. He wondered what this "important busi-ness" was. It must be something very serious to send Malik to see the landowner. Joachim knew that Old Malik avoided the landowner whenever he could. He exchanged glances with Giana and raised his eyebrows in a gesture of questioning but she responded only with a slight shake of the head.

The next day, Old Malik departed soon after the morning meal and was seen to be carrying several large books under his arm. During the morning, Giana tried to raise the subject several times with Maretta, to see what she could find out. Each time, Maretta just smiled gently and made a noncommittal reply.

At the midday meal break, Joachim and Giana met to discuss the matter in front of Joachim's house. 'What did she say?' Joachim asked.

'Nothing, really,' Giana answered, 'I tried three times to raise the subject – and I was very subtle about it – but she just smiled. She obviously understood I was trying to get her to reveal what it was all about. So I'm afraid I did not succeed. I didn't get any information at all.'

'Well, maybe we'll never get to know,' Joachim said. 'Maybe it's a very private matter between Malik and Maretta. If it is, it is none of our business. But I must admit I'm very curious.'

'Me too.' And the two young people, kindred spirits, looked into each other's eyes and giggled conspiratorially.

By evening, Joachim met Giana excitedly. 'I think I've worked it out, Giana. It's about the future of the farm. Malik is setting up for someone to buy the farm from him sometime in the future. After all, he's an old man and he may not want to work much longer. I hope the buyer might be Farmer Sistas; he could merge the two farms very easily. I'm sure he would employ both of us, too. But I'm a bit worried because the new owner might be someone we don't know and he may not want us. We'll have to try our best to persuade him to take us on when the time comes.' So the two young people were reassured in one way and rather worried in another.

The situation continued unchanged for the next two days. Each morning, Old Malik left immediately after the morning meal and did not return until early evening. Each time he carried a bundle of books with him. Meanwhile, Joachim managed all aspects of the farm work along with his four workers.

Since the new workers had started, it had been possible to make further good progress with the farm. Crops were now well tended and managed carefully to provide very good yields and all the farm animals were providing top class produce. In addition, all the farm buildings, fences and paths were now immaculate.

As he walked on a tour of inspection, Joachim looked around with pride and thought: 'Malik's farm is now as good as Farmer Sistas'. In fact, maybe it's better.' He grinned happily as he thought that. Still smiling, he added: 'And if it isn't better, I will work hard to make it so.'

Joachim was very proud of the work he had done at the farm. He knew he had put all his energy into it and had applied every bit of teaching he had received from Malik and Farmer Sistas. He also looked around him with a sense of sadness. 'Whoever buys this farm after Malik is gone will be a very lucky man indeed!'

After three days of absences, Old Malik returned to his work. On the first day back, Maretta and he spent a long time in deep conversation, sitting close together at the table in the farmhouse. Both Joachim and Giana strained their ears to hear what was being said but, apart from a few random words, they heard nothing but murmurs. Every so often, they met and compared notes but nothing they had heard made any sense.

'We'll just have to wait and see what happens.' Joachim was resigned. 'Maybe Malik will not speak to us about this at present. Perhaps he will leave it until he has decided to sell.' The young people looked at each other with dismay and longed to know what was to happen.

That evening, after the evening meal was finished, Old Malik spoke, looking at Joachim and Giana: 'You know I have been conducting important business in the last few days.

This is business that affects the future of both of you. We will speak about this tomorrow evening. Meanwhile Maretta and I must speak further and I would ask you to leave us alone.' This hardly reassured the young people. They withdrew to Joachim's house and he lit the lamp before they sat down in some dismay.

'It's going to affect our future.' Joachim was sombre. 'That sounds ominous. It must be about the future sale of the farm. Maybe he's selling it right now. Maybe he's sold it already.' Their faces mirrored their worry. Then Joachim, ever practical, tried to inject a positive note. 'Look, Giana, whatever it is we'll know tomorrow. And whatever happens, we have each other.' Giana was quite startled by this declaration.

'I suppose so,' she murmured uncertainly, looking anything but convinced!

The night passed restlessly. The day dragged by on leaden feet of worry. The evening meal was eaten distractedly and cleared away rapidly.

Then … Old Malik looked at Giana: 'First it's you I wish to speak to, Giana. I want to tell you a story. You'll be interested in this story, because it's a story about you.' The man paused and looked at Maretta. She nodded encouragingly. Old Malik continued. 'You will have seen that we have no children. We have never had any, although it was our wish to have many. After we had accepted this, one night the midwife of this village came to me at the village tavern and offered to sell me a new-born baby to be adopted as my own daughter. But I refused to take the child.' The last sentence was spoken very quietly.

There was a long pause, then the man spoke again.

'Do you know who that child was, Giana?'

'No, Master, I don't,' the girl whispered.

'Well, Giana, that child was you! You had been born in the middle of a violent storm and your mother and father were killed shortly after by a falling tree. You were found by a travelling merchant and his wife. They gave you to the village midwife so that she could find a home for you. That's when she came to me and I refused to have you. As a result, the midwife placed you in the handyman's family and I know you had a very bad time there. Years later when he decided to sell you, you were thin and ragged and starving. That's when I bought you. Maybe you remember?' Giana did remember. It was not a pleasant memory; Old Malik had frightened her. The man now ended his story. 'So you came here and you have been the Mistress's servant ever since.'

Giana had a question: 'Master, how do you know that the baby given to the handyman was the same baby you were offered?'

'A good question. I had to check that too. I went to the handyman the other day and asked him to tell me what the midwife had said about the baby. The story she told him was identical to the story she told me. The only extra bit of information he was given was your name. Evidently the merchant's wife had named you Giana after her grandmother who lived in a country far away. So there's no doubt there was only one baby – and that baby was you!'

There was a long silence. Then Giana spoke, tears in her eyes.

'Master, why are you telling me this? It is making me sad.'

'Giana,' the man spoke huskily, 'if I had accepted you all these years ago, you would have been brought up here as my daughter and Maretta would have been your mother. Now I am going to put things right.' He took out a thick piece of paper, rolled as a scroll. 'I know you are not able to read this, Giana, so I will ask Joachim to tell you what it says.'

Joachim took the scroll and opened it, reading its contents quickly.

'Giana, this paper says that from today you are the adopted daughter of Malik and Maretta and that you have all the rights and privileges of their daughter. It is signed and sealed by the landowner, in his position as King's Justice.'

There was complete silence in the room. Giana sat, wide-eyed, looking from Old Malik to Maretta, her mind clearly in the numbness of total surprise.

Then Old Malik spoke: 'Giana, you will no longer call us Master and Mistress. You are no longer a servant. It is your choice how you wish to address us. We hope you might choose Father and Mother. This would please us greatly.' Giana burst into tears of shock and joy.

'Of course I would wish to call you Father and Mother,' she said between sobs, 'this is the best day of my life.' The girl rose from her chair and threw herself into Maretta's lap. 'Mother,' she cried, 'I will be a good daughter, you will see. You will never regret taking me as your daughter.' Maretta put her arms around Giana and they rocked gently together.

Joachim was surprised but very pleased for Giana. What an incredible story! What a wonderful outcome. Admittedly, he had thought the "important business" would be about the farm. He had never guessed that Giana was to be Malik and Maretta's daughter. Within his feeling of joy for Giana, there was nevertheless an aching emptiness. Giana's life had been transformed. At one stroke she had changed from being a servant to a loved daughter of a successful farmer. On the other hand, his life, good as it was, was totally unchanged. As all these thoughts swirled around in his brain, he suddenly became aware that Malik was speaking to him.

'Joachim! Joachim!' The man tried in vain to gain the boy's attention and placed his hand upon his arm.

'Sorry, Malik, it's all been such a great surprise and I was thinking …' His voice tailed off.

'Joachim, the important business is not yet finished. We must yet talk about the future of the farm.' These words brought Joachim back to the reality of his life. Now Malik was going to tell him about selling the farm. How was this going to affect him? All his worries flooded back.

The man now spoke quietly into his ear: 'Joachim, Maretta and I are not adopting you as our son. You still have a father and a mother in the next village and you are still their son. But I want you to know we both think you are a very fine young man; if things were different, we would be delighted to have you as our son.'

Joachim sat totally still. Malik's words had disappointed him. He would still be a servant, just like he was before – and with a new master, when Malik sold the farm. He felt deflated, alone and abandoned. Malik was still talking quietly into his ear but, in his misery, the boy's hearing had ceased to function. Then he became aware that the old man was holding out another scroll of paper: 'What was this? What was happening?' The boy tried to listen to Malik's voice but was unable to comprehend the words that Malik was speaking. He gazed at the old man's face blankly.

Finally, with a great effort, Joachim was able to reset his hearing and he interrupted the older man: 'Malik, I am sorry, so much is happening and I have missed what you have been saying. Will you please start again?'

Malik smiled gently at him and, in reply, handed him the heavy scroll of paper: 'Joachim, are you listening to me now?'

The boy nodded.

'This paper makes you my sole heir. When I die, the farm will be yours. The farm and everything in it. I would only ask that you look after my wife and my daughter should I die before them. Will you do that?'

The boy was flabbergasted, hardly able to understand what had just happened to him.

'Of course I would,' he said faintly, 'I promise – I will write a paper to you recording my promise.'

'No, Joachim, your word is enough for me.'

The boy looked at the old man with great love in his eyes and they embraced warmly. 'You have made my life wonderful,' Joachim said, speaking through tears of joy, 'and I will never let you down.'

Meanwhile, the words "I will be the owner of this farm!" raced around inside his head, almost making him giddy. He had never been so happy.

So the months and years passed. Joachim became a man and took over the running of the farm as Old Malik withdrew more and more from the work.

'I am an old man,' he said to Joachim, 'I can leave the work to you, now.'

'As long as I can always come to you for advice,' Joachim would always reply with a fond smile.

The years had also transformed Giana. She had metamorphosed from a young and skinny girl into a beautiful, tall young lady. She and Joachim often sat and talked together in the evening after the meal had been eaten. They were firm friends and enjoyed each other's company very much.

One evening, they sat quietly in front of Joachim's house and tried to count the stars, soon having to abandon the attempt: 'There are too many stars to count,' Joachim said, 'Just think of all the worlds there must be up there.'

'I'm perfectly happy with this one,' Giana answered softly. 'I like it the way it is. I like the way everything is different …' The word "different" echoed in her ears and sent her mind back to something Maretta had said to her. What was it? Ah yes, she remembered now.

She turned to look at Joachim: 'Do you know what Mother said to me once? She said: "Boys are very different from girls."'

The silence lengthened as they both contemplated these words.

Then, for the very first time, she slipped her slim hand into his and breathed: 'I think I'm glad …'

CONTINUATIO I

At this stage, it would be easy to conclude that the Stone was an entity of power. That, however, would not only be incorrect but simplistic. Nevertheless it is true that the Stone, in a previous, unrecognisable form, had been a conduit of power – but that was a different measure of power; internal, pulsating, much more akin to the comprehensible power of motion, of flow, of life itself.

Humanity claims some understanding of this type of power, because humanity is bound up with life and motion. But there never had been any personal power within the basic structure of the Stone, within the scaffolding of particles that gave it its form and existence throughout the continuum of space and time.

On the other hand, there was a power *associated* with the reality of the Stone. Not a direct power that can be measured by sensitive scientific instruments, so often manifested as wave patterns of energy disturbance – those amazingly tiny but significant ripples in the ether of our world and beyond. More a pattern of mystically-transmitted influence, somehow able to flow directly into the mind of humanity, there becoming capable of significant psychological and physiological effect.

Perhaps the power associated with the Stone should be linked with the concept of "dark matter". Today, it is proposed by science that such matter is plentiful in our universe systems but its constitution, existence and reality are currently unknown speculations.

Now the Lord God had planted a garden in the east, in Eden; and there he put the man he had formed. And the Lord God made all kinds of trees grow out of the ground – trees that were pleasing to the eye and good for food. In the middle of the garden were the tree of life and the tree of the knowledge of good and evil.

Genesis Chapter 2 Verses 8-9.
The Holy Bible, New International Version (The Bible Society, 1973)

PART TWO

Kati

It was really very disappointing!

'Only a little stone! After all the trouble I've taken to get the box open.'

Kati had been pleasurably excited when she found the mysterious little wooden box. She had been searching for "treasure" in one of the old storerooms of the Manor House (one of her favourite Saturday pastimes) and, upon moving a very old and heavy trunk, had spotted the little box tucked into a shallow recess behind it. It looked like no-one had touched this box for a very long time, maybe even centuries. It had been quite a problem to reach but, by bending over the trunk and stretching her arm to the limit, she had just been able to grasp it and lift it from its hiding place.

Carrying it over to the single small window in the room, she examined it carefully in the stronger light. She saw that the small box was made of finely grained wood and that the top lid was adorned by a simple pattern that had been carved carefully into its surface. The girl attempted to open the box but the lid wouldn't budge. There were sturdy hinges at one side of the lid and a small keyhole set in the opposite panel. Clearly, the box was securely locked.

Now Kati could have looked around the area where the box had been concealed to see if the key had fallen from the lock at some time in the past. But this was not Kati's way – she had little patience and insisted on achieving what she wanted in the shortest possible time, no matter the method or the consequences.

Looking around, she seized an old, rusty broad-bladed knife from a box of tools. 'This will help me to get it open,' she thought, forcing the blade under the lid and levering the knife handle upwards. At first the box resisted her attempts but then the wood splinted around the lock and the lid flew open on its hinges to reveal its contents – a small yellow stone lying upon a thick layer of woollen cloth.

In her disappointment, the girl was about to throw the box and stone on the floor and kick both into a dark corner but, at the last moment, something made her change her mind. Instead, with finger and thumb she picked up the stone from its bed of cloth. It proved to be rather light in weight, roughly cylindrical in shape and with two peculiar depressions towards one end. As she held the object, her finger and thumb slipped along the length of the stone and fitted quite naturally into the two depressions near the top. It was then that Kati felt a strange momentary jolt within her, a strange feeling she had never experienced before; for a moment her head swam.

'That's funny,' she thought, 'I've never felt that before. I wonder what caused it? Maybe I've spent too much time in here. Maybe the air is too dusty.'

Now that the stone was much closer to her eyes, Kati could see that it reflected multicoloured light in quite an attractive way; the light appeared to come from vertical lines etched along its length. The girl now looked at the stone with mounting interest.

'You know, this would hang nicely on a fine gold chain,' she mused; 'a hole could be pierced through these depressions. What a good idea that is.' Once again, Kati was very pleased with herself. No sooner had that thought entered her mind than she was looking around for the means to make a hole through the stone. 'A large sharp nail would do it,' she said impatiently, her eyes darting around the storeroom.

'Aha!' A cry of triumph as she spotted a small iron spike on the floor. Within seconds, the stone had been placed like a sacrifice on top of a stout chest, the sharp end of the spike had been thrust into one of the depressions on its surface and Kati was hammering upon the end of the spike with a heavy baulk of wood. This was obviously a very dangerous way of achieving her aim, since there was a significant chance that the small fragile stone would split apart under the assault of such brutal tools. Kati was aware of this danger but did not care: 'If the stone breaks it just shows it has no quality and is worthless,' she had thought.

Concentrating on her task, Kati did not at first notice the sound that was building up around her; however, after several blows, the noise began to penetrate her consciousness: 'What is that terrible noise? It's like thousands of people screaming during a huge storm.' Meanwhile, each blow sent the brutal spike more deeply into the stone, without any sign of cracking. Each blow also increased the sound until Kati thought she might have to stop and hold her hands over her ears. 'I must find out who is making that terrible noise. And when I do, I'll tell my father and he'll deal with them severely.'

Despite the violence of the attack, the stone did not break. After six strokes, the sharp point of the spike emerged into the facing depression and proceeded to dig an ugly hole in the wood of the chest below. At that instant, the noise stopped abruptly and there was absolute silence. Dropping, the tools on the floor with a loud clatter, Kati ran to the window to observe who or what had been making the noise. Looking down, she saw no-one outside and no activity to be seen anywhere else in her field of view. She looked in every direction but still could see nothing.

'Oh well, I can't be bothered with that now. I'll try to find out later. I must finish my new pendant.' Returning to the trunk, she retrieved the stone and took it to the window for examination.

'Very good work,' she congratulated herself. The hole was rather uneven and distinctly jagged but Kati was more than satisfied. Her mind had already leapt to the next stage. 'Now I need to find a chain for my pendant.' She returned the violated stone to its broken box and carried both from the storeroom thinking: 'My stone sparkling on a gold chain around my neck would make me look even more beautiful.' Kati was very vain and this thought delighted her.

Suddenly she stopped and smiled widely: 'I know – my mother's jewellery box!'

The jewellery box was kept in the Master and Mistress's curtained sleeping area, a raised wooden platform near the large fireplace in the Great Hall of the Manor House. The box was always locked and the only key was hidden in a secret place, known only to the Master, the Mistress and the Mistress's personal maidservant. However, many years before, Kati had made it her business to find out where the key was hidden. Creeping into the sleeping area, she soon obtained the key and proceeded to search for a gold chain in her mother's jewellery box.

Her search quickly revealed the perfect solution – a slim elegant chain of pure gold. Kati knew this chain had been in the family for many years. Her mother had shown it to her when she was very small. There was a large, thin medallion on the chain with unusual geometrical patterns engraved on each face. The girl lifted the item from the jewellery box and noted that the medallion and chain were fastened together by a small gold ring. She tried to slide the ends of the chain through the small gold ring but the catches at each end were too large to pass through.

Without pause, Kati lifted a small knife and inserted the tip into the delicate ring. A simple twist broke it apart and the large medallion fell from the chain and rolled away across the floor to fall through a rather wide crack in the floorboards towards the corner of the curtained area. Out of the corner of her eye, Kati saw the medallion disappear.

'Well, who would have thought that would happen?' However, Kati was unworried. 'Fortunately it doesn't matter. It's only an old ugly medallion that Mother never wears. I'm sure she'll never miss it.' She gave the medallion no more thought as she threaded the chain through the hole in the stone and fastened her new pendant around her neck, joyfully admiring herself in her mother's looking glass.

Shortly after, Kati relocked the jewellery box and returned the key to its secret compartment. She made sure no-one saw her slipping out of her parent's private area.

Four members of the family came together for the evening meal in the Great Hall. Kati, her father, mother and younger brother all sat around the large table. Kati's father was an important man in the area and the family were rich, living for many centuries in a fine stone house built in the middle of an estate with extensive park and forested land.

It was a large house and, in addition to the Great Hall and the adjacent large kitchen, there were a number of smaller rooms on a second floor above that were used for various purposes, for instance, as bedchambers for the children. This was especially convenient when the children were young and there was a potential for considerable noise. Their parents did not wish to be disturbed by noisy children who were invariably in the care of their individual nursemaids or nannies.

Like all wives of important men with large houses, Kati's mother was in charge of the household organisation and dealt with the many servants who were employed to provide all the meals, to clean and maintain the house and look after the children. Additionally, there were other servants who worked outside – the gardeners and gamekeepers who worked on the land and the stable hands who looked after the horses, carts and wagons in the nearby stable complex. This comprised a large walled stable yard built close to the substantial river which flowed through the estate and continued downstream to water the nearby town. The stable yard had a range of buildings within its walls; these housed all the animals and vehicles and included the living quarters for the outdoor workers.

Kati was the only girl in the family. She had an elder brother who had been married for a number of years and now lived in the town nearby. She saw her brother and his wife only very occasionally – she had no liking for the wife and felt sure the feeling was reciprocated. The youngest member of the family was her "little" brother, a quiet, rather pathetic little boy of nine years old.

While Kati's father had been pleased enough to produce a son and heir on the family's first occasion of family expansion many years ago, he had never had any particular affection for his eldest son. When the child was young, his father had virtually no contact with him and the boy grew up as a stranger to his father. Although Kati's father did acknowledge the presence of his second son (advancing age often encourages the development of some degree of love and compassion), he spoke infrequently to the boy and his manner towards him tended to be formal and aloof. The little boy feared his father, was deeply respectful towards him and tried to keep out of his way!

On the other hand, the man was surprisingly enchanted by his daughter and always pleased to be in her company. Over the years, he had denied her nothing and the girl had no hesitation in making full and frequent use of his indulgence towards her.

'She becomes more beautiful every year but then, she has always been beautiful, right from the start,' the man had often said. Down the years, Kati's father had often remembered the very first time he had seen his daughter, not long after her birth. His wife had assumed that her husband would have no interest in the birth of a girl but, to him, this small wrinkled scrap of female life, already making her presence felt by the volume of her voice, was the most beautiful child he had ever seen. It is true that fathers and daughters often have a remarkably powerful bond. From an early age, Kati had always made sure that the bond was kept strong.

As Kati approached the table in the Great Hall, her father looked up with a smile of welcome. However, as she came closer she noted that the smile faded from his face, although he was still looking directly at her.

'That's very strange,' the girl thought, 'he must be worried about something.'

Unusually, the meal was eaten in silence; both her father and mother seemed to be preoccupied. Despite this, Kati could not resist boasting about her cleverness. When the food had been eaten and the plates cleared, she spoke across the table to her father.

'Father, do you not think I look very attractive this evening?' The man raised his head slowly and looked at her.

'You always look attractive,' he replied in a level tone. She was puzzled by this response.

'Father, look here, I am wearing a new pendant. It's a funny stone I found in one of the storerooms today. I wondered whether you would know anything about it. You always know everything, Father, don't you?' She finished with one of her best winning smiles.

He did not reciprocate.

She plunged on, disquieted: 'I pierced a hole in it and hung it on this gold chain I also found. The stone was in this little box when I found it. Do you know anything about its history?' So saying, she took the pendant from her neck, dropped it into the carved wooden box and passed it across the table to her father, who examined it gravely.

'I see the box is broken, Kati.'

'Yes Father, it was locked and there was no key so I had to break it to open it.'

The man said nothing but looked sharply at her. In the dim light, she could not see his expression. His next words shocked her deeply. 'It might have been a great deal better if you had left the box alone until you had found the key.'

A rebuke! He never rebuked her!

'I'm sorry, Father,' she said tearfully (tears always worked).

Her father said nothing as he lifted the stone from the box to examine it closely. Finally he spoke in a negative and off-hand voice: 'I have never seen this box before but I remember my grandfather telling me a story about a strange and beautiful stone which had been in the family for many generations. He couldn't tell me anything about it. It is possible this may be the stone. I do not know.'

He passed the box to his wife.

She looked disinterestedly at the stone without comment and was about to pass the box back to her daughter when she found herself looking more sharply at the gold chain: 'Where did you find this chain? It's very like the one on my great grandmother's gold medallion that I keep in my jewellery box.'

Despite herself, a slight shiver ran through Kati's body. She replied vaguely: 'Oh, that old chain was in the bottom of an old trunk. It was just lying there.'

Her mother said nothing and passed the box to her younger brother: 'Give this back to Kati, please.'

'Hurry up, give it to me,' his sister snapped, 'don't go into one of your silly dreams.'

The little boy flushed and quickly passed the box to his sister. Unusually, however, he looked into her eyes as he did so and she was taken aback by his forthright gaze.

Kati now withdrew to her bed chamber and placed the pendant on her dressing chest, leaving the lid of the box open so that she could see the stone sparkling in the flickering candlelight. She quickly attended to her ablutions and changed into her sleeping chemise. Then, extinguishing the candle, the girl snuggled down in her soft bed, ready to commence her normal routine of going over the day's activities and congratulating herself once again on how clever she had been.

'Finding my wonderful sparkling stone today was a real stroke of genius. And I was so clever at turning it into a beautiful new pendant for myself. I'm going to wear my new pendant every day from now on.'

Kati then relived each part of her day, marvelling at the many demonstrations of her skill and resourcefulness as she transformed a worthless piece of old junk into a thing of absolute beauty. When she had finished wallowing luxuriously on the events of this day, she now returned to the events of the previous day, Friday.

'I really must think about Friday again; it was the best day of my life! But I really need to start at last Wednesday, because that's when the experiment started to take shape; that's when the adventure began to be planned.' Kati hugged her body in an ecstasy of joy, because what happened on these days had exceeded her expectations.

It was on a fine Wednesday morning, while walking alone, that Kati had come across the nails lying in the mud on the riverbank. Probably a remnant of an old fence, long broken down and gone, the two large and rusty nails were driven through a small block of rotting wood. She had been drawn to pick it up and examine it. As soon as she did so, her fertile and inventive mind knew immediately where this unusual item could be employed in a wonderful experiment.

'That would certainly be a bit of fun,' she smiled dreamily, 'a real experiment and it would be fascinating to see what the outcome would be.' Undoubtedly, Kati had something of the experimental scientist in her. Opening her bag, she placed the item carefully within it, shielding the still sharp points of the nails with a handkerchief, so that the inside of her bag would not be damaged. 'I must plan this adventure very carefully,' she said to herself.

Thursday had been a quiet day for Kati, as she meticulously worked out the detailed plans for her experiment. She adopted the attitude of a military strategist.

'All details must be correct; I must adhere to the timings I have worked out, too. And, most important of all, *no-one* must ever find out the details of my unique experiment.'

The end of the experiment would involve a very important event which she, Kati, must control with precision: 'That will be the trickiest part. If I get that right, everything else should follow.'

By the end of the day, Kati thought she had everything planned perfectly and now she looked forward to the greatest adventure of her life.

Friday morning. Breakfast. Kati addressed her father: 'I think I'll take my horse out for a ride across the fields,' she announced, with a feeling of mounting excitement.

'Good idea,' her father had replied affectionately, 'today is a fine day and the fresh air will do you good.'

'Just be careful and don't gallop too fast,' her mother said, looking slightly concerned in a rather absent-minded way. Her mother was always engaged in organising the household, a task which filled most of her time.

The weather was notably fine, perfect for her adventure. Smartly attired for riding, Kati soon arrived at the stables. 'Boy,' she called in a loud and unfriendly voice.

A young man and a stable boy ran quickly from the stable and the man addressed her deferentially: 'Good morning, Miss Kati, we are at your service.'

'I know that,' she replied contemptuously, 'get my horse, saddle it astride.'

The man went to carry out her orders, leaving the stable boy outside with her. Kati ignored him totally and sat down on a box. After a few minutes, the boy suddenly spoke: 'Miss Kati, you are looking very lovely today,' he said softly with a smile of genuine admiration.

She was flabbergasted. This stable boy had spoken to her without permission – and furthermore he had been insolent to her! She sprang to her feet, recognising him as the youngest of the stable boys, a lad of around fifteen, not much older than herself. 'How dare you speak to me. You are insolent and I will see that you pay for this!'

'Miss, I am deeply sorry, I thought you would not mind. Please forgive me.' The boy's face crumpled into tears.

'I will not forgive you. I will make you sorry, you will see.' With that, Kati turned her back. As she did so, the stable hand appeared with her horse, saddled and ready. Furious, she snatched the reins from him and placed her foot in his cupped hands to be lifted into the saddle. Without another word, she galloped off noisily in a flurry of dust.

'I am done for,' the boy wailed to the man.

'What has happened? What have you done?'

'I spoke to her without permission. I told her she was lovely. She was furious. She said she would make me pay.'

'Don't worry, I'm sure it will be all right. She will calm down and, even if she doesn't, what can she do? The Head Stableman knows you are a good and honest worker and he would never believe anything against you. And if she says anything to the Master, he will always believe the Head Stableman rather than a silly little girl. Nothing will happen, you'll see.'

'I do hope so,' the boy dried his eyes, 'but I wish I hadn't been so stupid.'

'Anyway, she's just a weak little girl; no-one is going to listen to her.' The man was adamant.

Now thundering over the fields, Kati thought: 'I will deal with that boy later. I know how I will do it, too. It will serve him right. But now it is time for my experiment. It is time to have some fun with my horse. Let the adventure start!' If Kati had been in possession of a hunting horn at this moment, she would have blown a triumphant blast! She headed directly for a small copse of trees in the distance.

A few moments later, Kati slowed down and rode into the copse where she would be concealed from sight. She dismounted and located the small piece of wood pierced with nails in her bag. Now she loosened the horse's girth strap and lifted the saddle clear of the animal's back, placing the wood block with its vicious rusty nails pointing downwards, adjusting the position carefully to ensure the nails straddled the centre line of the horse's backbone. Satisfied, she retightened the girth and the horse, feeling the prick of the nails on its skin, jumped restlessly.

'Stand still,' she ordered angrily and swung into the saddle. The horse whinnied loudly as her weight drove the rusty nails through its skin into the tender flesh below. Shaking the reins, she drove the horse into a gallop and proceeded to bounce up and down as heavily as she could on the saddle. The horse screamed as the nails sank fully home and, crazed with pain, the tortured animal bolted back and forth across the fields, galloping faster than it had ever done before and covering many miles.

Kati was delighted: 'Yes, my experiment works; pain makes the horse go much faster. This is wonderful fun! I could keep this up all day.' Kati bounced violently up and down in the saddle to increase the pain even more. After at least half an hour of constant galloping at full speed, the crazed and lather-covered horse recognised the stable buildings some distance away and decided to head for home and security as fast as it could. Its rider, no longer in control, was now clinging on as hard as she could but still wildly elated at the wonderful success of her scientific experiment.

The loud clatter of hooves in the stable yard brought the same two stable workers running from the building, their faces showing their shock and concern. The horse, still in agony but now startled by their sudden appearance, reared up and Kati slid slowly from its broad back on to the ground without sustaining physical hurt or injury.

The young stable boy, acting with no thought for his own safety, ran beneath the hooves of the rearing and plunging animal and caught it by its reins, calming it to a quivering halt while his colleague ran to help Kati: 'Miss Kati, are you hurt? How can I help you? Shall I call the Master? Shall I call the Mistress?' The young man was shaking like a leaf.

She took his extended hands and drew herself to her feet, brushing herself down with her hands. 'Stand aside, you fool,' she said rudely and surveyed the scene with narrowed eyes. She knew she had to act quickly now. Striding quickly to the side of the horse, she loosened the girth and, with great difficulty, pulled the block of wood with its deeply embedded nails from the flesh of the animal, making sure that neither of the stable hands saw what she was doing. Quickly, as planned, she tossed the horrific blood-covered item over the stable yard wall where it fell into deep undergrowth close to the wall on the other side, in a spot where it would be concealed forever.

News travels fast. Before many minutes had passed, the stable yard was filling up with concerned men and women, many wailing and wringing their hands.

Kati's nanny came running up to her: 'Oh you poor baby, where are you hurt? You must come with me and we will look after your wounds and then you can rest for the remainder of the day.'

'Leave me alone, you stupid woman!' Kati's reply was spat out venomously. 'Where is the Master?'

The crowd parted respectfully as the Master appeared, very agitated: 'Where is she? How badly has she been hurt?' The man was beside himself with worry.

'Here I am.' Kati threw herself into his strong arms. 'I am unhurt; I fell softly from the horse when it reared and threw me off. It is because you have made me such a good horsewoman.'

'You must go to your bed and rest. You have had a terrible ordeal.' The man was so relieved.

'No, Father, there are things we must do here, now. There are two matters to be dealt with. After that, I can rest.'

Her father was greatly taken aback when his daughter then burst into loud weeping. 'Kati, darling, what is wrong, are you hurting somewhere?'

'Not physically, Father, but I am so ashamed. I am so humiliated.' Kati sobbed pitifully.

'Ashamed of what? Humiliated by whom?' The man was puzzled.

'Father, I am sorry, but I must tell you this. When the horse bolted into the stable yard and reared up, throwing me on to the hard ground here, these two stable hands laughed.' She indicated the man and the boy.

'Laughed?' The man was mystified. 'Laughed at what?'

'They were laughing at me being thrown off the horse on to the hard ground.'

'What?' The man now understood and his face became like a rock. 'Can this be true?' He addressed the man and the boy, now standing totally confused.

'No, Master,' the man replied.

Kati's father was about to speak when he heard his daughter's voice say: 'Father, that is not the worst part. I am so ashamed!' Her voice rose to a loud wail.

'What is it, Daughter?' the man spoke ominously, 'You must tell me.'

'When he was helping me up from the ground, he touched me. Here.' She pointed down to her lower body.

'Who touched you there?' Her father's face drained of colour. *'Who?'* he shouted.

'That stable boy.' Her pointing figure identified the young stable boy who had been so brave in dealing with the pain-crazed horse when it returned to the stable yard.

At this, there was a low howl from all those present, the howl of a ravening mob, instantly stilled to a bated breath silence as Kati's father stepped close to the boy: 'Boy, is this true? Did you do this thing to my daughter?' A growl of menace.

'No, Master. No.' The boy was wailing like a baby. 'I caught the horse, I wasn't …' The boy's voice merged into a scream as the Master's whip laid open his left cheek from lip to ear.

'Master,' the older stable hand tried to intervene, 'the boy did not …'

'Are you saying my daughter is a liar?' The Master's voice was frightening in its intensity. Silence. Then the same question repeated to the boy, now vainly trying to stem the blood from the gushing wound on his face: 'Are you saying my daughter is a liar?'

'Master …' the older stable hand began, before he was felled to the ground by a terrible blow to the head.

'Take him,' the Master pointed to the boy, 'lock him up and send for the Court Jailer.' Willing hands removed the boy very roughly, leaving a trail of blood on the ground.

'Now we must deal with the horse,' the Master said crisply. He looked kindly at Kati.

'You should leave us now so that you do not see this.'

'No Father,' she replied demurely, 'I feel I must stay. I have known the horse for many years.'

He looked at her with admiration: 'You are such a strong girl, Kati, I adore you.'

Of course, Kati was absolutely delighted with the outcome of all her plans. 'And now they will kill the horse. I must see this!' Her eyes gleamed in pleasure but she was careful not to show it.

The Head Stableman was called and he arrived with several assistants. The Master and he spoke together for a few moments and the Head Stableman departed to return with a small razor-sharp knife. The horse, now completely docile was led away to the back of the stable block. Kati and her father followed.

'Fetch the close hobbles,' the Head Stableman ordered his assistants. It was then, while waiting for his assistants to return, that the Head Stableman noticed a serious wound on the horse's back, now caked with a considerable amount of blood. Coming closer, he examined the wound carefully. The Head Stableman had been working with horses virtually every day of his life for over 30 years and he was an expert on these animals. His face impassive, he linked up his conclusions about the wound and associated them with the events of the day. He would write a few notes later to make sure he remembered what had happened on this dreadful day.

His assistants returned with the hobbles and these were fastened around the horse's fetlocks as tightly as possible. Warning Kati to stand well back, the men suddenly thrust the tightly-hobbled animal sideways; the unfortunate animal fell heavily on its side with a sickening crash, screaming in new pain as several ribs were broken by the impact with the uneven, stony ground. As the horse struggled and cried in pain and distress, the Head Stableman stepped forward and located the jugular groove near the base of its neck. Slitting the skin, he identified the large carotid artery and severed it with a single lightning stroke.

Kati loved learning new things and now her knowledge was about to be expanded considerably. She had always thought that the blood would just gush out in a steady stream but she saw it actually came out in powerful spurts, especially at first. Also, it took quite a long time to drain the horse of its blood, much longer than she imagined it would.

'Well, horses are quite big animals, so I imagine they must have a lot of blood inside them,' she mused. More minutes ticked by and she could see the flow of blood was diminishing now; furthermore, the horse's legs had stopped making these strange twitching movements and she noticed a change taking place in the large brown eye clearly visible from where she was standing. The eye was glazing over. She stepped forward so she could examine this eye from close range.

'How different dead eyes are from living ones,' she thought, 'I know this horse's eye so well but now it has become totally different; there's no life, no intelligence, no sense any more in this eye.' She shook her head in wonderment. 'There's always more to learn,' she concluded.

The girl was sure this had been the most interesting day of her life. Looking at the dead animal, she reviewed the situation: 'This is my horse – no, I must now remember to say it *was* my horse!' In fact it had been her horse for nine years. How well she remembered her father giving her the horse when she was only four years old. She remembered the horse was distinctly smaller than it was now.

'But then so was I!' This thought accompanied by a coquettish smile.

Thereafter, the horse had grown up to be a fine, good-natured animal who had always been kind and gentle and never given her any trouble. Down the years she had driven it harnessed to a light wagon and also ridden it on many occasions. Her father allowed her to ride the horse within their lands, across the fields and through the forests. How exciting that was at first. Over the years, Kati had become a very good horsewoman, able to ride both side-saddle and astride.

'It was different in olden days,' Kati thought, 'then, girls were not allowed to sit astride a horse but now in these times, we can go hawking with the men and everyone needs to be astride for that. Hawking is a very exciting way of hunting. Thank goodness it's the fourteenth century!'

As she completed her thoughts, Kati's father came over to her and embraced her with love: 'Don't worry, Kati, I'll get you another horse. I know how much you loved that one but sometimes they go a bit mad in the end. When they do, that's when you have to do the humane thing and end their lives.'

'I understand, Father, you are so good to me. I love you so much.' Kati was always artful!

Now there was another arrival. The Court Jailer had arrived in his black covered wagon. Having gone to the Manor House and enquired at the Servant's Door, he had been directed to the stable yard. The crowd, still milling about in the stable yard parted to allow the large and heavy vehicle through and then crowded around it.

'I am summoned by the Master.' The Court Jailer was a small portly man, dressed wholly in black. He was the first point of contact when there were matters of criminality to be dealt with. He was in charge of the Town Jail, a festering building in the centre of the town. He was also responsible for preparing the indictment which would be the basis of the case if it went to the Town Court. Someone from the crowd ran around to the back of the stable building to seek the Master. Here, he found the Master and his daughter sitting on a low wall, deep in conversation.

'Master,' the man said with great deference, 'the Court Jailer has arrived and requires to speak with you.'

'Bring him to this place for the conversation. We will be able to speak here and will not be interrupted or overheard. What I have to say is private.'

Shortly after, the Court Jailer arrived with his burly assistant who sat down some distance away. 'Greetings, Master.' The man removed his headwear in deference, 'I hear you may have work for me?'

'Yes, that is correct,' the Master replied, 'it has been necessary for me to arrest one of my stable boys. This is embarrassing to say but I must say it for my lovely daughter's sake. This boy deliberately touched her lower body when she was thrown from her horse earlier this afternoon.'

'I see,' the Town Jailor murmured, writing steadily. 'And does the boy admit his guilt?'

'No, quite the contrary, he protests his innocence. He maintains my beautiful daughter is a liar. And there is another stable hand who was present who also says the boy is innocent. He may need to be arrested, too, although his offence is not so grave. I have struck him grievously and this may be punishment enough. I will think about it and decide before you leave.'

The Court Jailer finished writing and heaved himself to his feet. 'Master, I think I have heard enough. Do you wish me to take this boy into jail custody, where I will examine him rigorously and construct an indictment for a Court case?'

'Yes, that would be satisfactory. Please do so.'

'And what of the other man, Master?'

The Master thought for a moment. 'You may leave him here with me. I will deal with him without the Court.'

'Thank you, Master. It has been a great honour to speak with you today. May we go and inspect the prisoner?'

Meanwhile, Kati had been sitting beside the men, listening raptly to their conversation – a real adult conversation – and she was only thirteen! What a joyous honour all this was. Mind you, she reminded herself, thirteen is not so young. Some girls get married at thirteen or even earlier. Not that she wanted to have anything to do with marriage or men. Men are brutes (except her Father, of course); all they want is sexual coupling.

Kati was not sure what sexual coupling was exactly but she knew it was concerned with something very nasty and painful. And she knew for certain that this thing happened to girls when they were married. So Kati's mind was made up; she wanted nothing to do with men or marriage or sexual coupling – and she had already told her father that.

'Don't worry, my lovely girl,' he would say playfully, 'I would never force you to do anything.'

Now she tagged along as they went to inspect the prisoner. He was held in a wooden cage which had been designed for hunting dogs.

'Goodness,' she breathed, 'he certainly is a sorry sight. But then he deserves it. He should never have been impertinent to me!' Her eyes shone with pleasure.

The boy lay in his blood-soaked clothes, weeping with pain and despair, still holding his gashed face in an attempt to stop it bleeding. He looked up with fear at the Court Jailer – of course he knew who he was and what it meant. He looked pleadingly at the Master, who turned his eyes away. Then the boy's eyes found Kati and his wailing ceased abruptly. He addressed her from his cage in a broken voice. 'Miss Kati, you know the truth. Tell them the truth.' She looked at him impassively.

'You know I have already told the truth, boy. I feel very sorry for you.' To say she felt sorry for him was a master stroke, she thought with glee.

'Kati,' the Master cried, 'you are so sweet, kind and generous but this boy is a criminal and he must pay the price for his crime.'

In the shadows, the Head Stableman listened silently and shifted uneasily.

The assistant of the Court Jailer dragged the boy from his cage and expertly placed his hands and feet in heavy manacles. Then he hustled him out to the stable yard where the waiting crowd spat on him and struck him with punches and slaps, opening up the wound on his face once more. Eventually, he reached the safety of the black covered wagon. The assistant lifted him high and threw him bodily into the back of the wagon, fastening the canvas cover securely. The crowd howled insults as the heavy vehicle manoeuvred to turn around and then rumbled away to head for the nearby town.

The light was now beginning to fade on this very eventful day – a real adventure, Kati thought, which could not have been planned more perfectly. The Master spoke to all the servants who were assembled in the stable yard and assured them that justice would be done. They should now return to their livings. The crowd dispersed slowly, everyone animated and having a great deal to say to each other. Kati and her father walked hand in hand towards the Manor House. It would soon be time for the evening meal and, after that, gleeful recollections in her soft, warm bed.

'I bet that boy will not be so comfortable where he is tonight. What an insolent boy he was – speaking to me without permission and making a personal comment about me. There is no doubt that he deserves everything that he will get.'

That night in bed, after she had reviewed once again the absolutely glorious events of the day, her thoughts turned to the boy in the town prison. 'I don't know what happens to criminals like him when they go there. I hope they beat him and make his body very sore. Kati liked to think about such things and tried to imagine what it would be like to be an observer at such an event: 'I'm sure it would be very interesting and it would add to my considerable knowledge,' she thought. She had seen public whippings before and they were very interesting – and they made her tingle with excitement!

Finally Kati turned over luxuriously, and, contentedly, drifted off to sleep with a serene smile on her lips.

Stable Boy

Along the bumpy and uneven road to the town, it had been a very uncomfortable journey in the darkness of the Court Jailer's wagon but the boy was relieved to have escaped from the stable yard. Tears welled up in his eyes as he thought about what had happened to him.

'All these people. They all know me. I've been a stable boy there for five years and they know I'm not the sort of boy who would touch Miss Kati. Why is she doing this to me? I'm only a poor boy who wants to do good work so that I would become a good stable hand when I'm older. If I'm really good at my work and I learn all I need to know, I might even have managed to become a Stableman. But now everything is ruined. Now I'll never be able to become a Stableman. Now everyone hates me – and I haven't done anything.' He burst into renewed tears, bitterly distressed at his situation.

The wagon rumbled and lurched on through the fading light and eventually entered the courtyard of the Town Jail. The heavy door of the jail clanged shut behind the wagon, a noise of finality for the shivering boy in the wagon. The stable boy had seen this building from the outside many times and had always regarded it with great fear. He had heard that bad things happened to the people held in there. Prisoners had to live in cold, dank cells infested with rats. They were given hardly any food to eat and sometimes they were beaten, too! The stable boy was petrified with fear.

'But surely the Court Jailer will listen to me when I tell him what really happened,' the boy thought, 'I must think very carefully what to say. I'll need to tell him about my impertinence to Mistress Kati and how angry that made her. And I'm sure he will believe me when I tell him that I was the one who caught the horse and calmed it down when Mistress Kati came back to the stable yard. I'll tell him my friend can confirm that – he's sure to believe me.'

The boy felt better and looked forward eagerly to the time he could tell his story.

He was pulled roughly from the wagon and, still in chains, was driven through a heavy studded door into the prison building. Here he was delivered to two jailers. To his surprise, both these men were pleasant, rather cheerful men who were eating and drinking together at a table.

The Court Jailer's assistant pushed the boy into the room saying: 'Here's another one for you. He says he's innocent!' The three men laughed uproariously. The Court Jailor's assistant bent down and removed the manacles from the stable boy's wrists and ankles and turned to leave the room. 'The Court Jailer is outside and will come to you in a moment,' he said.

'Sit down on that bench over there,' the First Jailer said to the stable boy with a smile, 'the Court Jailor will be here in a moment and then we'll see what is to be done.' The men returned to their food and paid no further attention to him.

The boy looked around. The room was warm, bright and cheerful, whitewashed and lit by several bright lamps. The walls had been decorated with some very old prison items, like heavy leg irons, chains and whips, etc. The boy had not expected it to be so pleasant in the Jail.

'Maybe it won't be so bad in here,' he could not help thinking.

Shortly after, the Court Jailor bustled into the room. The two jailers rose to their feet and greeted him respectfully.

'Good evening, Sir,' the First Jailer said, 'where will you examine the boy?'

'Here will be fine. This should not take long.' The Court Jailer sat down at the table.

'Boy, come and stand here.' He indicated the area in front of the table. The boy obeyed. Then the man gave close attention to his papers for some time. At last he looked up: 'Now, boy, can you read and write?'

'No, Sir.'

'Do you know right from wrong?'

'Yes, Sir, of course. I have always been honest.'

'Do you know what truth is?'

'Yes, Sir, I am always truthful.'

'Good. I have just one question for you. When you touched the Master's daughter on her body, was your hand on her bare skin?' The boy was shocked.

'Sir, no, I didn't …' The man interrupted: 'Be very careful how you answer this, boy. It's always best to tell the truth, you know that, don't you?'

'Yes, Sir,' the boy whispered, 'I always tell the truth.'

'Right, well, I'll ask you again. Did you touch the girl's naked body under her clothes?' This question asked testily.

'Sir, I beg you. You must believe me, I did not do the thing you ask about. I was not even there …'

The Court Jailer snorted. Paying no further attention to the boy, he wrote in his papers for a time and finally turned to the two jailers: 'Listen, men, you have heard my examination of the boy. My decision for the indictment is that the girl unfortunately fell off her horse (thank God she was not injured) and the boy took the opportunity to touch her naked body beneath her clothes, which, no doubt, were in disarray. Now I pass the matter to you for your action. I will return tomorrow morning with the indictment fully completed. Here is the confession for the prisoner to make his mark upon. As you know, he cannot read or write. You can return it to me tomorrow. Now I bid you good night.' With these remarks, the Court Jailer left.

In the ensuing silence, the boy wailed: 'But Sirs, this is not right. I am innocent of this crime. I would never …'

'Quiet now, boy.' The Second Jailer spoke for the first time. His tone was gentle. 'The Court Jailer has examined you and the matter is decided. Go and sit down on the bench.' The two men paid no further attention to the boy but sat down again to finish the remnants of their meal, talking cheerfully about everyday matters concerning their friends and families.

After a while, they rose from the table. Unhurriedly, the First Jailer unhooked a bundle of twigs from the wall (one of the wall ornaments) and handed it to the other man. 'I'll see him again when he's ready to make his mark upon the confession paper.' The man smiled as he said this.

'It shouldn't take too long, I think,' the Second Jailer said. 'I'll be as quick as I can.' Turning to smile at the boy, he crooked a finger. 'Come with me, boy.' Tucking the bundle of twigs under his arm, the man put his other arm around the boy's shoulders and led him gently from the room, closing the door quietly behind them.

The small windowless room next door was devoid of furniture, save for a long narrow table placed against one wall. Some leather straps were piled on the table. The most striking feature of the room was a large hook set into the low ceiling in the exact centre of the room. Immediately beneath it, there was the grating of a small drain. In this room, the man, though still friendly, became brisk and professional. Placing the bunch of twigs on the table, he said to the boy: 'Now just stand still and leave everything to me; I have done this before many times.'

A few minutes later, the boy had been made ready with his wrists strapped to the hook above his head. Now the man stood directly in front of him and looked straight into his eyes, saying quietly: 'I have an important question to ask you. Listen to it carefully and think before you answer. Will you put your mark on the confession paper next door? If you say "yes", I will unfasten you and you may get dressed. Then we can leave this room and all will be completed.'

'Sir, I cannot do that. I am innocent. You must believe me. I never did this …'

Unusually, the man was touched by what the boy had said. He looked at the beauty and sincerity of the young face before him and then down at the smooth perfection of the naked young body below. As he did so, he felt a pang of sorrow. Moments passed and then the man shook his head, as if to clear his thoughts. He raised his eyes to scan the boy's face once again. 'Just let me know when you change your mind.'

The boy hobbled back into the room painfully. Sobbing quietly, his face white with pain and shock, he accepted the pen and was about to make his mark on the paper when the First Jailer held up a hand: 'Just a minute, boy. You cannot read so first you must listen. It is the Law.' The jailer now read out the confession in a loud voice. When he had finished, he returned the paper to the table and handed the pen to the boy – but the boy's eyes now had a new light in them.

'No, Sir,' he whispered. 'You must hear me. I cannot make my mark on this confession. It is all lies. I never touched her. I would never do what this confession says. You can ask anyone …'

There was complete silence in the room. Then the Second Jailer sighed. Stepping close to the boy, he squatted down, gently cupping the bruised hips of the slim body in his hands and swivelling them around each way to inspect the ridged, swollen flesh with expert eyes. He addressed his colleague: 'I think the whip might be best for this. What do you think?'

'Either the whip or the scourge. I leave it to you.'

The light went out of the boy's eyes. Without a sound, he made his mark on the confession paper.

The jailers were not unkind to the boy. He was allowed plenty time to re-clothe his aching and tender body and afterwards they gave him a bowl of food and a cup of water to drink. He gulped down the water thirstily and managed to eat some of the food, which tasted sour and was of very poor quality. Nevertheless, he was grateful that they should give him anything and thanked them politely.

'You are obviously a well brought up boy,' they said to him. 'We don't usually get thanked for prison food!' They both laughed, thinking this a splendid joke. Then the men spoke quietly together, looking over at him from time to time.

At last, the First Jailer spoke to him: 'You're in luck, tonight. We're going to put you in a single cell. Normally, we would put you into the common cell – I think we have fifteen men in there tonight – but my friend and I think you might come to some serious harm in there. I'm sure you're sore enough already!' The men smiled at each other meaningfully.

So the boy stumbled down a long stone corridor with the Second Jailer, past a large wooden door from which a most frightening noise was coming.

'Excuse me, Sir, what is that noise?'

'Oh that? That's just the men's common cell. They always make that noise. There are always men fighting or someone being beaten in there.'

The boy was very frightened and was deeply grateful that he was not being put into that terrible cell. Through another heavy door, they came to a row of smaller cell doors and the jailer swung open one of these.

'You go in here,' he said to the cowering boy, 'you'll be all right, there's no-one else in there except maybe a rat or two.

We'll see you in the morning. The Court Jailer will come back to see you tomorrow and we must talk about that before he arrives.' Without another word, the jailer slammed the cell door shut with a deafening crash and turned the key in the lock. The boy heard his retreating footsteps and then the sound of the corridor door being closed and locked.

At first the trembling boy could see nothing in this dark cold place but gradually his eyes grew used to the glimmer of light in the cell and he started to see some details. It was a small cell with a little barred window high up in one wall. The boy was so pleased when he spotted a single star in the sky through the window. 'I hope that will be my lucky star,' he said, with a very small, careful smile. He did not want his slashed cheek to begin bleeding again.

Now he could make out a few more details in the cell. A rough truckle bed with a ragged blanket. A broken stool. A bucket in the corner, mercifully covered. The boy lowered himself carefully on the bed and reviewed his position. Just a few hours ago, he had been happy and content; warm, dry and pain-free, secure in his job as a stable boy at the Manor House. A popular and attractive young man who was friendly with everyone. Now, he was a prisoner; dirty, cold and desolate in a dank rat-infested cell. A person who has confessed to a disgusting crime for which everyone will despise him for evermore, with a face slashed by a whip and a body that had known the merciless bite of the birch upon all its parts. Here he was, with nothing but pain, suffering and deprivation ahead of him.

The boy sank on the bed and wrapped the dirty blanket around him: 'I am finished. Surely my life is over. Perhaps I will die here, in this cell. In some ways, I hope I do.'

For a whole series of reasons, the boy had hardly slept. These included rats, bedbugs, pain, cold, noise and terror. He was already awake when he heard the corridor door being unlocked and shortly after his cell door swung open.

It was the Second Jailer, carrying a bowl and a cup: 'Here is food. Eat it quickly and then come with me.' The man waited while the boy forced himself to eat the thin watery gruel and drink the cup of water. 'Right, come with me, we need to talk to you before the Court Jailer comes.' The boy stumbled along behind the man, gasping with pain, his body stiffened by its ill-treatment the previous evening. At last they reached the jailer's room.

'You certainly are a bit of a mess,' the First Jailer greeted him.

He addressed the Second Jailer: 'Take him out to the pump.' He waved his hand at the door. The boy was grateful for the fresh air of the courtyard, although the shock of the change of environment made him giddy at first.

'Give yourself a good wash down,' the Second Jailer said. 'Here's a cloth to dry yourself.'

The boy did look rather better when clean. The Second Jailer produced a set of thin prison clothes: 'Now that you are a prisoner, you need to wear these. Anyway, your other clothes are torn and blood-stained.'

Back in the room, the men directed the boy to sit on the bench once more. 'The Court Jailer will be coming to see you this morning and we just want to prepare you so that we don't have any more trouble.'

'Sirs,' the boy responded, 'I know I have confessed to this crime but I am innocent!'

The men sighed and looked heavenward.

The Second Jailer spoke quietly: 'Listen carefully, boy. If you say that to the Court Jailer when he comes you will be back in that room next door with me. Is that what you want?'

The boy paled. 'But, Sir, does the Court Jailer not want to know the truth?'

'Listen again, boy. Do you not think that every prisoner claims to be innocent? If the Court Jailer believed them, there would be no criminals in the Jail. They would all be out in the Town committing crimes. Anyway, you see this paper? It says you did the crime and it is signed with your mark. This means that the Court Jailer will take you to the Town Court and you will be tried for the crime.'

'But Sir …'

The First Jailer held up his hand. Now he spoke sharply: 'Stop speaking! Listen to me. The Court Jailor will speak to you when he comes. He will ask you two questions. It is part of the process of justice – that's why he's doing it. So listen carefully. When the Court Jailer asks: "Is this your confession, given without duress?" you are to say "Yes". And when the Court Jailer asks "Do you have anything else to say?" you are to say "No." Do you understand? First answer – "Yes", second answer – "No".'

'Yes, Sir, but I am innocent!'

The two men looked at each other. The First Jailer spoke slowly and clearly, speaking in an icy tone: 'Boy, if you do not obey me, do you know what will happen?'

'No, Sir.'

'I will tell you exactly what will happen. The Court Jailer will leave and we will whip you until you faint with pain. When you waken up, we will give you another confession to put your mark upon – and you will do it, just as you did last night. And, boy, we can repeat this every day until you answer the Court Jailer's questions in the way I have told you or until you die under our beating. It is your choice. Do you understand now?'

'Yes, Sir.' A whisper; the boy was totally crushed.

Noises of activity heralded the arrival of the Court Jailer, who hurried into the room.

'Good morning, men,' he said jovially, 'I trust you are ready for me?'

'Yes, Sir, we are quite ready. Here is the boy's confession with his mark upon it.'

'Excellent,' the Court Jailer was unsurprised; his jailers rarely let him down in these matters. 'Where is the boy?' The man looked round and saw the small, despondent figure slumped on the bench. 'Sit up, boy,' he said sharply, 'prisoners are not allowed to rest without permission.'

The Court Jailer now sat down at the table and perused the confession. 'Come and stand here,' he gestured to the boy, observing his slow and painful progress with a slight smile. (Perhaps he should examine the boy's body? The Court Jailer always enjoyed that. But, no, perhaps today there was no time!) He held up the confession paper to the boy's face: 'Is this your confession, given without duress?' Silence. The Second Jailor coughed loudly and was seen to be stroking the stock of a small whip.

'Yes.' Barely a whisper.

'What?' The Court Jailer sat forward sharply.

'Yes, Sir.' Slightly louder.

'That's better. Do you have anything else to say?' The jailers stopped breathing.

The boy's eyes had a spark of courage burning deeply within. His mouth opened and then: 'No, Sir.'

The relief of the jailers was expressed in a great explosion of jollification, sending almost visible vortices of gleeful energy around the room. 'A really skilled job, Sir,' they said in joyous, deafening tones. 'You are so skilled in these matters and you exercise them with such great aplomb.'

The Court Jailer smiled thinly and thanked them for their kind words. He would now start to prepare the case for the Court and would return with the date and time in due course. This would not be soon, he warned them, the wheels of justice proceed slowly: 'There is so much crime to deal with, you see.'

In the midst of all this spontaneous gaiety and congratulation, the stable boy stood forgotten. Head bowed, his slight figure faded to virtual transparency, a grey spectre half in an alternative dimension of hopelessness. However within that unmoving, amorphous body, a mind raced. In a brief moment of pure desperation, he considered throwing himself at the feet of the Court Jailer and pleading his innocence – but this spasm was quieted almost immediately at the prospect of being whipped to a certain and agonising death.

The Court Jailer had gone. The room was transformed into a more relaxed place.

'Now that we know where we're going, we'll need to make sure he doesn't get sick. He needs to look well-treated for his case in the Court.' For this reason, the jailers decided that they would keep the stable boy segregated in his single cell. 'More trouble for us but I suppose it's for the best,' they agreed. 'Maybe he can exercise with some of the other prisoners but we'll need to keep an eye on him. We don't want him getting damaged just before his case is heard. The Court Jailer would blame us for that and it would not go well for us.' They nodded at each other sagely.

Also, the jailers decided that the boy should be given better food than the dreadful meals that were served to the other prisoners. This better nutrition meant that the boy's body was able to recover from his wounds; it was not too long before his bruising had subsided and his skin healed. However, he had an obvious and permanent scar on his cheek where the Master had struck him many weeks before. He had seen his face in a looking glass and thought the scar might be an advantage to him in his new life:

'I can always tell them I got it in a knife fight – which I won!' The boy grinned.

In fact there was another reason why the jailers were being kind to the boy. One evening during their regular evening meal, the two jailers found that their thoughts about the stable boy were surprisingly in accord. They had been talking about their prisoners and how they always insisted they were innocent of the crimes for which they had been convicted: 'They say this even when they are caught red-handed!' The men laughed at this.

After an introspective silence, the Second Jailer said, very quietly and uncertainly: 'You know, I think he is innocent.' A silence of ten seconds. Then: 'I do, too.' The men looked at each other in surprise, a surprise that turned into conspiratorial grins of relief. 'If the Court Jailer could hear us say that …' The First Jailer drew a finger across his throat.

After a long pause, the Second Jailer spoke, his expression far away: 'I remember that first night so well. All routine to me, you know. You know how many beatings I've done – that's right, hundreds, maybe more. And it was all just the usual routine, the stripping, strapping the arms up, giving the warning; you know, nothing unusual. Then he looked at me. He kept telling me he was innocent, in such a sincere way. And I found, when the time came, I didn't want to do it. But I'm a professional. So I started, just as usual. I concentrated on all the usual places, then worked out to cover everywhere else and, yes, he cried, he screamed, just like all the others. But he did something else, too. In between the screams and the cries, he kept telling me he was innocent.' The man placed his head in his hands, his eyes becoming moist with tears: 'He is, I know it.'

'I know it, too.'

The two men sat pondering. 'What shall we do?'

'What can we do? We are nothing in the community, just jailers. Nobody listens to us.'

'He'll go to trial. He'll be found guilty. He'll be sent back here and we won't be able to protect him anymore, because by then he will just be a criminal serving his sentence.' The two men looked at each other with helpless dismay.

After a long silence, the First Jailer spoke: 'I have just had an idea. Listen …' The men talked together very quietly for some time.

Lying in his narrow bed, still cold and uncomfortable despite his three blankets – a gift from his jailers – the stable boy shifted and twitched in a fitful sleep, dreaming of the day when this nightmare would be over. In his waking hours, he never pursued such a dream, for he recognised the hopelessness of his position, not only for now but for the rest of his life, however long that may continue: 'One thing I have learned,' he thought, 'that poor weak people never receive justice from the Court. Even when they are known to be innocent, they will be forced to admit guilt and then punished severely for things they have not done.' The boy knew this was exactly what would happen to him in due course. He sighed with hopelessness.

'Excuse me, Sir, there is a man here asking to speak to you.'

'Who is it, lad?' The Head Stableman was not expecting any visitors at this time of the day; most of the tradesmen who came to sell him animal feeds and other materials came in the morning.

'I do not know who it is, Sir. He says he is from the Town,' the stable hand replied. Going outside, the Head Stableman found the man standing in the stable yard, dressed in neat working clothes and holding his headgear in his hands as a mark of respect.

'You wish to speak to me? Have we done business before?'

'No, Sir.' The man was very respectful. 'Many years have passed since we met. In fact we were boys together at the Town School. You were always very clever and were soon apprenticed to stable work.'

'I must say I cannot recall you at present. What work did you take up?'

'Sir, I went into legal work.'

'Ah, so you are a man of the Law?' The Head Stableman was impressed.

'No, Sir, forgive me for giving you the wrong impression. I am the Senior Jailer at the Town Jail. I have been doing this work for many years.'

The Head Stableman now recognised the man before him. 'Ah yes, I have seen you around the Town, you are sometimes seen with the Court Jailer – everyone knows him, don't they? However I am happy to say I have had no reason to make professional contact with you over the years.' The Head Stableman smiled briefly, then he said: 'So what can possibly bring the Senior Jailer to speak to me?'

'Sir,' the man said, lowering his voice, 'this is a matter of great delicacy which involves a former employee of yours; I refer to your former stable boy who is now in the Town Jail awaiting the date of his trial at the Town Court.' Lowering his voice even further, the man looked around nervously and continued: 'It is possible we could speak in privacy somewhere? What I have to say is of great importance but, as you will hear, it places me in some danger.'

The Head Stableman looked directly at this man and thought: 'Danger? I do not understand.'

Outwardly, he said: 'I will hear what you have to say; let us go to my rooms. Come with me, please.'

As the two men proceeded to the rooms, the Head Stableman was thinking: 'It is true that I am disquieted by the case of the stable boy. He was always a good and faithful worker and what he is said to have done was totally out of character. I remember he denied it vehemently at the time and this was backed up by the other stable hand who was the only other witness there. But the Master was adamant, Miss Kati reported what he did and the Master took the correct action at the time – if it is true, that is.'

This was not the first time the Head Stableman had thought about this. Also, there was the question of the injury to Miss Kati's horse. Somehow that seemed to fit in with this matter also. Nevertheless, the Head Stableman's loyalty was to his Master and, after the arrest and removal of the stable boy from his employ, the man had pushed the matter to the back of his mind; he had not forgotten, however.

'Sit down, please, and tell me what this is all about.'

'Sir, I work together with a colleague who is my assistant. We work well together. I do all the administration work and he usually attends to practical matters, like (the man hesitated) discipline, for instance. We are employees of the Town and are servants of the Court Jailer who, as you know, decides whether each case will be sent to the Town Court. When a criminal is arrested, he is brought to us for imprisonment before trial. We, that is, my colleague and I, assist the Court Jailer to prepare his case.'

The Head Stableman interrupted: 'You help? How do jailers help to prepare the case? I do not understand.'

The jailer paused and looked down at the floor. 'Well, the Court Jailer prepares the indictment for the Court and he, ah, requests that we obtain the prisoner's confession which will be submitted with the case.'

The Head Stableman thought for a moment: 'I understand that. But what happens if the prisoner refuses to sign the confession. What happens if the prisoner claims to be innocent?'

The jailer laughed: 'Sir, every criminal claims to be innocent!'

'So what happens? What do you do in these cases?'

'Well, Sir, we are instructed to examine the prisoners rigorously, you know, put pressure on them until they admit their guilt. They always do – and the case can then go to the Court.'

The Head Stableman was silent, introspective. Then: 'So tell me about my stable boy.'

'Sir, you know what happened here at the Manor House. The Court Jailer then brought him to the prison. He told us that the Master of the Manor House had asked him to prepare the case for the Court and the Court Jailer stated that he was about to do so. Meanwhile, we were to, ah, – obtain – a confession from the boy … which we did.' The last words spoken in a whisper.

'Did the boy claim to be innocent?'

'Yes, Sir, many times.'

'So why did he sign the confession?'

There was a long pause before the man answered: 'It was very difficult. We had to apply a great deal of pressure.' The silence stretched to minutes; then the jailer said, almost inaudibly: 'This is why I am here, Sir. My colleague and I, we both know that the boy is innocent.'

'How do you know that?'

'Sir, we have done this work for many years and we are very experienced. We know that virtually all of the prisoners we persuade to confess are in fact guilty. A very few aren't. Your stable boy is one. He is innocent. We know this with certainty.'

'So why do you tell me this?' The Head Stableman now spoke sharply.

'Sir, the indictment is complete, the confession has been submitted and we have emphasised to the boy that he must not insist on his innocence. If he does so he will merely be sent back to us for more … discipline. There is no doubt that he will be convicted; it is the Master's wish, it is the Court Jailer's wish and, presumably, it is also the wish of the young lady who made this charge.'

'So I ask again, why do you tell me these things?'

'Sir, if you were at the Court and spoke up for him, for his character, it could make a difference to his sentence, because you are a very respected man in this community. This is the only way in which we can help him. If he comes back to prison, my colleague and I will not be able to protect him from the evil and violent prisoners we hold, because we will need to treat him just like all the others. He will be held in a common male cell and many bad things are likely to happen to such a young man in there. So bad that some do not survive what happens to them.'

The Head Stableman looked at the floor and thought for a while. Then he lifted his head: 'I understand now why you came and why this is dangerous for you and your colleague. I will think about this deeply and I will keep it secret. You will let me know when the case will go to the Court and at that time I shall decide what to do. Meanwhile, should anyone ask, we will say that you were merely enquiring about future stable employment for one of your family, on the grounds of our earlier boyhood relationship.'

'Sir, I am most grateful to you. I will leave you now and wish you well.'

The jailer bowed low and left with a feeling of great relief. As he sat that evening with the Second Jailer, he reported all that had happened at the stable yard: 'I carried out what we decided. I went to see the Head Stableman and he was very fair to me, although he did ask some difficult questions. That's the trouble with our job, we need to keep quite a lot of it secret, don't we? Anyway, he listened to all that I had to say and said he would think about it. We have done all we can. The matter is in God's hands.'

Piously, they both looked up to the ceiling.

Brother

Kati's brother had grown up in fear of his sister. He did not understand why she was so unkind to him; after all, she was his "big sister," just four years older than him. Aren't big sisters supposed to love their little brothers? He had tried on many occasions to be very nice to her but her response was always brusque at best and sometimes downright aggressive.

When he was a very young child, her cruelty was physical, always taking any opportunity to prod him with sharp objects or stick pins into his tender flesh. At other times, she would deliver surreptitious blows to his body when no-one was looking. These attacks invariably made him cry loudly. Delighted, she would always shout: 'Listen to the cry-baby! Always crying about nothing.'

As the little boy grew up and acquired speech, he tried on many occasions to explain to his nanny and his mother that his big sister was hurting him but, invariably, they would be very displeased.

'You are a very bad boy to say that,' they would say, 'your sister loves you and would never do such things to you. You really must stop telling lies.' Sometimes this would be emphasised with a powerful slap to a convenient part of exposed flesh – which, of course, would make the poor child cry once more!

In fact the constant bruising and series of small cuts and punctures all over his body were clear evidence of his sister's attacks but, if noticed, they were never commented upon by his nanny, who believed that boys should be brought up to be strong, tough and aggressive.

'Be a man!' This is what the redoubtable lady would often roar. Such strident cries only succeeded in frightening the rather timid little boy! 'You'll never get anywhere if you sit about crying all the time. You need to be toughened up.'

When he was a baby and a toddler, Kati filled the little boy's life with pain and fear. As he became older, the physical attacks did not cease but Kati now added more subtle tortures, for instance singling out his most favourite possessions and destroying them. Toys were broken and his favourite books would somehow be ripped to pieces. Kati then refined this process by insisting that her brother had carried out this destruction himself:

'I actually saw him doing it.' She would report this artfully to her mother. Sometimes, if the occasion presented itself, she would report her brother's bad behaviour to her father, who doted upon her. These strategies sometimes worked so well that her brother was severely reprimanded and occasionally beaten by his mother or even by his father if the event was regarded as a particularly bad misdemeanour.

Another very cruel strategy that Kati applied many times was to prevent the little boy from emptying his bladder when he needed to do so. She would block the way to the toilet bucket in the room and keep the little boy in extreme discomfort until he wet his clothes. Then Kati would run and tell his nanny, who would burst into the room, tear the wet clothes from the boy and wash him roughly before slapping him hard on his bare flesh.

'You are a bad boy, you must not wet your clothes like this,' she would say grimly, 'and I hope this hurts.' The little boy's howls proved that it did!

Meanwhile, Kati stood back with her eyes shining with pleasure.

Years passed and Kati's attacks continued, becoming more devious and cruel. When the boy was seven years old, Kati had engineered a particularly traumatic event for him. This concerned the destruction of a valuable model of a Chinese junk. For a long time afterwards, every time the boy thought about this, the memory would send him into pangs of fear and inadequacy.

His father had largely ignored the boy as he grew up but, occasionally, the man appeared with small gifts for his son. These were usually small presentation items that he did not wish to keep; items that were meaningless to him. After a particularly successful trading deal with a merchant from a Far Eastern country, Kati's father had been presented with a model of a Chinese junk, beautifully carved from ivory. It was a wonderfully delicate piece of classical art but Kati's father was not interested in artistic beauty. On a whim, he decided to give the model to his young son.

The boy had been delighted with the gift – even more delighted that his father should have taken any notice of him! The man had appeared in his room and said: 'Here is a special gift for you. It is a Chinese junk, a type of trading ship from a land far away. It is a beautiful and delicate model so I want you to take very good care of it. It must not be played with roughly, otherwise it will break. Do you understand?'

The boy promised faithfully to look after the model. He placed it very carefully on his large dressing chest and thanked his father profusely.

At breakfast next day, Kati's father told her about the Chinese junk and how he had given it to her brother.

Of course, she was furious: 'Why did he not give this gift to me? Am I not his favourite?' However, as Kati thought about the Chinese junk, a clear plan came into her mind and she felt very much better. Within the hour, the door of the boy's room burst open. The little boy looked up nervously as his sister appeared, smiling falsely.

'Well, Father has told me all about this wonderful gift he has given you. Aren't you a lucky boy! And he's told me that you are to look after it carefully and make sure it doesn't get broken.'

'Go away, Kati.' The boy's voice was quavering with fear.

'Why are you telling me to go away,' the girl's voice trumpeted, 'I've come to see this wonderful gift, this wonderful model of a Chinese junk. You will be able to tell me all about it.'

'Don't touch it!' The little boy's voice was urgent and pleading, 'it's very easily broken.'

'I know,' the girl said brightly, moving towards the model on the dressing chest.

'You are not allowed to touch it!' The boy's voice wailed.

'Don't worry, if you don't want me to touch it, I won't touch it. You touch it. You pick it up tell me about all its parts.'

The boy looked at her with great fear. Then, falsely reassured, he approached the model and picked it up very carefully, turning round slowly to face his sister.

'You see,' he started, 'it's all carved in ivory which comes from elephant's tusks. You can see the deck here, where the sailors walk and if you look carefully, you can see where they steered it … aaah!'

The fragile Chinese junk hit the hard floor violently as the boy's words ended in a piercing shriek. As he spoke, Kati had suddenly swept her arm in a downward arc and deliberately knocked the boat out of her brother's hands, dashing it violently to the floor. Then, she stepped forward quickly and brought her heel down upon the fragile hull, splitting it apart.

'You clumsy fool,' she screamed, 'look what you've done to Father's present. You are a very bad boy and I'm going to tell him what you have done.'

Leaving the boy howling in inconsolable grief, Kati left the room in triumph: 'It was far too good a gift for him,' she thought, 'Father should really have given it to me.'

Moments later her voice echoed down the corridor: 'Father, Father!' Kati was weeping openly as she sought out her father who was working at his desk, 'I'm really upset and sad.'

'What is wrong, my dear Kati,' her father replied, putting a reassuring arm around her, 'tell me what is wrong and I will make it right.'

'It's my brother,' she wailed, 'I asked him to show me the lovely Chinese junk you told me about and he threw it down on the floor and broke it. He stamped his foot upon it.'

Kati's father was incensed. Not because the Chinese junk had been broken but because this had upset his beloved daughter so much. Grim-faced, the man said: 'I will go now and speak to your brother about this.'

Kati stood in the shadows as her father visited her brother's room. After a short time he left, soon to return with a horsewhip under his arm, entering and closing the door firmly behind him. As soon as the door was closed, the girl ran to the door and glued her eye to the large keyhole which fortunately accorded a view of much of the room. To her joy and delight, she saw her brother stripped of his clothes and tied to the post of the heavy bed. Then he was severely horsewhipped by her furious father. His screams were very loud and made her laugh with delight.

'Serves him right,' she thought. 'He should not have been so careless with such a precious gift from my father.' Memory of the little boy's whipped body made Kati smile throughout that day.

One fine day the following summer, Kati's father addressed his son at the first meal: 'How old are you now, Son?'

'I am eight years old, Father.'

'Are you a good swimmer? Do you swim in the river like I used to do when I was your age? I was the best young swimmer in the Town, you know.'

'Yes, Father, I can swim but I'm not very good yet.'

'Not good? You need to be good, my Son. You need to practice like I did and then you will become the best swimmer. Today is a fine day. Kati will take you swimming, won't you, dear Daughter?'

'Yes, Father, of course I will if it is your wish.' The boy looked stricken at this thought.

Kati then continued: 'Father, I have taken him swimming before. He is rather reluctant to go into the water. He says he does not like to get his linen under-breeches wet.'

'Breeches!' her father roared, 'you don't wear breeches for swimming. You swim naked. That's what all boys do. That's what I did and that's what you will do, too.'

'But, Father …' The boy's words were interrupted.

'We will talk about this no more,' his father said, 'you will go with Kati and she will tell me how you have improved.' Dismissively, the man turned back to his food. 'Breeches indeed!' The man was derisive, 'the children of today are so soft.'

So Kati and her brother found themselves on an open part of the riverbank, downstream from the Manor House.

'Stand there and wait.' Kati looked around carefully. No far away, she observed a large group of schoolgirls from the Town School approaching. She waited until they were quite near and then, despite his urgent protests, stripped her brother naked, smiling as the passing girls giggled and pretended to hide their faces. 'Do exactly what I say. Stand still. Remember what Father said about improving.' Kati then took off her stockings and hitched up her gown above her knees so that she could stand in the river. 'Come on in,' she ordered and the cowering boy stepped cautiously into the water.

As soon as he was within reach, Kati seized him by the back of the neck and pushed him down into the water, completely submerging his head and holding it under for at least half a minute. When she noted that the boy's struggles had begun to weaken she lifted his head from the water and let him go. Eyes rolling wildly, gasping for air and with dirty river water vomiting from his mouth, the boy stumbled back to dry land where he bent double, holding his stomach.

It was then Kati saw the opportunity to achieve something she had dreamed of doing for many years. With a powerful thrust, she sent the little boy's naked body hurtling into the centre of a lush and extensive patch of stinging nettles, where, to her great delight, he rolled and wallowed uncontrollably for some time, trying desperately to regain his feet. As he did so, the tens of thousands of tiny hollow trichomes on the leaves and stems of the plants sought out every square millimetre of his body, each one penetrating his skin with ease and injecting its toxic load of highly irritating histamine into the epidermis below.

His face mirroring his shock, the boy finally managed to stand up and stumble clear of the nettle patch. As he did so, the first effects of his whole body contact with the nettles began to develop. In an instant, his pale white body became blotched all over with huge red swellings and the explosive rush of sharp agonising pain almost rendered him unconscious. Screaming loudly, the boy threw his incandescent and pain-racked body into the river and started to swim faster than he had ever done before towards the middle of the stream.

'Don't go too far out,' his sister called casually after him but the boy had no ears for her. Within a short time, he was in the centre of the river where the current was much stronger. As the pain and shock of the nettle stings continued to increase, the boy's swimming weakened and, before long, he was carried away in the powerful current, by now struggling ineffectually in the water. Kati stood still and watched the black dot that was his head being swept away downriver.

'That's a pity,' she said to herself, 'now I will have to collect his clothes and begin to walk downstream. What a bother! My shoes will become stained with mud.' As the girl began to walk, she started to rehearse what she would say when she returned home without her brother.

'There was nothing I could do. He wouldn't listen to me and insisted he should become as good a swimmer as Father. I ran along the riverbank as fast as I could, calling to people to help but no-one would go into the river and rescue him. And then, his head disappeared. It was all because he wanted to please you, Father.' All this accompanied by inconsolable tears, of course. Kati rehearsed these words several times and felt quite satisfied with them. She was sure her father would be sympathetic towards her. Anyway, her younger brother had always been a bit of a nuisance, hadn't he?

So Kati continued to walk unhurriedly along the riverbank, carefully picking her way around the patches of mud. After some time, she saw a group of older boys near a narrow bridge across the river. 'I'll ask them if they have seen anything floating by,' she thought and quickened her pace slightly.

As she came closer, she saw that one of the boys was cradling a small body in his arms. As she approached them she called, 'Is he dead?' She expected them to answer, "Yes."

'No,' the boy answered, 'but he nearly was. I spotted a body floating in the river and swam out to retrieve it. It was this little lad. He had stopped breathing but I managed to start him up again. Now I'm trying to get him warm so that he will survive. He seems to have lost all his clothes.' He looked at the clothes in her arms. 'Are these his clothes? Is this your boy?'

'He's my brother.'

'What happened to him? Why is his body all red and swollen?'

'Oh,' Kati said casually, 'that's nothing. He fell in some nettles. He'll soon recover.'

The boy looked at her sharply. 'Let's get his clothes on. He needs to be warm.'

The clothes were slipped gently over swollen and burning flesh.

Kati now said, 'Just leave him there on the grass. When he recovers, we will walk home.'

'Listen, Miss,' the boy answered, 'this boy will not walk anywhere today. His body is badly injured because of what has happened to him.' He paused and looked at her thoughtfully: 'Maybe you should have taken better care of him?'

Kati flushed. 'I always look after him well. He just decided to go off …'

The boy looked at her and said nothing. After some minutes, he rose to his feet: 'Let us take him home. I will carry him; he is very light.'

They were a large group as they made their way back along the riverbank. As they eventually approached the Manor House and were walking beside the stable yard wall, Kati's attitude became increasingly haughty: 'I live here in the Manor House. I am the Master's daughter and the boy you are carrying is his son. You may leave us now. Put the boy down here. The river entrance gate is just here.'

The boy was respectful but adamant. 'No Miss, this boy needs to go straight to bed to recover from this terrible thing that happened to him.' As they entered the gate beside the stable yard, the Master appeared from the yard, having been out riding.

'What is this?' he enquired. 'What has happened here?'

Kati was quick to answer her father's question, tearfully giving a slightly amended version of events that was based on what she had memorised earlier. This, of course, placed her in a heroic rescuing role: 'These boys helped me bring him back,' she concluded.

'Kati,' the man said, 'you are always so good and brave.' He smiled at her warmly.

'Master,' the boy carrying Kati's brother spoke firmly, 'I am sorry but what your daughter has just told you is not correct. She was nowhere to be found when this young boy was drowning in the river. She was far away upstream and did not make any sound. It was fortunate I saw the boy's body in the water and swam out to retrieve it. Your son was drowned at this time and had stopped breathing but I have some knowledge of these matters and I was able to clear the water from his body and restart his breath. It was long after this when your daughter arrived. Also, Master, you will see that your son's body is covered everywhere with nettle stings; enough, I think, to kill him. Your daughter says he fell into some nettles but I have never seen a body so completely covered in the rash. The pain must have been extremely severe. It is like someone has thrown him into a bed of nettles without any clothes.'

'Yes, Master, what our friend says here is correct.' The other boys in the group spoke up to confirm their friend's version of events.

Kati's father was clearly puzzled and he turned to his daughter for explanation. Her face flushed deeply and she turned on her heel and stalked off towards the Manor House without another word. Her father looked after her with surprise: 'Why should she lie? She has never lied to me before.' The man would think about this later. Meanwhile a stable hand had alerted the little boy's nanny and she came running from the house with blankets.

'Oh, what has happened to the poor boy?' The nanny was shocked to see the boy unconscious.

'He has almost drowned and has fallen in nettles. Take him to his bedchamber and look after him well. I will come to see him later,' the boy's father instructed.

'I thank you, Young Man, for what you have done for our family today. Here is a reward for you.' The man proffered a bag of coins.

'Master, I am pleased to be of service. Thank you but I do not take money for saving a life. This is my duty to God.' Kati's father was deeply moved.

'You are a fine young man and I will not forget what you have done for us. Good day to you and may God bless you.' The group of boys departed and Kati's father looked after them thoughtfully before striding off towards the Manor House.

In fact the nanny was so horrified when she saw the condition of the little boy that she sent for his mother; after examining him, his mother sent for the town apothecary to come and treat the boy. Understandably, the boy was weak and barely conscious after his multiple ordeal, having suffered partial drowning at Kati's hands, torture by nettle stings all over his body and actual drowning in the strong current of the river. There is no doubt that the outcome would have been his death had it not been for the quick and expert action of the older boy downstream. So Kati's brother remained in bed throughout the following week, with the town apothecary ministering to his skin, which was still swollen and extremely sensitive as a result of the nettle attack.

Meanwhile Kati thought that the household was making too much of a fuss over her brother:

'After all, lots of children are drowned in the river every year,' she muttered crossly, 'so what's all the fuss about? It really is unfair and I don't see why I am not allowed to see my little brother.' This last comment referred to a meeting with her father the previous day.

On that day, Kati's father had called her to his desk.

'Kati, your brother is very ill and has to stay in bed until he recovers from his drowning and from the effect of so many nettle stings.'

'Do not worry, Father, I will go to him every day and read to him,' Kati replied solicitously.

Kati's father looked thoughtful.

'Kati, that is very kind of you but you are not to go to his bedchamber for the time being.'

'But Father …'

'Kati, listen to me, please. I forbid it.'

'But why, Father?' A shadow of annoyance crossed the man's face.

'Kati, your brother tells me he is frightened of you, frightened of things you have done to him. He would not tell me about these things but I am reminded of certain incidents in the past when I judged it necessary to whip him severely on evidence given by you.' The man paused and continued to look at her with a stern gaze. 'However there is another reason as well. When I put your younger brother in your charge, I expected you to look after him. It seems to me that you did not do so.'

Kati smiled her most winning smile at her father (her smile always worked) and adopted her most gentle tone: 'Father, you must believe me, I did look after him; I was very careful with him but he insisted on disobeying me …'

'Kati, that does not sound like your brother. You know he is not a bold or a disobedient boy. He knew he was in your charge and that he had to do what you ordered him to do. He knew that I had given you that authority. Furthermore, you told me about how you tried to rescue him when he was swept away, running along the riverbank, but …'

'Yes Father, that's exactly what I did and no-one would help me …'

'No, Kati, the young men who saved your brother all said the same thing. After your brother had been rescued by them, you were not there. You eventually appeared some time later, walking quite slowly. They all said this, Kati.'

Kati burst into noisy tears. The man continued: 'No, Kati. Dry your tears. I think you have lied to me about this. I do not know why. It perturbs me and makes me sad. I will think about this further. But meanwhile, you will not go to your brother's bedchamber. I forbid it, do you hear?'

'Yes, Father.' A whisper.

'You may go, now, Kati.' Her father's dismissal was unequivocal.

'We'll see about this,' Kati hissed furiously, as she stamped through the house, 'he may be ill now but he won't be ill for ever. And when he's better, I will find something to make him really sorry. All the other fun I have had with him will be nothing compared to this.' However, Kati's mood lightened when she thought of the fulfilment of her ambition to push her brother into the nettles: 'That was very clever of me to see the opportunity and take it. I know what one little nettle sting is like (that's really painful) but how wonderful that I was able to cover my brother's whole body with nettle stings. He had stings everywhere – absolutely everywhere!' Kati smiled broadly as she thought of all the very sensitive places on her brother's body that were now covered with nettle stings. 'Just you wait, my dear brother,' she whispered, 'you have a lot more suffering to come. Just you wait!'

Kati's brother slowly recovered from his ordeal although his skin retained a certain uncomfortable sensitivity which affected him for years. He was now approaching his tenth birthday and was in the middle of one of these jumps in development that children go through. He had cast off much of his "little boy" image and suddenly become taller and stronger. In part, this was due to the employment of a physical trainer for the boy who came regularly to the Manor House and schooled the boy in a range of games and physical exercises. The boy developed well and became strong and more coordinated.

His father was still keen that his son should be able to swim well but, instead of putting his daughter in charge of the boy's teaching, he himself took over this role. He had approached the boy some months after his recovery and suggested that he and the boy should go to the river for some swimming practice. The boy was pleased to have his father's attention though naturally still a little nervous at the prospect of swimming.

'Do not worry, Son,' his father said with a smile, 'I shall be there to save you.' The boy looked at his father rather doubtfully but felt he had to smile in return and say: 'I know I will always be safe if you are there.' Certainly the boy was much safer with his father than with his sister!

In this new-found father-son relationship, the boy felt he could raise the difficult question of swimming naked: 'Father, I know you always swam naked when you were a boy and, in obedience to you, I have done the same. But I think you will see that, in these modern times, the boys swim with some clothes on, usually wearing just their linen breeches, to cover their lower parts. I am pleased to obey you whatever you decide but I do not wish to dishonour the family by having people laughing at me if I am not covered.'

'Very well,' the man replied, 'you may wear your linen breeches when we go to practice. I am pleased to hear that you think of the honour of the family.' Remembering the supreme embarrassment of being stripped naked by his sister in front of many town children, the boy was delighted with the outcome of that particular conversation! Of course, it had never occurred to him that his sister had done this deliberately to make him suffer severe embarrassment. At that time, he thought it had just been an unfortunate coincidence.

In due course father and son went to the river for swimming practice. They went to an area where a number of the town boys were swimming and Kati's brother was pleased and relieved to see that all the boys wore a light garment of some type to cover themselves. Somewhat to his surprise, he found that his father was indeed a strong and expert swimmer and, under his schooling, the boy soon became a very good swimmer too, achieving a high standard within several months. His father was delighted with his son's progress and began to enjoy the boy's company very much, so much so that he took to seeking out his company for frequent conversations on many things.

The man was surprised to find that his young son had developed quite an academic bent. He noted that the boy's room was filled with many books and found that he was knowledgeable on many subjects. After a particularly interesting discussion about the stars – the boy was able to show his father a number of books on the subject – the man sat back, looking at his son with admiration. 'What will you do with your life when you are a man?'

'Father, I have been thinking about that. What I would like to do is study at the University of Yarlsvott (this was known as the "best" university in the Country). I thought I may study many matters of the world there; the stars, the science of our world, medicine, life, everything. Then, when I have learned everything there, I would return here and bring all my knowledge to the people. I would develop this knowledge and extend it.'

The man now looked at his son with great respect:

'You please me greatly, Son. I had no idea you had been studying so many things. I must think deeply on this. We must think how to prepare you for your great adventure to come.'

Needless to say, the young boy was very happy with this new and happy relationship he had with his father.

Meanwhile Kati worked hard to rebuild her father's trust in her, seeking to please him in every way she could. She had been artful enough to show sorrow and contrition about her brother's "unfortunate accident" and, in the end, the man decided that what had happened to the boy was just a serious mistake by his sister, a human error of judgement.

'After all, she's only a child, too. Perhaps it was my fault by placing too much responsibility upon her.' So saying, the man had forgiven his daughter and resumed his loving relationship with her. Of course, Kati would have dearly liked her father to return to his former opinion of his young son (disinterest, at best) but she realised there was little chance of this happening.

'That little brother of mine has ensnared my father into thinking he is clever! I'll watch him carefully and try to destroy their relationship in any way I can,' she resolved.

The months then rolled by without significant incident until the drama of Kati's accident with the horse. Kati's brother, deeply absorbed in his studies as always, was unaware of this incident on the day it happened. It was all over by the time he heard that Kati's horse had gone mad and had to be killed at the stables. However it seemed that even more trouble had occurred on the very same day; it was reported that the youngest stable boy had attacked his sister physically in some way and was now languishing in the Town Jail, awaiting trial for this crime. Kati's brother was amused at this thought, since he knew that few people, never mind the youngest stable boy, would have dared to attack the fearsome Kati!

'I wonder what really happened there,' the boy mused, 'I wonder what Kati was up to!'

Then the boy remembered that another incident that happened almost immediately afterwards (perhaps on the following day?). Kati had made a new decorative pendant for herself, using a funny old stone she had found somewhere in a storeroom. He remembered this because something very odd happened to him at on the day she had shown the pendant to their parents. He remembered that he had felt a little strange at the beginning of the evening meal in the Great Hall. Then, after the meal had been eaten, he found that his fear of Kati had completely disappeared. He remembered feeling this as he passed Kati's new pendant back to her. This change in himself puzzled him very much, because nothing had altered, had it? Afterwards, he had thought long and hard but could not find any positive explanation. Finally, he had concluded:

'It's probably because I'm growing up and my swimming and physical training has made me a lot stronger than I used to be. After all, I will soon be ten years old.'

A third family incident occurred only a few days later when an item of his mother's jewellery went missing. It was all very strange. The missing item was a very old medallion that he had never seen. A huge search had been carried out (extending even to his own body and belongings!) but nothing was found. For a time, he understood that his mother's personal maidservant was suspected of the crime but nothing came of this accusation: 'I suppose you can't accuse someone of theft if there's no evidence,' the boy had concluded.

One morning weeks later while the family were eating the first meal, his father announced he was making a business trip to a foreign country and would be away for a while: 'But I will return for your birthday,' he told his son, 'I am determined to be here for that.'

The boy flushed with pleasure. 'Father, I will be so pleased if you are here for my birthday.'

Kati lowered her head so that the family would not see her scowl as she muttered to herself: 'I haven't forgotten about you, little brother. Just you wait!'

Weeks passed and then came the glorious day when the boy's father returned, bearing with him a large box of fine polished wood.

'What is in this box is a secret,' the man said with a smile, 'all will be revealed in due course.' The box was placed beside the Master's desk in his room and everyone was forbidden to touch it or even approach it. 'You will all know what it is, soon enough,' the man smiled gently at them, giving his son a special smile.

'Surely such a large box cannot possibly be a birthday present for me,' the boy thought modestly; secretly, of course, he hoped fiercely that it was!

The day of the birthday came and Kati's brother was ten years old. On rising from his bed, the boy looked carefully at himself in the looking glass: 'I suppose I really am taller and stronger than I was before. This must be the reason I'm not frightened of Kati anymore.' Nevertheless, the boy was still rather mystified.

The family were instructed by the Master to gather in the Great Hall. All, except Kati, were excited and filled with anticipation. Kati was in a foul mood; however, she knew she would have to control herself and forced a rictus grin. The Master appeared, smiling broadly. He addressed the family in formal tones: 'I congratulate my clever son on his tenth birthday. You may not know this but he intends to become a highly-qualified scholar and then use his knowledge to benefit the world. He has asked me if he could study at the University of Yarlsvott and I have agreed that he may go there when the time is right. Meanwhile, I have obtained for him a birthday gift of true greatness, a gift which will enable him to expand his mind. It is in this large box here.'

The boy's heart leapt as two strong servants carried the large wooden box carefully into the room.

'Before I open it, I will tell you about my recent journey when I went to a foreign country far away to meet a very special man whose name is de'Dondi. This man is a very great scholar and he is the inventor of many fine scientific machines. This is his very latest invention, unique and considered by all who see it as the foremost marvel of these modern times. It is an incredibly complex astronomical clock and planetarium which he has named the "Astrarium". Until very recently, there was only one astrarium in the world (and that is in his possession) but I persuaded him to construct another in smaller scale, in fact exactly half the size of the original. I have purchased this unique machine from the inventor for a considerable sum of gold. It is here in this box and it is my gift to my brilliant son, who is already so knowledgeable in the science of time, stars and planets.'

With a flourish, the Master folded down the sides of the box to reveal an awesomely complex and elegant construction in silver and gold, its seven equal sides covered with dials, pointers and other indicators of varying size and shape. Each of the indicators was calibrated in a different way, so that at any moment an observer could tell the time, the day, the month, the year and the position of all the planets and stars in the solar system. It was truly a breathtaking work of scientific magnificence!

The ten-year old boy was at first struck dumb by the instrument's beautiful complexity but soon he drew near and, with incisive intelligence, began to seek out how its various parts worked and how they were all linked together by over one hundred (actually 107 – he counted them later!) toothed gear wheels, each one meticulously hand-cut to be a perfect fit with its fellow, each shaft and its means of mounting a vision of free-running perfection. His eyes shone with astonished delight.

'Father,' he breathed, 'this is the happiest day of my life. This is the most wonderful gift I have ever received and I will treasure it forever. I will study it and understand how it works. And then, Father, I will see whether it can be improved or whether it can be developed into an even more complex astrarium.'

'Bravo!' His father clapped his hands delightedly. 'What an intelligent boy you are. Now we will close the box and have it carried to your own room, where later you may study it at your leisure.' The servants were called and the box was carried carefully to the boy's room and placed upon a sturdy low table.

'Before we finish here, each member of the family will bless you on this, your tenth birthday.' The father opened his arms to his son and they embraced warmly. The man said: 'My son, I bless you on this occasion of your tenth birthday and promise you my love and support for ever.'

'Thank you, Father and I bless you too.'

His mother took her son into her arms and said: 'My beautiful, clever son, I bless you on your tenth birthday and I will love you forever, as I have loved you since the day you were born.'

'Thank you, Mother and I bless you too.

Smiling fixedly, Kati opened her arms to her brother and whispered in his ear: 'I do not bless you, you pathetic little fool. And, don't worry, I will smash it, I will find a way and there is nothing you can do to stop me.'

'Thank you, Kati, I wish you the same blessings.' As he said these words, the boy pulled back from her embrace, held her by her upper arms and looked straight into her eyes, something he had avoided doing throughout his life.

Kati was suddenly transfixed by those eyes; green ('just like Father's,' she thought with a jolt), calm, confident, resolute. Kati was totally unnerved and broke free from his grasp muttering: 'You cannot win against me. By the time I have finished with you, you will have nothing and Father will have disowned you.'

Maidservant

A "Great Commotion" had permeated all parts of the Manor House. It had started quite early that morning, not long after the breakfast meal. Kati's mother had gone to look in her jewellery box for a broach that she intended to wear later this day. Going to the curtained sleeping area in the Great Hall, she had retrieved the key from its hiding place, a well-concealed compartment in her largest dressing chest, and opened her jewellery box. She had found the broach she was looking for easily enough and was just about to close the lid and relock the box when she was struck with the feeling that something was missing.

The jewellery box was in the shape of a small chest and it was capacious enough to contain many pieces – broaches, pins, necklaces, pendants, all mixed and tangled together. So it was quite remarkable that Kati's mother should spot a single deficiency in the box. Now she began to sweep her eyes across the contents of the box in a methodical way, comparing what she now saw with what she expected to see; after some moments, she identified the deficiency. She could not see the large round disc of her great-grandmother's medallion, attached to its gold chain. Although this was an item that was never worn, it was highly regarded as a very important part of the family's history.

'Perhaps it's concealed below something else,' the woman thought and wondered whether she should bother to start a comprehensive search for the piece. 'After all,' she reasoned, 'it's bound to be in here. No-one ever unlocks this box except me and my maidservant. Of course my husband could look in here if he wanted but he is not interested in anything in this box.'

Kati's mother debated the matter for a few seconds and, inevitably, decided she had better make a thorough search for the medallion: 'It'll just worry me if I don't confirm it's here in the box.' A sensible, practical thought. So the woman immediately began to unload all the pieces of jewellery from the box, setting everything out neatly on her dressing chest. Within ten minutes or so, it became obvious that the medallion and its gold chain were not in the jewellery box. When the box was completely empty, the woman searched all the corners of the box meticulously, laughing at herself as she did so: 'That big medallion would never fit into a tiny corner!'

However, now she was puzzled and worried. Where had it gone? When did she last see it? She thought back carefully. It was probably about one week since she had opened the box. Frowning with concentration, she cast her mind back to that time and, yes, she thought she did remember seeing the piece then. She remembered seeing the large thin disk of the medallion standing on edge among all the other pieces. Therefore, it had gone missing in the last week! So began the Great Commotion in the Manor House.

Firstly, all the members of the family were assembled and apprised of the situation. They were then asked a number of questions:

Had they opened the jewel box? Had they seen the medallion and its chain? Could they think hard about this because there was no doubt the medallion was missing – and it was *very valuable!*

Her husband had not been in the box; in fact he couldn't remember the last time he had even seen the box open: 'The jewellery box is yours, my dear, I would not expect to have anything to do with it.'

Kati's brother looked blank, because no-one had ever shown him this piece of jewellery or spoke to him about its history. Kati's mother always had the intention of showing it to him – it was after all an important part of the family history – but until now she had thought the little boy would not be interested. Maybe when he's older …?

Kati was consulted. What box? (This said with total innocence.) Oh, her mother's jewellery box? Of course she never had anything to do with this box. She never went near it. Wasn't it kept locked and she, Kati, was not trusted to know where the key was kept? Did her mother think the medallion had been stolen? Obviously the servants were the suspects. Didn't she have a personal maid who knew where the key was? Didn't that make it pretty obvious what had happened? So Kati, the perpetrator of the crime, began to inject her special brand of poison into the situation.

The Mistress trusted her personal maidservant completely and knew she could depend upon her absolute honesty. However, she called for the girl to attend her and asked her the same questions that the other members of the family had been asked. Because she was the only other person who had regular access to the jewellery box, the Mistress questioned the girl closely, expressly asking whether she had noticed that any item was missing from the box. The girl projected her mind back to the times she had recently unlocked the box but could not remember anything amiss. The Mistress was satisfied that the girl had told the truth and instructed her to return to her duties.

The Mistress's maidservant had come to the Manor House as a little child of ten years old, a simple peasant from a poor family, greatly honoured to be given a job in such an important place. She had proved to be energetic, hard-working and quick to learn and, in addition, she had a very pleasant bubbly personality which made her popular with all her contemporaries, except of course, those who were jealous of her talents and attractive appearance.

Starting at the "bottom", where the tasks were always the dirtiest and least pleasant, this girl was assiduous in everything she did and, in the following years, was promoted to a series of more skilled jobs in the kitchen and household. As a teenager, she was given the unusual opportunity to train as a personal servant and proved ideal for this task, pleasing all those whom she served. She was always reported upon very favourably by her superiors and thus came to the notice of the family who were always on the lookout for good personal servants for themselves.

When the girl was just sixteen, she was called to the Housekeeper's Office to be informed that the Mistress wished to speak to her. The Housekeeper, a terrifyingly efficient lady who rarely smiled, instructed her to go to the Mistress's room immediately. No reason was given. Quickly donning a clean apron and checking her appearance in a convenient looking glass, the girl had felt very nervous as she went to see this very important lady in a part of the house she had never before visited. As she walked, she tried to remember whether she had made any bad mistakes recently. She knew that servants were sometimes called to the Mistress when they had made very bad mistakes. Sometimes, the Mistress ordered servants to be beaten! The girl felt a pang of fear as she walked.

She had knocked timidly at the large heavy door and was bidden to enter. The Mistress sat at a writing table completely covered with papers.

'Ah, yes. Stand there, please,' the woman said in a pleasant voice. The girl was taken aback. The Mistress had said "please"! Very few people ever said that to her. A few moments passed. Then the Mistress looked up. 'I hear you are a very good servant.'

The girl blushed with pleasure. The woman now looked squarely into the girl's eyes. The girl dropped her gaze.

'Look at me, girl.' The woman's voice was soft and friendly. 'I have a question to ask you. Would you like to be my Personal Maidservant?'

'Mistress, I would be honoured to be your Personal Maidservant but do you not already have such a servant? I would not wish to displace another.' The woman looked at the girl with respect.

'That is a very kind thing you have said. The answer is "no" because my Personal Maidservant has just left to work in a higher post in another household. I wish her well but now I have an immediate need for a new Personal Maidservant. You! If you will accept the position.'

The girl's heart was singing with joy. 'Of course I will accept, Mistress. It is an honour and I will serve you well and faithfully.'

'Then I will see you here tomorrow at nine. Thank you, you may go.'

The girl returned to the Housekeeper's Office, walking on air. The Housekeeper smiled her rare smile at the girl: 'You see! If you work hard you can have a very good life in a household like this.'

The following day, the maidservant arrived to serve the Mistress.

'You will stay with me throughout the day,' the Mistress informed her, 'and help me to dress and take my meals. You need to have access to all my clothes and also to my jewellery box so that you can bring the jewellery I wish to wear. We will go now to the sleeping area in the Great Hall and I will show you where all these things are kept.'

The girl followed her mistress to the sleeping area. The Mistress explained: 'These are the chests where my clothes are kept. You will be responsible for arranging them and keeping them in good order. Look here, this is the jewellery box that is kept on this dressing chest. It is always securely locked. Very few people know where the key is kept but you will be one of them. See, the key is kept here, in this concealed compartment. You press it here to open the secret door. Every time you have finished with the contents of the jewellery box, you are to lock it securely. Don't forget to check it carefully and return the key to this secret compartment. You must make sure that no one is observing you while you do this. And you will never tell any other person, no matter who, where this key is hidden. Do you understand all this?'

'Yes, Mistress, I do understand and I will be very careful. I will always obey you.'

Kati was not pleased when she heard the news of her mother's new maidservant. She had been quite happy with the old maidservant, a rather unattractive middle-aged woman who had learned to fear the Mistress's daughter. Even when Kati was a young child, the Maidservant had found herself put in the wrong on a number of occasions, all of which had resulted in her being rebuked by her Mistress. The Maidservant knew that Kati had been to blame for every one of these incidents. So after that, she had kept clear of Kati as far as possible and treated her with great care and respect on the few occasions they met. This power pleased Kati very much and she deliberately worked to keep the older woman in a state of nervous tension.

Kati had not known this girl servant before her elevation to this high position, so it was an especial shock to find an intelligent, friendly young woman in the position – and even worse still, she was actually quite a good-looking girl! Kati had immediately set about "smearing" her mother's new maidservant, by applying all her usual skills to the situation. To her

206

surprise, her mother would not react to any of Kati's sugges-
tions that her new servant was unsuitable.

'Don't worry, Darling,' her mother said absent-mindedly
as she perused her usual heap of papers, 'I know she is new but
I'm quite satisfied with what I've seen so far.'

Kati had also tried her father but he had just looked at her
and observed: 'Your mother is very capable of commanding
her servants, Kati.' Then he had turned back to his papers,
making it clear that the conversation was finished.

Of course, Kati also applied a range of tried and tested in-
timidation techniques on the girl herself. Kati knew that these
techniques had always been effective in the past. However, in
this case, she was astonished to find that none worked on the
girl. When Kati became haughty and overbearing with the
girl, she responded by treating her Mistress's daughter with
great kindness and respect. When Kati became abusive, the
girl defused every situation with quiet words of reason and
subservience. When Kati tried friendship (an inside position
from which she would be able to attack effectively), the girl
was friendly in return but always maintained the respectful
distance of employee and employer. All this left Kati deeply
frustrated and she vowed that someday, she would succeed in
destroying her mother's maidservant.

In the afternoon of the day of the Great Commotion, all the
household servants plus all those who worked outside the
house on the estate were instructed to assemble in the Great
Hall. They stood in complete silence as a grim-faced Master
addressed them. He told them that a very valuable piece of
jewellery had been stolen from the Mistress's jewellery box.
It was a large gold medallion on a chain. This had happened
during the last week and this was the jewellery box from which
it had been stolen. (He indicated the jewellery box, which had
been placed on the table.) Since the lock of the jewellery box

was intact, it had obviously been opened by someone who had access to the key. The family had no idea who the thief was but they knew that he or she was present in this room. They wanted the piece to be recovered right away. If this did not happen, it would become a criminal matter which would be referred to the Town Court.

So everyone who was assembled in the room was to search in all places for the stolen medallion. They were also to think about who might have carried out this crime. If any person had any information about the crime, they were to inform their Head who would pass the information to the Master. Meanwhile, the living quarters of all servants would be thoroughly searched; this to be organised by the Head Stableman for all outside workers and by the Housekeeper for all house servants. No-one would be exempt from the search and they would all be bodily searched also. They would have nothing to fear if they were innocent. The Master hoped this matter would be brought to a speedy conclusion. The servants were dismissed and streamed out of the Great Hall in a buzzing miasma of worry and puzzlement:

'Who could have done this thing?' They asked each other this in bewildered tones.

'You're not surprised, are you, Nanny?' Kati was stretched out in bed, having been awakened gently by her servant a few minutes before. It was the morning after the Great Commotion. Kati's first words to her nanny that morning had been: 'Of course, there's only one person it can be, don't you think? It's got to be her, hasn't it?'

'Miss Kati, I'm sure I don't know what you're talking about.' Her nanny was confused.

'I'm talking about the thief – who else would I be talking about?' Kati replied with her usual anger and contempt. 'It's her of course. Mother's maidservant!'

'Oh Miss Kati, you should not say such terrible things. She seems a sweet innocent girl to me.'

Kati levered herself upright and fixed her nanny with a baleful eye: 'Listen, you old fool, it's all a matter of who has access to the jewel box key, isn't it? *Isn't it?*' The words shouted angrily, making the older woman jump with fright.

'I suppose so, Kati, darling.'

Kati was clever enough to leave it at that. She knew her nanny would never be able to form her own opinion on such a matter; however she knew the older woman would go immediately to gossip with the other nannies and senior servants. In due course, Kati calculated that a significant number of accusations against her mother's maidservant would come from the servants as Kati's poison spread like an epidemic across the servant areas. Kati lay back on her pillows, satisfied with her morning's work.

'You see, you just have to wait. Then, when the opportunity comes, you need to recognise it and take immediate action. That's what I did when I pushed my brother into the nettles.' Kati smiled with genuine pleasure as she recalled the details of that event. How funny it had been to see the little naked boy rolling over and over in the nettles, making it absolutely certain that every part of his body would be stung. 'And now, Mother's Little Maidservant, you are going to experience the power of Kati!' Gleefully filled with vengeful thoughts, the girl now rose from her bed and prepared to enjoy the day.

Evil usually works fast and this case was no exception. By evening, Kati noticed that her mother and father spent a long time in deep conversation, perusing various pieces of paper on the desk before them. Nothing said at the evening meal; in fact the meal was eaten in almost total silence and the family left the table as soon as the last food was eaten. Her mother and father withdrew to their sleeping area and closed the heavy curtains around them. The murmur of conversation continued for a long time. While she was still in the Great Hall, Kati strained her ears but could not make out a single word. Disappointed, she withdrew to her room.

The next morning started a significant day. Kati suspected that this might be a day of drama and so she rose early. After the family had attended the morning meal, her father ordered that they should remain at the table while he called for the Housekeeper and the Head Stableman to attend him.

These servants arrived together, entered the Great Hall and bowed low. 'Master, how may we serve you?'

The Master addressed them both: 'I am aware that all the servants have been searching for the stolen medallion and that all quarters have been searched. Is the search complete?'

The Head Stableman replied: 'Yes. Master, we have searched all the quarters and the body of each servant has also been searched. Nothing has been found.'

The Housekeeper added: 'The same has happened in the household, Master. Nothing has been found.'

The Master paused and sighed. Then he said: 'You are both aware that I have received a number of accusations from the servants. Each of you have passed these to me yesterday. In fact I have received a total of nine accusations, four from the household and five from the outside servants. All nine identify the same person as the thief who has stolen the medallion.' The Master was silent for a few moments as he looked through the accusations once more. Then he addressed them once more: 'You know who the accused is. What is your opinion of that?'

The Housekeeper spoke first: 'Master, I find it very difficult to believe. I have known this girl for more than six years and, during all that time, I have never seen any sign of dishonesty.'

The Head Stableman said: 'Although I do not know this girl as well as the Housekeeper, I have always thought her to be a good and honest servant.'

'Very well,' the Master said heavily, 'I will examine the girl and I wish you both to be present.'

Behind him, Kati wriggled in pure delight. 'Everything is going to plan,' she thought.

The Housekeeper went to fetch the girl and returned within five minutes. The Housekeeper and the Head Stablemen were given seats at the side of the Great Hall.

'Stand there!' The Master's command to the girl was curt. She cut a totally pathetic figure, weeping silently, head hanging, hands clasped in front of her in an attitude of prayer. 'Look at me!' The Master's voice was loud and angry. 'Answer me truthfully.'

'Master, I have never told a lie in this house,' the girl whispered.

'Where is it? What have you done with it?'

'Master, I don't know. I have not taken it.'

Silence. The Master looked towards the Housekeeper: 'Has this girl's room been searched thoroughly?'

'Yes, Master, I conducted the search myself.'

'And nothing was found?'

'Nothing at all, Master. The girl has few possessions and everything in her room belonged to her, apart from her servant's clothes.'

'Was the girl's body searched?'

'Yes Master, I searched her body myself. I made her remove all items of her clothing and I searched these as well. I found nothing.'

The Master now turned back to the cowering girl: 'Where have you hidden it?'

'Master, I have not hidden it anywhere. I have not taken it.' The girl wept loudly.

'Be quiet! You will tell me where you have hidden it. I can have you beaten.'

'No, Master, please, no. I did not do this. I have stolen nothing.'

'Husband,' Kati's mother spoke quietly, 'I ask that you do not beat the girl.'

The Master paused. Then he addressed the Housekeeper: 'Take her. Put her in the Ice House without her clothes. I will see her again in two hours.' The girl was dragged away, protesting her innocence.

Hours later, the maidservant was brought back before the Master. White and shivering uncontrollably, she made no sound as she stood swaying in front of him, semi-conscious.

'Are you now ready to tell me where you have hidden the medallion that you have stolen?'

'Master. I have stolen nothing. You may kill me if you wish.' The girl's voice was a weak whisper and the Master had to crane forward to hear her words. He sat back in his chair, his face set in a mask of fury. 'Send for the Court Jailer. Tell him I have business with him. Take her and lock her in her room.'

Later that day, the Court Jailer appeared once again at the Manor House.

'Master,' he said, 'how may I serve you this time?'

The two men withdrew to a private area and were in deep discussion for a considerable time. Finally, the Court Jailer sat back and reviewed his copious notes: 'Master, this case is slim, I am afraid. I see how the girl can easily be identified as the thief because she was one of only three people who had access to the key. Since the other two people are yourself and the Mistress then the Mistress's maidservant is obviously the thief should anything be missing from the jewellery box. But unless the servant was extremely stupid (and you tell me she is not), she would never act to place such certainty of guilt upon herself. Furthermore, Master, since the medallion has not been found, there is, of course, no evidence. It is my opinion that the Court is very unlikely to convict the girl, given the complete lack of evidence. But even if it did, that would not achieve what you want – the return of the medallion.'

The Master held his head in his hands: 'So what am I to do?' A voice of despair.

'Master, I have a proposal for you. First you need to know with certainty whether the girl is guilty or innocent. You have already tried to do this by your own rigorous examination and the girl still insists she is innocent. At the Town Jail, I have men who are experts at finding out the truth and I suggest that you send the girl to the Jail for just one day, after which you will know the truth. If she is guilty then my men will make her tell us where she has hidden the medallion. If she is innocent, then we will talk again about the thief, because then we would know this to be someone who secretly knows where to find the jewellery box key.'

After some thought, the Master spoke: 'Sir, I must ask you one question. When I was examining the girl and threatened her with beating, my wife intervened to protect her. She is fond of the girl and does not think she is guilty. Will the girl be severely beaten during the examination at the Town Jail?'

The Court Jailer smiled.

'Master, she will not be beaten at all. After all, she is not a prisoner. The techniques my men will use are much cleverer than beating. We have moved on from the techniques of the Dark Ages; as you would expect, we are much more sophisticated now.'

The Master was reassured.

'Then I agree to your proposal and I thank you for your expert advice.' Without any further words, the Master slid a bag of coins across the table which the Court Jailer slipped into his pocket with a grateful smile. 'Thank you, Master, you can depend on me. I will arrange this for tomorrow if that is acceptable to you? My assistant will call at nine.'

Early the next morning, the maidservant was visited by the Housekeeper. 'Get cleaned and dressed. Today you are going to the Town Jail.'

'Am I to be a prisoner without a trial?' the girl wailed. 'Madam, I am innocent.'

The Housekeeper looked at the girl sympathetically: 'I am sorry this is happening to you. I don't know what it means. It is something arranged between the Master and the Town Jailer. Just go, be brave and tell the truth.'

'Madam, you know I always tell the truth.'

The Housekeeper nodded. 'I have certainly never found you to be dishonest. I have already told the Master that.'

'Madam, how long will I be held at the Town Jail. I am frightened to go there. I have heard there are many violent criminals there who may do me harm.' She burst into loud tears.

'Hush,' the Housekeeper said softly, 'you must be brave and tell the truth. I will come for you when the Town Jailer's man arrives.'

So the maidservant found herself in the darkness of the Town Jailer's wagon, rumbling and jolting along the road to the Town Jail. She heard the terrible sound of the Jail gates closing and, shortly afterwards, was marched into the building and into a bright warm room occupied by two men sitting at a table. There was also a dirty, ragged little boy sitting on a low bench against the wall.

'This is the maidservant from the Manor House,' the Town Jailer's assistant said as he pushed her rather roughly into the room. 'I must leave you now, I have other work to do.'

'Ah, yes.' The two men looked at her, quite kindly, she thought. One then said: 'Fetch yourself a stool and sit here at the table with us. I am in charge of this jail and this is my assistant. We want to speak to you about the trouble you are in. I suggest you tell us all that has happened.'

The girl poured out the whole story. She was the Mistress's maidservant, a very important position in the household, especially for a young girl like herself – she was only sixteen. She was completely trusted in her position and had access to her Mistress's jewellery box. She was the only servant who knew where the key was kept. Of course she had never divulged this to anyone – and she never would! Somedays ago, a valuable piece of jewellery had been stolen from the box, a large gold medallion with a gold chain. She had seen this item mixed up among the many other items in the jewellery box but had never examined it. It was not a piece that the Mistress ever wore. She understood it was a sort of family heirloom, something that was very old. Because of her position, she had been blamed for the theft but she was innocent; she would never have done such a dishonest thing or have been so disloyal to the Mistress. All the time the girl was speaking, the two men looked at her intently.

There was a short silence.

'So if you didn't steal it, who did?'

'Sirs,' the girl gasped, 'I cannot know. It must be someone who knows where the key is hidden. They must have taken the key, opened the box and stole the medallion.'

The men looked at each other. Then the First Jailer said: 'Miss, now listen to me very carefully. This man (he indicated the Second Jailer) and I are both experts in the truth. Experts, you understand? Hundreds of times each year prisoners are brought to us here and it is our duty to determine the truth about their crimes. And do you know what happens? These prisoners start off telling us lies but, by the end of our examination, they tell us the truth about their crimes. They tell us everything about them, down to the last detail and they are very glad to do it.' Now looking even more intensely at the girl, the man repeated: 'We are experts in the truth. You should believe it.'

Then the man continued: 'This is why you are here. You are not a prisoner but you will spend the day with us here while we examine you to determine the truth about the crime at the Manor House. You, Miss, will tell us that truth before you return to the Manor House. We will, of course, communicate that truth to our master, the Court Jailer and he will inform your master. Do you understand all this?'

'Yes, Sir, I understand, thank you. Your task is easy, for I have already told you the truth.'

The man looked at her kindly: 'Well, these are early times yet and we will see what happens. Meanwhile, we must start our day's work.' Both men stood up and stepped away from the table.

'Miss,' the First Jailer spoke again, 'do you see this little boy?'

'Yes Sir.' The girl looked more closely at the boy. 'He seems ragged and dirty. He also seems to be very frightened.'

'Yes, you are right, he is frightened; he is here because he is a thief. He stole an apple from the food shop. This apple.' The man held up a small, wrinkled apple. 'He was caught by the shopkeeper and had the apple in his pocket. So here he is with us now. Furthermore, we know him. He has been here before. He is a beggar boy from the town and we know that he is eight years old.'

The girl now looked at the frightened little boy with sympathy.

'I want you to help us now, Miss,' the man continued. 'Please ask him if he stole this apple.'

Reluctantly, the girl took the apple in her hand and addressed the boy: 'Boy, did you steal this apple?'

'No, Miss. It wasn't me, it was another boy who stole it and gave it to me.' The boy's voice was quavering and filled with terror.

The man sighed. 'You see what I mean? Is this the truth he tells you? What would you do now?'

The girl was confused.

'Maybe we should believe him. Maybe …'

The man interrupted: 'You see, Miss, you are forgetting that we are experts in the truth.' The two men now spoke briefly and the Second Jailer unhooked a thin springy branch from its hook on the wall.

'Come with me, boy.' He grasped the boy by a shoulder. 'You come, too, Miss.'

A mere ten minutes passed before the Second Jailer and the girl returned to the room, the man smiling and relaxed, the girl white with shock. The First Jailer looked up: 'What does he say now?' This with a cheerful grin.

'Oh, he admitted his guilt, of course. He said he stole the apple. In fact he told us every detail about how he did it; how he waited till the storekeeper's back was turned – you know, every part of the truth.'

'Have you dealt with him?'

'Yes, I took him to the gate and pushed him out. I also told him that worse would happen to him next time if he committed another crime. I told him I would use a whip next time.'

'Good!' The First Jailer turned to the girl. 'You see, Miss, you know what he told you when you asked him, don't you? But, you see, my friend and I, we are experts in the truth.'

'But if he is guilty, why does he not go to the Court?' the girl said faintly.

The man smiled: 'Miss, the Court might not convict an eight year old boy for stealing an apple. The Judge might be feeling kind-hearted on the day the boy was tried. It is part of our duty to apply the Law sensibly. That is what we have done this morning. That is what we do here all of the time.'

The man now gestured towards the table.

'Now, Miss, we will sit here and you will tell us the truth about the theft of the medallion at the Manor House. This time we will ask you some questions. Here is the first question: 'Did you steal the medallion from the jewellery box?'

'No, Sir, I have told you already, I did not.'

'The jewellery box was not damaged, was it? It had been opened using the key?'

'That is what the Mistress said. It was she who opened the box and noticed the medallion missing.'

'So, if you are the only servant in the whole house who has access to the key, it must be you who stole the medallion, mustn't it? That is precisely why you have been accused, is it not?'

'Yes, Sir, that is why I am accused but it is not true. It was not I who stole it.'

'Miss, is that not what the little thief said to you when you asked him about the apple?'

The girl looked shaken: 'Yes, Sir ...'

'And after he had been examined by my assistant in the next room, what did he say?'

'He said he was guilty, that he was a thief.'

'Is it not possible that you, too, are a thief? If we examined you rigorously, what would we find?'

The girl's face was a mask of terror. She replied in a quavering voice: 'Sir, you must not say that. It is not true. I did not steal the medallion.'

There was complete silence for several minutes. Then the man rose from the table and said: 'Now we must continue to show you what we do here at the Jail. My friend here will now educate you about the techniques we use to change lies into truth.' The man smiled pleasantly as he said this and patted the girl's hand reassuringly. 'Later, we will take you on a tour of the Jail. You must see everything before you leave us.'

218

The Second Jailer now conducted the girl around the walls of the room: 'You see, Miss, we are very neat and methodical. We keep most of our equipment here in the room; we have a place for every item – we take it, use and then return it. Sometimes, the item needs to be cleaned after use and I do this at the pump outside.' The man then worked around the room, showing her each item, explaining how it is used and describing the specific effects he would expect it to have.

'You see, Miss, you need to be an expert to get the job done as efficiently as possible – we don't want to waste time. So you need to plan, you know, maybe this one first to prepare the flesh and then, perhaps, this one to apply sharp persuasion to obtain the truth as quickly as possible.'

Finally the man led her back into the small room next door.

'You see, Miss, this is a very well-designed room. We fasten most of the adults to the hook there – it's a good strong hook and will take the full weight of a man, you know. When they are fastened there, all parts of the body are fully exposed and easy to reach, aren't they? Of course, if the prisoner is small, we can use the table and the straps, just like we did earlier today. You see how the straps are cleverly designed to hold the body still in absolutely any position we choose? As you have already seen, we are very precise in everything we do.'

Standing back, the man now said: 'Now, I have shown you everything. Do you have any questions?'

White and trembling, hugging her arms around herself protectively, the girl whispered: 'No, Sir.'

They returned to the main room. The First Jailer said: 'Please sit here, Miss, you must excuse us for a while; we have our work to do in the Jail.'

The two men were absent for some time, although, from time to time, one or other returned briefly to the room. Eventually, both men returned and the First Jailer said: 'Now we will all have our daytime meal. You must join us, Miss.'

Their meal was simple but good and they ate and drank leisurely, talking gently of many things, after which both men closed their eyes and dozed for a while.

When they awoke the maidservant said: 'Sirs, may I clear the meal away and clean the plates and cups?'

'Why, Miss, that would be lovely! The pump is in the courtyard, just outside the door.' The girl enjoyed the fresh air outside and was in no hurry to return! When finally she reappeared in the room, the First Jailer spoke kindly.

'Come and sit down, we need to talk again.' The men sat at the table, one on either side of the girl: 'Now, Miss, why did you steal the medallion?'

'Sir, I did not do that. I have told you the truth.'

'But Miss, you are the one who is accused. So answer me this – *If* you had stolen the medallion, why would you have done it?'

'Sir, I have no reason to steal the medallion. There is nothing I could have done with it.'

'Miss, we are seeking your help. *If* you had stolen the medallion, where would you have hidden it?

'Sirs, you must not ask me that. There is absolutely no place I could have hidden it without it being found.'

'You could have buried it in the ground, in a place only you know. Then, later, when all the hubbub died down, you could go to that place and retrieve it.

'No, Sir, I could not …'

'Yes, you could, Miss. And then you could sell it to a gold merchant, couldn't you? Then you would be rich and you would be able to set yourself up as a fine woman …'

'No, Sir!' The words screamed. 'I could never do that. I wouldn't know how to do that. I never touched the medallion. I never stole it. It was someone else who stole it …'

'*Who?*' The word was like the crack of a heavy whip.

'I don't know,' the girl wailed.

'Another servant? A member of the family? A thief from elsewhere?'

'I don't know.' The girl wept bitterly and slumped across the table. They gave her a cup of water to drink and the girl gratefully drank it down. Then the two men sat at the table attending to some papers while the girl recovered herself.

After about half an hour, the First Jailer looked up and said: 'Miss, it is now time we showed you the rest of the Jail. This is something you must see before you go back to the Manor House.' Going back to the Manor House was something the girl looked forward to, eagerly! 'There is just one thing,' the man continued, 'where we are going is very dirty and it is best that you wear clothes from the Jail. My colleague has laid some out for you in the next room. Will you change into them, please?'

'Yes, Sir,' the girl replied, 'I will do whatever you think is best.' The girl went into the next room, shivering a little at the sight of the hook, and found a thin shift and a rather worn but clean white gown spread out on the table. Obediently, she took off her own clothes and donned the shift and the gown, which proved to be quite voluminous. She returned a little self-consciously to the main room and the men looked at her with approval.

'That is good, now your own clothes will not be soiled or damaged. Let us go now.'

The men and the girl now made their way into the cell areas of the Jail. The First Jailer stopped by a large door and bid the girl look through the large grill. A frightening low moaning sound came from this room. Gingerly, the girl looked into the room. She could see that the large dark room had little furniture. The walls were steaming with damp and the smell was dreadful. Several miserable-looking women sat on rough bunks; the moaning was coming from them.

'This is the communal women's cell. If you were a prisoner here, this is where we would put you.' The girl held the grill bars tightly, feeling faint and nauseous. Suddenly, one of the women sprang up and ran to the door, screaming profanities. The girl jumped away from the door, her heart pounding.

'Get back,' the First Jailer shouted to the woman, 'do you want to be flogged?' The woman quieted immediately and disappeared.

'Sometimes, quite often, actually, they get quite aggressive.'

The men continued down the dank corridor, guiding the girl between them. Soon, they came to a large barred door from which emanated a terrible noise of screaming and shouting.

'This is the men's communal cell; they're always fighting in there. Do you want to look?' The man placed a hand in the middle of the girl's back and propelled her forward.

'No, Sir, please, I don't …' she screamed, resisting his push. As she was impelled forward towards the bars, suddenly, there were many hands and arms thrust through the bars, reaching out into the corridor, casting around, writhing in the air like snakes.

The First Jailer spoke quietly into the girl's ear: 'Sometimes we use these men to help us with the truth, you know. If someone won't tell us the truth about their crime, we put them into this cell with these men. Not for long, you understand, maybe only for an hour or even a half an hour. Funny thing, no matter how they're dressed when they go in, they always come out naked!'

As he spoke, the First Jailer had been pushing the girl towards the door. She struggled but could not stop the movement. Slowly, inexorably, the grasping, clawed hands came closer and closer until they could seize and tear at her clothes, her hair, her flesh …

'I am guilty,' she screamed again and again as loudly as she could, 'I did it, I stole the medallion!' Slowly, the men eased her back a little to the sound of ripping fabric. Then she was held at fingertip reach of the grasping, tearing hands; although flesh contact was now minimal, her clothing continued to be torn.

'Why did you steal it?'

'To get money, just as you said.' All her answers were screams of terror.

'Where have you hidden it.'

'I buried it in the ground, just as you said.'

'Where?'

'I can't remember.'

'You must remember.'

'I can't, I can't, I can't …'

'Why did you betray the trust of your Mistress?

'To get money, to become a fine lady, just as you said.'

'How did you think you would not be caught and accused?'

'I don't know, I didn't think, I don't know, I don't know …'

The men pulled her away from the grasping hands and sat her down on a rough wooden bench against the opposite wall. When she had recovered sufficiently to be able to walk, the men helped her back to the jailer's room and sent her out to change into her own clothes.

The girl crept back into the room, her face drawn with the horror of her ordeal.

'Sit here with us,' the First Jailer said. 'Do you remember what I told you about us?'

The girl was still traumatised, white, shaking uncontrollably. 'No, Sir.'

An almost inaudible whisper. 'Something about truth.' After another long pause: 'That you are experts in the truth.'

'That's right, Miss, I'm glad you remembered. My friend and I, we know truth. Now I know you're upset but listen carefully to what I'm saying. My friend and I, we know you were definitely *not* telling the truth outside that cell door. You were telling us lies, weren't you? You did not steal the medallion, did you?'

'No Sir, I did not and I never would do such a thing.' The girl wept hopelessly. 'And now that I have confessed you will make me a criminal and my life will be finished. I want to die!'

The man looked at her and smiled: 'Miss, you do not understand. Listen carefully. We know that you lied to us about stealing the medallion. You are innocent, we know that, too. And that will be our report to the Court Jailer. And I am sure our report will be believed by your master, too.'

The girl's head was now in a complete whirl. She had admitted guilt. She had confessed to the crime. But the jailers would report she was innocent? She was confused but gradually, a feeling of relief developed into pure elation! She had been examined and found innocent of the crime! Meanwhile, the two men talked together quietly, giving her time to recover.

After some time, the First Jailer said to her: 'Miss, we have now completed our examination on the matter of the medallion but there is one other thing we would ask you to do for us.'

'What can I possibly do for you?' The girl was mystified and fearful.

'Do you remember the stable boy at the Manor House who attacked the Master's daughter?'

'Yes, I knew him. I could never understand why he did that. He always seemed to be such a nice boy.' The jailers looked at each other.

'Miss, the stable boy is here in the Jail, awaiting his time at the Court. He is in a single cell and we are looking after him. He is well. We wondered if you would speak to him? He never sees anyone but us and we are sure he would like to speak to someone from his previous life. We could bring him here to this room and you could talk together.'

The girl thought for a moment or two: 'I feel very sorry for the stable boy,' she said. 'I will speak with him for a while if you think that will please him.'

The stable boy was fetched from his cell by the Second Jailer. He stood in the doorway, thin and rather dishevelled, blinking in the light and very surprised to see the girl sitting at the table: 'Miss,' he said in a surprised tone, 'what are you doing in this place? This is no place for you to be.'

The First Jailer intervened: 'This young lady has agreed to speak with you for a while.' Turning to the girl, the man said: 'We have some work to do; can we leave you alone to talk?'

The girl looked into the stable boy's eyes, seeing nothing but kindness and honesty.

'Yes,' she said simply.

'Sit at the table, boy, and don't touch the young lady.' Then, addressing the girl: 'We will be nearby, just call if you want us to attend you.'

So saying, both jailers left the room, not to do other work but in fact to eavesdrop on the conversation between the stable boy and the girl, this being the real purpose of the meeting.

'We might learn a lot more about what goes on at the Manor House,' the men had whispered together, 'in our position you can never have too much information.'

'I am sorry you are suffering here,' the girl said, 'but why did you do it?'

'Miss, I did not do it. This is what happened on that day. I was the one who caught the horse. It was my friend the stable hand who went to help Miss Kati and he only held her hands to help her to her feet.'

'But why did Miss Kati accuse you?'

The boy looked sad and explained: 'Earlier, I had been insolent to her. I had spoken without permission.'

'What did you say?'

'I told her she looked lovely. She was furious. She told me I'd be sorry.'

'Let me understand this clearly. You never touched Miss Kati?'

'No Miss; earlier, I had been insolent but I did not mean to anger or upset her.'

There was silence for a few moments. Then the girl asked: 'Why then are you pleading guilty for your attendance at Court?'

The boy flushed: 'The Court Jailer wished me to plead guilty and gave me a confession to sign.'

'Why did you sign it if you were innocent?'

The boy spoke quietly: 'The jailers were instructed to obtain my confession. This is what happens here.'

At that moment, the girl understood. Looking at the boy wide-eyed, she remembered the little apple thief and the means of obtaining his confession earlier in the day.

'What did they do to you?' The girl's voice was soft.

After a pause, the boy averted his eyes.

'It is no matter what they did. I put my mark upon the confession and that is what will be produced at the Court.' Outside the door, the jailers fidgeted uneasily and looked down at the floor.

'But this is monstrous!' The girl's voice was loud. 'What can be done?'

'Nothing, I am afraid. I will be convicted and must accept my punishment.'

The boy and girl sat together silently for a moment. Then the boy spoke: 'Enough about me. Why do I find you here at the Jail?'

The girl's face clouded: 'I, too, am in trouble.'

'You? How can you possibly be in such trouble that brings you to this terrible place?'

So the girl told the whole story of the theft of the medallion and how, as the only servant with access to the key of the jewel box, she had been accused of theft and been sent to the Jail for examination. The examination was now over and she thought the jailers believed in her innocence.

The boy's face darkened: 'Have you been beaten or ill-treated?'

The girl's hesitation was momentary: 'No, I have not been ill-treated but the examination has been rigorous.'

The boy nodded and asked: 'So has the medallion now been found?'

'No, everywhere and everyone has been searched but nothing has been found.'

The boy sat back and was deep in thought for a few moments: 'Miss Kati!' The girl jumped at the sudden, explosive exclamation!

'You startled me. What do you mean, "Miss Kati"?'

'I bet she has something to do with this. I bet it was she who stole the medallion.'

'Surely not!' The girl was shocked and protested against the boy's theory.

'Look, think about it.' The boy's voice was incisive. 'It can't be the Master or the Mistress because it's their own medallion. We know it's not you, the only other person with access to the key, so it must be someone who knows secretly where the key is hidden. Miss, is the key hidden in a difficult place?'

'Yes, I can assure you it is very well hidden.'

'So the thief needs to be a clever person. Now listen, most of the servants at the Manor House are not permitted in the Great Hall – for instance, as a stable boy, I was not. Of the house servants that are permitted to work there, many are not so clever and would not be able to find the key, even if they wanted to. Of those who are clever, I am sure none would dare to open the Mistress's jewellery box, let alone steal something from it, even if they knew where the key was hidden. That leaves only the two children of the family. The boy is young (nine or ten?) and he is a quiet, timid character. It is impossible to think that he would steal from his mother. What could a little boy like that possibly do with a gold medallion? That leaves Miss Kati, who, as I know to my cost, is capable of anything!'

The girl listened with an open mouth: 'But …'

The boy paid no attention to her and continued his line of thought: 'Let us think about Miss Kati. As a stable boy, I only saw her when she went riding and she was always very rude and unpleasant to the stable servants. And I saw her bullying her young brother a number of times. And wasn't there a time last year when she nearly killed the boy by neglecting him when they went swimming in the river? There was something about nettle stings, too. I always felt very sorry for that little boy. Then there was her horse, a fine animal that she had used for many years. I'm not exactly sure what she did to the horse but the horse bolted and finally threw her off in the stable yard. She insisted on being present when the horse was killed later that day. By then she had falsely accused me of attacking her and everybody believed her. I bet she is involved in what is happening to you, too!' The boy finished his analysis triumphantly.

The girl was quiet, introspective.

'You know, you may be right,' she murmured.

Outside the door, the two jailers looked at each other with knowing eyes and were pleased with their strategy. The First Jailer whispered: 'I think we have a lot more information, now. We must think on this very carefully.'

Breezily, the two men re-entered the room.

Kati

Kati was absolutely furious when the maidservant was brought back from the Town Jail. She had heard about the conditions for women prisoners in the Jail and had been congratulating herself that she had finally been able to criminalise the unfortunate maidservant whom she hated. She had assumed that the maidservant would be ill-treated and, hopefully, beaten as well. Although it was known that the male prisoners bore the brunt of most of the beatings, she understood that female prisoners were not immune either. She had heard they were stripped and flogged. Kati licked her lips at the thought. But now the maidservant had returned and, to Kati's great disappointment, she was told that the girl was unharmed and had been treated kindly by the jailers.

The maidservant had been delivered to the Housekeeper by the Court Jailer's assistant. The Housekeeper welcomed the girl back to the Manor House and spoke gently to her, saying: 'I have been instructed to take you to your room and lock you in it for tonight. Tomorrow I think the Mistress will speak to you. Meanwhile, I will send you food and drink and I wish you well. If there is anything else you need, please let me know.'

The maidservant was deeply grateful: 'Madam, I thank you for your kindness. I wish to tell you that I have been rigorously examined by the jailers at the Town Jail and it is my belief that they have found nothing against me. However, this is not for me to judge and I must await the Mistress's decision tomorrow. My fate is in her hands and, of course, in the Master's hands, too. Whatever they decide will be my fate.'

The Court Jailer arrived on horseback early the next morning and requested a meeting with the Master. The Master received him and, after polite greetings, the Court Jailer gave this report: 'Master, my jailers have carried out the work you required me to do and I wish to report that they are unanimous in their judgement of this case. As you know, the maidservant girl spent the whole day with my men in the Jail. During that time, she was examined rigorously using, as I explained before, the most modern questioning techniques, which do not involve violence or injury. Both my men have concluded that the girl is innocent of any involvement in the theft of the medallion and they have stated this unequivocally. Master, here is the paper inscribed with the report. I am pleased to be of service to you and thank you for your confidence in me.'

The Master accepted the written report and thanked the Court Jailer, who then left.

After a night of fitful sleep, the maidservant prepared with great care to meet the Mistress.

Shortly after the morning meal, the Housekeeper came to her room: 'I have heard nothing from the Mistress as yet but I understand that the Court Jailer has visited the Master. This means that the report of your examination will now be in his hands. We can only wait.'

Towards midday, the Housekeeper returned to the girl's room. 'Now I am to take you to see the Mistress. I say again to you what I said yesterday. Listen to this – it is good advice: "Be brave and always tell the truth."'

'Both of you come to my desk and sit here,' the Mistress said. Then she addressed the girl: 'The Master has received the report of your examination at the Town Jail. Do you know what it says?'

'Yes, Mistress, I believe it says I am innocent of the crime of theft. I pray to God it does.'

'That is exactly what it says, child. Furthermore I have never believed in your guilt. Of course the Master had to examine you rigorously – that is his duty – but he too is content that you are not the thief in this house. I have said to the Master that I wish you to continue as my Personal Maidservant and the Master has given his permission for this.' The woman smiled as the girl burst into tears of happiness:

'Mistress, I thank you. You are so good to me. I will work so hard for you. I will be the best maidservant ever …'

'Hush, girl. Go and compose yourself and then come back here to start your work.'

'Your day in the Town Court is next week on Friday.' This was the message the First Jailer delivered to the stable boy as he brought him his morning meal. 'Between now and then we will need to make sure you are healthy and well. To make sure of this, you will eat the same food we have. Also, I'll get you good clean clothes to wear.'

The boy was always polite: 'Thank you, Sir, for treating me so well.'

The jailer put down the tray of food and, avoiding the boy's eyes said: 'After you've eaten, I will fetch you so that you can wash thoroughly. Then you can spend the morning in the yard. You may do that every day until the day of the Court.'

'Thank you, Sir, I shall enjoy that. You are very kind.'

Simultaneously, the message about the Court was delivered to the Master at the Manor House. When he informed the Mistress, this was overheard by some of the house servants and, before long, the news was common knowledge throughout the workers at the Manor.

When Kati heard the news, she immediately approached her father: 'Father, is it true that the stable boy's Court is on

Friday of next week? If it is, I must prepare, for I am an important witness who will have much to say on that day.'

Her father looked up from his papers: 'Yes, Kati, it is true that the Court will judge the stable boy next week. However, there is no need for you to be present.'

'But Father, why? I am an important ...'

'There is no need for your witness, Kati. I think you already know that the boy has signed a confession of his guilt. Therefore, there is no doubt that he will be convicted of the crime against you. There is absolutely no need for you to be there. I will be there, as the accuser and the head of this family.'

After a short silence, Kati said: 'But Father, I would greatly like to be there.'

Her father looked at the girl sharply: 'Really, Kati? Why would you like to be there?' Kati hesitated:

'Because I wish to see justice done for the terrible thing this boy did to me.'

Her father looked at her impassively: 'I would have thought, Kati, that you would have preferred to wipe that very unpleasant crime from your memory. I would have thought that you would not want to see your attacker face to face again. Seeing him would bring back all the horror that happened to you. You would be upset greatly. Is this not so?'

'Of course I know you are very wise in all things, Father, but I just want to be sure that the Court knows everything about the terrible thing he did. He should never have spoken to me without permission.'

The room quieted suddenly. After some moments, the man spoke in a very soft voice, looking piercingly at his daughter: 'What is this about speaking without permission, Kati? It is the first I have heard of it.'

Kati was stricken. She had spoken without thinking! Now, she must think quickly and retrieve the situation: 'Oh, Father, I am sorry. I am so confused. That was another occasion at the stable yard. Then, that same stable boy spoke to me without permission. I was very cross with him.'

'What did he say, Kati?'

'I cannot remember, Father.' Kati's eyes filled with tears.

'Were his words rude? Coarse? Insolent? Were you offended by them?'

'Father, I cannot remember!' This accompanied by sobs.

After reflection, the man said slowly: 'It seems to me, Kati, that a harmless unremembered comment from a young stable boy is not a matter that should evoke anger on your part. It is our duty as an important family in this region to treat our servants fairly and with kindness. Furthermore, I cannot understand why you should have associated this harmless minor misdemeanour with an attack of the worst kind on your person, unless, somehow, the two are linked in your mind … or even in actuality.' The last four words were spoken almost inaudibly, almost as an introspective afterthought.

As he was saying this, the man remembered that the stable boy had vehemently denied his daughter's allegation and this had been confirmed by the older stable hand. In fact both had protested that the stable boy had not been involved with his daughter but had dealt with the terrified, plunging horse. Also, he had heard that the boy had not signed a confession of guilt until he had been a prisoner at the Jail for many hours. What was it the Court Jailor had said? Ah, yes, his jailers use "sophisticated techniques" to obtain the truth. An unpalatable suspicion was forming in his mind. The Master now looked coldly at his daughter: 'I am puzzled and disquieted by what you have just said to me. But I will leave that aside for the moment. Meanwhile, you may not go to the Court on Friday of next week. Do you hear this?'

'But, Father, please, I …'

The man was angered and spoke sharply: 'Do you not hear that your father is speaking? You will not go to the Court. Now leave me.'

That same day, a personal letter was delivered to the Head Stableman. It had been written by the First Jailer. Going to the privacy of his rooms, the Head Stableman opened the letter and read:

"To the Head Stableman at the Manor House,

Sir, I trust you will recall our meeting of three weeks ago on the subject of a coming case at the Town Court. I have now been instructed that the stable boy's case will be heard next week on Friday at 10 hours in the morning. I believe your Master will already have been informed. At the Town Jail, we have been looking after the boy, feeding him well and keeping him clean and healthy so that he will be of good appearance at the Court.

Of course you will know that the outcome of the case will certainly be a "guilty" verdict, for the boy has given us a written confession of his crime. However, I remain hopeful that you may speak up for the boy so that he has a chance of reduced punishment. I can only repeat that my assistant and I are convinced of this boy's innocence.

Finally, Sir, I plead with you to destroy this letter since its contents are such that my assistant and I would not survive its disclosure.

May God bless your heart as you do His work."

The letter was signed with the names of the two jailers.

The man read the letter carefully several times and sat thinking for a while. Then he rose and burnt it in a metal dish, reducing it to ashes.

Later that day, the Head Stableman requested to speak to the Master privately and was instructed to present himself at the end of the working day.

'Master, I come to seek your permission to attend the stable boy's case at the Town Court next week on Friday at 10 hours in the morning.'

'Tell me, why do you wish to attend?'

'This boy was always decent, honest and hardworking when he worked in your employ. I know this to be true and I had high hopes for his future. I am sorry that he appears to have committed a crime here at the Manor and there seems to be no doubt he will pay dearly for that crime. I would like to attend the Court to speak up for the boy's character. Of course I will do this only if I have your permission to speak.'

The Master's highly disturbing conversation with his daughter was still very much in his mind. Now, another strand of this puzzling case was being added by his Head Stableman, an employee whose judgement he respected greatly.

'You must give me a moment to think.' The Master was silent for some moments. At last, he raised his head and looked directly at the Head Stableman. 'You have my permission to speak up for the boy,' he said, 'furthermore, if I am asked to state whether I have any objections to what you have said, I will say that I have none.'

The Head Stableman was taken aback. This support was more than he ever expected!

'Thank you, Master,' he said. 'May God bless you.'

Kati was beside herself with rage! For months she had been looking forward to the stable boy's time in the Court and had given many hours of thought to what she would say in evidence – and, indeed, the exact way in which she would say it. She must be very precise about this, to make sure that this very insolent stable boy received the worst punishment for this terrible crime against her. This was what Kati kept reminding herself.

She had spent many hours thinking about all the various punishments for the stable boy and had decided on her favourites: 'I don't want him to be put to death, not because he doesn't deserve it but because that would end his suffering. No, I want whipping and beating, all in public where everyone can see it – especially where I can see it! I want him sent to the worst jail in the world where he will be beaten constantly, starved and worked to exhaustion.' Now she was to be denied the first part of her pleasure – attending the Court and giving damning evidence against him!

In her fury, her mind turned to her brother, who now spent even more of his time in his room, lovingly watching and manipulating his precious astrarium or intensely reading more and more books about the many subjects which interested him.

'It's time I gave that pathetic little boy a shock,' Kati thought. Although as she said the word "little" she acknowledged that her brother had grown almost as tall as her. 'I know he expects me to break his new clock or whatever it is and yes, I will do that – but not yet. For now, I think he just needs to be reminded who is in charge. Maybe he thinks that ten-year-old boys are too old to cry!' Kati smiled cruelly, felt very much better and began to plan what she would do.

Two days later, the weather was notably cold, wet and stormy and there was little activity in the Manor House. Kati's brother was sitting at his favourite table reading; nearby, his beloved astrarium whirred and ticked. Suddenly the boy became aware of another presence in the room. Looking around, he found that Kati had entered the room silently and was standing several metres away from him, completely still.

In her hand, she held a long sharp knife: 'Little brother, I have come to cut you in a place on your body which will hurt you very much.' This was said in a low, menacing tone. She had used this technique many times before and knew this would send the boy into a state of hysterical fear, begging for mercy. In this state, she knew she could do anything she wanted to him. She would then amuse herself by hurting him, rather in the same way she did when he was very young and could not resist. As she slapped, pricked or twisted his flesh without mercy, she would say: 'If you make a noise, I will hurt you even more.' At this, the boy's cries would die down to a whimper.

Afterwards, with her brother totally cowed, weeping with pain and nursing his injuries, she would stampede around his room, destroying his most favourite possessions, warning him to tell no-one about the destruction. On this occasion, she continued to set out her intentions: 'After I have you crying like a little baby, I'm going to take all your lovely new books and throw them out the window into the storm so that they will be ruined and destroyed forever.'

She was surprised when her brother did not move or make a sound. Instead, his eyes locked on to hers and she felt a bewildering sensation of fear coursing through her. Then her brother spoke, still the immature voice of a young boy of just ten years old but now somehow infused with a new lower tone, calm, unafraid and in control. 'Put the knife away, Kati. Don't be so stupid.'

Stupid? Her fury rose to choke her and she darted forward, the knife arcing down to slash across his upper leg. A piercing scream. The crack of joints twisted beyond their limit. An unbearable pain in her hand and arm. The knife quivering in the floorboards. Her brother re-seated, completely still but watching her narrowly. 'I said, "Don't be stupid",' he repeated.

Kati screamed like a banshee and lunged for the knife. His powerful sideways thrust against her body knocked her off her feet and sent her tumbling helplessly across the polished floor for several metres: 'Are you deaf, Kati? I said, "Don't be stupid".'

Unhurriedly, the boy pulled the knife from the floor-boards and put it in a drawer in the table. Then, striding across to his sister, he pulled her to her feet and pushed her towards the door. 'Get out!'

'He can't speak to me like that!' Her rage rekindled, Kati turned and drew back her fist to strike him as hard as she could in the face. (She would aim for his eye in the hope this would blind him.) He did not move but fixed his eyes upon hers – now she recognised a spark of anger within. The utter stillness of the scene was punctuated only by the ticking of the astrarium.

Moments passing, Kati's world contracting; his eyes seeming to fill her whole being … A howl accompanied by flood of tears as her hand fell limply by her side.

The boy spoke just once more: 'Get out!' The words quiet but uttered with great force.

Without conscious movement, Kati found herself outside the door, her mind in a whirl: 'What's happened? How can he have changed so much?'

The progress of days cannot be stopped. The sun had risen and set the required number of times and it was now the day of the stable boy's trial at the Court. A very early morning call had awakened the boy. He had already washed himself thoroughly and put on fresh, neat clothes. As he sat with the two jailers, sharing their food, they tried to tell him what to expect at the Court: 'Listen, boy, you will stand in the accused enclosure which is opposite the Judge's bench – it's set very high in the Court – you can't miss it. All the lawyers, notaries and court officers will be in the centre of the Court below you. One lawyer will accuse you of the crime and another lawyer will defend you. If anyone else speaks they will speak from an enclosure at the side of the Court. When all has been said, the Judge will pronounce the sentence. That is when you will learn what your punishment is to be. Do you understand all this?'

'Yes, Sir. It is good to hear that a skilled lawyer will defend me.'

The men looked at each other and shook their heads: 'Listen again, boy, you must understand. You have confessed to the crime – you know that, don't you – so there is no doubt that you will be convicted, that is, found guilty. What you must do this morning is make the best possible impression on the Town Judge, so that your punishment will be made as little as possible. Here is our best advice for you. You must stand up straight. Listen carefully and, if you are asked a question, speak clearly. Say as little as possible. Look directly at the Judge but do not be bold. Try to look innocent!'

'Yes Sir, I am innocent – but I will not say that …' the boy added with a slight smile as the jailers threw up their hands. 'May I now ask you a question?'

'You may.'

'Will Miss Kati attend the Court?'

'Boy, we do not know but, if she does, I do not think she will be called to speak.'

'Why not?' The boy was puzzled. 'She was the victim of the crime.'

'Boy, I say again, you have confessed, the matter of evidence is not required.'

'Will the Master be there?'

'Yes, I believe he will be.' The man hesitated, 'and it is possible that some others from the Manor House may also be present. If they are, they will be in the Citizens' Enclosure at the back of the room.'

After a short silence, the boy asked in a small voice: 'What is likely to happen to me?'

'You must expect punishment,' the First Jailer answered quietly, 'maybe prison with hard labour; perhaps whipping or time in the stocks. We do not know.'

The boy was silent, his face reflecting his terror, his eyes filled with tears. Then the rumble of the Court Jailer's wagon was imposed upon this scene from outside.

'Good luck, boy,' the jailers said, averting their eyes to hide their own tears.

The stable boy felt very nervous as he looked around the Court. It was a very large room and there were already many people assembled there, sitting at tables below him, talking loudly to each other and waving pieces of paper. No-one took any notice of the boy standing in the Accused Enclosure, his guard (the Court Jailer's assistant) standing behind him. Straight in front of him on the other side of the room was a very large panelled desk of dark wood; at present, no-one sat there.

On each side of the room, there were other enclosures with seats within them. In one of these areas, he recognised the Master, sitting with two other men who were busy writing. Behind the boy, there was a large enclosure which was rapidly filling up with ordinary townspeople, sitting on low benches. It was all very strange and frightening; he was glad the jailers had told him a little of what to expect. He looked down at the lawyers below and wondered which of them would defend him. He hoped that a good defence would be spoken.

The boy started violently as someone made a very loud noise by bringing a large wooden hammer down on the top of a table.

'The Learned Judge enters,' a very loud voice shouted. Everyone became quiet and rose to their feet. A small elderly man dressed in a long red robe and wearing a large complex head covering entered from a door behind the large desk. This man swept his eyes around the Court but did not even glance at the boy standing in the Accused Enclosure. When he had finished his inspection, he sat down in a large carved chair and began to read some papers. The hammer was brought down on the desk again with a deafening sound.

The loud voice shouted: 'The Town Court meets. All may sit.'

Silence, apart from the sound of fidgeting and coughing. Finally the Judge spoke without looking up from his papers: 'Is the boy in Court?'

'Yes, Learned Judge.'

'Who is accusing?'

'I am, Learned Judge.'

A tall impressive man in a black robe rose from the centre of the Court and spoke these words.

'Proceed.'

'Learned Judge, it is the Master of the Manor House who brings this case.' The Judge gave a nod of recognition towards the Master and the Master reciprocated. The lawyer continued: 'This is a very simple case. The accused worked as a stable boy at the Manor House. The daughter of the Master had been out riding and, on her return, the horse threw her from the saddle in the stable yard. Because of this fall, her clothes were in disarray and the stable boy took the opportunity to place his hand on the lower part of her female body, touching her bare flesh. The boy has confessed to this crime and you have his confession with his mark upon it. The boy is guilty without doubt.' The tall man sat down to complete silence.

'Who speaks in defence?'

A very young man, also dressed in black, rose nervously to his feet: 'I do, Learned Judge.' The stable boy gripped the front of his enclosure tightly.

'Proceed.'

'Learned Judge, the defence has nothing to say.'

A gasp followed by a hubbub of noise filled the Court. The boy went white with shock, his heart pounding in his chest.

'Quiet!' The loud shout was accompanied by deafening hammering. Order in the court was slowly restored. When all was quiet, the Judge said: 'I find the boy guilty of the charge. I will apply a severe punishment …'

As the Judge spoke, another voice was heard, emanating from the back of the room: 'Learned Judge, I would ask to speak on this case.'

The Judge looked up in annoyance: 'Who it is who speaks?'

'I am the Head Stableman at the Manor House. The stable boy worked for me. I wish to speak about his character.'

'What difference will that make?' The Judge was testy. 'The boy is guilty and I am deciding on his punishment …' As the judge was speaking, a considerable commotion was building up in the Court.

There were many voices from the Citizens' Enclosure shouting: 'Let him speak! Let him speak!'

The Judge assessed the situation. He could clear the Court but that would take a considerable time and he wanted to get through his case load quickly so that he could spend the afternoon in comfortable relaxation.

'Very well,' he said with bad grace, 'come forward and enter the Witness Enclosure.'

The boy was astounded when the Head Stableman came forward. 'Why should such an important man bother about me, a mere stable boy and now a criminal?' He looked fearfully at the Master to see whether this intervention had angered him. The Master sat impassively and the boy could not see whether he was annoyed or not.

The Head Stableman entered the Witness Enclosure and swore to be truthful in the formal words of the Court: 'God will see that I tell the truth.'

The Judge leaned forward angrily: 'What do you have to say? Be quick!'

'Learned Judge, I have known this boy for many years and he was a good worker at the stables. He had developed well and I believe that, in time, he may have progressed to a more senior position at the stables. He was always polite to everyone and especially to the Master and the members of his family. I have observed this myself many times. Therefore, Learned Judge, I ask you most humbly to take into consideration his very good character when you decide upon his punishment. As you know, he has already spent many months in the Town Jail.'

As the Head Stableman spoke, the Judge's irritation turned to anger: 'Is this all you have to say? You are wasting my time.'

The Head Stableman paused for a second and then spoke again: 'Learned Judge, there is one other matter I must bring to your attention. When the horse threw the Master's daughter upon the ground, there were two stable workers present in the yard, the boy and an older stable hand. The one caught the distressed horse and calmed it while the other went to the aid of the Master's daughter.'

The Judge interrupted loudly: 'Yes, yes, – and that's when the attack on the girl took place …'

'Learned Judge, the boy said it was he who caught the horse while the man went to the aid of the Master's daughter. The man confirmed that this was the case. There were many other witnesses there when they both said this, some of whom are here in the Court today.' Many loud cries of agreement came from the Citizens' Enclosure.

The Judge snorted loudly and his voice became very strident: 'Well, then, it's obvious; it must have been the older man who attacked …' His voice faltered and stopped as he realised the implication of what he had just said.

Utter silence filled the Courtroom. The Head Stableman's voice shattered this silence as he said quietly: 'But it is the stable boy that you have before you, Learned Judge …'

These words opened wide the floodgates of human tumult. Within a split second, the Courtroom was filled with the solid, deafening noise of many outraged voices, each shouting as loudly as they could. The Judge was clearly confused, paralysed, head lowered and staring blindly at his papers as he tried to decide what to do. How could he bring this troublesome case to closure? How could he recover the situation without loss of face?

A blessed intervention came with a folded paper which was passed up to him by one of the Court Officers. He opened it and read the words: "I have no objection to lenience." The paper was marked with the Master's seal. The Judge looked across at the Master and the Master nodded. Much relieved, the Judge began the difficult process of restoring order. This took many minutes but gradually, order and quiet were restored to the room.

The Judge then looked around the Court with baleful eyes: 'This is my verdict. The boy is guilty of the crime. I have his confession here. This is his punishment for the crime. At midday today, he will receive fifty lashes at the Whipping Post in the Town Square and then he will be placed in the Standing Stocks until midday tomorrow. I was going to imprison him for ten years with hard labour but now, because there are some difficulties in this case, I have decided to be lenient. I sentence him to four months in prison which he has already served. Therefore, at midday tomorrow he may be freed. This is my judgement and I record it now. Take the prisoner away and prepare the next case.'

There was an uproar of celebration in the Court. The boy was totally bewildered. As expected, he had been found guilty but his sentence meant that he would not return to prison!

He knew that the whipping would be very painful and would leave him with many scars on his back. In the past, he had occasionally seen criminals whipped and his flesh crawled as he thought of it. He knew that his time in the standing stocks would be humiliating, exhausting and very painful. Sometimes criminals put in the stocks were badly ill-treated and injured by town ruffians who enjoyed inflicting pain on others who were helpless.

'I'll just need to be very brave,' the boy thought. 'I know I'll scream and cry when I am being whipped (everyone does) and I'll just have to hope that the townspeople do not hurt me too badly when I'm helpless in the stocks. But after these ordeals, I will be free!' The boy felt a pulse of elation as he thought that, quickly extinguished as he remembered that his life afterwards would be the life of a convicted criminal: 'Afterwards, I'll need to leave here and seek my fortune elsewhere.' The boy felt sad because he had lived the whole of his life in the town and then at the Manor House.

The Court Jailer's assistant placed his hands and feet in manacles and said: 'You will be taken to the centre of the town in the wagon and kept there until it is midday. Then you will be whipped and put into the stocks. I think you are a very lucky boy; all the criminals I have known who attacked defenceless girls were sent to hard labour – and most of them died there. How you got off I'll never know.' The assistant shook his head in puzzlement as he bundled the boy into the back of the wagon.

It was not long before the details of the stable boy's sentence reached Kati at the Manor House. Predictably, she was absolutely furious!

'Only a whipping and time in the stocks! No prison, no hard labour. But he deserved to be beaten much more, he deserves to be starved and worked to death.' Kati knew that many criminals sentenced to hard labour did not survive. 'This is monstrous! I will not allow him to be freed like this. Meanwhile, I must not miss the punishment. I must hurry.'

So saying she left the Manor House and was soon leaving the estate driving a horse-drawn light wagon with a distinctive green painted canvas top – a small vehicle used only by Kati and her mother.

A considerable crowd had gathered at the Whipping Post. As always at these occasions, the mood was gay and festive. As midday approached, the Town Executioner appeared, carrying a large whip and accompanied by two Court Officials. A hush fell on the crowd. The boy was taken from the Court Jailer's wagon and the manacles removed. No words were spoken as his clothes were stripped off and his hands tied firmly to the ring near the top of the Whipping Post. The Town Executioner took up his position to one side of the boy and the officials stood nearby to record the strokes. As midday struck on the Town Clock, a light wagon with a green painted canvas top moved slowly to the edge of the crowd, its driver completely concealed within the cowl of its canopy.

The Town Executioner liked to take his time with his punishments, so that the crowd could derive the maximum enjoyment from the process. He was, after all, a public servant! Nevertheless, just ten minutes later, it was all over. The crowd had gasped and cried involuntary with the crack of each stroke. The lash had violated skin and flesh and now the boy hung semi-conscious. A bucket of ice-cold water brought him some way back towards consciousness and his reeling figure was untied from the Whipping Post and dragged towards the Town Stocks, conveniently nearby. The Court Officials studied their papers: 'The Standing Stocks are to be used. We will return to release him at midday tomorrow.' The boy, barely able to stand, was fastened into the stocks, head and hands thrust through the holes in the vertical wooden board set over a metre from the ground, then the heavy top board was locked down tightly over his neck and wrists.

By now the crowd was generally good-humoured. They had seen a really good whipping, there had been plenty of blood and they had heard a lot of screaming; now they were content and could go home and rest. Before they did, there was one more ritual to carry out. They gathered up any leftover food they had in their baskets and threw it at the unfortunate boy in the stocks. Bread rolls, soft fruit and the occasional egg splattered against the board of the stocks and some burst upon his face and hands. When this happened, the crowd cheered and clapped their hands in glee.

While all this was taking place, the Head Stableman stood back and looked at the scene with sadness. He was pleased with what he had achieved at the Court although he thought that luck must have been with him. In planning his strategy, he had decided to try for clemency first; then, if that did not work, he would suggest there was some doubt about the accusation. It had been obvious that the Judge had no sympathy for clemency so he had moved on to the second part of his strategy. In the event, that had worked brilliantly; the Judge falling neatly into the trap. Of course the Head Stableman did not know that his plea for clemency had been supported by the Master himself and that this had been a major factor in the outcome.

Looking over the heads of the crowd, the Head Stableman suddenly noticed a distinctive small green wagon. He recognised it instantly as one of two light wagons from the Manor House, the one which was used only by the Mistress and Miss Kati. He was unable to identify the driver because the canvas cover hid whoever it was. As he watched, he saw that the driver was speaking to one of the town urchins who were always present at public events of humiliation and he saw a coin changing hands. The urchin ran off and, shortly after, returned with a villainous-looking man, dressed in dirty peasant clothes. This man spoke to the driver of the wagon for some time; eventually, the Head Stableman saw a cloth bundle passed from the wagon to the man. Galvanised into action, the Head Stableman began to stride towards the vehicle but it drove off at speed before he could reach it.

Now that the crowds had all but gone, the Head Stableman went to the boy who had recovered full consciousness and was in considerable pain. He cleaned all the food and dirt from the boy's face and said to him: 'You need not worry because I am going to look after you until you are released from these stocks tomorrow. I am leaving now but I will return shortly.' The man soon returned with a healing balm which he spread on the boy's many wounds. Then, as the light faded and the temperature dropped, he wrapped a thick blanket around him to keep him warm. 'I will stay with you during the night so that you may be protected. I will watch over you,' he told the boy. The boy was bewildered but deeply grateful.

The night hours passed. Suddenly, the Head Stableman was aware of a dark shadowy figure approaching the stocks. The boy awoke with a start as a gag tightened over his mouth. As his eyes focussed, he saw a strange, bearded man standing in front of him. Speaking in a whisper, the man said: 'I have come to kill you, boy. But I have been told to kill you in a very special way. I am going to cut your neck with this small knife and you will bleed to death. It will take you a long time to die. I will enjoy watching you.'

The boy was terrified. He screamed but the tight gag stopped all sound. The man laughed: 'I really enjoy it when my victims are terrified. But I must not waste any more time. Are you ready to be cut? Are you ready to die?' His teeth gleamed briefly in the dim light as he seized the boy by the hair and twisted his head round to expose the area of the neck below which one of his carotid arteries pulsated strongly. He brought his other hand up and prepared to make the deep slicing cut which would sever the artery completely. The boy froze, his mind locked in total panic.

Suddenly the knife had gone. His head was free to move again. He opened his eyes to see his attacker's neck in the murderous grip of the Head Stableman. As he watched, the man's body slipped unconscious to the ground.

'I'll deal with him in a minute,' the Head Stableman said as he removed the gag, 'are you unhurt?'

'Yes, Sir,' the boy gasped, 'why should anyone want to kill me like a horse?'

'We'll see,' the Head Stableman replied as he threw a bucket of water over the assailant. The man spluttered and began pleading: 'Let me go, Master, I am only a poor peasant and I just wanted to steal from the boy …'

He screamed as the Head Stableman grasped him by the hair: 'Tell me the truth. You know that a criminal in the stocks has nothing to steal.'

'Please, Master, I am a kind and gentle man. I only wished to please the lady …'

'What lady?' The Head Stableman drew back his fist. The man answered in a panic: 'A lady in a green covered wagon. She told me the boy criminal was very evil and deserved to die. She asked me to kill him by cutting his neck so that he would bleed to death. She told me how to do it. She gave me the small knife to make the cut.'

'Was this lady young or old?'

'Master, do not hurt me. She was very young, dark-haired, no more than a girl.'

'How much did she pay you?'

'Nothing, Master, I did it only to please her. I took no money.' The Head Stableman smashed his fist into the body of the man. 'How much did she pay you?'

With a scream of pain, the man scrabbled in his pouch and produced a small heavy bag of coins. The Head Stablemen put the bag and the knife into his pocket: 'Go, before I decide to kill you.' The man staggered away into the shadows, bent double and clutching his body.

The sun rose over the horizon and the temperature began to rise. The boy had been dozing fitfully, supremely uncomfortable in the grip of the stocks but deeply reassured by the presence of the Head Stableman who had already saved his life.

The man now approached: 'I must now take this blanket away. You must be seen to complete your punishment,' he murmured to the boy.

Few townspeople paid any attention to the boy in the stocks as they passed. A few made rude or derisive comments and rotten fruit or eggs were thrown a few times. When a group of youths came with the intention of throwing stones at the boy, the Head Stableman chased them away with angry words; in the past, criminals in the standing stocks had been seriously injured in this way. The morning hours crept by with agonising slowness, each minute as dangerous and terrifying as the last. Eventually, the town clock wound its hands towards midday. The sound of the clock's midday bell marked the end of the boy's period of punishment but the Court Officials were nowhere to be seen. Some fifteen minutes later, they were seen to be walking leisurely towards the Town Square.

'Your punishment has come to an end,' they told the exhausted boy, throwing his clothes on the ground and releasing him from the cruel, constricting grip of the Standing Stocks, 'here is a paper to say that the whole of your criminal sentence has been served.'

Released from the stocks, the boy could not stand and collapsed in a heap upon the ground. The Court Officials dropped the paper on his limp body and left without a backward glance.

The Head Stableman came forward and lifted the boy in his arms, taking him and his belongings away to a secluded shady area by the river. Here, he washed the boy and helped him to dress. Then he encouraged the boy to sleep for a while: 'I will watch over you,' he said again.

The boy whispered: 'Why are you so kind to me? I am a despised and convicted criminal.'

The man smiled: 'It is because I know that you are not a criminal. I know you to be innocent of the crime for which you have been punished.' The exhausted boy smiled dreamily and passed into a deep sleep.

Back in the Manor House another boy was hard at work planning and implementing an important piece of work. Kati's brother knew that his sister would at some time mount an attack on his wonderful astrarium – indeed, on the very day of his birthday, she had told him that she would do just that. He knew this would be a total tragedy, because if the delicate machine was broken, it would be impossible to put together again.

'I know that this instrument is very valuable and that my father paid a very large amount of gold for it. Should it be damaged, he would feel betrayed and be extremely angry and sad. I, too, would be very sad, because I know that no one here would have the metalworking skill to repair its parts, even if I could tell them how it should be fitted together. So I must do all I can to look after its safety.'

This was the reason that the boy was constructing a very clever system of protection for the astrarium. When it was finished, he decided that he should be fair; he would warn Kati to stay away from the instrument.

As he worked, the boy mused: 'And to think I used to be so frightened of Kati. She used to terrify me and hurt me in so many ways. But now, I don't know why, I am no longer afraid of her. She hasn't changed. She's still as terrifying as ever but somehow she doesn't frighten me anymore.' The boy now remembered how he had dealt with Kati the week before when she came on a mission of torture and destruction. 'I think, in the end, she was the one who was terrified!' At the memory, the boy laughed out loud.

Several days later, the protection system was ready and Kati's brother installed its complex parts into the top of the astrarium case. He fastened a prominent notice on the case which read:

> This instrument is protected.
> Do not attempt to move or open the case.
> You will suffer serious injuries if you do.

The boy stood back and looked at his handiwork with satisfaction: 'The protection system is fine. Now I will be really kind and warn Kati personally about this.'

Later that day, the boy sought out his sister in her room.

'What do you want?' Kati voice was harsh and unwelcoming but she was surprised to see her brother. Normally he stayed well away from her and she could never remember him coming to her room before. Then she had a moment of inspiration – maybe he has come to apologise? If he has, she would certainly make him suffer! The girl looked at her brother coldly: 'What is it? Be quick, I'm busy.'

'I need to speak to you about my astrarium,' the boy said calmly.

'Oh really,' Kati said sarcastically, 'what about it? Have you broken it already? Don't think for a moment that's going to stop me. I'm going to smash it to pieces and then I'm going to tell Father that you did it.'

The boy looked at her with pity: 'If you told Father I had broken it, what makes you think he would believe you?'

Kati's face fell. It was true that her father and brother were very close these days. On the other hand, nowadays her father always seemed to be angry and impatient with her. He used to be so kind to her, believing everything she said. She didn't know why everything had changed. It was all very unfair! Tears of sadness, anger and frustration filled her eyes: 'So what is it you want?' This screamed loudly at the boy.

'Stay away from my astrarium, Kati. I have protected it with a special mechanism so that anyone trying to damage it will be injured. You will be very sorry if you touch it, Kati. Do you understand this warning?'

'Get out of my room. Do you think you can frighten me? You'll see …' Her face was suffused with rage.

Her brother did not move: 'This is the truth. You will be very sorry if you attempt to damage my astrarium. Listen to me and be warned.' With that, the boy left, closing the door quietly behind him.

The following week, it was the time for a complete cleaning of the Master's sleeping area in the Great Hall. The work involved the removal of the heavy curtaining that surrounded the large rectangle of raised flooring adjacent to the Great Hall fireplace and then moving the many items of heavy furniture – bed, tables, chairs and storage chests – from the area. The heavy curtains would be taken outside and beaten to remove all the dust, after which they would be examined carefully and any necessary repairs made. All items of furniture would be carefully cleaned and polished. Meanwhile, the exposed flooring area would receive a thorough cleaning. All this work involved many house servants and the operation was always overseen by the Mistress who delegated the detailed organisation of the tasks to her Personal Maidservant.

The maidservant had carried out her mistress's instructions on this activity a few times before the trauma of the theft accusation. She recalled that the very first occasion of the cleaning had been a nerve-racking experience for her; she was worried about her ability to command the workers (what if they would not obey her?) and whether the result would be in accordance with the Mistress's standards. In the event, she need not have worried. The house staff recognised her authority and no-one, not even those she had rather feared in the past, generated any difficulty for her. Although young, the maidservant had a very pleasant natural authority and was always reasonable and fair in her dealings with everyone.

The Mistress, while observing the progress of the work, had noted how effective her maidservant had been in dealing with the other staff. Now she congratulated herself: 'I certainly chose well when I made her my Personal Maidservant.'

So the curtains were removed and the large platform was once again stripped bare. The maidservant now carried out a personal inspection of the area before the cleaning work started. It was then that she noticed something gleaming in the light. On investigation, this proved to be a very small gold ring embedded in a crack in the floorboards; looking at it closely, she could see the ring was twisted and broken.

The maidservant had some difficulty retrieving this object as it was firmly wedged in the crack but eventually, she managed to lever it out with a thin knife blade. She thought it must have come from the Mistress's jewellery box, perhaps part of a piece of a long-broken jewellery; then, more recently, perhaps the broken ring had become attached to another item as it was taken from the box and then fallen unnoticed on the floor. She placed the small item carefully in her pocket. She would go right away to speak to the Mistress about this.

The Mistress was working at her desk and smiled at her maidservant as the girl entered the room after a gentle knock: 'Mistress, I have found this small gold ring wedged in the floor of the Sleeping Area.' She handed over the ring. 'As you see, Mistress, it is broken. I saw it was broken like that before I lifted it. I do not recognise it as any part of your jewellery, Mistress.'

The Mistress examined the ring carefully: 'Will you please go to the Master's room and ask him if he would attend me?'

Minutes later, the Master arrived and the Mistress showed him the small broken gold ring: 'I have thought about this, Husband. I think this may be the fastening ring from the missing medallion.'

The man looked puzzled: 'But how ... Who ...,' he faltered.

'I think we should have an immediate thorough search of the area,' the woman said, 'let us go and do this right away.'

As they left the room, they met their young son in the corridor outside: 'Come with us, my son,' the man said, 'you can help us to search, too.'

When the three family members and the maidservant arrived at the Great Hall, the Master said: 'Show us where the little gold ring was lodged.' They all examined the spot carefully. Then, each person began to scan the wooden floor carefully.

The boy was particularly meticulous and searched on his hands and knees, so that his eyes were closer to the floor. Then, in one corner of the area, the boy noticed that a wide crack had opened up in the floorboards: 'I wonder if anything could have fallen down there,' he thought, craning his neck for a closer look. The boy could see nothing except darkness below. 'Father,' he called, 'is it possible something could have fallen down here?' Everyone joined the boy.

His father knelt down and placed his eye close to the crack: 'I can't see anything, it's completely dark down there.' He looked at the maidservant: 'Girl, would you fetch a long, thin knife from the kitchen?' The knife was fetched and the Master inserted the long, thin blade into the crack, exploring the area below with the tip. After a moment, he said: 'I can feel something moving but it's impossible to tell what it is.'

The man thought for a moment: 'We must find out what it is. Girl, will you now fetch the carpenter?'

The carpenter was located and appeared about fifteen minutes later with his bag of tools. He bowed respectfully to the Master: 'What work would you have me do, Master?' The problem was explained and the carpenter examined the location. 'Master, I can remove part of a board in this area. You will then be able to see what is below.' The work took some time since the carpenter did not wish to damage the floor any more than was necessary. Finally, the man said: 'All is now ready for the cut floorboard to be lifted. Do I have your permission to do so?' The Master acquiesced and the board was prised out carefully and removed.

All present peered down into the void, immediately seeing the large gold disc of the medallion glinting in the dim light.

Kati had checked. Her brother was not in his room. She already knew her mother and father were downstairs in the Great Hall. A further quick check revealed that her brother was there, too. They all seemed to be very busy.

'The perfect time!' Kati breathed this with gleaming eyes. 'I'll show him. I'll destroy his stupid machine and, just like I did when that medallion was stolen, I'll just say I don't know anything about it – after all, no-one would ever suspect me. I'll pick one of the estate workers and say that I saw them in the Manor House. That should solve it.'

Kati was very pleased with this plan. She accepted it would be pointless to accuse her brother of the destruction. He was now such a favourite of her father's that her accusation would never be believed. On the other hand, one of the workers …

The girl had already prepared for the event. She had acquired a small but heavy hammer which she knew would be perfect for smashing the delicate parts of the astrarium.

'He said he's protected it against attack. My hammer will smash through anything,' she chortled with glee at the thought. 'I just wish I could see his face when he finds it!' Quickly, she fetched the hammer and, before making her way to her brother's room, made one final check on the other members of the family in the Great Hall. She was pleased to see that they were all still there – in fact, now one of the estate workman was there also and seemed to be carrying out some work on the floor. 'Wonderful,' she breathed, 'that will keep them busy while I do my work.'

Within a minute, she was inside her brother's room and standing beside the astrarium, hearing its soft whirring tick.

'You are about to die, little machine!' Kati thought it very amusing that she was speaking to an inanimate object and laughed gaily. She raised the hammer above her head and was about to strike a mighty blow on the astrarium case when suddenly she thought: 'It really would be much better if I opened the case and then smashed the machine to pieces. I'm sure I can do a lot more damage that way.'

As Kati placed her hand upon the case handle, she read the large warning notice in her brother's clear handwriting:

> This instrument is protected.
> Do not attempt to move or open the case.
> You will suffer serious injuries if you do.

She laughed sneeringly as she tore this notice from the case and threw it to the floor. Then she twisted the handle to open the case.

Kati found it difficult to remember what happened next – events moved so very quickly. She remembered the case falling open to reveal the elegant and delicate machinery within, pulsating and alive with its mysterious beauty and power. Almost in the same instant, her eyes focussed on the details of its construction, planning with devastating precision where the first of many bludgeoning blows would strike. As this decision was being made, she was raising the hammer above her head in a movement reminiscent of the deliberate elevation of an executioner's decapitating blade.

The very next instant totally transformed the static reality around the astrarium into a maelstrom of sound and movement. As Kati's hammer reached its zenith, a very loud click heralded the almost invisible appearance of many thin flexible steel wires, rotating around the astrarium case at incredible speed while cycling rapidly up and down to create a beehive-shaped volume of whirling motion, extending to two metres in diameter and reaching two metres high above the machine. Any object within this dense volume of rotating wire would be struck grievously very many times.

Kati's immediate reaction to the astonishing deployment of these whipping steel wires was to step backwards out of their reach and this is exactly what she did. However, even the fastest human reaction time is not instantaneous. The brain needs to react to sensory information, analyse the event and decide what action to take. Only then will the appropriate limb movement instructions put that decision into practice. By the time Kati stepped backwards to escape the volume of high velocity motion, she had been whipped from head to toe many hundreds of times. Thus, she looked down with bewilderment at sliced clothing and bloodied limbs.

'My face!' She raised her hands to her face and found that this too was wet; inspection of her hands revealed this wetness to be her own blood. Whimpering, she dashed back to her room and, with a feeling of acute dread, peered in her looking glass. Her worst fears were confirmed immediately. Her face and neck were criss-crossed by an extensive matrix of fine cuts, many oozing blood. Similar injuries covered hands, arms and legs as well as other parts of her body that had been exposed when her clothes were cut apart.

Kati's instinct was to scream with terror and sorrow; this is certainly what she would have done in any other circumstance. However she controlled herself with great difficulty because her mother and father would immediately demand to know how she received these injuries and her intention to smash the astrarium would surely be revealed. Sobbing with grief, she removed her pendant and tended to her injuries by gently washing her face, neck and limbs. When she had patted the skin dry, she found that the injuries to her skin were mostly shallow but there were many long and obvious cuts.

Now she needed to decide upon a plausible explanation for her injuries before her parents saw her. She tried to work out a way of implicating her brother but could think of nothing that would ring true. She considered accusing one of the male workers of the attack and injury but had to reject that idea too. 'Too similar to the stable boy affair,' she thought. In the end, she decided she would claim she had slipped near the river and had fallen into a large thorn bush which had scratched her very badly.

Kati now crept downstairs and slipped out of the Manor House. Then, weeping loudly, she entered the Great Hall where the rest of the family were still assembled.

'What is the matter, Kati,' her mother called, 'what has happened to you?' The story about the thorns was told and her mother immediately sent for her nanny. 'She will make sure all your scratches are clean and treat your skin with balm.' She looked closely at the scratches, 'Some of these are quite deep,' she said, 'it will take a long time for the scars to go away.'

Now Kati howled even more loudly! Then her mother spoke again: 'Kati, listen to me, I must ask you an important question before you leave us. We have found the missing medallion here beneath the floorboards. But the gold chain is missing. I want to look at that gold chain that you used for your stone pendant. Are you wearing it now?'

At this, Kati felt a wave of pure panic. 'No, Mother, I'm not wearing it. In fact, I've lost it. I think the chain was so weak it must have broken some time when I was outside. I lost it last week. Anyway, I don't care about it – it was just an ugly old stone.'

'Are you sure you are telling us the truth, Kati, because I think that chain might have come from the medallion. Your father and I have talked about this and he agrees with me.'

'No, Mother, I found that old chain in a trunk in the storeroom. I told you before. Surely you cannot think that I stole the chain? Why would I do that?' Kati burst into fresh weeping. Her mother and father looked at her neutrally.

'Well, if you find it, I want you to bring it to me immediately. There are some special marks on that chain and I will be able to tell right away whether it belongs to the medallion or not.'

Kati was saved from further interrogation by the arrival of her nanny who took her away to treat her wounds. As soon as she reached her room, Kati scooped up the pendant and hid it carefully.

In due course, Kati's brother was informed about Kati's injuries; he also heard her explanation for the cuts and scratches. Of course, he knew exactly what had happened. On returning to his room, he found that his astrarium protection had been deployed and he was pleased to see how effective it had been. On the floor, not far from the astrarium case, lay a small, heavy hammer. The boy picked it up and examined it carefully: 'A lot of damage could have been done with this hammer. I'll keep it as evidence.' The boy put the hammer into a chest. Then, smiling, he dismantled the protection system, knowing it had done its work and would not be required again.

The following morning Kati glared furiously at her brother over the breakfast table. When they had finished she sought him out for a private conversation: 'Look what you've done to me. You've cut me in many places. You've scarred my face, you horrible little boy. I am going to kill you for this!' Kati was deadly serious.

The boy looked at her coldly: 'You've already tried to kill me several times, Kati – and you very nearly succeeded. You certainly hurt me badly many times in my life and made my life a misery. But all that is changed now, because I am no longer afraid of you. Regarding your injuries, I did warn you. And there was a warning notice on the machine. So you have only yourself to blame ...

'Now, here is another warning; listen to it carefully. If you attempt to damage my astrarium again, or arrange for someone else to damage it, I will tell Father how you received these injuries. I will be able to show him your hammer, which you left behind on the floor. I will also tell him about all the other terrible things you have done to me throughout my life. I think you know he will believe me. I leave you to imagine what Father might do, Kati, but I don't think you would be living in this house any more. Personally, I would be quite happy with that outcome.'

As the boy spoke, his eyes never left hers and she felt real fear building up within her. Then the boy continued: 'From now on, I want nothing more to do with you. Stay away from me and do not speak to me. In particular, do not go near my room or my belongings. I know you are evil, Kati.' With that, the boy walked away.

'He's only a stupid little boy!' Kati muttered this as she thought of that recent conversation with her brother. Despite her bravado, she had been shaken by her brother's accurate judgement of her. Her disquiet was not that she had been recognised as evil (she was if anything rather pleased to hear it stated so unequivocally) but rather that her brother had been sufficiently perceptive to recognise that quality in her.

It was abundantly obvious that her brother had changed and Kati knew it would be best if she kept out of his way: 'From now on, I'll just ignore him,' she resolved, 'anyway, I have other important problems to deal with. Maybe later he'll lose his new-found power then I'll deal with him and his precious clock or whatever it is.' In fact, Kati's "other problems" were twofold and she now concentrated her whole mind on these.

First, there was the problem of the pendant. Clearly, if her mother was able to examine the gold chain, she would identify it as belonging to the medallion. In that event, Kati knew that the truth would follow inevitably and she would be fully exposed as the thief. Although in fact the medallion had never been stolen, Kati's utter selfishness and disregard for her parent's property would brand her forever as unworthy of her position as a loved and respected daughter. She had spent many hours trying to concoct various explanations to fit the facts of the medallion "theft" but, in the face of what had happened, she knew that none of these were remotely plausible.

'The only solution is to lose the chain,' she thought, 'and I have already said I have done that.'

So Kati decided that she should act immediately to dispose of the chain. However she was unsure about the stone; should she keep it or throw it away with the pendant?

After making sure that no-one could see what she was doing, Kati retrieved the pendant from its hiding place and removed the chain from the stone, experiencing once again that odd jolt as she handled it. She looked at the stone speculatively: 'Maybe this is a magic stone,' she thought. 'Maybe that's why it makes you feel funny when you touch it. Not many people have a magic stone; I think I'd better keep it, just in case.' So she wrapped the stone in a piece of cloth and put it into an obscure hiding place in her room. Then she took the gold chain and left her room to walk from the Manor House down to the river. Here, she walked a little way upstream and looked around carefully to see if anyone was in sight. Seeing no-one, she quickly took the gold chain from her pocket and, bunching it into a tight little ball, hurled it into the middle of the river. The chain made no sound as it disappeared into the swiftly-flowing water. Kati smiled: 'That's one problem permanently solved!'

Returning to her room, Kati now began to address her second problem – what to do about the stable boy. Her wishes for his punishment had not been fulfilled and she was determined that he was not going to get away with a mere whipping, even although it had been enjoyably severe, plus only 24 hours in the stocks. Kati had attempted to apply proper justice to the situation but her hired assassin had failed to carry out the deserved execution; someone (she knew not who) had prevented her solution from being applied and, as a consequence, the boy was still alive and well. This was completely unsatisfactory and needed to be corrected. She knew she had to act quickly because now that the boy was a convicted criminal, he would surely move away from the area to seek a new life elsewhere. In fact, there was not a moment to lose.

Some hours later, a comprehensive plan had been formulated: 'This time, I'll deal with it myself but I still need others to be involved to prepare the stable boy for his meeting with me.' Kati smiled at the ingenuity of her plan. It took two days to put all the arrangements in place. Kati had been very busy, going several times into the town in the light wagon. At last, the plan was ready to be executed.

So it was that the stable boy received a letter the very next day. Not being able to read, he took it to a kindly shopkeeper and learned that the writer of the letter wished to meet him on the riverside beside the Manor House stable yard at midday the next day. This meeting would be very much to his advantage, the letter said. There was, however, no indication of who the writer might be.

'Well,' the stable boy said to himself, 'I have nothing to lose, have I? Maybe this is someone who can offer me work, perhaps on a remote farm, or somewhere like that.'

The next day, scrubbed clean and dressed in the best clothes he had, the boy walked from the town to present himself at the riverside alongside the wall of the stable yard where he used to work. He arrived there in good time and sat down on a fallen tree trunk to wait for the writer of the letter. He looked sadly at the high wall, remembering how happy he had been when he had worked there. As tears welled up in his eyes, he thought: 'All that is over. Now I am a criminal convicted of a dastardly crime and no-one wants to have anything to do with me.'

The boy was so engrossed in his reverie that he failed to notice four men approaching from the direction of the town. Suddenly, his arms were pinioned from behind and blows began to rain upon his head and body. The boy was strong and fought back as best as he could but he was soon overcome by the ratio of four to one. Systematically, the men beat him unconscious, stripped him and tied him securely to a tree adjacent to the wall of the stables. Then, having placed a gag in his mouth and fastened it tightly, they disappeared, leaving him totally alone and defenceless.

Time passed. The boy stirred, groaned inaudibly because of the gag and began to regain consciousness. As his eyes opened, he saw a pretty girl sitting on a fallen tree opposite him: 'I must be dreaming,' he thought hazily and closed his eyes again. As his consciousness increased, he began to recall what had happened and became aware that he was securely tied to a tree. Looking down, he realised he was naked. Now he looked up again and, sure enough, there was the girl. With considerable shock, he now realised who it was. Miss Kati! He would have spoken the name aloud but could not because of the gag. Kati was watching the boy closely and was pleased to see recognition in his eyes. She rose to her feet and came to stand directly in front of him: 'Well, my little stable boy, now that you are awake I'm going to punish you properly.'

So began the first part of Kati's carefully worked-out plan. With long years of practice on the body of her brother, she was of course an expert in pain. The boy's cries were almost inaudible although, just once, the gag slipped and the boy's hoarse cry rang out before being cut off by the gag's rapid replacement. However, Kati was rather disquieted by the way the boy's eyes never left her face, no matter how much she was hurting him.

There was a disquieting power in these eyes: 'I could blind him so that he couldn't look at me. It would be easy enough to do.' Kati considered this seriously but decided she wanted him to see and be able to anticipate the whole process of his punishment. Thus the boy's eyesight was saved.

Eventually, Kati's appetite for torture was sated and she was ready to move on to the second and final part of her plan: 'Now I am going to kill you, little boy. I'm going to cut your neck and you will bleed to death. It will take a while and I'll sit here and watch you. You deserve this for the crime you committed against me. Afterwards, I'll throw your body in the river and it will be carried away downstream. When your body is found, no-one will care that you have died, because you are just a convicted criminal. And certainly no-one will ever suspect me.' Kati now produced a small knife and twisted his head around to expose the area of the neck below which his carotid artery pulsated strongly.

'Stop!' an authoritative voice roared. Having heard the single cry when the gag slipped, the Head Stableman had recognised the boy's voice and had come through a small door that led from the stable yard to the riverside. Fortuitously, he had been working in the stable yard close to where the door was situated. It took the man only an instant to assess the situation: the naked boy tied to the tree like a sacrifice, the body bruised and bloody in many places – Miss Kati holding his hair with one hand and clutching a small razor-sharp knife with the other, his neck taut and ready to receive the slashing cut that would sever the artery and begin the expiration of his life.

'No, Stop,' the Head Stableman repeated as loudly as he could.

A silence of suspended animation as Kati looked directly into the eyes of the Head Stableman. Then a rapid movement of her hand as she drove the knife into the boy's neck, releasing a powerful spurt of blood.

The scene exploded into action.

The Head Stableman rushed forward with a hoarse cry. Kati dropped the knife and streaked away towards the riverside entrance of the Manor House, plunging through the deep undergrowth beside the stable yard wall. The bound boy strained at his bonds with blood pouring from the ugly wound in his neck. The ground was turning dark with his blood.

The Head Stableman reached the boy as quickly as he could. With one hand, he jerked the gag from his mouth before tearing at the ropes that bound him to the tree. His other hand pressed on the gaping wound in his neck.

'Lord God, let it not be cut.' A prayer thought, not spoken. The man knew if the carotid artery was severed, the blood flow could not be stopped and the boy would die.

Releasing the boy from the ropes, the man lowered him to the ground and immediately examined the wound minutely. To his great relief, he saw that both the carotid artery and the jugular vein were intact. Although the wound was deep, by good fortune the knife had not caused fatal damage.

Gratefully, he cradled the boy in his arms and said: 'You will survive. She did not succeed in cutting your artery. You will recover from this.'

'She did it. Now I remember.' The boy was whispering in an urgent tone.

'What are you saying, boy?' The Head Stablemen spoke gently.

'She wounded the horse. Below the saddle. There was an old block of wood with long rusty nails driven deeply into the horse's back. I saw her lifting the saddle and pulling the nails out, all dripping with blood. I saw her throwing the nails over the stable yard wall. It was horrible. She did it. That's why the horse was out of control. It was wounded and in very great pain. She had caused that pain deliberately.' His voice faded away as his consciousness diminished.

After some time, the Head Stableman managed to diminish the blood flow from the boy's neck and it became possible to move him. The man stripped off his own tunic and shirt and wrapped them around the slight body to keep it warm. Then he lifted the boy in his arms and began to walk towards the riverside gate to the Manor House, where he would seek help. As he walked, he suddenly heard the sound of weeping and, peering through the deep undergrowth in front of the stable yard wall, he saw Kati sitting on the ground.

'Miss Kati,' he called, 'what has happened to you?' Kati stopped weeping: 'You,' she called imperiously, 'Never mind about that stupid criminal boy, he does not matter. Drop him there on the ground. Go immediately to the Manor House and bring my nanny here to me. If you do not obey me immediately I will tell my father to whip you severely.'

The man stepped closer to the girl and was able to see exactly what had happened. As Kati ran through the undergrowth next to the stable wall, she had trodden heavily on something that was concealed in the deep grass. Now the spikes of two very large rusty nails protruded from the top of her right shoe, having entered the sole of the shoe and been driven by her own weight right through the foot it contained. The nails were fixed to a very old and rotten piece of wood, which was now fastened snugly to the sole of her shoe.

The Head Stableman was an intelligent and loyal man who had worked for the Master for many years, starting as a boy and rising to the highest position in the stables. He had always been unfailingly grateful to the Master for his tutelage and support. He had developed a strong belief in obedience towards his superiors and he applied this not only to his direct employer, the Master, but also to the other members of his family and any guests who visited the Manor House. Even the extraordinary nature of what he had just witnessed today would not have altered these deep-seated beliefs. Thus, there is no doubt that the Head Stableman, in loyalty to his employer, would have obeyed the commands of his daughter, no matter how rude and unpleasant she had been to him.

But something had happened. Something that had changed him radically. As the Head Stableman had approached Kati, he found his normal thought processes altered. Looking at her impassively, his brain processed the recent series of events at lightning speed: It was obvious that Kati, the daughter of the Master, had arranged for the stable boy to be attacked by town ruffians hired by her, beaten unconscious, stripped, gagged and tied to a tree in a remote area where few people walked. Clearly, these assailants had been given very precise instructions about what they were to do. – after he had been left alone, trussed up and unconscious, she had come to him and, when he had recovered consciousness, subjected him to an extended period of extreme pain and severe torture. The man knew this because he had heard the boy's cry when the gag slipped; also, the ugly bruises, abrasions and cuts on his body were clear proof of what had happened to him.– she had then attempted to murder him by cutting the artery in his neck. He had seen this with his own eyes. Had she not been interrupted by his call, it is very likely she would have succeeded; she would have kept hacking away within his neck until the artery was severed.– in her flight, she had badly injured her foot by standing on large rusty nails which were protruding dangerously from an old rotten piece of wood. He now knew that these were the same nails she had used to injure (and indirectly kill) her horse. He remembered the pattern of the wounds on the horse's back and linked this positively to what the stable boy had told him a short time ago; after pulling the wood and nails from the horse's flesh, the boy had said she had thrown the horrific item over the stable wall; it would have fallen into this exact area of undergrowth.

The Head Stableman had experience of many people penetrating their flesh with rusty nails. This was recognised in the community as one of the main hazards of life. It was common knowledge that these accidents led to the "lockjaw", a serious and extremely unpleasant illness from which most infected people died. Before death, they suffered weeks of severe illness, during which their bodies were often locked in agonising rigidity. The physicians and barber surgeons who tended to the ills of the people in these days recommended immediate action when such injuries occurred; the sooner the penetrating item was removed from the flesh, the greater the chance of survival.

For many centuries, it was thought that the illness was caused by the action of rusted iron within the wounded flesh; indeed, five more centuries passed before nineteenth century scientists found the cause to be a type of anaerobic bacteria which are able to develop and live in such environments; once transferred to a wound, the bacterium multiplies rapidly and the neurotoxins it releases cause the symptoms of tetanus (lockjaw) to develop.

Although this procession of thoughts through the Head Stableman's brain took only an instant, Kati was screaming at him again: 'Go! What are you waiting for, you stupid man? I will certainly have you whipped for this. I will tell my father to cast you out of the Manor House. I will see to it that you die a beggar.'

Still the man did not move, his eyes fixed on hers: 'No.' This single word spoken quietly.

'What!' Kati was dumbfounded. 'You disobey my command? Now you are finished here. I will speak to my father immediately I see him.'

Silence. Then the man spoke again: 'You may do what you wish, Miss Kati. When I see the Master, I will certainly tell him what you have done today.'

With that, the Head Stableman turned around and, with the boy in his arms, walked to the riverside gate and disappeared within.

The following weeks and months were times of exceptional trauma at the Manor House. On that first day, the Head Stableman took the injured boy to his rooms at the stables and sent for a physician to attend to his injuries. That evening, it was discovered that Kati was missing and an extensive search commenced. When it became clear that she was not within the immediate grounds of the Manor House, the search extended to the areas outside the gates and it was then that Kati was found, still lying in the undergrowth beside the stable wall, unable to move because of the severe injury to her foot. The physician and the surgeon barber were summoned to the Manor House and, in due course, the nails were removed from her foot.

Despite the application of the best medical treatments, Kati began to show the symptoms of lockjaw five days later and this developed into the full-blown disease. She spent the next weeks in various stages of horrific rigidity as the disease took its course. However, because she was a young, strong girl and perhaps because she was receiving the best medical treatments that fourteenth-century medicine could devise, eventually she began to recover slowly. Nevertheless it was many weeks later before she could begin to walk and it was then apparent that the lockjaw plus the injury to her foot had left her with a serious limp. Meanwhile, the other young patient continued to be in the care of the Head Stableman and some trusted workers at the stables. The boy healed quite quickly but was left with a large ugly scar on his neck.

The trauma at the Manor House was not confined to injury and illness. The day following the awful events on the riverbank, the Head Stableman requested a meeting with the Master and intimated that he needed to discuss a series of very serious matters. The spur for this initiative was the presence of the injured boy in his rooms; if the boy was to recover there, he must seek the Master's permission. After all, in the eyes of the law, the boy was convicted of a serious assault crime against his Master's daughter. However, the Head Stableman remembered that the Master had promised to support his plea for lenience in Court; this suggested that he was sympathetic towards the boy. Of course the man was unaware of the Master's unsettling conversation with his daughter which was the true origin of his note to the judge.

The Master received the Head Stableman in his private room that evening.

'Master, I am sorry to bring this report to you,' the Head Stableman began, 'but it is right that you should be aware of the truth of the terrible events that have happened here. Will you permit me to speak the truth?'

'Yes, you may speak and I would welcome the truth, however terrible.'

So the Head Stableman spoke of the events of the previous day; how he had heard the boy's cry, how he had investigated, what he had seen and what had happened thereafter; how, by good fortune, the wound had not been fatal. He told how he had eventually been able to stem the flow of blood. He had then brought the boy to his own livings and called for medical help. Finally, he produced Kati's blood-stained knife and placed it on the Master's table: 'This is the knife she used, Master. She dropped it on the ground as she ran away.'

There was silence as the Master looked sadly at the knife. Then the Head Stableman spoke once more: 'Master, I seek your permission to keep the boy with me until he is well.'

'I give you that permission,' the Master said, 'and thank you for all that you have told me. You may leave me now. We will speak further about the boy after he recovers.'

The Master sat at his desk for a long time with his eyes closed. At last, he stood up and went to the room of his young son and found him studying by the window. 'You have heard what has happened?'

'Nanny told me that Kati is injured and in danger of the lockjaw illness.'

'This is true. She stepped upon some rusty nails on the riverbank and now she is in the hands of the physician. But this is not why I came to speak to you, Son. I have some questions to ask you.'

'Ask, Father, and I will tell you the truth if I know it.'

'My questions are about Kati, Son. When you were younger, did she ever attack you, hurt you?'

The boy was silent for a time, head bowed, his mind racing with memories. Eventually he replied, speaking hesitantly: 'Yes Father, I regret to say that she did. Often. When I was very little and learned to speak, no-one would believe me when I said she hurt me; in fact my nanny and sometimes my Mother punished me for suggesting it. So I soon learned to take the hurt and say nothing.'

It was the man's turn to be silent. Then, in a soft voice: 'The Chinese junk …?'

'She broke it, Father, then told you I had done it.'

'The drowning in the river …?'

'She held my head under the water until I nearly drowned and then threw me naked into a large patch of nettles. I was mad with the pain and jumped back into the river. I did not know what I was doing and swam away into deep water. Kati made no attempt to rescue me. I understand I drowned and my body pulled out of the water by some boys downstream. One of them knew how to bring me back to life.' The man sighed deeply and looked at his son with tears in his eyes.

'My Son, I have been responsible for the pain you have suffered. How will you ever forgive me?'

'Father, my life has been wonderful since you have become my friend, teaching me to swim and giving me the best birthday present that any boy could ever receive. Father, I love you so much!' Father and son embraced.

'Thank you for telling me the truth about your life with Kati.' The man prepared to leave but the boy held up a restraining hand: 'Father, there is one other thing you must know about …'

The boy now told his father about Kati's threats to destroy his precious and valuable astrarium from the very day of his birthday. He explained how he had developed and installed a system of protection within the case of the instrument and showed his father a drawing of the mechanism and a sample of the steel wire he had used. He then told how Kati had actually attacked the instrument on that day when the medallion was found under the sleeping platform in the Great Hall: 'You will remember how we were all fully occupied by that search.' He produced the hammer that she had abandoned on the floor

273

when she rushed from the room, after being extensively but superficially injured by the whipping wires of the protection system. 'I did warn her personally,' the boy concluded, 'and there was a clear warning notice on the machine but I knew it was almost inevitable that she would disregard my warning. I had to protect my wonderful astrarium.'

The man was devastated by this news. His own daughter bent on destroying an extremely valuable instrument which had cost him a considerable part of his wealth! It was unbelievable, heart-breaking. After a final embrace the man thanked his son once again and stumbled from the room. Seeking out his wife, he recounted all that he had heard from the Head Stableman about Kati. Then he added the account of his son's sufferings at the hands of his daughter, finishing up with her attempt to destroy the astrarium. After he had finished, holding his head in his hands, he said: 'How can she have done all these terrible things? How can I have been so duped? The terrible thing is – there is even more I must speak about to you.'

His wife listened carefully as her husband now told her about his conversation with Kati when she tried to persuade him to permit her to attend the trial of the stable boy: 'Suddenly it seemed that the boy's crime had been to speak to her without permission. The boy always insisted that he had never touched her – in fact he was never near her, because he was the one who caught the horse and calmed it. This was confirmed by the other stable hand who still works here. It was this other man who went to Kati's aid when she fell. This is what the Head Stableman said in the Court when he was giving evidence. I have become convinced that the boy has been severely punished for a crime he did not commit. In fact – I must go further – punished for a crime that never existed! Kati's accusation was a complete lie.'

Husband and wife sat together wordlessly for some time. Finally the woman spoke, her tones calm and practical:

'Listen, Husband, at this time, we do not know what will happen to our daughter. In the circumstances, it is not unlikely that she will develop the lockjaw disease; this is what the physician and the barber surgeon have told us. The rusty nails were within her foot for many hours. So we must now wait for the Lord's judgement upon her. Once that judgement has been delivered, if she is still alive, we will know that the Lord has transferred the next part of the judgement to us. Meanwhile, we should wait and make sure that our daughter has the best treatment for her ills. Regarding the stable boy, it is clear that he should remain at the stable yard in the care of the Head Stableman and others. It will be for you to decide what should happen to him in the longer term.'

Several months crept past on the leaden feet of worry. Kati's illness took its course and eventually she was able to return slowly towards a semblance of good health. When she was at last able to limp rather painfully around the Manor House and the immediate grounds, her father and mother sought her out for a private conversation.

They all sat around a table and her father spoke quietly and without emotion: 'Kati, your mother and I are pleased that you have been able to recover from your illness. However we have been appalled to learn of your actions towards the stable boy on the day you were injured on the riverbank. We know everything that happened, Kati. We also know how you have hurt and abused your brother over the years. For instance, we know that you almost succeeding in killing him when you took him swimming in the river – and we know how he came to be stung by nettles so severely. Finally, we know about your attack on your brother's very valuable astrarium – you bear the marks of that attempt on your face and body, Kati, and will do so for the rest of your life.'

Kati interrupted her father by bursting into tears and saying: 'Father, all you have said is not true. I have not done any of these things ...'

'Be quiet, Kati, I suggest you should not attempt to deny anything I have said because I know that everything I have said is true. Furthermore, I suspect that you instigated at least some of the other bad things that happened here over the years. However, I have heard enough and your mother and I have come to a decision about you. It is clear that you cannot stay here because your murderous actions would come to light sooner or later and I would be required to hand you over to the town authorities for justice. I cannot have the good name of the family besmirched in this way.'

Kati was terrified. What was to happen to her? Her father was speaking again but her hearing had been temporarily disconnected from her brain.

'Do you?' Her father was looking at her quizzically.

'Sorry, Father, I ...'

'Do you remember Master Ottvid? He is a very rich merchant who lives over the mountains.'

'Yes, Father, I do.' She remembered a rather small portly man who had a serious speech impediment and would not look anyone in the eye. Her father had introduced her to him and she had treated him with extreme rudeness and contempt. As a result, the unfortunate man became more and more tongue-tied and uncomfortable in the face of her aggression towards him. She had thought he was pathetic in every way! But why was her father speaking about this peculiar little man? Kati's brain raced. Then, suddenly, she knew! Father would send her to this Master Ottvid and she would live with his family. There would be children to bully, perhaps. Certainly there would be servants to abuse. She would be very nice to Master Ottvid and he would give her a lot of money to spend. Kati cheered up considerably but controlled herself carefully. Her mother and father must not see that she was pleased!

'Kati!' Her father's voice was sharp and brought her back to reality. 'Are you listening to me? What is wrong with you? You should be listening carefully because this affects your future.'

'I am very sorry, Father. I have developed a sudden pain in my head.'

'I will tell you again, Kati. Listen! Master Ottvid is a very rich merchant. You are very fortunate indeed that he has agreed to marry you …' – her father's voice droned on but Kati heard nothing more. Her mind was in turmoil once again. 'Marry! Marry! Marry Master Ottvid! No! No!' Her thoughts were hysterical. She could not possibly do that. She did not want to marry. She did not want anything to do with men. She had told her father that many times and he had always said: "Don't worry. I would never force you to do anything."

As she thought this, Kati cut across what her father was saying and blurted: 'But Father, you always said you would never force me to do anything.'

Her father sighed deeply: 'I said that in the days when I thought I had a daughter who was kind and gentle. Now I find I have a daughter who is cruel and selfish. Listen to me, Kati. You will marry Master Ottvid and this will happen as soon as it can be arranged. Then you will go to live in the town over the mountains with your husband and you will not return here, ever again. Do you understand?'

Kati wept. However she knew that her presence at the Manor House and, indeed, in the local area, was now untenable. She recognised that she was in danger of being arrested and brought to Court so she must now make her escape as soon as possible. But marry Master Ottvid? That was unthinkable … or was it? Now her mind began to rampage through the new situation into which she found herself catapulted. Master Ottvid was a pathetic weak little man who could not even speak properly. She could dominate him! Yes, she was sure she could do that. From the beginning she would be cold and haughty and order him about. She would treat him like a dog. And she would make it clear from the outset that she would have nothing to do with sexual coupling, whatever that involved. She would insist that she lived in a separate part of his house, have her own servants and be given plenty of money to spend on what she liked: 'Yes,' Kati mused, 'this can be the start of a wonderful new life for me.' She felt quite elated.

'Do you understand?' Her father repeated his question.

'Yes, Father.' Kati was demure. 'Of course I will always do as you wish.'

The wedding was hastily arranged for the following month and life became extremely busy at the Manor House. As befitted an important family in the region, it had to be a lavish affair with hundreds of guests invited from the local area and from the town over the mountains where Master Ottvid lived. Kati's father invited Master Ottvid to come to the Manor House and make further acquaintance with his future wife but the merchant's business commitments prevented this; he would only be able to arrive on the day of the wedding. However he sent a letter to Kati which she received the following week:

> Dear Miss Kati,
>   I am greatly honoured that you have agreed to marry me. I know that we have met only once before when I was visiting your father on business. At that time, I gained the impression that you did not choose to like me much. However, I think you are a very attractive person and very suitable to join me in my life as my wife. I will do my very best to make you happy and I am sure that you will find life with me very rewarding.
> Your humble servant,
> Gar Ottvid

Alone in her room, Kati smiled wolfishly:

'Yes, my little man! You will indeed do your best to make me happy! I will make sure you do. Once I have you to myself, I'll soon have you trained like a dog.'

The day of the wedding arrived. Early in the day, Master Ottvid rode in with his friends and supporters. All were taken off for a morning meal in the Manor House where they were welcomed by Kati's father, who was in fine spirits. He knew that Kati's marriage to Master Ottvid was an almost perfect solution to all his problems. Secretly, he felt a little sorry for the bridegroom.

'I hope he learns to stand up to Kati,' he thought, 'at least occasionally. But perhaps she will be sensible and just manipulate him cleverly.' For Gar Ottvid's sake, he hoped so.

By contrast, the bridegroom was clearly feeling tense and nervous. Despite the support of his friends, his stammer and shifty manner were just as bad as ever and he wouldn't look anyone in the eye as he tried to force out the words he was attempting to articulate. Kati's father looked at him with sympathy and hoped that the little man would be able to cope satisfactorily at the wedding ceremony. 'I do hope Kati will be nice to him,' he thought – although he suspected she would not. 'At least she cannot upset him before the betrothal ceremony.' Traditionally, the bride and bridegroom were kept apart – they would not meet until the ceremony in the afternoon.

The time arrived and all was in readiness. The priest and his assistants were in place. The bridegroom took his place and awaited his bride. She came, deeply veiled, on the arm of her father. The ceremony proceeded and bride and bridegroom were borne through it on the usual gossamer wings of unreality that are so often a characteristic of such events. The bridegroom was deeply grateful to find that he could speak his words of promise with clarity. 'I wish I could speak like that always,' he could not help thinking.

The ceremony over, the veil was lifted from her face and she turned contemptuous and hostile eyes upon the man who was now her husband, expecting his gaze to be firmly fixed on the floor. It was not. Two calm grey eyes were looking deeply into hers; eyes so powerful that she had to look away, feeling a pang of bewilderment.

With so many guests and well-wishers, both bride and bridegroom were kept very busy in the next few hours and had little opportunity to speak or be together. The banquet had to be served and eaten, much wine drunk and long speeches made. Master Ottvid was now is extremely good spirits, laughing and joking, looking confident and, to everyone's surprise, speaking quite fluently. On the other hand, Kati sat confused. This was not the Gar Ottvid she had expected to marry.

She looked at him and suddenly had the explanation: 'It's the effect of the wine! That's why he's so much more confident. He'll revert to his usual nervous and inarticulate self when the wine wears off. I'll need to make sure he doesn't drink wine in future. I'll deal with that tomorrow. I will forbid it.' Kati sat back and smiled. 'I'm really clever at solving problems,' she thought.

It was evening and time for the departure of the bride and bridegroom. Kati had changed into travelling clothes and boarded the large covered wagon that her husband had brought with him. As befitted a rich and important man, he would make the journey on horseback. Kati was exhausted by the events of the day and, despite the bumpy and uncomfortable progress of the wagon, she quickly fell into a fitful sleep and did not waken until they arrived at her husband's home town. Of course the wagon also carried all Kati's possessions in several large trunks. Just before leaving, Kati had suddenly remembered her "magic stone" and ran to recover it from its hiding place. She kept the stone in its wrapping of cloth and placed it in a deep pocket of her clothes.

Darkness had descended by the time Kati arrived at her new home. She was pleased to note that her husband's home was a very fine manor house, as far as she could see, considerably larger than her own family home. It was also gratifying to see that there were many servants to greet them. As soon as the wagon came to a halt, ignoring her husband completely, Kati alighted and addressed the assembled servants in icy tones: 'I shall retire immediately to my rooms. Take me there immediately.'

'Mistress, I am the Housekeeper,' a tall lady dressed in black replied, 'I shall take you there now.'

Kati glared at the woman: 'I don't care who you are, just conduct me to my rooms.'

Her rooms were large, spacious and very lavish, containing everything that Kati could possibly want. There was a large bedroom, an adjoining dressing room and a pleasant sitting room next door.

'Leave me,' Kati snapped to the woman, 'send my personal maids to me and tell my husband that I do not wish to see him tonight.' The woman bowed and left. When the maids came shortly after, she ordered them curtly to prepare a bath for her. After a long and leisurely bathe, Kati donned her sleeping chemise and prepared for bed. As she undressed, she remembered her magic stone, took it from her gown, unwrapped it and placed it on a convenient dresser: 'Maybe it will bring me luck,' she thought, 'although I don't think I need luck now!'

Her orders to her maids were equally curt and unpleasant: 'Go! Bring food and drink to me one hour after sunrise tomorrow. Make sure it is properly prepared or you will be punished.'

'Yes, Mistress.' The frightened maids departed.

Kati stretched out on the soft and very comfortable bed.

'This is the start of a new and wonderful beginning for me, just as I planned. Here I am, a very rich wife, married to a pathetic little dog of a husband. I'll just study him carefully for a little while and then I can work out what are the best ways to make him terrified of me. I'll find all the best ways to hurt him, physically and mentally. And I'll do the same with all the servants – they will soon be dancing exactly to my tune.' Kati drifted off into a luxurious and happy sleep, looking forward to the wonderful and totally fulfilled life she was starting.

It was the strengthening daylight that woke her. She stirred and opened her eyes, just a little. Light streamed through the partially opened window shutters. It was morning! She had slept blissfully throughout the night. Now she lay without moving, luxuriating in the moment. Finally she opened her eyes fully for the first time and began to examine the large room, noting its very spacious proportions, its fine decoration and expensive ornamentation: 'Beautiful,' she breathed.

'Yes, isn't it?' Kati started and jerked her head around to identify the origin of the voice. Her incredulous gaze came to rest on a figure sitting in a large carved chair not far from her bed. It was her husband, although, in a way, she hardly recognised him. Yes, he was still the same small man that she had married yesterday but, now lightly dressed, he looked much more solid and muscular. Also, the voice she heard was not weak, stammering and hesitant but strong, powerful and without impediment. Even more startling was the fact that he was actually looking directly at her, steadily and confidently, his lips set in a slight smile.

'What are you doing in my room?' Kati's voice was shrill. 'I told that servant that I did not want to see you. She must be punished for this ...'

His voice cut across her hysterical tones: 'I am here in your room because I am your husband. You belong to me now. I can come and go as I please in my own house.'

Suddenly remembering that the only garment she was wearing was the thin sleeping chemise, Kati drew the bed covers up to her chin and lay with only head and whitened knuckles visible: 'Go away! You are not allowed here while I am in bed. Go away or I will call the servants.'

The man laughed: 'I have told the servants to stay away from this part of the Manor House until I instruct them further. As your husband, I have business with you; we have things to talk about and there are things that I intend to do with you.'

Kati was horrified! Was he talking about sexual coupling? He must be! She had long decided that she would not permit this and had intended to inform him as soon as possible. 'No, you must not. I will not allow it. Keep away from me.' Kati burst into hysterical tears.

The man waited until she had quieted down. Then he spoke in calm, level tones: 'Listen to me very carefully. I understand that you have already been rude and unkind to the servants. You will not do this again. The servants are to be treated with respect. I remind you again that you are my wife and I will enter your room any time I like; or I may order you to come to my rooms, if this pleases me. As my wife, you will do exactly what I want you to do; you will do it today, tomorrow and for the rest of your life. If you don't obey me and please me in every respect, you will have reason to be very sorry indeed.'

'What would you do?' Kati's voice was spirited. 'I will contact the law authorities here and report your misdemeanours and then …'

'Be quiet!' Her husband's voice was like the crack of a heavy whiplash. Measured tones followed. 'This is what I would do. I would take you back across the mountains to the town you came from. There, I would hand you over to the town authorities to be examined for the serious crimes that I know you have committed there. I understand that the court and prison authorities there have interesting ways of dealing with the bodies and minds of fourteen-year-old girls who try to avoid the justice they deserve. Ways, my Dear Wife, that even you may never have imagined.'

For the first time in her life, Kati was totally frozen in horror, lying rigid, her eyes staring sightlessly into his in complete disbelief, her mind short-circuited in utter capitulation and defeat. Minutes passed; there was no hurry. Then the man said quietly: 'Now we will begin the first part of what I have come to do.' From his pocket he withdrew a compact multi-tailed whip of fine medium-weight leather and strode purposely towards the bed.

Kati's eyes were fixed upon this fearful implement as it occupied larger and larger proportions in her field of vision. Then, as her husband reached the bed and seized the bed covers with a powerful fist, her eyes refocused past the whip to the glowing Stone visible on the dresser; in that instant, a dreadful understanding began to dawn in her mind: 'My God,' she whispered, almost to herself, 'you've changed. Suddenly. You, all of you, have become exactly like …'

Her final utterance was drowned out by the unique sound of leather thongs striking uncovered flesh at high velocity.

CONTINUATIO II

It is obvious that a stone has no memory, even if it has a distinct history that could translate into a memory when it was formed over millions of years. In such processes, large objects are sometimes preserved intact as recognisable fossils of what they were, now presenting as replicas in stone. These cause great amazement when found by the intelligent minds of humanity. However, in most cases, the large prehistoric constructions are split and broken apart, crushed, extruded and reformed in ways that have already been described in an earlier section. The origin of the constructions remain an unchanging reality but their precise existence is not preserved anywhere but in memory; so if there is no memory, then all is lost ... or is it?

The Stone is an example of notable exception. It had been completely reformed and, as an inert entity, it had no memory. However, it had a mysterious *awareness*. At the core of this awareness was the conviction that its birth had been within a growing living construction, one which became larger and larger until its influence was overbearing. Growth, life, means energy is involved.

In many ways, it seems that energy is there to be captured and utilised. It is clear that humanity have been ingenious over the centuries, indeed, the millennia, in doing just that. Generally, energy is power to control – but not all energy is like that. Some energy is like that associated with the Stone; predestined, powerful, never to be controlled by mankind.

So the Stone stirred, not with physical movement but with the mysterious movement of that energy within. In the Stone's awareness, it "knew" its part, its role, was to belong; to become possessed by a member of the human race. With the possession of the Stone, an essential, unbreakable link would be formed and the power focussed precisely to become a mysterious beam of influence. An influence that will always, in a very real sense, change everything.

And the Lord God commanded the man:
    "You are free to eat from any tree in the garden: but you must not eat from the tree of the knowledge of good and evil, for when you eat of it, you will surely die"

Genesis Chapter 2 Verses 16-17.
The Holy Bible, New International Version (The Bible Society, 1973)

PART THREE

Julian

It was a busy day at the sandwich bar. The boy behind the counter was alone and flustered. 'Was it a ten or a twenty you gave me?'

'A twenty,' Julian replied immediately.

The boy hesitated and looked despairingly into the drawer of his till. 'Are you sure?'

'Absolutely!' Julian always believed in being positive about these things. Pocketing the change from the transaction and clutching the brown paper bag containing sandwich and bottle of water, he walked out the door, smiling broadly, and waited on the kerb for the traffic to stop at the red light thirty metres up the road. When the traffic light did its work, Julian and many others streamed across the wide road and entered the public park through its large wrought-iron gates. This was a part of the day that Julian always enjoyed – his lunch break. 'That office can be a bit stuffy and so it's a real treat to get out at lunch time and come to the park.' This was a thought that came to him almost every day – every day, that is, that the weather was suitable for eating lunch outside.

As always, the park was busy but Julian usually managed to find a place on one of the many park benches. Today was no exception; look, there was a place on a comfortable wooden bench, next to a pretty girl! Julian smiled at the pleasure to come. 'I'll be my usual friendly and charming self and she will be enchanted.' This pleasing thought came to him with smug satisfaction. He considered he had a special way with the opposite sex. However his smile faded as he noticed a grim middle-aged "businesswoman-type" approaching from the other direction. It was all too obvious that she was steering a direct course towards the bench in that particularly determined way that middle-aged businesswomen have!

Julian quickened his pace to a shambling trot and arrived just in time to plant his bottom on the vacant seat as the middle-aged lady was on "final approach" for a landing on that same seat; Julian was reminded of the majestic landing manoeuvre of a jumbo-jet. This thought amused him and he gave a little private smile, greatly admiring the inventiveness of this imagination.

Even when faced with such a frustrating situation, it is true that many people in the world would not seek to engage with it but would pass by without overt comment. However, middle-aged businesswomen are unlikely to be so retiring!

'Young Man, you have just taken my seat,' she roared in a loud and frightening voice. Even the birds hushed as everyone in the immediate vicinity fell silent and looked around; with the vivid curiosity of humankind, all were fascinated to see how this confrontation would now develop.

Julian knew that he was a very kind-hearted and generous person. After all, did he not help old ladies across the street when it was required? Was he not always kind, pleasant and honest in everything he did? He squinted up at this formidable lady and addressed her in a smooth and pleasant voice: 'Madam, I am very sorry you seem to be upset but I'm afraid you have misunderstood the situation. I was sitting beside my friend here (he indicated the pretty girl next to him) and I left my seat to retrieve somebody's hat that had blown away in the wind. I have just returned at this moment to resume my seat.'

Julian was taken aback when the businesswoman looked quizzically at the girl and spoke to her: 'I thought I knew all your friends. Who is this?'

'I've never seen him in my life before, Aunt Matilda,' the girl replied.

This reply imposed a dramatic hiatus upon the scene as the information was received and processed by all who were listening intently.

Release was provided when a new voice moved the action forward: 'You are welcome to have this seat.' A boyish young man who had been sitting at the other end of the bench now stood up and was smiling at the businesswoman. 'I'm quite happy to sit on the grass.' So saying, he moved several metres away and sank down on the grass, returning his attention to the slim eReader tablet in his hand.

'Thank you for your kindness and generosity,' the woman called to the young man before sitting down heavily on the bench beside her niece. As she did so, she unleashed a ferocious glare upon Julian. This, however, was totally wasted because Julian had been quick to turn his back on the girl, at the same time expertly wiping the details of the recent situation from his mind. Julian was very skilled and experienced in such matters.

'Time for my free lunch,' he was thinking equably. 'I hope tomorrow will be another fine day so that I can enjoy another free lunch in the park. I'll go back to the sandwich shop and spend the other five euro I was given by mistake. That boy will have a little problem today when it's time to cash-up; he really should be more careful.' Julian smiled proudly, well pleased with his victory.

Now sitting completely at ease in the warm sunshine and fortifying himself with his tasty (free) sandwich, Julian reviewed his life with considerable satisfaction. He held an important position in his workplace, a large legal firm that dealt primarily in commercial matters. As Head of Document Control – the department was known as "DC" throughout the Firm – he knew that everyone depended upon him to provide them with the correct paperwork for the particular task they were about to carry out. Absolute accuracy was essential and a high standard was called for and expected.

'Well, there are mistakes very occasionally,' he conceded, 'but that is of course inevitable in such a complex organisation.' If pressed on matters of error, this is how he always responded, smiling charmingly. Apart from that occasional admission on behalf of his department, Julian always claimed that DC was extremely efficient. This, he said, was due to the quality of his personal management and organisational skills: 'I am very skilled at recruiting good quality staff and training them to the highest levels,' he would insist to the Partners and senior lawyers of the firm, 'that is why you find our operations so reliable.'

Now in his early thirties, Julian had been employed by this large legal firm for around eight years. When he talked of his employment with the firm, he presented quite a rosy picture of his recruitment, followed by a rapid progress through the ranks: 'I agreed to come here after I had completed my Law degree,' he often said loftily, 'and they were very pleased to be able to recruit a person of my quality.'

However, the reality was actually quite different.

Julian's father was a skilled and successful solicitor and it had been planned that his only son would follow in his footsteps. The family were rich and lived in a large and expensive house where they wanted for nothing. As a child, Julian was thoroughly spoiled and his every desire was provided by his doting parents. From his youngest schooldays, Julian had been sent to the best schools and it was expected that he would study at his father's "old" university, a prestigious establishment that had a significant reputation for its Law courses. Having gained an excellent degree, like his father had, Julian would then become a top-class solicitor.

However this plan and strategy did not work out as expected. Over the years of his boyhood, the various schools saddled with a lazy, reluctant and far-from-bright Julian worked tirelessly on him (as such schools do) and eventually managed to secure him a place at the prestigious university of his father's choice – the establishment that he himself had attended. Here, Julian was to study Law.

In fact his acceptance at the university was touch-and-go, with his father and others having to plead the boy's case to the Selection Panel. Fortuitously, some of those on the Panel were old friends of Julian's father. So the indolent and conceited Julian was enrolled at the university, unaware that he had almost been rejected; his father did not wish to upset him by informing him of this. Predictably, the subsequent Honours Degree Law course had not gone well and Julian had been very lucky to acquire a degree at the end of it; the award was at the very lowest level – a mere Pass Degree.

This was the reason that Julian was not a practicing lawyer but worked at an administrative level. All attempts to join a law firm as a trainee solicitor had failed totally when his prospective employers read his C.V. While Julian had acquired a superficial sophistication, a combination of his poor C.V. and his uninspired technical performance at interview was enough to preclude him from any of the solicitor posts he applied for. While his father was deeply disappointed, Julian himself was largely unconcerned: 'I believe life is here to be enjoyed,' he often told himself, 'I'm sure I really don't need to work my fingers to the bone just to earn a living. If they don't want me as a solicitor (and I'm sure that's just because they have a prejudice against me), something else will come along. After all, I am an intelligent and personable fellow; whoever gets me as an employee will be very lucky.' Modesty was not one of Julian's virtues!

After some time, now with the help of his father's contacts, Julian was employed in a junior administration post in the large legal firm where he still worked. In time, his veneer of sophistication and unjustified confidence in himself gained him several promotions within this firm; some managers can be fooled by superficial qualities such as Julian's. Then, by scheming, dishonesty and some luck, he finally managed to land the job of Head of Document Control (HDC), a medium-rank position in the organisation. Here, he gained a small, dingy office of his own and had a group of mainly junior staff working for him. He also gained a small, rather cramped parking space in the underground garage of the building. Whereas Julian had previously arrived by bus, he now took great pleasure in shoehorning his rather elderly 3-Series BMW into this space. As he did so, he usually thought: 'A suitable high quality car for an excellent senior manager.'

In actuality, Julian was a poor manager. In addition, he was personally disorganised and suffered from a poor memory. Most seriously, he was lazy and unreliable; he took no pride in his own work and had absolutely no regard for detail or timeliness. Consequently, he often made mistakes, some of which were very serious and cost his Firm a lot of money in loss of trust, as well as lost or cancelled contracts. However, his cunning led him to conceal his errors carefully, usually by passing the blame to his subordinates in DC.

Because of all these problems, DC suffered from a frequent turnover of junior staff; many were dismissed in disgrace from their posts for committing serious errors, although often they were blameless, while others were sufficiently perceptive to recognise the degree of scapegoating that was swirling around the department and arranged to leave before the axe could fall upon them.

In such cases of inefficiency and poor management at the top, there has to be someone competent in a position of authority, someone who can adequately hold the departmental functions together. This "someone" was the Deputy Head of DC, Margarite, who was considerably more organised than Julian, in addition to being significantly more intelligent. Even so, Margarite did not escape the effects of Julian's inefficiencies. Periodically, she was rather irritated to be blamed for DC errors that she knew she had not made. However, in her loyalty to Julian, she always accepted the blame without demur, remembering that everyone is bound to make mistakes occasionally: "Nobody's perfect!" This was a favourite saying of Margarite's. Secretly, however, she was convinced she was fairly close to infallible!

At this time, Margarite had worked with Julian for three years – ever since he had been promoted to be HDC. She had also been a candidate for the post, having already been Deputy HDC for two years but, as so often happens to those who occupy second-in-command posts, she fell victim to the popular attraction of "fresh blood" and was passed over. When Julian arrived to take up post, relations between HDC and his deputy were a little strained at first but his charm and good looks soon solved any suggestion of animosity. Thereafter, they had developed a close relationship; so close that they had shared his flat (and his bed) for the last two years.

It was here in the cosiness of this small flat that Margarite had developed a love for the slim and handsome Julian. For his part, he was unsurprised by her love and accepted it with neutral equanimity. He admitted to himself that it was very pleasant to have someone with whom to share life, to eat and drink together, to exchange thoughts and opinions.

However, although Margarite shared her most innermost thoughts, Julian was generally private and reticent in personal matters. When Margarite commented rather plaintively that he kept his thoughts secret, he would smile at her and say:

'Well, not everyone is a chatterbox like you. You know I can hardly get a word in!'

Shortly after they started to live together, Julian had made it a rule that they should not talk about the work that they shared. Margarite was a little taken aback but was content to allow Julian to have his way.

On the other hand, Julian was always happy enough to share a bed with Margarite: 'You are a lovely woman,' he would tell her affectionately, especially after their lovemaking, which was almost invariably instigated by Margarite. Sometimes, especially on a Sunday when they did not go to work, Margarite would waken early and look with pleasure and tender love upon the still-sleeping Julian, admiring his handsome features and the contours of his masculine body. By contrast, Julian rose from bed as soon as he wakened, rarely glancing at Margarite, whether still sleeping or not.

'You don't love me,' she would sometimes complain.

'You know I do,' he would reply, usually perfunctorily.

A Monday morning, grey and drizzly outside. Julian answering his telephone:

'HDC.' This said crisply. 'Ah yes, Oberto, I will come right away.' A hush fell in the General Office of DC as Julian strode across the room to poke his head into Margarite's office – not much more than a cubbyhole in the corner of the room: 'I have been called to see Oberto. I'm going there now.' He left before she could respond.

The elevator carried him smoothly upwards to the top floor of the building where the senior staff worked. Julian walked along a wide corridor, thickly carpeted, until he arrived at a large, polished wooden door. The sign read 'Senior Partner.'

Julian knocked and entered. The Senior Partner's Personal Assistant, an unsmiling woman about Julian's age, was typing at breakneck speed at her computer keyboard. She ignored Julian's presence.

'Excuse me,' Julian said. The woman continued to type.

'Excuse me.' Louder. Still no action for a few moments; then the woman sighed and turned towards him: 'Yes?'

Julian looked at the woman with dislike.

'Oberto wants to see me.'

The woman turned to her computer screen. 'When is your appointment?'

'I don't have an appointment. Oberto called me and asked me to come up.'

The woman sighed again: 'You can't see the Senior Partner without an appointment,' she intoned and turned back to her keyboard.

Julian felt his face reddening: 'Would you tell Oberto that HDC is here.'

'HDC? What's HDC? I've never heard of it.'

'Head of Document Control, HDC, my name is Julian.' He knew he was shouting.

'All right, all right, no need to get excited,' the woman was now saying. With bad grace, she picked up a telephone handset: 'Someone called HDC is here. He says you asked him to come.' She listened. 'Well, if only you would tell me what you're doing, we could all work together more effectively.' So saying, the woman slammed down the handset. As she turned back towards her keyboard, she gestured briefly towards a door.

The office was huge and lavishly furnished. The Senior Partner was a small bald man – a friend of his father who had known Julian since he was a child. 'Ah, Julian,' he waved a welcoming hand, 'come and sit down.'

'Good morning, Oberto. Who's the dragon?' Julian jerked his thumb towards the door he had just entered.

'Oh, don't worry about that. She's a very good secretary,' the Senior Partner said absent-mindedly, shuffling through many papers on his desk.

'Ah, yes. Here it is.' He turned to Julian. 'We have a very important contract coming up. It's worth half a million to us. So we need to be sure to get everything right – and that certainly includes the documentation. Here are the details. I need a full and totally complete documentation pack first thing tomorrow morning. Any problems with that?'

'Of course not, Oberto. Could you send your PA to pick up the pack at 0900 tomorrow?' Julian was determined to get his own back on the unpleasant woman in the outer office.

The Senior Partner acquiesced and made a note in his diary. 'Fine, Julian. You make sure personally that the documents are correct. No mistakes, please. It's too important.'

Julian left Oberto's office. As he passed the unpleasant secretary, still ostentatiously rattling away at her keyboard, he called to her in an authoritative voice: 'See you tomorrow at my office. 0900 hours. Room 156a. Don't be late!' He left with a covert grin before she had time to reply.

Julian strode back purposefully to his office. On reaching his desk he called Margarite's office:

'Margarite, can you come and see me? We have an important priority.' A few moments later, Margarite arrived and they sat down together to examine the requirement for the documentation pack. Finally, Julian sat back: 'You know, I think this will be a very good training exercise for the staff. They should learn quite a lot from this.'

Margarite looked worried: 'Do you think we should involve everyone? Doesn't that increase the chance of getting something wrong? That's the last thing we can afford to do, is it not?'

As always, Julian was resolute: 'Nonsense. Everything will be fine. We'll do this as a training exercise.' He held up his hand as Margarite was about to speak again. 'No, let's not discuss it any further. I have decided. Follow me.'

Julian now strode into the General Office, followed by a solemn Margarite.

'Attention, everyone.' The office became quiet. 'We have an important job to complete before tomorrow morning and I want everyone to be involved. Margarite will allocate all the tasks you have to do but I have decided that Jana will be the Base Co-ordinator.' Julian looked at a young slim blonde girl who looked both pleased and apprehensive to be singled out for this extra responsibility.

Julian continued: 'Jana, you will raise the initial document pack and we'll build from there. This will be a full and comprehensive pack, so we will need to use the deep A3 format. Is that clear?' He looked piercingly at the girl, who blushed and nodded. 'While Jana starts that, the rest of you wait for instructions from Margarite.'

'Julian, could I have a word?' Margarite indicated her small office.

'Why Jana?' Margarite's first question.

'Oh, I thought it was about time she took on some responsibility. Had her confidence built up again. She was reprimanded for a serious mistake a while back, wasn't she?'

'Yes, although it was never positively established that it was her fault.'

Julian looked at Margarite sharply: 'Of course it was her fault! I investigated the matter and that was the outcome.'

Julian now became even more authoritative: 'Right, here are the details of what we need. Could you look through it and get the others organised. Make sure you pick the right people for the tasks. You know we cannot afford to make any mistakes.

I will need the completed pack on my desk at the end of today so that I may carry out the final HDC signoff check.' Without another word, Julian left and returned to his office where he relaxed and read a tabloid newspaper contentedly, checking his watch to see how long it was until lunch time.

So it was a day of high activity in DC. Staff were instructed and despatched to stores and filing rooms to return with carefully-checked items. The large and sturdy document pack on Jana's small desk grew throughout the day with items meticulously checked against the comprehensive Document List that had been drawn up initially by the Senior Partner's legal and administrative staff, then refined, added to and cross-checked by Margarite in DC, with further lists and sub-lists made and checked off. It was an impressive example of staff organisation and Margarite felt quite proud as she watched her staff (very much her protégés) scurrying around.

Unusually, she decided that staff lunch breaks should be taken in groups, so that the office was always manned by several people. This, she told them, was to ensure that nothing went amiss. The young staff were pleased and excited by this important task, their flushed, cheerful faces reflecting their delight. In the centre of this web of activity was the slight figure of Jana, also flushed with pleasure; having been allocated such an important role in the procedure, she felt she had been redeemed.

As the afternoon progressed, the document pack began to take on impressive proportions. All the items within it were filed within folders and sub-folders, each folder fronted by clear and concise document lists. All the folders were arranged in a specified order, so that the legal team could quickly lay their hands on whatever they required. Everything was topped by a master list, a sheet of high quality heavyweight paper printed with the proud masthead of the Firm and then with a bold sub-heading declaring 'Document Control Department.' Eventually, it would be this impressive paper that HDC himself would sign before releasing the pack to the legal staff – in this case, no less than the Senior Partner himself. By late afternoon, the pack was completed, checked by Margarite and ready for transit to HDC. All staff agreed that it had been a great day in the department.

The large pack was carried almost ceremoniously to Julian's office. At the knock, Julian hurriedly concealed the newspaper he had been reading and called:

'Come in.' The door opened and the pack was carried in by Jana, followed by Margarite.

'Ah, yes, just put it on my desk. I'll be checking that later. First, I have some other work I must do.' The girl left and Julian addressed Margarite:

'Is everything checked? Can you guarantee no mistakes?'

'Everything is checked,' she replied firmly.

'Just go home ahead of me,' Julian now said, 'I want to finish something and then I'll sign off the pack.'

'Are you sure?' Margarite was anxious. 'I could stay and help you.'

He looked at her coldly: 'No thanks. I'm perfectly capable of doing it myself.'

Margarite knew the meaning of Julian's tone. It meant: "Go away and leave me alone!"

'I wonder why,' she thought, 'no good arguing – I know him – I'll just leave and maybe he'll be in a better mood by the time he comes home.'

Most of the staff in the building had now gone home and Julian luxuriated in the quietness. He recovered his newspaper and finished reading the racing pages – Julian fancied himself as a racing expert; however, his bets rarely paid off. Noting that all of his bets had been unsuccessful, he now threw the paper across the office in a fit of pique. As he did so, his elbow caught the edge of the large document pack, knocking it to the floor where it spilt its contents.

'Damn!' he said loudly, 'why didn't these fools next door pack it more securely?' However, there was nothing for it. Julian had to scramble around the floor to repack the documents, placing them in what he thought was the right order. Finally, he found the front page and appended his signature to it: 'That's done and dusted,' he said with satisfaction, 'and now I'm looking forward to that PA woman coming to pick up the pack tomorrow.'

Julian would need to think about this carefully and see how he could best humiliate her.

Shortly after 9 o'clock the next day, Julian waited in his office with pleasurable anticipation. At last, a knock at the door. Julian waited until the knock was repeated.

'Come in,' he called and the Senior Partner's PA entered, looking extremely bad tempered.

Julian held up a hand without looking up: 'Just a moment, please,' he intoned, pleasantly. After a moment, he raised his eyes: 'Yes?'

'I've come for the package.'

Julian looked puzzled: 'What package?'

Then: 'Who are you?'

The woman was furious: 'I'm the Senior Partner's PA,' she snapped.

Julian smiled: 'Ah, the Boss's secretary. Now I know what you want. The Document Pack. There it is on the table. Sign here for it.' He slid a form across the desk. The woman signed angrily and prepared to leave with the bulky pack.

'Did we meet yesterday?' Julian called as she was opening the door.

'Of course we did. Yesterday morning.'

'Ah yes, I remember talking to someone in Oberto's outer office. That's the trouble with support staff, you don't really remember them – rather below the radar, if you know what I mean. Goodbye, then!' Julian finished cheerfully and grinned broadly as she slammed the door hard.

The business meeting in the client's boardroom was extremely affable and everything was proceeding well. It seemed very likely that the whole contract would be sewn up by lunchtime. The clients were very impressed by the knowledge and efficiency of the legal team headed by the Senior Partner. Details of the various projects had been discussed in detail and the proposed actions of the legal team appeared to meet to client's wishes at every turn. And the coffee was delicious! Finally, the Managing Director of the client company sat back in his chair and beamed at the assembled company:

'Does anyone have any other points to raise before we formalise the contract?' Music to the ears of the Senior Partner. Murmurs of assent from the others. The MD continued: 'Fine, can we now proceed to the contract documents?'

The Senior Partner now turned to his team and said jovially: 'Can we have the contract documents, please?'

'Of course,' his subordinate replied smoothly, snapping open the document pack, 'just a minute …' Minutes passed with much rummaging in the pack. Silence gradually fell on the room. The subordinate eventually lifted a stricken face and spoke in a low tone to the Senior Partner: 'Sir, we do not seem to have the major contract document here.'

The Senior Partner blanched: 'Look again,' he hissed. Further searching revealed nothing.

'Sir, it definitely isn't here.'

Silence while the Senior Partner collected his thoughts; then he addressed the MD in a tone of extreme regret: 'Hektor, we have a missing document – I will send for it right away …'

The MD looked at his watch: 'Sorry, Oberto, there is no time. I leave for South America in an hour. I will return in four weeks. We will have to wait until then to complete the documents. Of course, this will delay the whole project and, unfortunately, I think you will agree that puts you in default. This is a financial matter we will need to discuss next month.'

'Hektor, I am very sorry …'

'Mistakes will happen, Oberto. It's a great pity.' The MD was cold as he rose. 'I am sorry but I must leave you now.' The rest of the client's team followed with only murmured goodbyes. Soon, the legal team were alone in the boardroom.

HDC barely had time to conceal his newspaper as the Senior Partner burst into his office. Julian knew something extremely serious must have happened. The Senior Partner had not been seen in DC for years. One glance at his face told Julian that his conclusion was correct. He decided he had better play this one formally – no First Names!

'Good afternoon, Sir, I hope there is nothing wrong?'

There was! Julian listened in silence as the Senior Partner angrily told the story of the missing document: 'I emphasised to you that there must be no mistakes and you assured me ….' The Senior Partner was speechless with rage.

Julian moved to defuse the situation: 'Sir, I cannot understand what has happened. I will institute an in-depth enquiry immediately and report to you. Meanwhile, I will find the document and bring it to you.'

'Too late!' the Senior Partner bawled and stamped from the room.

Without pause, Julian began to search his extremely untidy desk, knowing that this was where the document pack had spent the night. After some time, he was sure the document was not on the desk. He then rummaged through his desk drawers, finding nothing there also. Banging all the drawers shut, he concluded: 'Just as I expected. It's not my fault. I should never have suspected myself. The document must have been missing from the pack when it was delivered here. Someone is going to pay for this.' Julian was extremely pleased with this outcome. He would need to think carefully about the next move.

He sprang up and began to pace back and forward in front of his desk. He always thought that this action helped him to think. After some minutes of pacing, he noticed a sheet of paper lying on a side table against the wall. The sheet was partially covered by a raggedly-torn scrap of paper with some writing on it. Striding across to investigate, he lifted the torn piece of paper and read the following scrawled message: "i find this undr your desk an thougth you might need – Cleaner."

Julian picked up the crisp expensive paper from the table and regarded it with widening eyes; it was the Formal Contract Document that had been missing from the document pack!

'How could it be under my desk?' Julian was puzzled and then he remembered his accident with the Document Pack the previous day.

Now he sat down with the paper in his hand: 'This requires some thought,' he concluded gravely.

Jana

On the morning following the assembly of the Senior Partner's Document Pack, the DC staff arrived for work in high spirits. Yesterday had been a considerable amount of hard work but they had all coped very well and DHDC had commended them all for their excellent and conscientious work. Praise works! She had even bought cakes which had, of course, been devoured with delight by the always hungry young men and women.

Perhaps the most delighted of all was Jana. She had been singled out by no less than HDC himself to be the Base Coordinator for the task, which meant that she was the assembly point for all the documents as they built up. It was she who had made the initial check and inspection of the documents as they arrived; she had then assembled them into their first informal groupings. Of course, this did not mean she was in a position of authority; the only authority in the DC General Office was DHDC.

However, Jana hoped she would have authority someday. She was a serious and intelligent girl who had always applied herself assiduously to her lessons at school. In consequence, she had achieved good results in her final examinations and this had helped her when she sought work with her current employer. She had clear ambitions for the future and hoped for advancement in this large and prestigious law firm. Her eyes filled with tears when she remembered the reprimand she had received from HDC about six months before. Her tears flowed faster when she remembered it would be a stain on her record forever!

Jana had been born into a poor but loving family. Her father was an Assistant Storeman in a local factory, a position which paid little and involved long hours of work. By his own admission, he was not very bright – as a rebellious teenager, he had been disruptive at school and, as a result, his education had been minimal. Now he used his plight to warn his children of the dangers of undisciplined living, citing his own case as a perfect illustration. Jana's mother had achieved a higher state of education than her husband but marriage at an early age followed in short order by children had prevented her from following up her talents. Because the family was always short of money, she contributed by working as a cleaner at various industrial premises, jobs which were a certainty for wages set at the very lowest level.

Nevertheless, their rather small and cramped flat was always a happy place. Jana had a sister two years older than herself and a younger brother who had arrived five years later. Their parents were very proud of their children. Jana was judged to the academic of the family, although her young brother's talents were also developing well. Her parents considered it right that she had a good job in an important law firm. By contrast, Jana's elder sister did not show an academic bent in her education at school and was regarded as the stylish, flamboyant member of the family. Several years before, she had secured a job in one of the town's department stores and was able to take advantage of staff discounts when buying the latest clothes styles. She had always had a streak of independence within her and Jana had learned everything about being a teenager from her!

The two girls were firm friends and Jana admired her sister greatly. The younger girl was allowed to try on any of the new clothes that her sister brought home triumphantly. This was always a time of great happiness. Gusts of laughter, also occasional screams, could be heard emanating from the girls' bedroom when garments were being tried on experimentally. On one occasion, a fifteen year-old Jana had expressed a desire to try on the very latest in feminine underwear, a style of garment that had been adopted by her sister for everyday wear. The beautifully made peach-coloured garment had been slipped on and Jana was admiring herself in the mirror, blissfully unaware that that the minimalist thong design left her bottom completely naked. That particular scream was the result of turning round for a back view! However, it seems that fashion is an overpowering force for the young, especially the commercialism of the 21st century. It would not be long before Jana succumbed to the straightjacket of fashion conformity.

Months passed. School for Jana was coming to an end. She had been looking for employment opportunities and had seen this advertisement in the local newspaper: "Administrative staff required for large commercial law firm."

She knew this firm and the impressive building it occupied in the town centre. This was the chance that Jana had been waiting for and she applied immediately. After several weeks, just when she was giving up hope, a large stiff envelope arrived and she was overjoyed to be called to interview. She had consulted her parents and her sister about dress and it was decided that she must have a formal suit for the interview. Jana was adamant that she would not attend in school clothes. A neat grey suit and white blouse were obtained by her sister from the department store (along with correctly fashionable underwear) and Jana was ready. On the day, she was careful with her makeup and arranged her long blonde hair neatly.

She was interviewed in a rather dingy office on the first floor of the building. Her two interviewers, a man and a woman, were kind to her and she was able to lose some of her nervousness.

'Anyway,' she told herself as she was about to go in, 'at least I look quite nice.'

The man introduced himself. Jana knew it was vitally important to remember his name and immediately forgot it! He identified himself as the Head of the Document Control Department. Then he introduced the woman as his deputy. He explained that Jana was being considered for a post in his department and he outlined its functions and how it fitted in with the other activities of the Firm. She was, of course, in competition with other applicants for the post. After her interview, his deputy would show her around the department and she would be able to ask questions. Did she have any questions now, before they started? She didn't.

The interview passed in a confusing blur, as so many interviews do. Eventually, the man intimated that the questions had come to an end and thanked her for attending. Did she have any questions at this time? She didn't. Then the Firm would be in touch with her as soon as decisions were made.

The woman stood up and smiled at her saying: 'Come with me, Jana, and I will show you what we all do here.'

Jana said goodbye to the man (he was really quite nice) and left with no memory of all the questions she had answered well but vivid, agonising memories of those that she considered had been answered badly!

The woman had taken her to a large room next door; the sign on the door said: "Document Control Department" and then, in smaller letters below: "General Office"

Inside, the room was quiet and seven or eight young men and women were working quietly at small desks. Jana thought that most of them looked little older than herself. Later, they told her they were instructed to look busy any time there were visitors. This was a Standing Order from HDC and so it had to be obeyed: 'Normally, we're not as quiet as this,' they smiled, 'or as hard-working!'

The room was lined with cabinets of varying sizes and there were also a good number of computer terminals, printers and copying machines around the walls. The woman explained that there were document stores throughout the building that were under the technical control of HDC and his department:

'When the legal teams need document packs for their contracts and other work, it is our responsibility to supply them. You will appreciate that this means a lot of meticulous work – we can't afford to get it wrong. It also means quite a lot of running around. That's why the Document Control team are generally quite young; the young tend to have more energy.' This final remark was accompanied by a pleasant smile.

She also explained that it was possible to obtain documentation from the computer terminals: 'Then we print them out here in this room. So you need to know how to operate the terminals, printers and copying machines.' Jana thought that all this sounded quite thrilling. As she was shown round, she asked a few intelligent questions and Margarite was duly impressed: 'A nice girl, looks and sounds intelligent and serious. Probably a good bet for us.' She would intimate this to Julian after the girl left.

Jana left the building impressed and excited. However, with every step she now revisited all the interview questions where her performance had been, in her opinion, below par: 'Oh dear, why did I say that?' She murmured this over and over again as she walked towards the bus station. By the time Jana alighted from the bus near her home, she was thoroughly depressed, knowing that she must have come across as a complete dullard, quite unsuitable for such a prestigious job. The trouble was – now she had to face her family. They would all be waiting to hear how she had done; she decided she could not possibly tell the truth. She would just have to be noncommittal, she decided.

As she had predicted, all the family were agog to hear what had happened to her. Forcing a degree of gaiety (extremely difficult to maintain), Jana told them all about the Document Control Department at the law firm, emphasising how complex, difficult and responsible the work was: 'You need to know all about computers and a whole range of other very expensive office machinery; there's absolutely no room for mistakes, that's what the deputy head of the department told me.'

Her father's face fell: 'But, Jana, you don't know anything about computers. We've never been able to afford one.' He looked thoroughly miserable, convinced that he had let his lovely daughter down.

'Don't worry about that, Daddy,' she responded cheerfully, 'I've used computers at school (in truth, not very often!) and anyway, the lady told me that I would receive full training on everything I need to know.'

'If only we had a bit more money,' her father said mournfully to her mother, 'then we could have prepared Jana better for this important job.'

'Look everyone,' Jana said firmly, 'let's not get ahead of ourselves here, no-one says I've got the job yet. There were a lot of other young people being interviewed as well as me (Jana crossed her fingers as she told this lie). I'm in competition with them. We won't know for one or two weeks.' Of course Jana was completely convinced she had failed.

Just seven days later, the Great Day arrived. A large white envelope, reassuringly thick, fell through the letterbox and fell on the floor with an audible thud. Feigning nonchalance, Jana sauntered into the hallway and saw that the envelope was addressed to her. Her mother came out from the kitchen and observed the frozen figure of Jana, wide-eyed, clutching the envelope to her chest. Without a word – sometimes speech is impossible – the girl slipped past her mother and disappeared into her bedroom, closing the door firmly behind her.

Ten minutes passed, little temporal blocks of tension. Jana's mother hovered nervously around the kitchen door, often popping her head into the hallway to pick up any sound from the bedroom. Worryingly, all was completely silent. Annoyingly, a saucepan on the cooker required attention and the woman had to leave her post to deal with it. When she turned around, her younger daughter stood in the doorway, clutching a veritable sheaf of papers in her arms and grinning broadly. That grin took her mother back many years – a much smaller, younger Jana used to grin like that when she was especially pleased with herself; a grin that had been overlaid over the years by the sophisticated smile of a young lady! Speech was unnecessary but there was no way that silence would prevail: 'I've got it! I knew I would! I felt it all along! I thought I interviewed well and asked some very good questions. I think it was a foregone conclusion as soon as I walked in!' Jana knew she was lying but you are allowed a few lies at a time like this, surely? The girl threw the papers on the kitchen table and hugged her mother tightly. 'Oh, isn't it wonderful! I can't wait to tell Daddy. He will be so pleased, won't he? Everybody will be so pleased. Wait till I tell my friends, they will all be so pleased – well, maybe they will be a bit jealous, too, but I can't help that …' A delighted Jana was unable to stop talking and now started to dance around the room.

'That's wonderful, Darling.' Her relieved mother finally managed to speak. 'You are a very clever girl, I'm so pleased and, yes, I'm sure Daddy and everyone else will be very happy for you, too. When do you start work?'

'The week after next,' Jana exclaimed joyfully, 'that will give me time to get myself organised. There are some things I need to buy – a document case, for instance.'

'What do you need a document case for? I thought the Firm would provide everything?'

'Yes, they do, but I'll need it for my sandwiches.' They looked at each other gravely for a moment and then burst out laughing. The laughter rapidly became hysterical as the linking of document case and sandwiches provided the trigger for an explosion of pure joy: 'Sandwiches!' her mother screeched, holding her sides.

'Yes, sandwiches!' Jana could hardly get the words out, she was so breathless with laughter. In the end, they both clung on to each other in an ecstasy of love and joy.

It was all so strange and thrilling. The man at the desk gave her a temporary pass with her name printed boldly on it. 'You'll need to get proper ID from HR,' he said incomprehensibly, 'your department will sort that out. Meanwhile, I'll call someone to take you up.'

Jana sat in a sumptuous armchair, feeling like she was waiting outside the Headmaster's Office! A few minutes later, a young girl arrived, wearing a green plastic-covered ID card on a chain around her neck. Jana thought this looked extremely official and decided this girl must be a very important person. The man behind the desk pointed to Jana and the girl approached: 'Jana! Welcome. I'm Marie, one of the DC girls. Let's go.' She skipped over to the elevator and pressed the call button. A few minutes later they were both in the DC General Office. Everybody called "Hi!" to her in a very friendly way and the woman who had interviewed her came out of a small office in the corner of the room:

'Jana! Here you are. Let's get you sorted out. Come into my office.' She closed the door and invited the girl to sit down. 'I'm Margarite, the Deputy Head of DC. You can call me Margarite. We are going to be working together closely.

The Head of DC is Julian (you remember him?) but you call him "Sir".'

There were a few papers to sign and a form for an ID card to fill out. Then Margarite asked Marie to take Jana to HR – this turned out to be "Human Resources" – where she was photographed and received one of these wonderful plastic-covered ID cards on a chain. She was surprised to see it was the same colour as Marie's card. When she queried this, she was absolutely delighted when Marie replied: 'My ID is the same as yours because you're the same grade as me.'

'I thought you were someone really important,' Jana gasped.

'Wish I was!' smiled Marie.

On returning to the DC General Office, Margarite took Jana to a small desk. 'This is your desk, Jana. This is where you will work; here's the key to the drawer. I will give you the work you need to do every day. If you have any queries, come and see me, although you can also ask any of the other staff here. You're all the same grade in here but sometimes staff are given special positions of responsibility, as you will soon find out. For the time being, I'd like you to read the contents of these folders, which will show you the structure of DC and how it fits with the rest of the organisation. These are things you need to know in order to do your job well.'

Jana sat at "her" desk, in that peculiar spirit of euphoria and strangeness that all new employees experience, reading and re-reading the first page of the first document in the folder. Just at the moment, she felt she had lost the ability to read! She read the words, understood them and then lost their meaning as her mind cartwheeled to a different plane of thought: 'I must stop this, I must concentrate,' she thought, fortunately with a certain degree of amusement. Jana knew that the strangeness and the euphoria would soon wear off.

'This is a bit like my first day at school. I thought I'd finished with such experiences.'

Meanwhile, her colleagues came over to introduce themselves. They seemed very nice, all offering their help if she needed to know about anything. Jana began to feel much more relaxed and settled down seriously to read.

Six months passed. Jana had now become something of an old hand. She knew her way about and she found she could cope with the tasks that Margarite gave her without too much effort. However, she was always careful and meticulous in everything that she did. This was recognised by Margarite and she began to trust Jana with some of the more tricky document assemblies. Every time, Jana completed the work with no problem. Margarite was delighted to see her latest staff member make such good progress and she made sure that Julian knew her views about the girl.

Periodically, Julian himself would assemble a document pack for the most senior people in the firm. He was always very careful to have his work checked by Margarite. At these times, she often found mistakes and omissions in the packs; usually, because she loved Julian, she would just rectify the errors and return the pack to him, assuring him that all was correct. Occasionally, she mentioned an omission to him if the error was particularly serious. At such times, Julian would listen to her gravely and then deny that the error had been his, insisting that someone else must have been responsible. He usually suggested Margarite *herself* was responsible: 'You must have lost the sheet,' he would say, looking at her affectionately, 'you know "nobody's perfect!" You tell us that often enough.' Having said this, Julian would refuse to speak any more about the matter but, of course, they both knew where the truth lay.

One morning, Margarite woke with the symptoms of a dreadful cold and felt very ill. It was decided that she should stay at the flat and spend the day in bed. The previous day, Julian had received a request for a senior staff document pack. 'This is very important, Julian, we'd really appreciate if you would handle it yourself.'

In his usual, casual, slapdash way, he had assembled the pack ready to give to Margarite the following day. Now, as soon as Julian arrived at his office and saw the pack, he panicked. Margarite was off sick – she was not here to check his pack! What would he do? Distinctly wild-eyed, he considered the options. He could send it out unchecked but he knew that was too dangerous. Anyway, it was against DC Rules. A large notice on the wall trumpeted:

"ALL DOCUMENT PACKS MUST BE
INDEPENDENTLY CHECKED."

Suddenly, Julian had a solution. 'Margarite is always telling me how good that girl Jana is – I'll get her to check it.'

Jana was surprised and pleased to be asked to check HDC's pack. 'Of course, Sir, I'll do it right away. I'll have it done within two hours.'

The girl made a start right away. She did not expect to find any errors – after all, he was HDC, wasn't he? However, her face was soon wreathed in concern as she spotted error after error. The Schedule was wrong. The dates were wrong. The cross-checking was wrong and some of the documents referred to other contracts. Jana was at a loss. What should she do? In the end, she felt she could not embarrass HDC by pointing out all these errors to him, so she decided to rectify them herself. It took her some time but, just before the two-hour deadline, she had printed a new corrected Schedule and re-assembled the pack meticulously.

A gentle knock at HDC's door. Jana entering shyly and presenting the pack to Julian: 'Here you are, Sir, everything is ready for your final check.'

'Thank you, Jana.' Julian was feeling expansive, 'are you sure everything is correct?'

'Yes, Sir, but it still needs your final check.'

'Leave it there on the desk, Jana, I'll get around to it later. I'm busy with something else now. Could you ask someone to bring me a coffee?'

'Yes, Sir. I'll do it right away.' Shortly after, Jana appeared again with a steaming cup of coffee which she put down carefully on the desk. Julian, absorbed in some work pretence at his computer terminal, ignored her.

After the girl had left the room, Julian returned to his desk and newspaper and stretched luxuriously in his revolving chair, spinning it around until one arm struck the edge of his desk.

'Damn!' he said as some coffee was spilled from the cup. Most of the spillage went into the saucer but some large drops splashed on to the open document pack. Julian sprang to his feet and tried to mop the liquid from the paper before it stained it – a vain attempt, of course. The all-important Schedule was now marked with several ugly brown stains.

'Damn,' he said again, wondering what to do. Then, a solution: 'I know – I can print out another Schedule from my computer file.' The Schedule – Julian's first error-filled attempt – was duly printed out, signed by Julian as checked (of course it wasn't) and incorporated into the pack. Jana's corrected Schedule was crumpled and tossed into the waste paper bin. The document pack was sent off to the Senior Legal Team.

The next morning, Margarite was sufficiently recovered to come to work. The morning was routine and the General Office was filled with the usual buzz of activity. After lunch, everyone was taken aback when a white-faced Julian appeared. He marched into Margarite's office and slammed the door behind him.

'Whatever is wrong, Julian?'

'Yesterday, I had to raise a Document Pack for the Senior Legal Team,' Julian grated, 'you weren't here so I had to use your wonderful girl Jana to check my pack. I've just heard from the Team. Everything went wrong. The Schedule was rubbish and they couldn't complete the deal. They're thinking of raising a Formal Complaint against the Department.'

'Oh, Julian, I'm so sorry everything went wrong. Let me talk to the girl and try to find out what happened; I'll report to you as soon as I can.' Julian left without a word and stalked out of the General Office.

'Jana,' Margarite called, 'can you come in please?' The woman and the girl were closeted together for some time. The question was asked and the story was told. Margarite was not surprised to hear that there had been many errors in the pack that Julian had assembled.

Jana was extremely upset to hear that errors in the pack had been the cause of the failure of an important negotiation. 'I'm sure everything was right when I gave it to him,' she wailed, deeply distressed, 'I was really careful. I checked it all again and again. You know how careful I am.'

'Jana, did you change the Schedule?'

'Yes I did. I had to raise a new one. There were so many mistakes …' The girl's voice tailed off.

'Do you have a copy of the schedule you produced?'

'Yes,' Jana sobbed, 'just a minute … I'll go and get it. It's in a folder on my desk.'

Margarite cast an expert eye over the schedule. Everything looked to be in order: 'I don't see any problem with this,' she said, 'leave this with me. Dry your eyes. I have to go and see HDC.'

Julian and Margarite were together in his office. The offending document pack was on the desk. One glance at the top sheet told Margarite that the pack schedule was different from the one in her hand. Furthermore, the pack version was clearly wrong. 'Julian, this is the schedule she gave you. It's correct.' She looked at him quizzically. 'What happened?'

The man's face went pale: 'I don't know,' he stammered, 'I really don't know …' Then he brightened: 'She must have given me the wrong one. That's it! She must have done a new one and then given me the old one. She's to blame for this. I'll tell the Senior Legal Team we have had a full investigation and a member of the staff has been reprimanded. Then, hopefully, they won't raise a complaint against me … er … I mean, the Department.'

Margarite looked at him coldly: 'Julian, it wasn't her fault, it was yours …'

'Nonsense,' he cried, 'she is to blame and she will be reprimanded.'

The reprimand was duly delivered to a shocked and tearful Jana. Margarite was sure she knew what had really happened but her love and loyalty meant that she had to take Julian's side. Even so, she tried to soften the blow for Jana.

'Jana, I know you did your very best and that the work you did was good. Sometimes, life in big firms like ours gets very complicated and people get wrongly blamed. But you saved the Department from an Official Compliant.'

However, Jana was inconsolable: 'Margarite, I didn't do it. I didn't make a mistake and I didn't deserve to be reprimanded.'

Margarite took the girl in her arms: 'Hush, now. I know you're a good and reliable worker and I'll always trust you.'

Now it was months later, early afternoon. A grim-faced Julian stood in the centre of the General Office. Margarite stood behind him. All the staff were there, sitting at their desks. The room was completely quiet, no coughing, no shuffling. Everyone had been transfixed by his words: 'There has been a catastrophe. The Senior Partner's Document Pack was incomplete. There was no Formal Contract in the pack.

Because of this, the Firm is in default and the mistake will cost a considerable amount of money. Tens of thousands of euro.'

After a long pause, he continued: 'Someone in DC has caused this error.' There was another pause while Julian looked directly into each face in the room. Finally, he said: 'I have already searched my room thoroughly and the Formal Contract sheet is not there. Now, we, all of us, will search this room – starting NOW!' The last word was a whiplash of sound.

It took ten minutes to find it, standing vertically in thick dust behind a filing cabinet – the filing cabinet nearest to Jana's desk. It was discovered when one of the young men (Alex) strained at the heavy cabinet and was able to slide it a little way from the wall. Now Julian stood silently, holding the stiff sheet of paper with one finger and thumb while once again looking at each of his staff in turn. Finally, he turned on his heel and walked out of the room, growling: 'Margarite, come with me, please.'

Two armless upright chairs were set in front of Julian's desk, about a metre apart. He indicated that Jana should sit on one of them. He then reopened the office door and set the "DO NOT DISTURB" sign before returning to sit on the other chair, turning it so that it was at right angles to hers. (Julian had been impressed by an article he had read about staff contact techniques; an important recommendation was: "Do not speak to your staff across a desk. This is negative and suggests aggressive confrontation.") Nevertheless, his face was grave and unfriendly as he looked at the trembling girl: 'I take it you know why you are here?'

'Yes, Sir.' A tiny whisper.

'You were the Base Coordinator yesterday, is that right?'

'Yes, Sir.'

'Can you explain to me how the Formal Contract Document came to be behind the filing cabinet nearest your desk?'

'No, Sir.' The girl's voice was filled with hopelessness. A lengthening pause. Then: 'Sir, I am sure the Contract was in the Pack when I delivered it to you. It was just below the Schedule and I can remember seeing the margins of the paper.' At last, a slightly more spirited voice.

He sighed deeply, then he spoke in a harsh voice, his eyes boring into hers: 'Listen, Young Lady, if the Formal Contract sheet had been there it would have gone with the Pack to the Senior Partner and the Firm would have signed the contract with the client. And we would not be in this mess. You see that, don't you?'

Numb, she did not reply. 'Don't you?' His voice loud and sharp. The girl jumped in fright.

'Yes, Sir.' The man sighed again. Now he spoke in clipped tones. 'You give me no choice. I will refer you to HR for immediate dismissal.'

The girl was frozen in horror and then she started to weep bitterly: 'Please don't,' she sobbed, 'please give me another chance.' Then, after a pause: 'Please, Sir, could you not discipline me yourself?'

The man smiled sardonically: 'You mean I should smack your wrist and say you're a naughty girl? I'm sorry but I don't think I can do that. It's not so long ago that I had to reprimand you for another mistake, is it? You were warned then about the next time.' The man sat back in his seat, indicating that the situation was hopeless and that the interview was drawing to a close.

The girl sat completely still, a small fragile creature, large eyes locked to his but now unseeing. Behind those eyes, her thoughts were a raging torrent, conceiving and rejecting a myriad of hopeless courses of action. Suddenly, her memory of lovingly-read Bible stories provided a joyful solution. She would offer herself as a sacrifice. She would accept the penance and he would then grant her mercy!

Within that same magical microsecond, her actions were planned. In a fleeting whisper of movement, she would propel her slim, thinly-clad body across his lap, unmistakably offering him a sacrifice of utter submission. Then she would speak: 'I accept my penance … Afterwards, forgive me … Please …'

These words of total capitulation would cut through his astonishment and fright and set the process of atonement in motion.

The woman in HR was very experienced and looked at Jana kindly: 'Could you just sign this, Dear,' she said, sliding paper and pen across the desk.

'What is it?' Jana asked calmly.

'It's the beginning of the dismissal procedure,' the woman replied gently. Jana's calm was replaced with alarm: 'There must be some mistake,' she said urgently, 'I'm not being dismissed. He, HDC, said he'd changed his mind, that he'd forgiven me. He definitely said it.'

The woman looked at the papers in the folder: 'There's nothing in here about a change,' she stated flatly.

'Please, she said … Can you check? Can you ring him up?'

The woman was reluctant. 'I don't know if I have the authority to do that …'

Jana pleaded. She even fell to her knees in front of the woman and held up her clasped hands in a classical pose of supplication: 'Please … he said he had forgiven me, he did, he really did …'

'Get up, Dear, don't be so distressed. I might get into trouble but I'll do it, just for you.'

The woman picked up her phone and consulted an internal telephone directory: 'Hello? Is this HDC? Good morning,

Sir, this is Marta at HR. I am very sorry to disturb you but I have your girl Jana with me. That's right, you referred her for dismissal. She insists that you've changed your mind. I thought I'd better check. I know it's not normal procedure but I thought …' Silence while the woman listened, then: 'Yes, Sir, I understand completely. No, it's absolutely no problem for HR. I am so sorry I had to disturb you. Thank you for speaking to me. Goodbye, Sir.'

For a moment, the woman looked down at the papers on her desk and then she lifted her head to look sadly at Jana: 'Sorry, Dear. You must have misunderstood. Could you sign the paper …'

The day was unpleasant, dank and drizzly. The small disconsolate figure of Jana slipped almost guiltily through the large glass entrance doors of the Firm for the last time, agonisingly divested of her coveted ID card. Head down, document case in hand, she began to trudge slowly towards the bus station. On reaching it she did not board a bus but sat down on one of the many benches near the ticket offices. Buses came and went but Jana continued to sit motionless on her bench, unaware of the bustle and activity around her. After half an hour or so, she rose to her feet, left the bus station by its main entrance and began to walk purposefully along the busy road which led away from the town centre. After just a few hundred metres she stopped and leaned pensively against a stout, well-constructed wooden gate. Here, she raised her eyes and gazed into the distance, seeing nothing, totally preoccupied with two sentences that continued to spin endlessly, round and round in her brain: 'Here is your Dismissal Pack, Dear. I'm sorry we cannot offer you a reference – we have a responsibility to the business community, you know.'

Still leaning on the gate, Jana felt her inner resolve strengthening. After all, she had always been a completely level-headed person, hadn't she? Good at making decisions. Always able to cope with whatever life threw at her.

Now she put her thoughts into unspoken words: 'I'm bound to feel like this right now. It's really awful to feel such a failure. And I thought I was doing so well. I never thought I could make such a dreadful mistake.' After a few seconds, a fleeting smile lit up her young face. Then, for the first time since she left the Firm, she spoke out loud, stirring words of encouragement and decision addressed solely to herself: 'Come on, decision made, time to get going; time to start solving these problems!'

With these words, the girl opened the gate resolutely and walked steadily forward for about three metres before turning at right angles and standing quite still to look straight into the shocked eyes of the train driver, as his white-knuckled hand strained to pull the handle of the Emergency Train Brake Lever beyond its maximum.

Train brakes, even Emergency Train Brakes, are not known for their speed of action; this is because they are attempting to overcome the momentum of hundreds of tonnes of rapidly moving metal.

The Coroner had received six folders in the afternoon of the previous day and, in accordance with his usual practice, was working through them in order.

'Case Number 3. Ah, yes, the girl on the railway line.' He located the Police Report and read it carefully. Then he removed the stack of photographs from a large envelope and flipped through them. There were several photographs of the girl; large, starkly focussed images of a disturbingly life-sized, impossibly twisted rag-doll lying beside bleak rail tracks. Then two photographs of her only possessions, found later under the train; a crushed document case containing a small leather bag of feminine essentials, a splintered mobile phone and a large torn envelope, spilling papers; everything heavily stained by the remnants of dismembered tomato sandwiches.

The man turned next to the Autopsy Report. Death was instantaneous and caused by "multiple external and internal injuries to the head and body (listed)." There was an envelope of photographs but the Coroner set them aside; he had seen so many mangled bodies stretched pathetically naked on the pitiless stainless steel of autopsy tables. The Toxicology Report showed no alcohol or drugs in the body. Stomach contents were normal. There was no evidence of sexual activity. The Coroner was about to close the folder and pass on to the next case when a final item caught his eye. It read: 'Unrelated injuries: There was extensive bruising to the buttocks. This injury had been sustained 12 to 24 hours previous to death – see photographs, Envelope D.' The Coroner located Envelope D and held it in his hands. Then he laid it aside without opening it.

'No one ever knows what goes on behind closed doors,' he said quietly, shaking his head sadly.

In practiced official tones, the policeman and the pathologist confirmed the evidence in their reports and stood down. The train driver was called and took the Witness Stand, still white with shock: 'She just appeared from nowhere, Sir, looked straight at me – I'll never forget those eyes. Of course I applied the Emergency Train Brake as soon as I saw her but we were doing 100 kilometres per hour – that's the designated speed on that stretch of line. The train took 437 metres to stop. I got out of the cab and ran back, meeting my Guard along the way. We found her beside the track, hopelessly smashed, broken, dead.' Tears welled into the man's eyes.

'I heard the impact, you know. You wouldn't think you would – hundreds of tonnes of steel against a little light girl like that – but I heard it and I felt it too. I still do …'

Now the man was weeping openly.

Julian, tight-lipped, shifty and uncomfortable – unequivocally instructed to attend by the Senior Partner – confirmed that the girl had been dismissed from the Firm on the morning of that day. Why? There had been a serious problem. He did not know all the details. Such things are handled by the Human Resources Department of the Firm. Could he add that the Senior Partner of the Firm had asked him to extend his deepest condolences to the girl's family? He looked towards her parents sitting in the court, two shrunken traumatised figures, frozen in absolute disbelief.

The Coroner summed up and concluded:

'This was a great tragedy. A terrible waste of a young life. Perhaps the law firm should review its dismissal procedures to ensure that vulnerable staff are suitably supported at such traumatic times.' Julian looked at the floor and gritted his teeth.

Finally, the verdict: 'That she took her own life while the balance of her mind was disturbed.'

Julian

The fresh air felt very good to Julian as he walked away from the Coroner's Court.

'I'm very glad all that is over! Of course I'll say nothing about the criticism the Coroner made about the Firm. It was a load of nonsense, anyway. After all, once you have dismissed someone, especially for a serious misdemeanour, they are no longer your responsibility, are they?'

Julian had to admit he felt a little depressed about the whole affair. Hearing all the details about Jana's suicide had disquieted him. He hoped fervently that her actions would not reflect badly upon him at the Firm. Surely Oberto would see that it was not his fault in any way? Yes, he felt sure Oberto would be on his side – after all, his father and the Senior Partner were such old friends. Nevertheless he was strangely worried and now sought to soothe his fears by rational analysis: 'I wonder why she did such an extreme thing? After all, she was only dismissed from a low-level administrative job and she had the whole of her life before her. I suppose it was a pity she had to take the blame for the mistake in the Senior Partner's document pack, but Top Management were absolutely furious about what had happened and someone's head had to roll. All the DC staff were involved in the catastrophe but Jana did have the lead position. So she must be responsible for the loss of such an important document.'

Typically, Julian had already schooled his mind to believe his own fabrication of events. He continued his justifying thoughts.,

'Obviously, as Senior Staff, neither Margarite or I could take any of the direct blame. That would have been very bad for the whole Firm and could have led to a general loss in morale in the Department. As HDC, I am afraid I just could not allow that to happen.'

Now he felt better!

Julian's next thoughts were about Margarite: 'Poor Margarite! I know she was rather fond of that girl. I hope this doesn't make her unhappy and angry with me for insisting on dismissing Jana. I don't want our relationship to be damaged by what has happened. We're thoroughly used to each other now and I don't want to be forced into finding another partner. I'll just have to be extra charming to her. I know – I'll get her some flowers. That always works.'

A few minutes later, Julian had entered the flower shop near the law firm building and soon emerged with a large bunch of red roses which he carried into the Firm's underground car park.

'I had better leave these flowers in the car and give them to her when we get home. If I took them into the office, everyone would wonder why I have bought her flowers. They might suspect it has something to do with Jana and I want to dampen all that down as soon as possible.'

The flowers seemed to work. Margarite was very pleased to receive them; even more pleased that Julian should have thought about her so lovingly. Nevertheless, she remained in a quiet and introspective mood. In truth, she had been deeply shaken by what had happened. Of course she was very upset by Jana's untimely death but somehow the terrible suicide seemed remote and unreal. By contrast, the sequence of events in the

Office was terrifyingly vivid, a dreadful procession that led inexorably to the girl's dismissal in disgrace.

Margarite knew the quality of Jana's work and, although she had queried Julian's selection of the girl as Base Coordinator for this very important task, she had been pleased that he had appeared to recognise the girl's talents. She was even more pleased to see how Jana proceeded to organise the work. It had been a large and complex document pack to set up and it took considerable time and manpower. Several times, Jana had spotted that wrong documentation had been brought in by her colleagues and initiated the necessary rectification procedures. When all had been assembled and checked by Jana, Margarite had taken the heavy pack away for the DHDC check and found only very minor errors – the odd document slightly out of date order.

Margarite knew that the Formal Contract was certainly in place during her check. There was absolutely no doubt about this; this was a very important document in the pack and she could actually remember seeing it. After she had completed her comprehensive and meticulous check, she had signed it off as DHDC, closed the pack up and returned it to Jana's desk. This was routine procedure. After the disaster, when the document was found behind the filing cabinet, Julian had proposed that Jana must have opened the pack again, for some reason removed the Formal Contract sheet and placed it temporarily on top of the filing cabinet nearest to her desk. From there, the sheet had somehow fallen down the back of the cabinet where it was completely concealed from view.

That Jana would have done such a thing was completely illogical; not only illogical but dangerous, because this would be interfering with the pack after the DHDC check – something the staff were forbidden to do. Margarite knew that Jana would never have disobeyed orders. In any event, she was sure that the girl would never have separated a single document from any pack and placed it temporarily on top of a general-use cabinet away from her desk. Finally, no one, not even Julian, could explain how this crisp, heavy sheet of paper fell down the back of the cabinet; the building was sealed and air-conditioned and the General Office of DC was never subject to sudden gusts of wind!

Margarite's final thought concerned Julian himself and this made her feel very uncomfortable. The Record Sheet indicated that Julian had carried out the final HDC check. Why did this final check not reveal the absence of the document? Love and embarrassment prevented Margarite from following this particular thought process any further. Instead, she shook her head in sorrow and despair and concluded: 'It really doesn't add up.' Then, with considerable effort, she forced her mind away from the catastrophe: 'I really must snap out of this, for Julian's sake. It was lovely of him to buy me flowers. I must cheer up.'

With Jana gone, DC was now short-staffed. After a week had passed, Julian and Margarite met to initiate a new recruitment exercise. Newspaper adverts were placed by HR, responses received and passed to HDC for consideration. Subsequently, Julian and Margarite met again to decide on a short-list of candidates.

'This boy Alain will take some beating,' Julian said decisively, 'did you see his qualifications?'

Margarite had also been impressed by this particular candidate. 'I agree. Maybe it would be a good idea to interview him first?'

'Yes. I agree to that. Could you set it up for next week? We'll interview the other four after we've seen him.'

The day of the first interview arrived. The candidate Alain arrived at the front desk in good time for his interview and, in due course was conducted to Julian's office where Julian and

Margarite were waiting. Alain impressed at first sight, being a tall, good-looking boy of eighteen, confident and well-spoken. The interview explored his education, motivation, other achievements and interests. His replies were intelligent and comprehensive, expressed in clear, respectful tones. Interview over, did he have any questions?

The boy responded with a slight smile: 'I'm sure I will have many questions in the future. But first, I have a lot to learn.'

Even Julian smiled with admiration at that answer! 'Thank you for coming,' Julian said, 'my deputy will show you around the department and you can see what goes on. Please don't hesitate to ask any questions.' He nodded at Margarite and shook hands with the boy before he left.

By contrast, the next three candidates did not inspire. Two girls and a boy, they came across as disinterested and generally rather dull; their educational achievements confirmed that impression.

'Those last three were dreadful!' As usual, Julian's judgement was unequivocal. 'I wouldn't employ any of them, even if there was no-one else.'

Margarite often thought that Julian's judgements were extreme but, in this case, she was in general agreement. It began to look as of their favourite candidate had the job "in the bag" – until the last candidate appeared, that is!

Sunia was a seventeen year-old girl whose father was Chinese and her mother Brazilian. In her, this combination of race had produced striking physical attractiveness. Her large almond shaped eyes, fine features and perfectly smooth skin gave her a classical beauty, while her body had developed to be quite tall, slim and perfectly proportioned. Even as a small child, her prettiness had always been greatly admired and she augmented this with a sweet, gentle and loving personality. Now, on the brink of adulthood, it was obvious that her beauty was proceeding towards perfection.

She had been born in Switzerland but her father's work for an international company meant that the family often moved to different countries around the world. In consequence, Sunia had attended many schools as she grew up – always the very best ones wherever they were. With each change, the latest school did its best to raise her educational standard and develop her other talents – the trouble was, she remained contentedly passive and could not be persuaded to learn at the same rate as the other children. Because of this, she eventually left school at the age of sixteen with distinctly sub-standard educational achievements.

Of course Julian and Margarite had noted the poor educational qualifications at the sifting stage. They were about to reject her application when Julian noted the unusual pattern of her upbringing and schooling: 'What a peculiar background she has,' he had said, 'I think we should interview her just to see what she is like.'

Margarite was unimpressed by this idea: 'It's probably a waste of time, Julian. However, if you really want to see her, we'll see her.' Margarite knew better than to argue – she never won in the office. Thus, Sunia was invited to attend.

The interview day arrived and Sunia had been ushered into Julian's office. As she stood, waiting to be asked to sit down, Julian was strangely silent. Margarite looked at him with surprise and found he was staring fixedly at the girl with a sort of frozen expression on his face. As the silence lengthened, Margarite took over: 'Come in. You're Sunia, aren't you? Please sit down.' She went on to introduce Julian and herself to the girl. Meanwhile, Margarite's words had brought Julian back to life and now he took over the interview.

'I wonder what happened to him,' Margarite thought, 'it's like his engine stalled!'

As Julian spoke, she studied the girl. She certainly was pretty – no, really beautiful was the correct term. Softly spoken, simply dressed in expensive clothes, she appeared to radiate a sort of calm, gentle serenity. However, when Margarite began to listen to what she was saying, it was immediately obvious that she was coping badly with Julian's questions, sometimes silently perplexed, sometimes completely misunderstanding the question, often ignorant of the simplest everyday topics. Even when invited to speak about her own life and experiences, she was far from fluent.

'What a waste of time,' Margarite thought and then she realised that something strange was happening. Although the girl's answers were poor and often monosyllabic, Julian was reacting as if they were totally splendid! He was smiling encouragingly at the girl. Anytime there was a possibility of any humour in the answers, Julian was laughing heartily. It was all very strange.

'I wonder if he sickening for something,' she thought, looking at him carefully.

He noticed her look and blenched a little. Turning to her, he said, 'Would you like to ask Sunia some questions, Margarite?' Out of politeness, Margarite did so but it proved to be a sterile experience. Although the girl's voice and manner were pleasant enough, her answers were hugely disappointing. Soon, Margarite indicated she had no more questions and thanked the girl.

At the end of the interview, Julian was effusive. He thanked her very much for coming. She would hear about her application as soon as possible. His deputy would now show her around the Department and he hoped that she would enjoy this. She would be able to ask questions about any aspect of the work.

'Bet she asks nothing,' Margarite thought wryly!

Ten minutes later, Sunia had left the building. Margarite was amused to see that her presence caused some interest among the young men of the General Office. She had outlined the functions of DC and described the work the girl would do. Sunia smiled at the staff and remained silent. She shook her head when Margarite asked finally if there was anything else she would like to know. Shortly after, the girl departed and, in accordance with their normal procedure, Margarite made two cups of coffee and joined Julian in his office.

'Well,' Margarite began, 'that was more than a little painful, wasn't it? She certainly was a lovely looking girl but I'm not sure if she had any brains at all in that pretty head. That's definitely one of the worst interviews I have ever been involved in.' She paused for a moment. 'So shall I now go ahead and have a formal offer sent to the boy Alain? We might as well get on with it. He certainly was an outstanding candidate and he probably has a very good future with the Firm. I'll go and get the papers for you to sign and take them up to HR, shall I?'

Julian sipped his coffee introspectively. 'Don't go yet, Margarite. You know, I've been thinking. If we took the boy it would unbalance the sexual distribution in the General Office. I think it would be much better to employ a girl in what was Jana's position. It will keep everything on an even keel.'

Margarite looked at him in puzzlement. 'Julian, we have never needed to consider that sort of balance before. I mean, when Jana came, she replaced a boy and, before that, there were always more boys than girls. Anyway, as their immediate Line Manager, I am absolutely sure it doesn't matter. What matters is that everybody is sufficiently bright, energetic and motivated to do the work reliably and that they all get on well together. Although I know we're not considering her, the last thing we need in DC is someone like that stupid girl we've just seen. We need to employ the best person for the job – and we know who that is, don't we?'

Julian looked into his coffee cup as he spoke, 'Margarite, I have decided that Sunia will be the successful candidate. I liked her. I thought she would develop well.'

Margarite looked at Julian in utter astonishment. 'Julian, I'm sorry, but have you gone mad? That girl would be a disaster in the General Office. At best, she would be useless but, more likely, she would cause serious problems for us and the Department.'

Julian now lifted his head and looked at her with steely eyes. She knew that look!

'I have decided, Margarite. The job is to be offered to Sunia. See to that immediately.'

So Sunia joined DC and took Jana's place. Margarite did her very best to train her. She spent a lot of time with her – more time that she had ever spent with any other trainee – but to no avail. Sunia seemed incapable of assimilating even the simplest of procedures and had to be supervised by Margarite or other members of staff in order to avoid serious mistakes being made. Although some of Margarite's young men were quite happy to have contact with Sunia at first, they soon grew tired of her lack of effort. Rather than learn, Sunia was quite happy to let her supervisor do all her work while she sat and stared out of the window!

Margarite was furious. She reported Sunia's lack of progress to Julian:

'The girl is totally idle and stupid, Julian,' she raged, 'I can't trust her to do anything. All the other staff have to pick up what should be her work. She does absolutely nothing. I've taught dozens of trainees in my time and never had a failure – until now. We must get rid of her.'

Julian demurred:

'Don't be so hard on the girl, Margarite, she has had a really disrupted life, travelling around the world. I'm sure she will improve. You'll see! I tell you what – I'll do a little training with her when I have time and I'm sure everything will soon be fine.'

'Julian, I wish you luck. You are welcome to have her anytime – she's just sitting around doing nothing anyway.' Margarite stumped out of the office angrily.

Julian was absolutely delighted. How clever of him to have achieved that! He would have Sunia to himself in his office. Now he sat and thought about her. He hadn't changed his mind since their first meeting. She was the most beautiful girl he had ever seen and he was absolutely bowled over by her. This would be a wonderful chance to get to know her better.

Not long after, Julian appeared in Margarite's office, diary in hand.

'About Sunia, I'll try to spend a little time with her every morning next week. Tell her to bring in my coffee at 1000 hours. Oh, and Margarite, tell her to bring her own coffee in too.'

Margarite was far from pleased but there was nothing she could do.

'Well, it's your funeral,' she said shortly and made a note in her diary.

The rest of that week and the weekend passed on slowly lumbering, plodding feet. Julian was agitated and fretful, impatient for Monday to come. Monday would be the start of a very exciting week and Julian was carefully planning his meeting with Sunia. He practiced the words he would use. He even practiced facial expressions in the mirror to make sure he would look as attractive as possible. Where would they sit? He must make sure that he did not talk to her across a desk. Then he had a brainwave; they would sit together at his computer terminal – he could show her how skilled he was, how extensive his knowledge and how he knew all the important people in the Firm. He hoped she would be pleased and impressed. Maybe she would smile at him? Julian felt quite faint with the rush of pleasure that came with that thought.

Finally, with agonising slowness, Monday morning came. Julian sat tensely in his office. Surely that clock has stopped! He rose several times to check. Each time the creeping progress of the second hand revealed that the clock was operating normally. Finally, a soft knock. Coffee. She had come! Julian was frenetic: 'Come in!' His voice booming joyfully. 'Yes, just put it there; come and sit here.'

Oh, she was so beautiful, so elegant, so perfect, so fragrant, so feminine, so desirable! She, looking at him with a slightly uncertain smile as she sat down. He, grinning hugely, sitting as close to her as he dared. Perhaps their hands could touch momentarily as he offered her a biscuit? They did! Julian nearly fainted with the intense thrill of it.

So the delight of the training sessions proceeded. In truth, Julian made very little attempt to train Sunia for her work. There were two reasons for this: firstly, he was far too busy showing her how clever and knowledgeable he was about the matters of the Firm. Secondly, his knowledge of the work of the General Office was quite sketchy; he left all that firmly in Margarite's control.

By the end of the week, he and Sunia sat closely together at the computer terminal, he showing her what to do and sometimes even guiding her soft hands on the keyboard. Each blessed occasion of touching her hand or arm was a golden moment for him.

During the following week, while the "training" continued unabated, Julian discovered that Sunia sometimes ate her lunch in the nearby park.

'Why, so do I,' he exclaimed gleefully, 'why don't you allow me to buy you lunch from the sandwich shop and then we can eat together in the park.' This seemed a good idea to Sunia; she was quite happy to strengthen her relationship with her senior manager. She thought this might be good for her prospects in the firm. Julian was delighted when she agreed and seemed to be pleased with his offer. This provided him with a new and wonderful opportunity; on the narrow park benches, it was possible that their thighs might touch! A further escalation of bliss for the infatuated Julian.

Although Julian's strong attraction to Sunia could so easily have been based on sexual lust, this was far from the truth. At first sight, Sunia had literally transfixed Julian with her beauty. Months later, she remained a truly magical creature to him. With closer contact, he had judged her as feminine perfection itself and their relationship had grown as she responded to his attention, smiling when he joked, showing (simulated) grave attention when he was serious. As a result, Julian's attraction to Sunia had turned into a pure, deep and incandescent love. He worshipped her and would never have attempted to take advantage of her in any of the traditional male ways. Day and night, she was in his thoughts.

It was during one of their lunchtime visits to the park that Sunia informed Julian it was her eighteenth birthday on the 15th day of the following month. Julian immediately decided that he should give her a birthday present on that day. He knew this would require serious thought. While he always marked Margarite's birthday with a card and a present, casually selected, Julian knew it would not be appropriate to buy something expensive or lavish for Sunia – although he would dearly have liked to. If he gave her something expensive, it was likely to cause problems in the Department – laughter, derision or even jealousy among the staff. No, it would have to be something relatively inexpensive but unusual. Something that would express his love to her without giving the game away.

For some time now, the evening meal at the flat had become a silent affair. When Julian and Margarite were first together, they used to chat quite happily on a whole range of trivia. As time passed, Julian became increasingly keen to expound his views on the vagaries of world politics, international finance or global sociology. If not that, there was always the theme of the World/Region/Country going to the dogs! While Margarite did not always agree with Julian, she admired the energy he put into expressing his views on such a diverse range of subjects. And, more importantly – she loved him. So, even in disagreement, she would sit quietly and regard him fondly, often employing the popular lover's strategy of switching off meaningful hearing!

It was no longer like that. The situation at the Department was worsening and Margarite was becoming more and more worried and frustrated that Julian would not listen to her warnings about Sunia. Suddenly, the silence was broken with shocking brutality: 'I want you to leave.' Julian's voice was harsh and flat.

'Leave? What do mean leave? Leave what?' Margarite's response was full of puzzlement.

'Leave the flat. Stop living here.' Margarite was dumbfounded.

'Julian, what's wrong? What have I done to upset you so much? Whatever it is, I'm sorry. You know I love you, Darling.'

He shook his head. 'I want you to go. Now.'

NOW! She was transfixed in panic: 'What do you mean? You don't mean *right now*, do you?'

'Yes. I mean right now.' His voice hard and unyielding.

'But I have nowhere to go – where would I go?' Her response was shrill.

'Oh, ring up one of your friends. I'm sure they will take you in until you can find a new place to live. Go on – do it now!' His tone was offhand and callous.

Margarite stumbled from the room, her mind whirling. He was deadly serious – she knew that. It was his flat. She would have to obey. She started to weep as she packed some essentials in a suitcase. Then she rang a friend and asked if she could stay the night.

'What's wrong?' The friend could not help asking.

'I'll tell you when I come,' Margarite sobbed. She returned to the main room of the flat. Julian was still sitting motionless at the table.

'Can't you even tell me what's wrong?' Margarite wailed. 'You know I love you so much. Tell me what's wrong, I will apologise and you could forgive me. Don't punish me like this.'

His face was stony. 'No. You can collect your belongings when you find somewhere else to live. Goodbye.' He turned away and completely ignored her as she stumbled from the flat.

Fortunately, her friend's house was not far from Julian's flat. Margarite wept bitterly as she trudged along. The doorbell was rung. The door opened and Margarite fell limply into the arms of her friend.

The situation at DC worsened further. Julian spoke to Margarite only when necessary and, although she looked at him with pleading eyes full of love, he ignored her approaches. His manner towards her was cold and unfeeling. On several occasions, she had tried to speak to him about their relationship but he refused to talk about it: 'I'm far too busy to talk about out-of-office matters. Anyway, you and I have absolutely nothing to talk about.' As he said this, he looked at her with hard and hostile eyes.

Inevitably, this friction at management level had its effect on the staff. Where the ambiance in the General Office had always been one of efficiency and cooperative cheerfulness, now everyone was subdued and nervous, suspicious of the appearance of either of their managers in the room. Everyone, that is, except Sunia, who had been taken over by Julian as a sort of informal Personal Assistant – a PA who in fact did no work but often joined him in his office.

Margarite, still technically in charge of the girl, had long ceased to allocate her any work; Sunia's attempts at DC work were always hopelessly disorganised and riddled with mistakes. Margarite regretted that she had to spread Sunia's workload among the other staff but there was nothing else she could do. Meanwhile, Julian remained enchanted by the beautiful Sunia and sought to be with her as much as possible. Making her his informal PA had been a masterstroke! Now he could be with her for hours each day and they could get to know each other even better.

The days and weeks passed and Julian had certainly not forgotten about Sunia's eighteenth birthday. As the date approached, he really had to get down to the task of finding the right present for here. Nothing too expensive; something unusual, preferably beautiful, (just like her) and relatively inexpensive. He started searching in the town, peering earnestly in shop windows. Then, one day he noticed a rather scruffy Antiques and Collectables shop in one of the narrow side streets. Now there was an idea – maybe he would be able to find something unusual for Sunia in such a shop.

Moments later, he had opened the flimsy creaking door and entered the shop. The door banged shut behind him noisily, propelled by a powerful closing spring. Julian had never visited this particular shop before and was surprised to find how dark and depressing it was inside. He was the only customer and he started wandering around rather self-consciously under the incurious gaze of an elderly man perched on a stool behind a small rickety counter.

'What a load of old junk,' Julian thought as his eyes ranged over a bewildering range of items, piled high on every side, 'everything from tumbledown tables to tawdry trinkets!' Julian smirked, pleased with these apt alliterations. He paused by a battered glass case and, through smeary glass, scanned the antique jewellery jumbled inside. There were one or two quite attractive pieces but he quickly concluded that a gift of jewellery might be too ostentatious for the occasion.

Just as he was despairing and beginning to work his way towards the front of the shop, with the intention of darting gratefully into the fresh air, he noticed a shallow, splintered wooden box filled with a number of stones of various shapes and sizes, all pierced with holes, presumably so that they could be assembled on a cord or chain. Sitting on the top of the pile was a beautiful smooth piece of rose quartz, a roughly oval shaped disk about four or five centimetres long.

Julian paused and picked up the quartz, examining each face of its smooth, cloudy surface by the light from a nearby dim bulb and then holding it up to the daylight of the shop window. Against the daylight, the quartz now glowed rose-red, with a characteristic, star-shaped diasterism projected on its surface. Certainly it was a very attractive item.

'I think I might have found the perfect birthday gift for Sunia,' he thought joyfully, 'how clever of me to have thought of coming in here.' He saw that there was a tattered ticket stuck to the side of the box. Scrawled words read "Unusual Stone Collection €20."

Julian approached the motionless man behind the counter:

'How much is this?' he held up the rose quartz stone. The man sighed and heaved himself from the stool to lumber across and look at the label on the box.

'Eighteen euro.' The voice gruff and laconic.

Julian responded sharply: 'I don't want the whole box. I just want this particular stone.'

'That's right, eighteen euro for that one.'

Julian felt his face flush: 'Look,' he said hotly, 'the whole box is just twenty, isn't it? So how can one stone be eighteen?'

The man looked at him with pity. 'Because it's a collection, see? The collection is twenty but if you're breaking up the collection, that one is eighteen.'

'That's ridiculous!' Julian was raising his voice, 'you're trying to cheat me.'

The man regained his seat on the stool: 'Suit yourself,' he said, 'that's the price. Do you want it or not?'

'No I don't,' shouted Julian, 'I'll take the whole box for twenty!' Julian would show this appalling man who was going to win this particular contest.

'Just as you like,' the man said, handing him the box, 'give me twenty euro.'

Seconds later, Julian was back in the street, distinctly bemused that he had just bought an "Unusual Stone Collection". However his disquiet was soothed when he lifted the beautiful rose quartz stone from the box: 'This is very beautiful, a perfect gift for my perfect love. I'll get a little thin silver chain for it.'

As he replaced the stone in the box, he could see that there were a few other semi-precious stones there, possibly agate, onyx or even amethyst. At the same time he could see that others were variegated pebbles of the type found on seashores.

'Maybe some of the others will be nice, too. I'll have a look at them later. You never know when they will come in useful.' So saying, he entered the firm's garage and placed the box of stones in the boot of the BMW.

That evening, he had locked his car and was walking away when he remembered Sunia's birthday gift. Returning to the car, he retrieved the box of stones and carried it to his flat, placing it on the kitchen table.

'I'll have something to eat first, then I'll have a look at these,' he told himself. Julian prepared himself a simple meal and drank some wine. Then, after clearing up, he removed the rose quartz from the box and tipped the rest of the stones out on the table.

'Some of these are very nice,' he said to himself as some semi-precious stones were revealed. Even the pebbles were quite nice, some having been machine-polished. Then his eye was attracted to a slightly rough yellow stone that sparkled in the light. Its shape was roughly cylindrical and there was a jagged hole pierced through it towards one end. He lifted it up to examine it and his finger and thumb slid naturally into the depressions where the hole had been made.

The slight jolt he felt was the evidence that the power associated with the Stone had registered its "handshake" contact, while the momentary giddiness and loud rustling sound which followed marked the transfer of a mysterious energy of influence. For a moment, he imagined the stone had glowed brighter. Certainly, everything was altered.

Sunia

There is always a reason for the way people turn out – and Sunia was no exception.

Here she was, approaching eighteen and, like everybody else, being judged in two fundamental ways. The first is by physical appearance and, here, it is clear that Sunia scored highly. Of course many people acknowledge beauty and transmit admiration and goodwill towards it; however, not all people react like this. Some examine the beauty they see before them and compare it to their own. Then, if they find themselves wanting (as they often do), they transmit dislike, rejection and malice.

The second is by perceived intellectual ability, a judgement that is often based on tangible academic achievements. Here, Sunia achieved a low score. People acknowledge high intelligence and are impressed, even awed, by its presence – although their reactions may be contaminated by feelings of inferiority as they compare their own achievements.

People know that beauty is "skin deep" but intelligence is far more complex. However, low intelligence, allegedly demonstrated by poor academic achievements, is much simpler to judge; universally, it is looked down upon, derided or even reviled.

It was the first day of a new term. Arriving in the sunshine, the girls were hugely and noisily excited, enjoying making contact once more with their special friends after the long parting of the summer break. Their parents stood beside the laden refreshment table, sipping coffee and exchanging comfortable trivia with that special quality of comradeship which is a feature of such gatherings at "good" private schools. Across the neatly paved driveway, the car park area was filled with shiny, top-specification cars; Mercedes-Benz, Jaguar, Range Rover, Cadillac and the like.

Suddenly a hush fell on the easy chatter as a gleaming, pure white Bentley Continental whispered into view, its open top revealing a sumptuous interior of figured walnut and finest cream leather. In the silence of arrested time, the assembled parents were struck by that unsettling blend of admiration and dismay.

From this wonderful car stepped a new girl, a hesitant fourteen-year-old Sunia, immaculately turned out in the uniform of the school. Her future classmates examined her with hostile impassivity. Observing the transfixed onlookers, Sunia blenched and thought, 'I hope at least one person will be kind to me.'

This proved to be a vain hope. Although she was politely received by her classmates in the presence of a teacher, it was not long before the verbal attacks started. Sneering hurtful questions about her parents, her previous life, her interests and achievements; insults about her appearance, speech, dress and other qualities. Then came the exclusions, total rejection by the group; any individual attempt to be compassionate to her brutally supressed.

This was soon followed by the cyberattacks through mobile phone and social networking sites; a plethora of deeply distressing messages and misinformation transmitting hurt and hatred. Finally, the physical violence, with Sunia often emerging from changing areas or wash rooms, bruised, dirty and considerably dishevelled. If she was particularly unlucky, a mobile phone video of the attack and its embarrassing result would be posted on the Internet for the world to see – until the authorities acted to remove it as "unsuitable".

Happily, Sunia's life had not always been like this. Fourteen years before, she had been warmly welcomed into her cosmopolitan family, a much loved baby daughter. Both her parents were people of considerable intellect and, with their teaching and encouragement, Sunia developed well in her early years and showed a lively intelligence. At the age of five, she attended her first school in Europe and established herself successfully, coping well with the initial lessons and becoming popular with her classroom peers.

Unlike the majority of her classmates, within two years Sunia was no longer a pupil at that school – and no longer living in Europe either. She was now in Asia and had to cope with the trauma of starting at a new school, not as a pupil starting her education but as a new girl amongst the "old hands" who had been together since the beginning of their formal education.

This is often a difficult transition to make because the new pupil is in danger of becoming an outcast. After some struggle and unhappiness, Sunia's outgoing and pleasant personality overcame the adversity of the situation and all was well. Unfortunately for Sunia, this pattern of movement continued to be repeated every few years.

In life, most people can recall situations where it was necessary to develop a survival strategy; for many, school was (and is) such a place. Unfortunate children like Sunia, who are compelled to move schools frequently, are extremely vulnerable as they become the unwelcome stranger parachuted into the middle of the fragile microcosm that is a school class. Many times, the new pupil is seriously attacked – the world knows this as bullying and it has always been a problem.

Sunia had experienced this treatment at previous schools but, as time passed, she noted that the bullying was becoming more intense and brutal. As children become older, they begin to adopt the more venomous actions of adulthood, without the offsetting compassion that the experience of adult love brings. This is why children can be unbelievably cruel; it is the application and enjoyment of power without the moderation of experience and responsibility.

It had taken much thought but Sunia had developed a survival strategy that usually worked in the end. Now, as a young teenager struggling with frequent psychological and physical attacks, she was applying that strategy as assiduously as she could. She knew she could not change her looks very much. She did what she could to be less attractive – dressing untidily and having her hair cut inappropriately. However the main plank of her strategy was to convince the bullies that she was stupid and inept. If she could achieve this, they would categorise her as greatly inferior to them and no longer regard her as a threat. Hopefully, she would then be free of their attention.

So Sunia made sure she was consistently poor at her classwork, despite the strenuous efforts of all her teachers. Soon she was regarded as the dunce of the class and she continued to emphasise her stupidity to the bullies, as well as fawning upon their greatly superior abilities. In addition, she worked hard to become a clumsy and uncoordinated athlete and, in consequence, was never selected for any of the sporting teams. As before, her survival strategy worked – eventually. The bullies decided she was too pathetic for them to waste their valuable time upon. They started to ignore her totally and, with extreme caution, Sunia was able to establish friendly links with a few kindly girls at the school.

There is always a reason for the way people turn out – and survival was Sunia's reason.

Unfortunately, every action has consequences and Sunia's consistent efforts to be academically poor had become a fixed part of her life. She had long given up any thought of educational advancement and had settled comfortably into her role as a beautiful, kindly and placid girl who had no talent for learning of any kind.

This was, of course, the persona she presented to Julian and Margarite when she was interviewed for the job in DC. On the basis of her performance at interview, there is no doubt that she would have been unsuccessful in her application but that outcome was instantly reversed when Julian fell in love with her "at first sight". Such unexpected things do happen to people, even to people like Julian.

The girl had not expected to be successful when she applied for the job at the law firm. She had applied for other jobs before and experienced rejection. Her applications had been made to please her parents, who were keen that she should make the best of whatever talents she had and gain some experience of the world of work. They knew that the outcome of her schooling debarred her from pursuing any career or position that required reasonable academic qualifications and encouraged her to apply for lower-skilled office jobs where she might be able to work her way up by means of her very pleasing personality and appearance. In any event, they expected this phase of her life to last for a few years only because they were convinced that their beautiful daughter would soon be borne away on the wings of marriage!

Sunia had not been nervous when she arrived for interview at the law firm because she expected to perform badly. In the event, she was surprised when it turned out to be a rather strange experience. The woman was just as she expected, brisk and professional, seeing through to her stupidity right away but the man had acted very strangely. He was extremely nice to her as she stumbled inadequately through her answers – she could not understand why; in her experience, people do not usually react kindly to stupidity.

After the interview, she had been taken into a large office of the Department and thought the staff working there seemed to be very nice young people. Having been educated exclusively at all-girl's schools, Sunia had virtually no experience of boys and, in truth, she had little interest in them either. However, she found herself thinking that one of the "boys" in the room was actually quite attractive. The frisson of excitement that passed through her body was very pleasant and mildly surprised her.

For the rest of the time, she had walked silently and passively around the various parts of the Department, not really listening to what was being said. Eventually, she found the woman looking expectantly at her and realised she must have asked a question.

'Sorry ... Pardon me ...?'

The woman was kind: 'Sunia, do you have any questions about what I have told you? Is there anything else you want to ask about?' Of course she had no questions to ask – Sunia never had any questions to ask! As she left the building, she mused gently: 'It's a pity I won't be able to work here. It might have been quite nice.'

It had therefore been a total surprise when she was offered the job a few days later. She was totally taken aback. Her parents were delighted. This would give her something to do until she was married, they thought, looking at each other with knowing delight.

On the day that Sunia started work at the law firm, her father rather unwisely dropped her at the main entrance in a flame red Lamborghini Countach, causing a considerable stir within the building. Staff at the reception desk were astounded when they discovered that the elegant young lady who entered the building was just a new recruit starting her first day. In due course, Sunia was inducted into DC, provided with an identity card and shown her desk. Margarite had welcomed her warmly and intimated that they would have a chat later in her office. As soon as she had returned to her office, the rest of the DC staff, especially the young men, crowded around to introduce themselves. Sunia was very pleased to be welcomed so warmly: 'What a change from my terrible school days!' she thought with relief, 'maybe I'm really going to enjoy this.'

Sunia's school survival strategy was so much part of her life that she had come to believe she was a stupid and physically uncoordinated person. She knew that she was an attractive looking girl – the mirror told her that – but she did not regard that as an advantage either. After all, her appearance was one of the things that caused her so much trouble in the past. However her parents had persuaded her that this job was going to be a completely new start for her and, reluctantly, she had changed from the baggy shapeless clothes she had cowered in during her earlier teenage years and now dressed somewhat nervously in elegant, stylish clothes that enhanced her beauty. Because of this, she now looked poised and confident; unfortunately, this was soon revealed to be an illusion.

Of course Margarite already had some experience of Sunia; left to herself, the woman would have rejected Sunia at the paper sift stage of the selection process. Nevertheless, Sunia was now an employee and Margarite had to try her best to train her to be adequate in the job. Margarite was a kindly person and she did not want to make Sunia's life miserable – after all, she thought, it wasn't the girl's fault that she was stupid, was it? So when Sunia was called into Margarite's office, she was treated with kindness and gentleness. Instinctively, Sunia treated Margarite as if she was her schoolteacher. This meant that she had to convince her superior that she was inadequate and hopeless.

Firstly, Margarite had tried to put the girl at her ease by starting with an informal, innocuous "ice-breaker" chat. It was obvious that this tactic rather alarmed Sunia. Why was her manager being so nice to her? After a while, Margarite saw that her attempts were having a negative effect if anything and decided to move on to the next stage of the process. She smiled and said briskly: 'Right Sunia, Here is a notebook and a pen for you to make notes in. We'll start with the basics. You know that DC is responsible for raising Document Packs for the legal staff?'

Sunia felt panic rising in her: 'Raising …?' Her voice a bewildered whisper.

'Sorry, Sunia. That's the word we use when we're starting a new Document Pack. We *raise* it – raise it to life, as it were.' Margarite smiled encouragingly. Sunia felt she should write something in her notebook to show Margarite that she was listening. Margarite continued: 'When we receive a request for a pack, the first thing the DC staff have to do is start a new Document Pack folder. Now you and I will go to the DC Storeroom where all our supplies are kept. Any time you need to go there, you get the key from me. If I'm not in my office, the key is kept here on this hook.'

Sunia wrote busily in her notebook.

The DC Storeroom was along the corridor from the General Office. Margarite unlocked the door and swung it open.

'Switch on the light, Sunia.'

Sunia looked rather wildly into the darkness. 'Please, Margarite, I can't find it!'

'It's there by your right hand, Sunia. Switch it on.'

The light revealed a fairly small, windowless room with a large range of stationery items piled neatly on tall shelving that extended all around the room. There was a table in the middle of the room and a substantial set of metal steps so that items on the highest shelves could be reached with ease.

'I'd like you to notice this, Sunia. When you switch on the Storeroom light, a warning light comes on in the corridor, just above the door. Do you see it? That's right, it's that red light.'

'What is the light for, Margarite?' Sunia asked, 'Is it just to remind you to switch off the Storeroom light when you come out?'

'Well, yes, it does that – but that's not its most important function. You see, the Storeroom isn't very big and you need to shut the door when you're inside, so that you have space to move around. And sometimes you may be standing on the steps near the door to reach something on the high shelves. The light outside means that the door should not be opened suddenly. In the past, we have had the odd accident and that's why we had the warning light installed. People knock at the door and the person inside opens it. So it's a very good idea to check that the warning light comes on when you switch on the light.'

Sunia wrote in her notebook.

'Come in and close the door, Sunia. Come over here. This is where we start. These are the various types of document folders we use to make up a Document Pack. Sometimes the request will specify a particular size. If it doesn't, you must decide which size of folder to use.' Sunia's heart leapt into her mouth.

'Margarite, how do I do that? I won't know what to choose!'

'Yes, you will, Sunia. You will look at the request and it will tell you approximately how many documents will go in the Pack. If it's just a few, say, less than twelve, you choose a small folder, if it's a longer list, take a large folder. Don't worry, Sunia, it's easy, you'll see.'

The instruction continued in much the same vein. Margarite did her best to make things as simple as possible for Sunia and the girl kept writing earnestly in her notebook, in the hope this would impress her superior. However it was soon clear she was panicking and near to tears.

Margarite noticed that the girl was distressed and sighed, saying: 'We'll leave it at that for today, Sunia. But you should come down here to the Storeroom and make yourself familiar with all the items here and where they are kept. That's something you really will need to know. You'll do that, won't you?'

'Yes, Margarite.' A small voice filled with hopelessness.

'And don't forget about the warning light.'

'Yes, Margarite, I have written it down.'

When they returned to the General Office, Margarite tried to instruct Sunia on a few simple aspects of the office routine but it was clear that Sunia's brain had now switched off. Margarite looked at the girl and smiled once more: 'Don't worry, Sunia. Just relax. It will all become clear.' However, by this time, Margarite knew it would take a miracle to bring Sunia up to an acceptable standard.

'I just don't understand it.' Sunia was having one of these irritating conversations with her parents – the sort where every word she utters is greeted with praise, enthusiasm and celebration! 'For some reason, I have become a sort of Personal Assistant to the Head of Document Control – and I'm the most junior person there. I've only been there four weeks.'

'But that's really wonderful,' her mother trilled joyfully, 'he's probably a very clever man who recognises your true talents. Do you think you might be promoted over all the rest of the Office staff?' Mothers always ask questions like that!

Her father was also very pleased: 'Your boss probably wants someone beautiful to be his PA. And you, my beautiful daughter, are certainly that.' The man did not know how close he was to the truth.

'Just concentrate, Darling,' her mother continued, 'I'm sure everything will work out for you. It was such a pity that some of these schools you went to didn't suit you.'

Sunia's parents had never suspected the truth. The girl had been skilled at concealing her bruises or, if they were seen, attributing them to her clumsiness on the sports field. Her parents had long accepted the school reports which identified Sunia as a "lovely, kind and gentle girl without any ambition to succeed academically."

The weeks passed and Sunia spent large parts of her days with HDC in his office. She still could not understand why such an important person could devote so much of his time to her – and, in addition, be so nice to her. However, she was content to sit beside him at his computer terminal and, at times, let his strong hands guide hers on the keyboard. She felt she was learning something about computer operation; however it never occurred to her that this skill was not required for the job she had been employed to do.

At other times, she sat silently while he worked at his desk or spoke to various people on the telephone. She would watch him gravely, admiring his masterly skill with people and situations. Sometimes, he would ask her to make cups of coffee for both of them. She was happy to do this and felt she was being helpful.

Occasionally, he would send her on errands to deliver material to other people in the building. At first, this worried her; she was afraid she would not be able to find the office she was looking for but, having done this a number of times, she now enjoyed this very much. She felt rather important as she found the office and delivered the folder or envelope. 'This is from HDC,' she would say proudly.

One day while they were drinking their morning cup of coffee, HDC surprised her. 'Sunia, when we are alone here in the office, you need not call me "Sir". I give you permission to call me Julian. Would you like that?'

Sunia was nonplussed and not at all enthusiastic. It all sounded very complicated. How would she remember what to do? However, she realised this was a considerable honour. The only person who called HDC by his name was Margarite – and she was DHDC. Everyone else was instructed to call HDC "Sir" at all times.

'Thank you, … Julian.' She found it difficult to speak his name, it somehow felt wrong. 'You are so kind to me, I don't know why.' Her voice was low and hesitant.

'Sunia, I'm kind to you because I like you and you are proving to be a good assistant to me.' Julian was looking at her tenderly, pleased with the outcome of his initiative. Then he said: 'However this new arrangement is just for us when we're working in here. Don't use my name in front of Margarite or the others. This is something special between you and me, something secret.' Julian twinkled conspiratorially and treated her to his most attractive smile.

Although Sunia spent a considerable part of most days in HDC's office, there were times when he was busy or out-of-office for one reason or another. At these times, she took her place at her desk in the General Office. Margarite had given up trying to train her to do the DC work for which she was employed but she continued to be kind to her, greeting her pleasantly when she was there and sometimes pausing for a brief chat.

When she was present in the General Office, Sunia had decided to see if she could attach herself to Alex, one of the more experienced members of DC. Coincidentally, Alex was the young man to whom she had been attracted on her first visit and he had been especially friendly towards her when she joined the Department. So she had appeared at his desk and, in a respectful voice, had asked: 'Alex, would it be all right if

I followed you around and saw what you were doing. I'll help you, if I can – just tell me what to do.'

Alex had looked at her doubtfully, thinking how such an arrangement might slow down his work. On the other hand, he had to admit she was a *very* attractive girl. It would be unkind to say no, wouldn't it? So after a brief hesitation, he had smiled and answered: 'OK, Sunia, stick with me and we'll see how it goes.'

Sunia was very pleased. Now she had three things to do. Work for HDC as his informal PA, learn DC work from Alex and sit looking out of the window!

In fact the liaison with Alex began to work quite well for Sunia. Because she was able to regard him almost as an equal rather than a superior (e.g. a teacher) she began to feel that it was not necessary to establish herself with him as a stupid and inept person. In other words, she began to allow her long-buried natural intelligence to surface, the intelligence that had been demonstrated in her early school days, before bullying destroyed her life and her education. Alex was pleased when he noticed the difference in Sunia and reported it to Margarite.

'That's fine, Alex,' she said, 'keep it up if it's not making your work too hard.'

Alex was becoming increasingly happy to have such a beautiful girl at his beck and call! 'Not at all,' he demurred, 'she's actually becoming quite useful and it's really good to see her confidence developing.'

Of course Margarite kept a keen eye on the situation but had to admit that all seemed to be going very well.

The following week, HDC was going to be away on a prestigious training course for two weeks and would be totally absent from his office during this period. This meant that Sunia would be with Alex every day. On the first day, Alex came to Sunia's desk.

'Right, Sunia, what about you doing this simple document pack? I'll be here to help you and to check that everything is OK.'

At first, Sunia looked stricken and responded that she could not possibly do it. She wouldn't be able to remember what to do. She would make mistakes and everyone would be in trouble. Alex was insistent: 'Look, I know you're good enough to do it. Have a go! I'll watch over you.'

So, feeling that something momentous was happening in her life, Sunia obtained the storeroom key from Margarite. Standing in the storeroom – warning light checked – she made her first real decision and spoke out loud: 'A small folder, I think.' At that instant, she felt wonderful!

During that morning, the document pack built up. Sunia had to obtain various documents and forms from a number of different sources and she checked with Alex several times to make sure she was doing it correctly. At last, the Schedule Sheet had been produced and the Check Sheet raised. The pack was complete! Sunia was elated as she passed her "very own work" to Alex for the initial check. He worked through it steadily and found everything correct apart from a minor error on the Schedule Sheet.

He pointed this out to Sunia and invited her to correct and reprint the sheet. 'Don't worry about this, Sunia. We all make mistakes that need to be corrected. That's why we have such a rigorous checking procedure. When you have made the correction you need to take the pack to Margarite for the DHDC check.'

A widely smiling Sunia appeared in Margarite's office with the Document Pack. Margarite looked at the Check Sheet: 'Sunia, were you the Base Coordinator for this pack?'

'Yes, Margarite, I was. Alex watched over me but I did all the work.'

'Sunia, this is very good work. You've been hiding your light under a bushel, haven't you? Someday you'll have to tell me why.'

Sunia looked thoughtful and serious: 'Yes, Margarite, there is a reason and I'm just beginning to realise what it is. I'm so grateful to Alex. He is such a wonderful person and a very good teacher. When I've worked everything out, I will tell you all about the reason for my slowness.'

The following two weeks passed happily with Sunia becoming steadily more competent at DC work, under the tutelage of the ever-patient and pleasant Alex. Margarite was extremely pleased. In addition, it was obvious that a special bond was developing between Sunia and Alex.

Sunia's eighteenth birthday was now fast approaching. Some months before, her father had sought a discussion with her mother on the question of birthday presents.

'Oh, we'll get her some really good clothes, handbags, shoes, cosmetics, that sort of thing,' her mother had said.

'Yes, that's fine, but I think we need to buy her a car,' her father replied.

'But she can't drive,' her mother said, 'we offered to buy her lessons but she refused.

'That's true, but I think she is different now. Much more confident. Anyway, I'm going to buy her a car – just a small one. That'll make her want a Driving Licence. And we can buy her driving lessons, too, as part of her birthday.'

Sunia's birthday was at the weekend. When she awoke on the morning of her birthday, there were many lavish presents piled around her bed. However her eyes widened when she saw the shiny car key on her bedside table. She immediately leapt from the bed and flew to the window. There, standing in the driveway below was an extremely pretty Fiat Cinquecento

Gucci Special Edition in sparkling white paintwork with perfectly gorgeous alloy wheels. It had a broad pink ribbon tied around it, saying "Happy 18th Birthday Sunia". Within seconds, Sunia was outside in her dressing gown and slippers, unlocking the car door and slipping into the soft two-tone leather seat behind the wheel. As she looked at the specially styled Gucci interior, her eyes shone with pure delight.

'What a fabulous car! It's like a film star's car – somebody really famous,' she breathed.

'Do you like it?' Her father, also in dressing gown and slippers, stood smiling beside the car. Sunia jumped from the car and threw herself into his arms.

'It's absolutely wonderful,' she cried, 'it's the very best present ever!'

'Yes,' her father said. 'It's the very top of the range in Fiat 500s and the very latest model.' Sunia's father was a car enthusiast and would not dream of buying anything but the top of the range! He continued, looking at his daughter affectionately: 'You'll need to start driving lessons as soon as possible. Meanwhile, you will be able to drive it in here in our grounds. It'll give you a start. I'll teach you the basics, then it's up to you. One of your birthday presents is a course of driving lessons.'

'Papa, when can we start?' she cried. 'Can we start right now?'

Her father smiled: 'Well I was thinking we should get some clothes on first and, I don't know about you but I'm looking forward to some breakfast. Let's do that and we'll start after breakfast.'

They went into the house, arms around each other affectionately.

On Monday morning, HDC returned. Yes, it had been an interesting course, he told Margarite, quite useful. Had anything been happening here? Nothing much? Well, that was what he expected. He had organised things before he went so that it would be a quiet two weeks for the Department. He wanted to make sure that there would be nothing difficult to deal with while she was in charge.

Margarite said nothing but felt her jaw muscles tightening. How she wished that Julian would not treat her like this. Love does not die easily and Margarite still loved Julian despite what he had said and done to her. She always hoped that he would revert to his former self and they could start again, living together in the love she had enjoyed so much.

'Fine, Margarite, that's all. You can get on with your own work now. Would you ask Sunia to come and see me?' Pointedly, Julian turned to his In Tray and started to read the top sheet.

A few minutes later, a reluctant Sunia knocked at HDC's door. Suddenly, she felt completely different about her association with Julian. Where before she would have come with passive obedience, now she wished she could stay as she was, working in DC with Margarite and Alex. She felt a surge of love as she thought of Alex: 'And I think he loves me too.' Sunia had noticed how happy Alex always was to see her.

'Come in, Sunia,' Julian's voice was filled with joy. 'Come in. Happy Birthday! You see, I haven't forgotten. Even although I was away on this important Management Course, I still remembered.' Julian, smiled at her expectantly, waited to be congratulated.

With some effort, Sunia smiled palely. 'Thank you, ah, Julian.' Saying that name still felt wrong.

'Sit down here, Sunia. Here is a birthday card and, "Surprise, Surprise", I've bought you a birthday present. It's just a little token of my … affection … for you.' Sunia said nothing as she took the small box and opened it.

'It's very nice, Julian,' she said, neutrally. The rose quartz glowed pink in the light and she did think it was quite a nice, unusual stone. 'It needs a thicker chain,' she thought, 'this thin silver chain does not set it off correctly. Gold or platinum would be better.'

'Put it into your bag, Sunia, you had better not wear it now. We don't want all the other staff to get jealous, do we? We just need to keep it a secret between us. But you can give me a kiss, if you like!' Julian was becoming emboldened and leaned forward enticingly.

Sunia was taken aback by this request. She certainly did not want to kiss him. Yes, she had appreciated his kindness and friendliness, making her his informal PA, and so on – but kissing him? It didn't seem right. She hesitated for a moment, then leaned forward and kissed him very lightly on the cheek. 'Thank you, Julian, it was very kind of you.' Her words were spoken perfunctorily, an echo of the trained words of childhood.

Julian, oblivious of her reluctance, was over the moon. She had kissed him! Her lips felt so soft and warm. His desire for her almost boiled over. He ached to hold her in his arms. He reached out, intending to grasp her arm and draw her closer but she moved back out of his reach.

'Julian, I have a headache and I'm not feeling very well. Unless there is something you specifically want me to do for you, could I continue my work in the General Office? I can just sit quietly and do it. I have been doing some work for Margarite while you have been away and she is quite pleased with my progress.'

Julian was very surprised. Margarite satisfied with Sunia's work? He never expected to hear that. He would have to have a chat with Margarite about this. 'It must have been all the training I have given her,' he thought, although, deep down, he was rather puzzled. In truth, he knew that he had not done any training with her that would be useful for the work of the General Office. Then he became aware that Sunia was still there, standing motionless, looking at him impassively.

'Ah, yes, Sunia. I'm sorry to hear you don't feel well. Do you want to take the rest of the day off?'

'No thanks, Julian, I'll be fine. I'll just work quietly at my desk.' Julian followed her slim, beautiful figure hungrily as she left the room and closed the door quietly. But now he felt uneasy, unsettled, uncomfortable. Something had changed. What? How? Why?

Julian

In truth, Julian had not had a good time on the management course. In fact, it had been a traumatic experience. He had gone there eagerly, knowing that his intelligence and easy charm would soon establish him as a leading light on the course. He had been on other courses and, in his perception, that was what usually happened. However, this course had been very different. The Course Tutors and the other attendees seemed to be a very peculiar group. He had approached them all in his usual friendly, informal manner but they had not responded well. They were offhand with him and excluded him from their conversations. Julian was seriously perplexed.

'Normally, I am the centre of attention in such circumstances; everyone, even the tutors, welcome my interjections and listen carefully to what I have to say.'

It had all started when his car had refused to start on the first day of the course. By the time he had organised emergency help to boost the battery, he was well behind schedule and arrived late at the venue of the course. As his rather old BMW arrived at the car park, he noted that almost all the cars there were recent models. Then he saw two almost identical Audi saloons parked alongside each other with their drivers deep in conversation. Julian proudly swept his BMW alongside.

'Good morning,' he called incisively. The men acknowledged him briefly and continued their conversation. Julian listened. They were talking about their cars, about the impressive working of their automatic gearboxes. Now Julian considered he was an expert on the workings of automatic gearboxes!

Looking rather disparagingly at their shiny cars he interrupted their conversation: 'I know you will both have the standard 5-speed auto but I greatly prefer the 4-speed that I have in my trusty BMW. People keep offering me later BMW models but I always refuse; the older model is a much better car, particularly with the superb 4-speed gearbox. The ratios are finely tuned to the power curve of the engine – and you know how much more torque you get from four cylinders, don't you?' The men looked at him rather blankly.

'We have CVT,' one said crisply, 'I think you would find that CVT is much better. It means that the torque distribution is optimal through the power range.' Julian flushed. He did not know what CVT was! The man recognised his confusion.

'CVT, Continuously Variable Transmission. Much better.'

He turned his back on Julian and resumed his conversation with the other man.

Julian stumbled into the building to register. There was an elderly man in uniform behind a small reception desk.

'Yes?' the man said, without looking up. Julian gave his name.

'You're very late,' the man said, 'you've been allocated the very last room. It's on the top floor. Used to be servant's quarters up there, you know. Pretty compact, it is.' The man smiled derisively as he said this.

Julian thought it was time to put this officious man in his place: 'I am afraid that is unacceptable, my good man. I require a more spacious room. At my firm, I am Senior Staff, a Head of Department. Would you just sort that out, immediately?' Julian was at his most haughty.

'Can't do it, I'm afraid,' the man said, 'everyone is Senior Staff on this course and the rooms are allocated on a first come, first serve basis. You didn't exactly come first, did you?

In fact you came last.' The man smiled at his joke. Then he reached behind him and threw a key across the desk. 'Room 509, there's no elevator, you'll have to walk up.' He turned away and paid no further attention to Julian.

Julian was furious. His legs were quite tired by the time he had walked up five long flights of stairs. The fifth floor was a rabbit warren of narrow, dark corridors and he had some difficulty locating Room 509. When he finally found it, it proved to be small and very cramped with a low ceiling.

'Quite unsatisfactory!' he raged, 'I shall complain to the Course Director. And I will place a complaint about that insolent man at the Reception Desk, too.' Julian consulted the Course Schedule. He saw that all tutors and members of the Course were to meet in the Lounge for coffee. There, the Schedule said, they would meet the Course Director.

'Good,' he thought grimly, 'I have business with that gentleman.'

Most of the course attendees were already drinking coffee in the Lounge when Julian arrived. He looked around and identified the Course Director by the badge pinned to his lapel. He was standing in the centre of the room, talking affably to a small group of attendees. Julian marched across and interrupted: 'Excuse me,' he said loudly, fixing the Course Director with a dominating eye, 'can I have a word? In private ...'

The Course Director did not move. He looked at Julian's name badge and said in a quiet but penetrating voice: 'Ah, yes. I want to speak to you. There's been a serious complaint against you from a member of my staff. It seems you were very rude at the Reception Desk. We treat such matters very seriously here. I suggest an apology is in order. Now would be a good time to put things right, don't you think?'

The Course Director returned to his conversation with the others. The room was hushed and all eyes were on Julian. He was absolutely mortified and went bright red. He had been humiliated in front of the whole Course! He wished the ground would open and swallow him up as he slunk from the room.

The rest of the Course continued in the same vein; Julian seemed unable to get anything right. He had apologised to the man at the Reception Desk with his eyes on the floor. He had tried to recover from his public humiliation by turning on the full force of his considerable charm and wit, all to no avail: 'I normally get on with people splendidly,' he thought with despair, 'but here, I just seem to fail all the time.' He spent all his free time closeted in his small unpleasant room, thinking: 'If I just stay in here, hopefully, I can't get into any more trouble.'

So the Course proceeded with agonising slowness and a depressed and nervous Julian counted the days until he could leave and return to the familiar life he knew.

'It will be lovely to return to the work I do so well.' Julian had lost none of his modesty! Eventually, the wonderful day came. The Course was finished and he could leave. As he drove out the impressive gateway, his spirits soared: 'Soon, I will see Sunia. I'm sure she will be very pleased with her birthday gift.' The thought of seeing Sunia again made him shiver with the delight of pure love and adoration.

'So what's all this about you being pleased with Sunia's progress?'

Julian had appeared in Margarite's office and the tone of his voice was derisive: 'This is what Sunia is trying to tell me. It can't be true, can it? You've always had a down on that girl and I can't imagine you changing your mind.'

Margarite was stung by Julian's tone and answered with some irritation: 'Well, you're wrong about that, Julian. While you were away, Sunia asked Alex if he would help her and, to my great surprise, it seems to have been a great success. So successful that Sunia assembled a simple Document Pack last week as Base Coordinator. All by herself, I am told. I never thought I would see the day. I have congratulated her and authorised her to work with Alex as much as possible. I doubt whether she will ever be our top scorer, but at least she seems to be gaining confidence and becoming useful at last.'

Julian was greatly alarmed. What was this? Sunia working with Alex? He had never paid much attention to Alex, considering him just one of the unimportant "foot soldiers" in the Department. Now he would pay a great deal more attention to him! Meanwhile, he must put a stop to this right away.

He addressed Margarite in his gravest tones: 'I think that sounds like a very bad idea, Margarite. Junior staff training junior staff? That's very dangerous and it's inefficient, too. I will not have such a thing happening in my Department. I insist that this liaison be broken up immediately. That's an order.'

To his surprise, Margarite demurred; she normally backed down right away when he adopted his most serious tone. 'I really don't agree, Julian. The training with Alex has been highly successful and the girl is now learning well. I think it is essential for her to work with Alex. He is very good with her and he is one of my most reliable workers.'

Julian gritted his teeth and looked angrily into Margarite's eyes: 'Listen, Margarite, I have given you my decision on this matter. I am extremely surprised that you should be arguing with me.' Suddenly, he had a brilliant idea. 'Anyway, I have decided that Sunia will now work full-time with me; I have been finding her very effective as my PA.' He turned to leave the office.

'Fine, Julian. I'll get on to HR right away and tell them to organise a recruitment exercise for a replacement in the General Office. Do you want me to tell them about your acquisition of a PA, or will you do it? One way or another, HR will need to know. It's an overall staff increase for the Firm. You know they're very hot on that.'

Julian froze in the doorway, his mind racing. If Margarite contacted HR, they would report a staff increase request to their Director and an Internal Staffing Review would need to be set up. He, Julian, would need to make a strong case for a PA. He would probably have to be interviewed by the Partners' Board. If his case failed, it would be a humiliation for him and he would lose Sunia. However if his case was successful, they would insist on a Fair Recruitment Exercise and the best and most experienced candidate, internal or external, would be chosen. This would definitely not be Sunia, since she had no PA skills or experience. Success or failure, this course of action would be a disaster for him! Julian turned back slowly to Margarite, his face ashen: 'Ah … Let's take no action on any of this for the moment, Margarite. You will appreciate it's a very complex matter and I need to think it through properly. I'm very busy at the moment with other things. I'll let you know in due course. For the time being, Sunia can stay under your control.'

No mention was made of Alex.

'OK, I have noted that, Julian. No action, no change, at least for the time being.' She watched him go with a slight smile.

Moments later, Julian was back in his office, wild-eyed, heart pounding. Margarite had outmanoeuvred him! It had never happened before. Worse still, he had lost Sunia completely. Now he could not insist on having her for training or informal PA work, as he did before. If he did, Margarite would insist on asking HR for a replacement for the General Office. He knew it was very unlikely he could construct a successful case for a PA for HDC. None of the Heads of Department at his level had PAs and he was sure the Firm would not wish to make an exception for him. But even if they did, his PA would certainly not be his beloved Sunia. Julian slumped forward in despair and held his head in his hands.

The weeks passed and Margarite was astonished at the progress Sunia was making. She was like a different person! Instead of the dreamy, detached and rather inarticulate person who had come to DC, panicking if asked to do anything and seemingly quite happy to spend the whole day staring out of the window, here was a bright and determined girl, hungry to learn everything she could and approaching every task with meticulous enthusiasm.

'It really is a miracle to see,' Margarite thought. 'Who would have thought she was capable of this?' As yet, Margarite still insisted that Sunia work with Alex and use him as her informal supervisor. However, she thought it would soon be time for Sunia to "go solo".

A few days later, a cheerful Sunia popped her head around Margarite's door and asked if she could speak to her.

'Yes, Sunia, come in,' Margarite replied with a smile, 'I'm really pleased with your progress, you know. You're becoming a bit of an expert.' Sunia blushed with pleasure.

'Margarite, I want to tell you why I've improved. Finally, I've worked it out.'

'Let's make a cup of coffee and then you can tell me all about it.' Margarite was curious to hear what Sunia would say.

So Sunia told Margarite the whole story of her childhood and the horrifying bullying she had experienced as she moved from school to school in various parts of the world: 'All the schools were different but the bullying was the same,' she said sadly. 'It only takes one bully and their pathetic followers to make the lives of their victims a misery. It's no good trying to stand up to them. I tried that many times at first and always got beaten – sometimes psychologically, often physically. Bullies like to hurt people. I know now it's because they feel inadequate. So a long time ago I worked out a survival strategy. If I could make them despise me as an inferior, they would leave me alone. At all the schools I made myself stupid, clumsy and pathetic and it worked. I survived! But unfortunately that became a way of life for me and I carried it with me after I had finished school. When I came here, you and Julian (I mean, HDC) were the authority figures here and I automatically wanted to establish myself as stupid and inadequate in your sight. If I made you believe that, you would leave me alone and not ask me to do difficult things that I would get wrong; because if I got things wrong, I would get punished – and that would hurt me, just like the bullying did. Do you see? It was just another application of the survival strategy.'

Margarite looked at this beautiful girl with sympathy, deeply aware that she had misjudged her: 'Sunia, I think you are really brave and very clever to have worked all this out. But how were you able to overcome it with Alex?'

'Margarite, I like Alex. He was always very nice to me, even when I was being stupid and pathetic. Recently, I suddenly realised that I didn't need to make myself stupid to him. He was not an authority figure like you (sorry, Margarite!) and he was not going to bully me. So I thought if I could persuade him to put up with me tagging along behind him, I might learn something and become a little bit more useful in the Department. After a while, I began to realise I wasn't so stupid and became a bit more confident. Alex is so nice to me. I really like him.'

Margarite smiled: 'Well, I imagine that pleases him quite a lot.'

'Do you really think so, Margarite? I want him to be pleased.'

Margarite smiled again: 'What young man is going to object to a beautiful girl following him around, hanging on his every word?' After a short pause, Margarite said: 'Sunia, I was very surprised to hear you calling HDC "Julian". No one in the General Office calls him by his first name.'

'I'm very sorry about that, Margarite. I made a mistake. I hope I'm not going to get into trouble.' Sunia looked very worried.

'No, you're not,' Margarite said, 'but why did you do it?'

Sunia looked uncomfortable: 'He told me to call him Julian when we were together in his office. He told me not to do it anywhere else. But I made a mistake. I forgot. I knew I would.' The girl was silent for a moment. 'Margarite, I don't like doing it. It doesn't feel right. But he's HDC and I felt I had to do as I was told.'

Margarite thought for a moment and then said somewhat hesitantly: 'Sunia, was everything … all right … when you were alone with HDC in his office? I was always a bit worried about you.'

Sunia replied thoughtfully: 'HDC was very nice to me. He was kind and I really appreciated that because, in my life, so many people have not been kind to me. He seemed to like me.'

'What did you actually do, Sunia?'

'Sometimes he gave me training on the computer terminal. Not the sort of training I need to do my DC job. Really it was training to do the job that he does. I thought that was a bit strange. At other times I sort of looked after him, got him coffee, ran errands for him. The best thing of all was delivering envelopes or folders to other people in the Firm. That made me feel quite important. There were also times when he was busy and I did nothing. I just sat there. It's what he wanted me to do.'

'So you were always very happy with HDC?'

'Yes … in a way … But …'

'What's the "but", Sunia?'

Sunia looked uncomfortable. 'Well, I thought he touched me rather a lot – just on my hands and arms,' she added hastily, thinking about the kiss he had insisted upon. After a moment, Sunia continued quietly: 'But, Margarite, I've changed. I think it's because I'm doing real DC work now. I don't really want to work with HDC anymore. I just want to be one of the General Office staff. I just want to get better and better at my work.'

Margarite looked at the girl with real pleasure: 'Well that's exactly what you're going to do from now on. Thank you for telling me about your life – and your secrets.'

Sunia was smiling happily as she left Margarite's office. Alex was busy, head down, working hard at his desk. As she passed, Sunia ruffled his hair affectionately.

'Hi!' he said, smiling at her, 'you're spoiling my good looks.'

'Nothing could spoil your good looks,' she riposted, leaving him to interpret what she meant.

The following week, Margarite appeared at Sunia's desk. 'Sunia, we have an important Document Pack to raise for Legal Team Three. I want you to assemble the Pack as Base Coordinator. Here are the Request Details.'

Sunia looked at Margarite, wide-eyed, startled but delighted, too. 'Oh, Margarite, I'll do my very best; but do you think I'm good enough to take on such an important Pack? I might make mistakes.'

'Listen, Sunia, you've heard me say it hundreds of times: Nobody's perfect – not even me! Mistakes are inevitable and, if there are any, they will be picked up on the checks. I am confident that you are ready to do this standard of work. I expect it to be on my desk by the middle of this afternoon. If you have any queries or you need any help, Alex will help you, or you can come to me. Don't worry, you'll be fine. You're ready to do this. I trust you.'

When Margarite had gone, Sunia sat back in that heady mixture of pride and fear. She noticed her hands were trembling. 'Come on, get a grip!' she reproached herself. 'Stage 1:

Understand the Request.' She opened the Request Folder and began to read.

'Congratulations, Sunia.' Alex was standing by her desk. 'Don't worry, I won't interrupt you – I know you have plenty to do. I'll be here if you need me for anything.' Sunia looked at Alex, her eyes shining with pride.

'You're a real friend, Alex. You're my favourite person in DC. It's lovely to know you're on my side. Thank you.' Alex flushed. He was glad she liked him so much.

'I certainly like her – a great deal! Perhaps a lot more than she imagines.'

By coffee time, Sunia had constructed a draft Schedule and Document List, the first essentials of the task. She was ready to start assembling the documents. Pleased with her progress, she decided that she needed a coffee break. For the first time in DC, Sunia felt she deserved her coffee – and it was a very heady feeling. She happily joined the other staff of the General Office as they chatted about their lives outside the Firm.

To her surprise, Sunia found that she was actually quite an expert on clothes, unaware that the other girls had always admired the simple but expensive clothes she wore. And, of course, she was always ready to talk about cars, being the proud owner of a gorgeous Fiat Cinquecento SE Gucci! She also reported upon her driving lessons and her accounts of some of her errors were hilarious! At times, the room rang with laughter.

Sitting unhappily in his office, Julian heard the laughter and wondered whether he should go and complain: 'They are distracting me from my work,' he said to himself peevishly – in fact he had only been reading the racing paper. Then his mind turned to Sunia, as it often did: 'I hope Sunia is not becoming too familiar with that pathetic little boy Alex.' Julian had become ragingly jealous of Alex. 'It's absolutely dreadful that this stupid boy now has complete access to her.' Julian's expression hardened into hatred with the thought that the boy might be touching her hand. How was she responding? Where else was he touching her? You know what young people are like nowadays!

Now Julian was working himself up into a rage. Why he could even be taking advantage of the fact she is an innocent little girl! So powerful was this emotion that he gasped for breath, flushed with a raging love. At last, he calmed himself and became resolute: 'I must protect her. I must watch them together. I must make sure nothing untoward is happening. If it is, that boy will be in trouble!' Julian smiled unpleasantly at the thought and felt much better. That's it, he would keep a very close eye on them.

Coffee break over, Sunia was ready to go to the storeroom to raise the Document Pack Folder.

'Margarite, can I have the key to the storeroom, please?'

'I don't have it, Sunia. Alex took it about ten minutes ago. It's not come back, so he must still be down there. How is everything going?'

'I think it's going fine, Margarite.' Sunia's voice was full of pride. 'On schedule,' she added proudly with a little smile as she left the office. In the corridor outside, she met Julian. She thought he was acting rather shiftily.

'Hello, Julian,' she said in a friendly tone, 'how are you?'

She was taken aback when he held a finger to his lips and spoke very quietly: 'Where are you going, Sunia?'

'To the storeroom to raise a Document Pack Folder.'

'I'll come with you, Sunia. I can help you.'

'It's all right, Julian,' she replied, 'Alex is already there. He can help me if I need help.' She was astonished at his reaction. Without a word, he turned on his heel and marched into his office, slamming the door behind him.

'I wonder what's wrong with him,' Sunia mused as she walked down the corridor. As she approached the door, she could see that the storeroom warning light was illuminated. In accordance with procedure, she knocked at the door and waited.

'Just a minute, I'm on top of the stepladder.' Alex's voice. A moment later, the door swung open. 'Hello, it's my favourite girl! Come on in.' Alex was greatly struck by her elegant beauty as she entered. He had been busy with his own Request and had already assembled a heap of papers and folders on the table. 'Are you OK?' he enquired solicitously, 'do you need any help?'

'No thanks, Alex. I want to do everything myself. I need to start by getting a large Document Pack Folder. My Request involves quite a lot of material.'

'Do you know where they are?' Alex was eager to help!

'Of course I do, Alex. You taught me where they were. On the top shelf just beside the door.' Sunia wheeled the tall metal stepladder into position and prepared to ascend.

'Where is everybody? The place looks empty.' Moments before, Julian had come to the General Office to check up on Alex and Sunia. Now he burst into Margarite's office in a distinctly agitated state.

Puzzled, Margarite glanced out of her office door. 'Everybody's here – except Alex and Sunia. They're both down in the storeroom.'

Both in the Storeroom! Still there. Alone together. Julian swayed with the shock of it. This was extremely dangerous. He had better take action right away. With these thoughts racing through his fevered mind he left the General Office and ran towards the storeroom as quickly as he could.

As the storeroom door came into view, he felt a wave of pure panic. The door was closed tight! The warning light glowed! Anything could be happening in there!'

Now he pressed his ear tightly against the door, hearing the low murmur of conversation. He strained his ears but could not hear what was being said. Then he heard the sound very clearly – she was laughing, that beautiful little laugh that he had heard in his office so many times.

Something was happening in there! Something that should definitely not be happening!

Immediately, he worked out his precise course of action. He would surprise them. He would throw open the door and find out precisely what was going on. He would fix that boy! After all, he was the boss, wasn't he? He was in charge. This was *his* department. This was *HIS* storeroom.

A final listen at the door; now a worrying silence from within. Then – CRASH!

Julian had twisted the handle and flung the door wide open with great force. However, the door only opened about ten centimetres before it was blocked by an obstruction inside. An obstruction which fell over with a gigantic metallic clatter. Julian's mind worked with blinding speed: 'He's blocked the door, that's what he's done! He's used the heavy stepladder to do it. But that won't stop me getting in.' Julian threw his weight against the blocked door and pushed with all his strength. The door gave way slowly as the overturned steps were pushed across the floor. Now Julian was able to see into the brightly lit room. Alex lay on his back on the floor with Sunia on top of him. He had his arms around her slim body.

There is a special roar that a lion gives when it assumes its most intimidating persona. This roar is deep, long and very, very loud. It sends an almost primeval fear into all who hear it, even those who are far away. Julian started his "conversation" with Alex and Sunia by emitting such a roar! In the following stunned silence, he continued in an exceptionally loud voice, stentorian and razor-sharp with fury. Inevitably, it began with a question directed at the unfortunate Alex: 'What are you doing to that young girl in my storeroom?'

'Saving her from injury.' A small voice filled with shock.

'Saving her!' The answer repeated in an apoplectic scream. Girl and boy now disentangled themselves and stood up. Sunia ran to a corner of the room and stood, wide-eyed with fear. Alex remained where he was, next to the table.

Stepping forward quickly, Julian swung a punch at Alex's head. The punch was blocked by Alex's forearm. Another punch followed, similarly blocked.

'What on earth is going on here?' Margarite's voice, a sharp-toned question from the open doorway. Alex switched his attention momentarily from Julian to Margarite and the man took the opportunity of landing a heavy blow on the young man's cheekbone, splitting the skin open. As he fingered the bloody wound, Alex turned back to Julian who had drawn back his fist, preparing to strike again.

'Listen, Sir, if you try to punch me again, I will need to retaliate. If I do, I will knock you down, possibly unconscious. One of my hobbies is boxing and I'm quite experienced.'

There was silence as Julian digested this information; then, wisely, he discontinued his attack. Now he turned to Margarite in blazing fury. 'This evil boy was attacking Sunia sexually. They were lying on the floor and his arms were around her. I will not have such behaviour in my Department. This is a criminal matter.' Julian was beside himself with rage.

Margarite stayed calm. 'Is this true?' She asked the question of Alex but it was Sunia who answered in a quavering voice from the corner of the room.

'Margarite, it certainly is not true. Alex saved me from serious injury by catching me when I was thrown off the top platform of the stepladder. For some reason, HDC threw open the door without knocking or observing the warning light outside. The edge of the door caught the stepladder and knocked it over with me on it. Lucky for me, Alex was near enough to catch me in his arms as I fell. The force of my fall knocked him to the floor. That's when HDC saw us and became furious. I think Alex is wonderful to have saved me.'

Alex added ruefully: 'Yes, and I think I will have a bruised chest as well as a bruised face.'

Another silence. Then, Julian's voice, still taut with rage, 'Get this mess cleared up. You will be hearing from me.' He looked balefully at Alex and stalked out, stony-faced.

One hour had passed. Alex had just been summoned to HDC's office. Julian sat at his desk, glaring at Alex, who was standing at the other side of the desk, not having been invited to sit down.

'I will not have it! Junior staff rolling about in a sexual embrace on the storeroom floor. I regard this as a misdemeanour of the worst kind. You are here to do your work, not attack innocent young girls. I know all about you young men – always trying to seduce young girls and attacking them physically. It's absolutely disgusting, criminal, in fact. I have constructed a comprehensive report which I am about to submit to HR, in which I set out all the circumstances. In the report I accuse you of gross misconduct and criminal behaviour – attempted rape of an innocent office junior, newly turned eighteen. I also accuse you of insubordination and threatening behaviour – threatening to strike a senior officer. I have recommended immediate dismissal with no reference and I have no doubt that HR will carry that out. I have also directed that the report be passed to the police for a criminal investigation. When I am finished with you, not only will you have no job but if I hear of anyone else thinking of employing you in this town, I will personally ring them up to warn them off. In any case, by that time it is highly likely you will have been convicted of attempted rape and will have a criminal record. No one will ever want to employ you again.' Julian was virtually foaming at the mouth as he roared this at the top of his voice, every word clearly audible to the staff in the General Office, crouching over their desks, barely breathing, trying to make themselves as small as possible.

In the silence that followed, Julian swayed in his seat and gasped for breath, mopping his face with a handkerchief. 'I must be calm,' he told himself, 'I will make myself ill.'

Now he lifted a sheaf of papers from his desk and, fixing eyes of hatred on the boy standing opposite, said triumphantly: 'In five minutes, this report will be with HR and you will be finished. I'm certainly finished with you right now. Get out of my office.'

He was surprised when the young man did not move.

'I said, "Get Out!"'

'Don't send it, Sir.'

'What?' A veritable explosion of sound.

'Don't send it, Sir. You'll regret it if you do.' The voice was quiet and calm.

Julian's mind raced. What could the boy mean? Then – understanding. Of course! He was asking for mercy. As this thought registered, another fleeting memory was recalled for a microsecond. Hadn't someone else asked for mercy? Didn't he grant it? The word "penance" flickered in his consciousness. He shook his head to return to the situation in hand. Then, leering unpleasantly, he said harshly: 'You want mercy, do you? Well, my boy, the answer is "No". I would not have mercy on you even if you begged on your bended knees, even if you promised to be my personal slave for the rest of your life!' Julian was enjoying himself.

'I'm not asking for mercy, Sir. I'm saying, don't send it to HR. You'll regret it if you do.'

'Really!' Julian emphasised his sarcasm as unpleasantly as he could. 'And why would I regret it, pray?'

'Because I've already been to HR for a personal interview with the HR Director. I wanted to make sure that the truth was told – and recorded.'

Julian's mind blanked. His vision switched off. Everything went black. In that blackness, it seemed to Julian that the room was performing 360 degree rotations in a number of planes. He slumped back in his chair. He must think this through. It was important to get this right. But, try as he might, his brain would not work. It felt as if a power source had been switched off. Completely disconnected, in fact. Panic surged through his body and he felt he was losing consciousness. He needed help!

Suddenly, a shaft of blessed reason! Sunia would help him. He could trust her. He loved her. Her very presence calmed him. If she was here, he would be able to work out what to do. Greatly relieved, he opened his eyes and was surprised to find Alex still standing in front of his desk. In an almost normal tone of voice, he said: 'Go back to the General Office. Ask Sunia to come and see me right away.'

She came, with hesitation, looking greatly alarmed. He smiled at her, his best smile. She did not smile back.

'Sunia, come and sit beside me here at the terminal. We must talk. You must help me. I am unwell. I have many worries. I try to run the Department with the greatest possible efficiency but staffing problems keep occurring. For instance, that event that happened today in the storeroom. I am a very moral man and I was horrified to see what was happening.' As he spoke, he was edging closer and closer to the girl. She moved away pointedly.

'Sir – Julian – I am very sorry. I cannot advise you on Department problems. I am only a young, inexperienced girl. Today was an accident and Alex saved me from injury by

384

catching me as I fell from the stepladder. I'm very grateful to him. Otherwise, I think I would have been hurt badly.'

Julian ignored what she had said and again moved his body closer to her. 'Sunia, you must tell me the truth. This boy Alex, do you like him?' He waited with terrible dread for her answer.

'Yes, Julian, I do. I think he's very nice. And he's very kind and helpful.' Julian flushed deeply and his hands began to tremble.

'But Sunia, what about me? Do you like me?' This time his heart stopped beating. Time was arrested as she paused before answering.

'Yes, of course I do,' she said slowly, 'but you are HDC, you are the Head of Department. You are an important man. You are my superior officer. You are like a father to me.'

As she spoke, she recognised this was a lie. However she knew that she dare not tell the truth. She knew her former passively neutral feelings for him had changed abruptly – she didn't know why. Now she felt nothing but unease and a clear feeling of dislike. She dearly wanted to flee from the room. She sensed growing danger.

He smiled delightedly. His heart sang – she said she liked him! He could stand it no longer. He grasped her slim body with both hands and drew it close to his own: 'Sunia, I love you so much. I want to marry you. Will you?' He was really surprised when she started to struggle and cry.

'Julian, please let go, you mustn't do this, stop it, please.' Her cries were becoming louder and more desperate.

'Oh, Sunia, Sunia, you are so beautiful. Do not run away, please. Marry me, please. Say you will!'

'Julian, no, please.' She jumped up and pulled away from him as hard as she could, pulling him from his seat. He fell on his knees on the floor and grasped her even more tightly. Her struggles intensified even more and, with a sudden violent

385

twist, she was able to squirm out of his tight grasp and rush away towards the door, leaving almost all of her light summer dress in his clutching hands. As she approached the door, it suddenly opened, framing the tall figure of the HR Director. Sunia, now clad only in two items of minimalist underwear, ran screaming into his arms: 'Help me, please, save me!'

The scene was immobilised in "freeze frame" mode for several seconds before the release of the imaginary Pause Control introduced animation once again. Julian, dropping his gaze to look incredulously at his clenched hands, still grasping the fine material that had been Sunia's dress. The HR Director, astounded, trying to decide on an appropriate course of action when a beautiful almost-naked girl throws herself into your arms. Then, with admirable presence of mind, stripping off his jacket to wrap around the girl. The door of the General Office bursting open, with the staff, led by Alex, pouring out in a veritable torrent of humanity. Margarite, bringing up at the rear, hurrying forward and assessing the elements of the situation with impressive precision.

It was Margarite who took charge and initiated a series of essential actions: two young men instantly instructed to restrain Alex from attacking HDC and remove the young man from the scene– Sunia retrieved gently from the comforting safety of the HR Director's arms and taken to Margarite's office where the jacket was replaced by the more suitable covering of Margarite's overcoat – the rest of the General Office staff instructed to return to their desks and not to move from there – then, Margarite and the HR Director joining HDC in his office and closing the door firmly.

The police were called.

The HR Director had insisted, 'I am sorry, Julian, I hear what you say but the Firm simply cannot take the risk. After all, you were alone here in your office with the young girl and the fact is, you tore off her clothes. Yes, I know you didn't tear off *all* her clothes but you certainly tore off most of them, didn't you? I was coming to see you about another staff matter when I heard the screaming. If I hadn't opened the door, goodness knows what would have happened! Now, while we're waiting for the police to get here, what's all this about a boy called Alex and something that happened in your storeroom?'

Margarite interrupted quickly, 'Julian, I think it would be useful if I showed the Director the storeroom and explained the details, don't you? After all, he has already heard Alex's account.'

Julian picked up the report he had intended to submit to HR and opened his mouth to speak. As he did so, he saw Margarite, standing behind the Director, shaking her head violently.

'Well … yes,' he said weakly, 'I suppose that's a good idea.' He realised suddenly that Alex, Sunia and Margarite would give similar accounts of what happened at the Storeroom; accounts that would be markedly different from his own. He would need to think about this.

'Could have been a very nasty accident, that.' Minutes later, the HR Director was back. 'Very unfortunate – your mistake, I think? Opening the door without knocking?'

'Well, yes, I suppose so.' Julian was reluctant, 'perhaps the warning light wasn't working? It's not like me to make a mistake.' The Director consulted his notes.

'Well it certainly is working now. Now Julian, another matter, the young man says that you struck him in the face. He certainly has a nasty cut there.' Julian had forgotten about hitting the boy. He thought quickly. 'I think he must have received that when the stepladder fell over. Perhaps I bumped against him in the confusion afterwards. I'll apologise to him for that.'

The Director looked at Margarite. 'Did you see what happened?'

'Not really, there was so much confusion. I'll think about it and see what I can remember.' Margarite looked significantly at Julian.

A knock at the door heralded the arrival of the police, a man and a woman.

'Rape Investigation and Support,' the man said in an official tone, 'we've been directed here by your Human Resources Department. Are we in the right place?' On receiving an affirmative answer, the policeman continued: 'Right, I've been given an outline of what happened. Is this the room where it took place? First of all, I would like to speak to the accused and my colleague will speak to the victim. Which of you gentlemen is the accused?' The HR Director was quick to identify Julian and declare he was returning to his office!

'Were you a witness, Sir? I'll need to speak to you later. Shall I come to your office in a while?

The policeman made a note of the HR Director's room number and then turned to Julian. 'May I sit down, Sir? Thank you. Now, tell me what happened in your own words and I'll make notes. Oh, and by the way, do tell me the truth, it always comes out in the end.' Julian started with the storeroom incident but was soon stopped by the policeman.

'Excuse me, Sir, what's this got to do with the attempted rape?' Of course a confused and often incoherent Julian denied attempted rape. The policeman asked searching questions. It became unequivocally clear that Julian had torn the girl's dress off. What was she wearing underneath? Very little? Precisely what? Did he attempt to remove these garments also?' Time crawled past. All other relevant staff were interviewed and statements taken. The HR Director was visited in his office.

Finally, the two police officers withdrew to a corner of the General Office and conferred for some time, comparing the statements they had recorded from Julian, Sunia and all the other staff members. Finally they both came to Julian's office and knocked on his door.

'You'll need to come with us, Sir. We are arresting you for attempted rape.'

This was the stuff of nightmares. Julian had never even visited a police station before and here he was, locked in a prison cell. Numb, he had been processed by the station officers. Details were taken, information and warnings given, papers read sightlessly and signed, searches done ('yes, we need your tie and your shoelaces …'). Finally he was taken to a lower level of the building, where a brightly-lit corridor gave way to heavy, barred doors on each side. Here, it was hot and noisy, with the pungent smell of disinfectant almost masking more noxious odours. A heavy door was opened. Julian was shocked by the smallness of the cell now revealed.

'These are only holding cells,' the accompanying police-man explained, 'you'll get a much bigger cell when you get to a proper prison, though I expect you'll have to share it.' This was certainly not what Julian wanted to hear at that moment!

The door closed with a deafening finality. Traumatised, Julian sank down on the hard, narrow bed. Now he was alone and confined, he felt panic building up within him, the panic of fear, reality and claustrophobia. For a few seconds, he considered hammering upon the door with his fists, crying: 'Let me out! I'm innocent. This is all a terrible mistake.' However he realised this would be pointless and achieve nothing. With great difficulty, he calmed himself and lay down on the bed, closing his eyes and trying to slow his racing thoughts.

'I must be dreaming, I really must. I'm a totally law-abiding citizen who would never do anything criminal. I'm deeply and madly in love with Sunia. How can I possibly be accused of attempting to rape her? I worship the ground she walks on. I love her so much. I can't possibly have done anything wrong.' He paused and pictured her beauty, remembering how her slim body had felt when he held it in his hands. 'When she thinks about it, surely she will recognise that what happened was just an accident. Surely she will recognise my love for her. I do hope she will think seriously about what I said. I'm sure she will. I think there's quite a good chance that she will change her mind and decide to marry me.'

He suddenly felt much better and smiled: 'It's all a ghastly mistake. Everybody knows I'm a kindly, generous and highly moral man. This will be recognised and I will be acquitted of this alleged crime, probably with an apology. I wonder if I could claim compensation?' Julian pondered this final thought carefully.

'Do you think he did it deliberately?'

It was the next day and Margarite was talking to Sunia in her office. The tone of her question was gentle and friendly. The girl looked deeply into her coffee cup.

'I don't know. One minute he was normal and the next minute he went mad! He grabbed hold of my waist in such a tight grip. I couldn't get free. It was like being back at school when the bullies trapped me in the washroom. I often had my clothes torn off …' Tears welled into the girl's eyes. 'I thought all that was over … I thought I didn't need to suffer that anymore.'

'Yes, I understand why you are so upset, Sunia. But do you think he did it deliberately? Do you think he meant to tear your dress off?'

'Margarite, I really don't know. He was shouting. I couldn't understand what he was saying, I was in such a panic. I just needed to escape.' Sunia was weeping at the memory.

'Goodness knows what would have happened to me if I hadn't broken free.'

After an introspective silence, Margarite spoke quietly: 'You know there will be a court case, don't you, Sunia? You know he's being accused of attempted rape? Do you know what that is?'

'Oh, yes, Margarite, all that was discussed at school. We even had lessons on it.'

'Sunia, sometimes young people, especially young girls, don't really understand about sex and rape, so you and I are going to talk about it now, so that I can be sure you know what you're talking about. Because you will be the victim, a key witness at the court case, you know that, don't you? You will be asked all sorts of questions and it's essential that you are very clear in your mind what happened exactly and why it happened.' The woman and the girl were then deep in conversation for some time.

'It's a bad business,' the Senior Partner sighed.

The HR Director nodded his acquiescence: 'It isn't something I will forget in a hurry. I've never experienced anything like it in my life.'

'What do you think will happen? What do we need to do now, in your opinion as HR Director?' It was the turn of the HR Director to sigh.

'I think the outcome is pretty obvious, don't you? I'm talking about the outcome for the Firm, by the way. I don't think it matters to us whether he is convicted or not.'

The Senior Partner replied in regretful tones: 'I suppose you're right. So we need to do a few temporary moves, don't we? And then, in due course, make things final.'

The HR Director nodded. 'Do you want me to arrange things for the interim period?'

'Yes, please. The woman, the Deputy, Margarite is it? She's reliable, isn't she?'

'Yes, I think so, although HDC had a few criticisms. Anyway, it's the only solution in the short term. She stands in for him when he's not there. We'll see how she does in the next months.'

'How did you manage to swing that? I've never seen anything like it.' The lawyer was derisively incredulous as he packed away his papers into his briefcase. His words were directed at a silent Julian slumped over the table.

'What do you mean?' a flat, despondent voice.

'You're the boss of an eighteen-year-old girl, you get her alone in your office, grab her and tear off her clothes … and you manage to swing a suspended sentence? People are put away for years for much less than you did. Have you got a lucky horseshoe at home, or something?' Julian looked with dislike at the man who had been his defence lawyer.

'Look, I've told you hundreds of times – I'm not guilty, it was an accident. I love the girl. I would never have done anything to hurt her. I'm innocent of attempted rape. I think I ought to appeal.'

'Listen, my friend,' the lawyer said, 'you've achieved a superb result here, you'll soon be a free man and you can get back to your life. If you appeal, you could easily get your suspended sentence changed to a custodial one – and not a short one, either. I expected you to get at least five years for this. So, keep quiet and thank your lucky stars.' Julian's face darkened: 'A superb result, you say? I've lost four months of my life, sitting in a stinking prison cell on remand. Now I've got a criminal record for a serious crime I didn't commit. I would hardly call that a superb result, would you? I should have been found "Not Guilty".'

The lawyer ignored Julian's response: 'Goodbye, then,' he said cheerfully, 'best of luck!' He departed, leaving Julian with his thoughts.

Julian had to admit that it was nice to be free, to be able to go anywhere you want, to eat what you want – if you could afford it, that is. He reflected angrily that he had been compelled to pay a large fine and this had drained his bank account.

'I'd better get back to work,' he thought, 'to start building up my resources again.' He felt in his pocket and pulled out his money – a single 20 euro note. 'Twenty euro. Enough to buy lunch for several days.' He headed towards the sandwich shop beside the park. It was a nice day and Julian looked forward to relaxing in the park for a little while before making contact with the Firm. 'Plenty of time for that,' he thought.

As usual, the sandwich shop was busy. The boy behind the counter was working as hard as he could to serve his customers. Julian joined the queue and eventually placed his order for a ham sandwich and a bottle of water.

'Five euro, please,' the boy said, perfunctorily. Julian handed over his twenty euro note. The boy rummaged in the till drawer and handed Julian his change, a single green five euro note.

'Next?' he called.

'Just a minute,' Julian said firmly, 'you've given me the wrong change. I gave you a twenty. You still owe me ten.'

'I'm sorry, Sir, but you gave me a ten. This is your note in the clip on top of the till.' He pointed to the red note fixed in the clip: 'You see, Sir, we have a fixed procedure here. It's what most shops do. When the customer pays with a note and change is required, we always place the customer's note in the clip until we give the change. So, you see, this is the note you gave me – and it's a ten.'

Julian reddened: 'You're wrong. I gave you a twenty – you must remember.'

'No Sir, you didn't.'

Julian stiffened: 'I want to speak to the Manager – immediately.'

'Sir, I am the Manager. You gave me a ten; and this is it.'

Angry voices began to sound from the waiting queue. A few moments later, Julian was outside the shop, his purchase in one hand and only a single five euro note in his pocket.

'I've been cheated,' he thought angrily, 'I'll never buy another sandwich in there and I'll make sure I'll tell everyone else this story. He'll be sorry by the time I've finished with him.'

Inside the shop, the young man allowed himself a brief smile of satisfaction.

'Hello, Oberto,' (Julian had decided it was best to use his family connections), 'as you probably know, I'm available to start work again as soon as you like; today, even! Shall I come round to see you?'

'Ah, Julian. Could I just ring you back? I need to have a word with HR. There are things to organise, you know. Give me your phone number, please.'

About one hour later, Julian's cell phone rang. It was not Oberto but the HR Director:

'Hello, the Senior Partner has asked me to have a word with you. Would you like to come in to see me? 10.30 tomorrow morning would be fine.'

'Ah ... I was rather hoping for today ...'

'Can't do it, I'm afraid; stacked out with meetings. See you tomorrow at 10.30. Goodbye.'

Time passed at a snail's pace. In the afternoon, Julian had walked around aimlessly; he had even gone to the Museum and tried to interest himself in the dusty exhibits whose details were explained in tiny writing on small faded cards. Standing in front of a large Roman pot, broken and reassembled rather haphazardly, he thought, he realised he had read the exhibit card four times and still did not understand the words.

'Time for a cup of coffee and a pastry,' he thought, then remembered he did not have enough money. Finally, he gave up and went back to his flat, to stare gloomily at daytime television trivia.

The only bright spot in his life was Sunia. His face relaxed into a tender smile as he thought about her. He loved her deeply and was absolutely obsessed with her. He longed to be together with her in marriage. How wonderful that would be. There had been many girlfriends and relationships in his life but he had never before felt like this about anyone. 'She said she liked me; I'm sure that means she loves me! I might have made a mistake when I took her in my arms that day but I wanted to show her how much I loved her.' This was the one thought that had kept Julian sane in prison. He would sit for hours, thinking and planning: 'When I am found "Not Guilty" and get out of here, I must make contact with her as soon as possible. I'll need to leave it until I get back to work, though, because I don't know her cell phone number and it wouldn't be appropriate for me to ring her up on the office phone without warning. We have a lot to talk about, Sunia and I.' Oh what bliss that would be!

After a rather fitful night's sleep, Julian prepared himself for his meeting at the Firm. His elderly BMW took him to the town and, for the first time in months, he drove into the Firm's underground car park and attempted to park it in his allotted space; however he was greatly annoyed to find another car parked there.

'This is very annoying and totally unacceptable; I'll need to sort it out as soon as I get back to DC. And I'll give whoever it is a serious piece of my mind.' With some difficulty, he turned his car around and eventually parked at a nearby public car park. Looking at his watch, he found he would need to hurry to arrive at the HR Department for 10.30.

The familiar doorway was entered. Julian greeted the security staff smoothly as he passed, flashing his Security ID. Should he call in briefly at DC? He knew that everyone would be very pleased to see him – and he might see Sunia. He looked at his watch again. Better not, he didn't want to be late for the meeting with the HR Director After all, he would be going to DC after the meeting – returning to his office to start work.

As he stood in the elevator, he mused: 'I wonder what this meeting is all about. Maybe he wants some advice from me.' Moments later, he arrived at HR.

'I have a meeting with your Director,' he said loftily to the HR Receptionist, 'HDC, 10.30.' The girl consulted a list.

'Nothing here about HDC,' she said. 'What's your name?' Somewhat testily, Julian gave it.

'Ah, yes, your name is here on the list. Will you come through to the Waiting Room?' Julian was irritated again: 'Will you tell the Director I am here, please?'

'No need, Sir. The procedure is that his PA will come for you when he is ready to see you.'

About fifteen minutes later, a girl came in and requested that he should accompany her.

'About time,' he grunted but she did not react. They reached a door marked "Head of Staffing"; the girl knocked and opened the door, indicating that he should enter. A rather grim middle-aged woman sat on a comfortable overstuffed swivel chair behind a large polished desk. She glanced at him briefly and introduced herself: 'I am the Head of Staffing here. Sorry to keep you waiting. The HR Director has asked me to see you.'

'I'm sorry,' Julian replied icily, 'there must be some mistake. My meeting is with the Director himself.'

The woman lifted a bulky folder from a tray on her desk and read the title. Without looking up, she said: 'He isn't here this morning. He's playing in a golf tournament. He has asked me to see you and explain things before we get started with the action.'

'Explain what? ... What action? ... ' Julian began but the woman interrupted him: 'Sit down, please. She pointed to a small plain chair opposite her.

Julian sat down, smiling thinly and thinking: 'Not much idea about interview technique. A cross-desk confrontation; a pathetic little chair to sit on. I could teach her a thing or two!' The woman opened the folder.

'Perhaps the simplest thing is for me to read out what the HR Director has written to me?'

'Yes, can we get on with it? I want to get back to my work.'

The woman looked at him sharply, before saying: 'Here is the relevant part: "Julian (that's you, isn't it?) is an employee of the Firm who has been convicted of a serious crime against a junior member of his staff. The Partners' Board have taken the decision that the Firm cannot employ anyone with a Criminal Record, especially when the crime is connected with sexual molestation. Therefore he is to be dismissed immediately from his position in the Firm. Will you please inform him of that decision and put into action the usual procedures for Dismissal without Reference." The woman sat back and looked at Julian with a neutral, professional expression.

'This cannot be true,' Julian said, 'I am a personal friend of the Senior Partner. My father and he were at university together. Oberto would never do such a thing to our family. Furthermore, my work here as HDC was exemplary and I am innocent of the crime of which I was accused. I demand to speak to the Senior Partner. In fact, I will go to his office now – I have been there many times before.'

The woman tried but she could not stop him. Julian stormed out of HR and made his way to the Senior Partner's office. His PA was in the outer office, rattling at speed on her computer keyboard.

'Yes?' She didn't look up.

'I want to speak to the Senior Partner immediately. Tell him it's HDC and it's extremely urgent.'

The woman sighed, looking up. 'Oh, it's you, is it? Have you got an appointment?'

Julian was now shouting. 'Tell him I want to speak to him immediately.'

The woman hesitated, then picked up her phone, spoke quietly and listened. Then she replaced the handset quietly: 'No.' she said.

'What?' he exploded.

'No, he doesn't want to see you. That's what he said.'

At that moment, the door of the outer office burst open and two security staff appeared with the Head of Staffing.

'That's him!' she said, triumphantly.

The men grasped Julian by his arms. 'Will you come with us, please?' Words spoken with authority.

Julian went quietly. He had spent four months in prison and was used to such treatment. He knew it was useless to struggle against it. You wound up worse off – very much worse off at times!

The woman in HR was very experienced and looked at Julian kindly.

'Could you just sign this, Sir,' she said, sliding paper and pen across the desk.

'What is it?' Julian asked dully.

'It's the beginning of the dismissal procedure,' the woman replied gently.

It did not take long. Papers were signed and put in a large envelope. He was given a cardboard box filled with his personal belonging, removed months before from his office. He was required to hand in keys, ID card and Car Park Pass.

'You will remove your car from the Car Park right away, won't you, Sir. You use this temporary card. You return it to Reception after you've used it.'

'I don't need it,' he said mournfully, 'someone had parked illegally in my parking space and I had to come out again and park elsewhere.'

'That's probably just as well.' The woman smiled sympathetically. 'Saves you the bother of coming back into the building, doesn't it?'

She handed him the bulky envelope. 'I wish you good luck, then.'

He put the box and envelope in his car. He considered going home to his flat but could not stand the loneliness and sense of loss that would bring. He needed to be alone but with lots of other people, he decided, recognising this as something of a contradiction in terms. He needed to walk, to think. But somehow his mind was frozen, numb. He needed lunch, coffee, but he had almost no money. He had only five euro. Almost without thought, he bought a supermarket sandwich and a small bottle of water. One euro 20c left. He wandered into the park, found a bench to sit on and ate his lunch, largely unaware of his surroundings.

Gradually, as the raw shock of his dismissal began to diminish, his mind cleared to some degree. Suddenly, a wonderful thought. Sunia! He had to make contact with Sunia as soon as possible. With joyous urgency, he began to assemble his strategy: 'She finishes work at 5.00. She usually parks her car in the public car park round the corner. I'll check if it's there (I hope she still has the Cinquecento) and I'll wait for her.

Oh, it will be so lovely to see her.' Julian felt very much better. Then he had another wonderful thought. 'Her father is a very important man. Maybe he can get me a job – maybe a better job than I had at the Firm! I'm sure if Sunia spoke to him, he would be sympathetic. He would understand how unreasonable the Firm had been, just tossing me out like that for a little mistake on my part.'

So Julian walked purposely to the car park near the Firm and surveyed the vehicles. There it was, the distinctive Fiat Cinquecento with its attractive red and green Gucci stripe. She would come here just after five o'clock. Julian almost hugged the little car in joy.

'Hello, Sunia, how are you?' The familiar voice was a shock; he had concealed himself behind a bush at the entrance to the car park. Word had filtered down to DC that afternoon that the former HDC had been released from prison – Guilty but Suspended Sentence – and that he would not be returning to the Firm. On hearing this, Sunia hoped fervently that she would not see him again. She had shuddered at the thought! Now her worst fears were realised. Julian had sought her out as soon as he could and jumped out at her when she least expected it. She looked at him fearfully, trembling and wondering what to do. He was smiling at her – his best smile!

'I hope I didn't startle you, Sunia. I would never want to do that. I am hoping we can arrange to get together for a good, long chat. Would you like that? I have so many important things to say to you.'

The girl and the man were seen to stand close together for some time at the entrance to the car park. At first, the man was animated, smiling, waving his arms energetically, encouragingly. By contrast, the girl was subdued, uncertain, looking down at the ground, unsuccessfully edging away from the man as he followed her backward movements to maintain their closeness. From his body language, it was clear he was trying to persuade her to do something; it was equally clear that she did not want to comply. His words were a torrent of energy, becoming ever louder; her replies hesitant and monosyllabic as she shook her head in negation.

He became more and more persistent, finally grasping her urgently by her upper arms, causing her to pull back in an attempt to free herself. By now, passers-by were looking at the girl with concern but were reluctant to intervene, not least because any interruption to their progress homewards would upset the absolutely fixed schedule that determined this extremely important journey. Nevertheless, it was obvious that a degree of ugliness was beginning to emerge at the entrance to the car park.

'Let her go, Julian.' Alex's voice, firm, clear and confident. Julian recognised the voice.

He did not release his grip or turn around: 'Go away, boy, this is between Sunia and me. This is adult business.' His tone was harsh and unpleasant.

'It is my business. Sunia is my girlfriend. We love each other. We have been together for four months now.'

Julian's face altered dramatically to register shock, dismay and disbelief. How could this be happening to him? He loved Sunia strongly and passionately and he believed she loved him. He looked into her beautiful eyes. 'Do you love me, Sunia?' His voice at once urgent and pleading.

This was her chance. She must tell the truth, now. She spoke clearly and decisively. 'No, Julian, I don't. Not at all. In fact, I dislike you. I'm frightened of you. Let go of my arms or I shall scream!'

His mind awhirl, he released her and she jumped back out of his reach. Then he swivelled around to stand toe to toe with Alex. Silent and motionless, standing within an invisible, isolating cocoon of crackling negative energy, the two men glared with pure animal aggression deep into each other's eyes, while many other grown men and women scuttled by, flitting shadows of humanity with eyes carefully averted. After a full twenty seconds, Julian's eyes suddenly dropped and the energy field around them collapsed, instantly dismantled. Muttering incomprehensibly, he stumbled back in capitulation and, seemingly in an instant, melted away, defeated, diminished, emasculated …

He walked. He did not know whether he walked slowly or quickly. He did not know where he walked or for how long. Although his eyes were open, he saw nothing.

'I have lost her.' Within the confusion that was his brain, these words were repeated endlessly in a whirling mantra of utter despair. This was the truth and he recognised it as an endgame reality. Unmeasured time passed.

It was midsummer so the light remained strong. Now, as he walked, he began to add up the totality of what his life had become. He had lost her, the love of his life, the only love he had ever had. She hated him. He had no job and no prospects. He had no money. He had been convicted of a serious crime and sent to prison. He had a criminal record that would follow him for the rest of his life. And now, everybody disliked him, he who used to be so popular, so sought after. 'Negatives, negatives, negatives,' he muttered, 'I'm done for, finished.' Suddenly, he had to stop walking, his progress brought to a halt by a stout, well-constructed wooden gate. Bells were ringing and road barriers had been lowered. He looked across the polished steel rails which, within minutes, he knew would carry the speeding tonnes of steel that was the train from the city. As he leaned upon the gate, it moved freely; it was unlatched, unfastened from its automatic lock; it was ready to be entered.

The train driver still had nightmares about it, such is the sensitivity of the human brain. He did not like driving this stretch of line and tried to avoid being scheduled for it. Every time he approached this particular crossing, he had a powerful urge to slow the train right down, preferably to walking pace; he would then be in a position to stop if anything happened. On several occasions after the accident, he had actually done this. Unfortunately, this unexplained speed reduction was recorded each time by the train's tachograph system and the District Manager had called him to his office to demand an explanation.

'I'm sorry, I know how you must feel but your job is to run your train to the schedule. So, in future, do it, or I'll have to take further action.' The driver had been compelled to sign a paper saying he would obey the rules in future.

Now the train was approaching the crossing and the driver's breathing quickened. He could not help resting his hand on the Emergency Train Brake Lever. He checked the speed – 99 kph, correct for this stretch of line. The crossing was coming up fast now – he could see the closed barriers and the warning lights flashing. Then he noticed a man leaning on the pedestrian gate – the same gate *she* had stepped from. The driver's stomach leapt within him as he saw that the gate was slightly ajar! The hand on the emergency brake lever tightened, quivering with the tension of indecision. He would dearly have loved to apply the brake to its maximum extent but memories of his interview with the District Manager prevented the hand from moving.

Frozen with dread, he waited for the man to move forward on to the track. For a split second, their eyes met, then the train thundered through the crossing in a deafening cacophony of metallic sound, accompanied by sharp-edged gusts of dirty fume-filled air and vibration of earth-tremor proportions.

Borne inexorably away, the driver squinted anxiously into his exterior rear-view mirror but could see nothing as the track bent around. His eyes flicked to the speedometer, reading 98 kph. He sighed with relief; on target, thank goodness.

Thirty minutes later, the train pulled into its destination. The driver set the brakes, shut down the engines and carried out the closedown checks. Then he scribbled his report:

'Journey uneventful. No problems. Nothing to report.' He removed the tachograph chart from the machine and stapled it to the report. Finally, he collected his belonging, locked the train and went to file his report at the office, familiar actions done hundreds of times before. But now he was apprehensive.

'Nothing to report,' he grunted at the Recording Clerk, 'anything from your side?' He waited tensely, feigning indifference. The clerk checked his log.

'Nothing much. Somebody thought they saw a dog on the track earlier this afternoon.' The tension flooded out of the driver and he expressed his relief in uncharacteristic joviality.

'Good,' he said in a joyful voice. 'Well, I'll be off home now.' He left the office, humming tunelessly. The Recording Clerk followed his exit with puzzled eyes; this driver was known for his constantly taciturn manner.

Julian pushed the gate open and walked forward about three metres before turning at right angles to look along the shiny, converging lines of the railway track that led to the city: 'It's incredible! People actually throw themselves in front of speeding trains. I can't understand it. I remember there was that girl from the office – she did just that. What a strange thing to do. Now what was her name …?' Julian turned and walked to the gate at the other side of the tracks, racking his brains. After a few minutes he thought: 'I think it began with "F". Maybe "Frieda" or "Fran", something like that.' Suddenly he stopped with a little wan smile, 'How typical of me! Always thinking about other people instead of looking after myself. That's probably the reason I get into so much trouble!'

It was several weeks later and things had settled down at the Firm. Margarite had been confirmed as HDC and was firmly established in Julian's old office. The promotion procedure for DHDC was under way and it was likely that Alex would be promoted into the post; he had been working as Acting-DHDC while Margarite was filling in as HDC. Although the formal decision rested with HR, Margarite had made it clear to them that she expected Alex to be successful. None of the other candidates measured up to his experience and skill and she considered he would make an excellent DHDC.

It was now obvious that DC had a serious office romance in progress. Sunia and Alex were deeply in love and Margarite thought it was only a matter of time before engagement and marriage would follow. She understood that Sunia's parents had met Alex and that they approved of his liaison with their beautiful daughter. Her father had looked speculatively at this intelligent young man and could see him successfully occupying some higher-level posts in the international organisation he worked for.

'But that will be for some time later,' he thought.

It was now 6.30 p.m. Margarite had finished work half an hour earlier and come home to her house, rented some weeks after she had been unceremoniously ejected from Julian's flat. Her friend had been very kind and allowed her to live with her until she could reorganise her life. It had been very unpleasant to return to Julian's flat to recover her belongings. He had ignored her and had not even said goodbye when the time had come for her to leave. It had all been very upsetting and Margarite could not understand why he had treated her so badly. After all, she had loved him and, truth to tell, she still did. Love endures, with those who love remembering the halcyon days of their relationship rather than the problems and acrimony that may follow later. Now she thought she had come to terms with everything that had happened:

'Maybe it's all for the best,' she mused, sadly.

Her doorbell rang. The opened door revealed a silent, subdued Julian. Despite herself, her heart leaped within her; love will not be controlled by logic.

'Come in, Julian,' she said quietly, 'let me make you a cup of tea and we can chat.' At first he was silent, staring into the tea in his cup but gradually he began to talk. Yes, prison had been a dreadful experience and the trial had been a nightmare. He was innocent of the crime – he would never have hurt Sunia (he hoped Margarite believed that). He loved Sunia but she did not love him; now, she was in love with that boy and that was that. He shook his head in disbelief and was silent for several minutes. Finally he spoke again, telling how a combination of no job, no prospects and no money had compelled him to move out of his flat.

'So where do you live now?' Margarite's question was gentle. He did not reply but pointed to the rather battered, dirty BMW outside.

They sat quietly for some time as the light began to fade.

'Julian, would you like to come and live here with me until you can get on your feet again?' Julian looked up, meeting her eyes and smiling sadly – his best sad smile!

'Margarite, could I really do that?'

'Yes, Julian, you could. She may not love you, but I do.'

With tears of self-pity in his eyes, Julian said: 'You know, this is the first good thing that has happened to me for so many months.'

In the small splintered wooden box in the boot of the BMW, the Stone glowed, somehow aware of an opposition to its functionality; its power of influence, transmitted through its possessor, had been countered by a greater force.

EPILOGUE

And the Lord God said, 'the man has now become like one of us, knowing good and evil.'

Genesis Chapter 3 Verse 22a.

The Holy Bible, New International Version (The Bible Society, 1973)

From its earliest existence, it is clear that the entity that became the Stone had been a conduit of power. Starting from a simple molecular structure, this was a conduit that had grown physically. At this stage, it had an integrated living function and physical nutrients were transmitted through it. Although it could not have known, it was but a small part of a very large and living whole, an edifice of size and solidity, set deep in the earth and yet reaching high into the heavens above, huge, heavy and immensely solid in its centre, tapering to be thin, delicate and fibrous at its farthest extents. Humanity were informed that this was a tree, not an ordinary tree but one with a very special function.

In the due course of time, the tree was no more as a living construction and its physical form returned to the earth, decayed but not disappeared. Altered, changed, split, broken and remade into large and small pieces, then further remade as eons of time passed. But the power remained, unaltered, ever present. And the physical tree that had been a million conduits was still precisely that. Of course, there was no longer any necessity for the transmission of physical nutrients; fossilised materials do not need such nutrients but the power, the other power that was the meaning of the tree was still there in all its parts.

During its physical existence, latterly within the Unusual Stone Collection, the Stone was *aware* that power, function and action constantly defined its task. It was also *aware* that it had once been part of a huge mysterious whole. By contrast, it was *unaware* that the amazing whole still existed, though now as many units of remade fossilisation. It is a sadness that the Stone was *unaware* that it was not alone. *Unaware* that there was a multitude of other inert, *aware* objects in many places across the Earth, each one mysteriously power-charged, ready for its prescribed action. In reality, a proportion of this multitude would already be in operation, carrying out their designated functions of mystery. Many others would be awaiting human discovery, possession and physical contact – again.

Then, as the Stones were found, owned and achieved that inevitable physical contact, the mysterious power that was the purpose of the Tree of the Knowledge of Good and Evil would flow to their new owners instantaneously. This would *not* alter the character of these owners *in any way;* instead, it would turn them into powerful transmitters of their own knowledge and conviction of good and evil. From that moment, all other people coming into contact with the Stone owners would be instantly transformed into their psychological and spiritual likeness for that period of contact. In other words, the people they met would instantly assume the attitudes of the Stone possessors – for good, for evil or both. There was, however, just one thing that could not be changed by this mystical power. Love could not be changed, altered or suppressed, for love transcends *all* other powers.

For the possessors of the Stones, there was no going back. Once found and activated, each Stone was in that particular owner-ship for the rest of that person's life. Throwing the Stone away, destroying it or otherwise disposing of it was pointless. The current ownership link would continue unchanged. During ownership, the Stone was totally inert to anyone else's touch; even if they slipped finger and thumb into the depressions on its surface, they would experience nothing. On the other hand, the Stone would become ownerless with the physical death of the possessor. At that moment, there was a disconnec-tion; then, the Stone would return to its active *waiting* mode, ready for human contact.

Julian, totally self-centred, dishonest, false and manipulative, neither *knew* nor *understood*. He was totally bewildered at the sudden reversal of his fortunes. After prison he faced a life of complete despair and his future looked totally bleak; nothing but aggression, unkindness, rejection and indifference filled his life. No matter how hard he tried, no success, no prospects, no money. Worst of all, no Sunia in his life. How could she have rejected his love? (He could not know that it was her love for Alex that shielded her from his transmitted desires.) How could all these terrible things be happening to him? Had he not always been kind, helpful and generous to everyone? Of course he could not grasp that it was the power and con-stancy of Margarite's love for him that was his only lifeline to the future.

Joachim, unfailingly genuine, good-hearted and kind, *knew* but he did not *understand*. He knew that the Stone was magic. He knew that it was somehow responsible for what had hap-pened to him. He was immensely grateful that his extremely hard, brutal and hopeless existence had been changed by the Stone. From that time he had lived an absolutely wonderful life, trusted, integrated into a wonderful family, loved and respected by all. And, unknown to him, his transmitted love kindled and rekindled a lasting love in those he met; a reawakening of the love which lies within everyone. Perhaps, in time, Joachim would come to understand how all this came to pass.

Kati, evil, cunning and incredibly cruel, *knew* and *understood*. She knew that her life had been changed irrevocably by the Stone. She knew that her feelings towards others were now reciprocated, reflected back at her with equal power. She knew that there would be no love in any of these reflections of power, for she never transmitted love. Her spoken words demonstrated complete understanding of her situation, specifically by the words she uttered at that moment her husband was advancing upon her for the first time:

'My God, you've changed. Suddenly. You, all of you, have become exactly like ... *ME.*'

In fact, Kati was only at the threshold of understanding. She had understood *how* but she had no concept of *why*. Her journey towards true understanding would certainly be slow and unreliable; her inexperience of goodwill towards others was a crippling handicap that she would need to overcome to make any progress. Only then could she begin to have some sort of appreciation of the awesome strategy that had been put in place for the stability and development of the world in which she would continue to live. Would she ever understand that her destiny was in her own hands?

Down the ages, human thought and action has invariably included clear concepts of good and evil, so clear that it is unnecessary to define them. However the effects of good and evil have always been of paramount importance in human life;

the growth and strengthening of goodness, manifested as love, have led to all things positive while the growth of evil has been a pathway to negativity, destruction and hatred. The fact that mankind is completely free to choose good or evil at any time has made life dangerously precarious for all.

However, mankind is not left completely alone. The Knowledge Stones are part of the strategic intervention applied by the Power who has created and continues to create the Universe. It is not the Stones that carry out the work of this intervention; in this scheme of great elegance, the Stones are merely the conduits, the catalysts, which allow their possessors to apply the full effects of the intervention. Notably, the possessors are not changed; they retain fully their convictions about good and evil, along with the free will to apply them. Amazingly, there is no need for external pre-selection of the possessors, because the strategy operates unfailingly for the common good, simultaneously weakening and destroying evil while strengthening goodness through love.

When evil is projected by the owner/possessors and reflected back, the perpetrators are seriously afflicted by their own evil. The effect of this is to discourage, diminish and destroy evil. The stories of Kati and Julian were illustrations of this. However, there is also a wonderfully positive dimension available to such people. Those like Kati and Julian are offered the real possibility of restitution; by understanding the purpose of the Stones, *the why,* they can be redeemed and saved by changes of their own hearts. By learning love.

Conversely, when good is projected it not only is reflected back to the possessor but also acts powerfully in the recipients to awaken or re-awaken their own goodness. Consequently, love, the true spirit of goodness, is strengthened and made anew. This is how the lives of Joachim, Malik, Maretta and Giana were transformed. Love begets love. The effect is as the ripples from a stone dropped in a pool of water, ever widening to infinity.

This is the purpose of the Power's intervention. The strategy is perfect. The effect is awesome.

And the Knowledge Stones are waiting.

Love does not delight in evil but rejoices with the truth. It always protects, always trusts, always hopes, always perseveres.

And now these three remain: faith, hope and love. But the greatest of these is love.

1 Corinthians Chapter 13 Verses 6-7, 13.

The Holy Bible, New International Version (The Bible Society, 1973)